Flesh and Blood

The leaves collided with the door yet again. This time the wood frame splintered, and one of the hinges popped. Iris pressed her shoulder against it, but Emily kept tugging at her wrist and screaming, 'Let him in! You have to let him in!'

The leaves crashed against the door again, and yet again, and yet again. Iris's shoulder was badly jarred, and she felt as if her neck had been whiplashed. But her whole system was flooded with terror and adrenalin and she knew that she had to keep this thing out of her house.

Terry had warned her: the Green Traveller will come knocking at your door, and he will knock and knock and go on knocking until somebody lets him in. And then God help you.

Graham Masterton is a master of the horror genre. His previous books for Mandarin include *Black Angel*, *Prey*, *Burial* and *The Sleepless*. He lives in Surrey with his wife and three sons.

GRAHAM MASTERTON

Flesh and Blood

An Arrow Paperback
FLESH AND BLOOD

First published in Great Britain 1994
by William Heinemann Ltd

This edition published 2002
Arrow Books
Random House Group Ltd.
20 Vauxhall Bridge Road
London SW1V 2SA

A GIP catalogue record for this title
is available from the British Library
ISBN 0 7493 1671 3

Printed and bound in Germany by
Elsnerdruck, Berlin

For Wiescka

One

They had been driving for less than an hour when Terence said, 'This is it, kids.' He steered the battered black Mercury station wagon off the side of the road so that it was tilted up against the bank, and shut off the engine.

Emily peered out of the window at the stormy wheatfield and the flying chaff and the sky that was darker than Daddy's eyes.

'Why are we here?' she asked him. 'We're going to miss *Deep Space Nine.*' Eleven years old, she wore a yellow flowery print dress that was one size too small for her, and her spectacles were stuck with a BandAid. Her coppery hair was braided and tied in ribbons.

Beside her, Lisa stirred, and opened her eyes, and frowned. Lisa was nine, and blonde, with skinny wrists and skinny legs and anklesocks, and complicated dental braces that always made her lisp. George was sleeping with his mouth open, dribbling down the armrest. George was only three and had sticky-outy ears.

'It's time, kids,' Terence told them, with an oddly-sloping smile. 'Time to do what's right.' He climbed out of the station wagon and wrenched open the passenger doors. Then he paced around and around it, slapping his hand on the roof, slapping his hand on the hood. Impatient, edgy, couldn't keep still. 'Come on kids, hustle, it's time.'

They climbed out and Daddy slammed the doors. They stood by the side of the road with the wind whistling and sizzling and the dry soil snaking across the bitumen surface. They didn't know what to do. They didn't know why they were here. But Daddy had kept on telling them in the car that they had to be saved.

'I love you, all of you. Do you know how much I love you? That's why you have to be saved.'

Daddy opened the tailgate and lifted out his old sack. The children didn't like his old sack. It was the same old sack that he had used to drown that Labrador puppy that was born strange. The same old sack in which he regularly carried home the heavy bleeding bodies of rabbits that he had shot. The old sack was stained with all kinds of terrible stains, and it always smelled bad.

'Come on now, kids, come on up here,' Terence urged them, and together, still dazed, they scrambled after him up the crumbly earth bank. A fleck of chaff blew into George's eye, and made him stop, and blink, and furiously rub it. Daddy came back and put down his sack and looked at it for him.

'Can you feel where it is? Look up . . . look sideways. I don't see nothing, George. I think it's gone.'

Together they made their way into the vast rustling ocean of ripening wheat. Emily and George, hand-in-hand, Lisa a little way behind. And Daddy just up ahead of them, talking and fidgeting and turning around, never too close, never too far away.

'What do you think, kids!' Terence whooped. 'Isn't this one of those days!'

Emily looked up. The sky was darkly maroon – *maroon!* – and the clouds were rushing like hell-let-loose. The clouds were rushing so fast that the whole world felt as if it were rotating around them; as if the whole of Iowa were going around on a gigantic rumbling, rocking turntable. Terence sang, '*Alouette, gentille Alouette*', and then whistled it, and jumped, and turned. He swung the old sack around his head, around and around. 'Remember that song? Remember that song, Emily? You used to love that song when you were a baby.

I used to have to sing it to you night and day, day and night, and that's the God's-honest truth!'

The children trotted and stumbled. Spots of rain began to prickle their faces.

'Save us!' Terence shouted, striding knee-deep through the wheatfield. 'Save us, God, please save us!'

'Save us!' George piped up, in his funny little trumpety voice.

Dust and chaff whirled all around them. 'Save us!' Terence sang. 'Save us-save us-save us!'

'Save us!' the children screamed. 'Save us!'

'And save us from *what*?' Terence demanded, turning to confront the children wide-eyed, but still stalking backwards at the same long-legged pace. 'Save us from *what*, kids? Save us from *what*?'

'Save us from the woogah-boogah man!' shouted George.

'Oh, no!' Terence replied, shaking his head. 'Not the woogah-boogah man!'

'Save us from bad blood?' Lisa volunteered.

Terence took three long backward paces, staring at Emily all the time. Then he held up the old sack and whooped, a high harsh whoop like a hog-call. 'You betcha!' he shouted. 'Save us from bad blood! Save us from that bad, bad blood! Save-us-from-evil-and-the-flesh-and-the-devil!'

'Save-us-from-evil-and-the-flesh-and-the-devil!' George chanted. 'Save-us-from-evil-and-the-flesh-and-the-devil!'

About a half-mile into the field, they came across a deep furrow in the soil, which looked as if it had once been a wallow or a creekbed, or dug deliberately as a fireguard. It was overgrown with broad-leaved mulleins, which trembled incessantly in the wind, which trembled and shook like nervous hands.

Terence stopped, and frowned all around him, his eyes narrowed against the wind and the dust. He looked down into the furrow first. Then he arched his neck back and stared right up at the hurrying sky. The clouds were moving so swiftly that he became momentarily disoriented, and almost lost his balance. Yes! It was twister weather. Catastrophe weather. A tornado was up, he could feel it. Sure as eggs, this was no time to be dancing through wheatfields.

'Oh God in heaven, save us from that bad, bad blood!' he shouted at the sky. And the children chorused, 'Save us!'

'Save us, O Lord!' he raged; and the children obediently chorused, 'Save us!'

He strode off a short way, swinging the old sack. The children stayed clustered together on the edge of the furrow, holding hands, all three of them, and waited for him. Terence was very tall and skinny and loosely jointed, and one of his shoulders was noticeably hunched-up, and one side of his chest stuck out at an angle, as if his mother had dropped him when he was a baby. His head was large and angular, too, like an axe-head. His reddish hair was cut very short, so that it sprigged out at the back. Although he was wearing a washed-out denim jacket and baggy washed-out jeans, fieldworker's clothes, he had white unhealthy skin and plum-coloured circles under his eyes, like a clerk, or an accountant, or a puppeteer. Somebody who spends all of their days indoors, and smokes too much, and rarely speaks to real people.

He came walking back through the knee-high wheat. He sniffed and coughed and wiped his nose with the back of his hand. 'We have to pray,' he told them, his voice much lower now, much more serious. 'That's what we have to do next. We have to pray.'

Lisa raised her left hand to shield her face from the wind. 'Daddy – it's raining so hard! I'm cold. I want to go home.'

George said, 'I want to go home, too.'

Emily was shivering but said nothing. She watched her father warily, her eyes magnified by her glasses. She had seen him acting strange before; she had heard him talking about bad blood ever since she was little, not to mention the Bible and Things That Women Should Never Do. He talked about something else, too, which she had never been able to understand, but which always frightened her, although she never knew why. The Green Traveller, whatever that was.

She remembered him shouting at Momma: 'You may hear knocking, Iris, you surely may! But don't you never go opening your door to the Green Traveller. Don't never even *think* about opening your door, even in your wildest dreams.'

When she was very little, she had asked him innocently what the Green Traveller actually was. With awful suddenness, the blood had drained out of his face, and he had started to shudder, as if he were having an epileptic fit.

She never asked him about the Green Traveller again. She didn't dare to. But that didn't stop her from having endless nightmares about doorknockers unexpectedly banging in the night, banging and banging, and something green and unspeakable trying to force its way into the house. A rotting man who could still walk, with moss on the backs of his hands instead of hair, and a tangle of weeds covering his face.

The Green Traveller!

Sometimes, in the early hours of the morning, Emily had seen her daddy standing motionless in the yard – seen him standing naked, pale as veal, staring at the fence, staring at the dark alleyway behind the house, or maybe staring at nothing at all, while her mother slept and murmured in her sleep.

She had heard Ms Van Dyke at the Medicap Pharmacy say that her father was 2 per cent human and 98 per cent Valium.

Terence never abused his children, never spanked them, scarcely ever scolded them. He kissed them and tucked them into their beds at night and told them stories. They knew that he loved them, and most of the time he was fun. But there was always the feeling that something was badly wrong. Too often, the fun was desperate fun – the jokes too manic, the tickling too violent. And for some inexplicable reason Emily knew that what was wrong was *them.*

Some evenings, when Terence came home from work, he was unapproachable. He would brood and pace and cover his face with his hands, and rail at God. He railed at himself, too, over and over. 'Why did I do it? Why did I do it? Why did I do it when I *knew.*'

And, by the time she was eight years old, Emily had guessed what he meant by 'why did I do it?'

What he meant was, 'Why did I ever have children?'

But why he kept on asking himself that, and what he had known that would have made the slightest difference, she never found out.

The rain speckled her glasses. Lisa squeezed her hand and Lisa's hand was cold and sticky but Emily didn't mind. Emily kept her eyes on her father and didn't look away.

Terence laid down the old sack and approached the children with a warm, muzzy, unfocused expression on his face. 'Emily?' he said. 'We have to pray.'

Lisa said, 'Daddy, I want to go home. It's raining and it's horrible and I don't like to get wet.'

George stamped his feet and trumpeted, 'Doctor Foster! Went to Gloucester! In a shower of *rain*!'

Terence took Emily in his arms and held her tightly against him. 'My sweetheart,' he said. 'My darling girl. Don't ever forget how much I loved you.'

He hadn't been drinking. He smelled only of antiseptic soap, and cigarettes, and that funny sweetish smell that always seemed to cling to his clothes, especially when he came back from work. He worked in 'feed'. That was all he ever told her.

'I love you, too, Daddy,' said Emily, carefully.

Terence gave her an extra-tight squeeze, and then he took

hold of Lisa, and hugged her, too. 'Lisa, my darling, if you knew just how darned special you are to me. If only you knew.'

Lisa said nothing, but looked across at Emily with an expression that was partly possessive (this is *my* daddy) but partly quizzical (what has he brought us here for? why is he acting so extra-specially loving?).

Last of all, Terence hunkered down and ruffled George's hair, and pulled him close. 'Hey, George . . . you know what it means to a man, when a man has a son of his own?'

George nodded. 'I know,' he said. Then, 'Can we go home now?'

Terence ruffled George's hair in a brief gesture of infinite tenderness, and George irritably smoothed it down again. Terence smiled. Then he eased himself up. The rain was crackling noisily through the wheat, and the wind was rising all the time. Sure as eggs, this was no time to be dancing in wheatfields. This was no time to be dancing at all.

'We have to pray,' said Terence. 'Come on, kids. It's time to do what's right. Let's get down on our knees now, and thank the Lord, and ask him to save us from our bad blood.'

'He fell in a piddle, right up to his middle, and never went there again!' George bellowed.

'George, it's "puddle", not "piddle",' Emily admonished him.

'It is *too* piddle,' George shouted.

Terence said, with a rising key of urgency in his voice, 'We have to pray, kids. You understand me? Get down on our knees – get down on our knees in the eyes of the Lord, and *pray*.'

The children all stared at him. The rain was falling harder and harder, and he was asking them to kneel in this field and pray?

'*Pray!*' he screamed at them. 'For Christ's sake, *pray!*'

Lisa knelt first. Then George. Then Emily. The rain was so heavy now that Emily could hardly see, and she had to take off her glasses and wipe them on the hem of her skimpy dress. The soil felt stony and knobbly and hurt her bare knees, but she thought that the sooner she did what she was told, the sooner this would all be over, and they could climb back into the station wagon and go home for supper. Momma was baking ham. She always baked ham on Saturday afternoons. She always gave Emily the first slice, too, which was dark with honey, and pungent with cloves. And always corn to go with it, or butternut squash.

'Close your eyes,' said Terence, and the children closed their eyes.

Emily could hear the rain, sweeping across the field. She could hear the wind blustering, and her father's feet, chuffing backwards and forwards through the stalks. She said, as loud as she could, 'Our Father, which art in heaven, hallowed be Thy name . . .'

Lisa joined in, and then George. George didn't know the Lord's Prayer very well, and kept missing words out.

'Save us from our bad blood, O Lord,' said Terence, and the children said, 'Save us!'

Emily could hear her father circling around behind them. She opened her eyes, and turned around, trying to see where he was, but he shouted at her, 'Keep your eyes shut, Emily, sweetheart! Keep your eyes shut tight! And pray! Because you won't be saved, else!'

Obediently, she closed her eyes again. But then she heard the most nerve-tingling sound she had ever heard in her life. Her father singing – not in his normal voice, but in a strange falsetto warble, as if he were trying to sing like a woman. She shivered with cold. Her dress was soaking, and she desperately wanted to go to the toilet; but she didn't dare to open her eyes, not until her father said so.

'*Lead, kindly Light . . . amid the encircling gloom,*' he was singing. '*Lead thou me on!*'

She could hear him circling, hear him circling.

But she couldn't see him open the old sack, and carefully reach inside, and take out his largest sickle, the sickle he usually used for cutting back the bramble hedges. She couldn't see him run his thumb down the edge of the blade, slicing his thumb open, right to the bone, that's how sharp it was, and then thoughtfully sucking the blood that welled out of it.

'*The night is dark,*' he sang, '*and I am far from home, Lead thou me on.*'

The blood from his sliced-open thumb ran in two streams down his left wrist and into his sleeve. He approached his children with the specially-sharpened sickle in his hand and his face very calm and compassionate. *Save us* was all he could think. *Save us from our bad, bad blood.* The wind was blowing so wildly now that silvery wheat-serpents snaked across the field, and the chaff stung his cheeks. Little George's exposed neck was so thin and white, with just a fluff of hair on it, and one tiny mole. Had George ever grown old enough to be vain, and self-conscious, he would have had an operation to fix those sticky-outy ears. But it was better this way – better for George than for any of them, because George would never know vanity, or embarrassment, and George would always stay pure.

Bless'd are the pure in heart, For they shall see our God.

Terence stood close behind George and a little to George's right. George was whispering, '*Father father art in heaven hallowby thy name, thy willby done, thy kingdom come.*'

Terence lifted the sickle and it winked silver in the sky. Then he whacked it down and took George's head off in a single blow. The head tumbled into the thickest part of the mulleins, so that they stopped their trembling and gave a sudden convulsive shudder. George's neck spurted out a walking-stick of bright red blood, and then his body collapsed forward, onto the dirt.

Immediately – taking a quick, jerky step to the left – Terence whacked at Lisa's neck, cutting through braids, skin, flesh and spine. Not all the way through. Lisa cried out, *ow!* – as if he had done nothing worse than slap her face. But then Terence adjusted his grip and whacked her again, upwards this time, into her larynx, and her head tumbled off her shoulders and fell onto the ground behind her back. Her face stared up at him in surprise, her blue eyes wide open, her dental braces glistening. Blood pumped out of her severed neck in a sudden, S-shaped spray, spattering Terence's face and hands.

Emily heard the whacking and the rustling and all the commotion and dared to open her eyes. She turned and saw her father standing with his face birthmarked in scarlet and his arm lifted. She didn't even see the sickle – but she saw that Lisa had fallen over onto the dirt. She saw that Lisa's pink checkered blouse was decorated with blood. She saw that George was lying sprawled on the ground, too.

'Daddy?' she squeaked, in a tight, constricted voice.

Daddy smiled at her. A slow, sure, welcoming smile.

It was then that she understood that he meant to kill her.

She felt the grip of absolute terror. She climbed to her feet – slowly, wobbling – and began to inch away. The rain stung the side of her face and dripped from her eyelashes and dribbled from her chin. Terence approached her with his arm still raised, and said, 'Emily – Emily?' as softly as a lullaby. 'Are you listening to me, sweetheart? I love you! You have to be saved! You can't let George and Lisa go on their own! You have to be *saved*, my beautiful girl!'

He dropped his arm, very quickly, and she felt something brush against her shoulder. It stung sharply, like a bee sting – but it was only when she pressed her hand against it, and felt a flood of sticky warmth, that she understood what it was that her father had done to her. He lifted his arm yet again, and this time she looked up, and saw the sickle.

She wanted to speak to him, to tell him to stop. She was Emily, she was Emily! She was Daddy's first and dearest girl! But she couldn't find the words to explain. She couldn't find the words to tell him. Her chest was too tight and her throat was too tight and her whole brain was locked with panic.

Instead of trying to talk to him, she turned and ran.

She didn't know where she was going. All she knew was that if she wanted to live, she would have to run and run until her father couldn't keep up with her any longer.

'*Emily!*' he roared at her. '*Emily, come back here!*'

She plunged into the wheat. It whipped at her ankles and the rain lashed at her face. She heard animals rushing off in all directions, mice, rats, wheat-monsters. Usually, they scared her, but not today. Today she had to run. She had to run and run, even if she never stopped until she reached home.

She stumbled over one furrow after another. Her face was scratched and she had picked up pebbles and grit in her sandals. She knew that her father was close behind her. She could hear his heavy, champing footsteps, like something terrible that chases you in a dream. Like the Green Traveller, banging and banging and banging at your door. She could hear him gasping for breath and calling and cajoling. 'You can't leave your brother and sister alone, Emily, they need you!'

Emily was so seized with fear that she could barely remember how to run. She was almost tempted to stop, and drop to her knees, and let Daddy do whatever Daddy wanted to do. But she had seen so much blood, and Lisa's bloody fingers curled up, and she knew for certain that Lisa was dead, and probably George, too. She was completely convinced that if her father caught up with her, then she would die, and that was why she kept on running.

Behind her rain-blurred glasses, her eyes were popping like a rabbit's.

Terence wasn't especially fit, but Terence had never been a man to give up easily on anything. Terence didn't enjoy pain, but pain was the only way to get what you really wanted, his father had always told him that. His father had rapped his knuckles with a steel rule and said, with sly delight, 'Nothing's worth squat less'n you've suffered to get it.'

And Terence's father knew all about suffering. Terence's father had been married to Terence's mother.

And Terence's mother – that night in 1962 –

Terence couldn't allow himself to think about it, not now. It paralysed him, when he thought about it, it gripped his central nervous system like an ice-cold engineer's vice. And he had to catch Emily. He had to! He had to atone for conceiving his children. He had to atone for so many acts of squalid selfishness. He had to release them, he had to set them free. He wanted their freedom more than anything. The thought of releasing them blazed inside his brain, as bright as burning magnesium, as pure as fire.

That was why he kept on running after Emily with such doggedness. She was young, she was frightened. She would tire and stumble soon. Then he would have her. Then he could save her, as Lisa and George had already been saved.

He was gasping now. The Lord in heaven be praised! The Lord! In heaven! Be praised!

Emily was nearing the highway, not far from the embankment where their station wagon was parked at a tilt. The afternoon was so dark now that it was difficult to tell where the wheatfields ended and the sky began. The rain was hitting the tar road at an acute angle, so that spray was rising up from it like an endless procession of drifting ghosts. Thirty or forty miles away, over to the west, lightning crackled, and thick black curtains of soil were rising, hundreds of tons of agricultural dirt, lifted up into the air, and blotting out the sun.

Emily turned around just once, to see how much her father had gained on her. Terence lifted both arms and shouted, 'Emily! Emily! You don't know what you're doing, sweetheart! You don't know what's in store for you!'

Terence caught his foot on a grassy tussock, and stumbled, and dropped to one knee. As he got up again, he saw a winking light in the middle-distance – the brief, bright glitter of automobile headlights. Emily must have seen it, too, because she began frantically to wave her skinny arms; and over the rain and the blustery, roaring gusts of wind, Terence could hear her screaming in a high-pitched voice.

Now Terence ran flat out, his legs pumping, his fists clenched, his face grim. He could hear his heart thumping like somebody furiously and pointlessly beating a dead spaniel with a stick.

God, if he didn't get her, she wouldn't be saved, she wouldn't be saved!

The car came closer and closer, and its headlights set the rain sparkling. A saddle-bronze E1 Camino pick-up, bouncing and dipping on the uneven road. Emily was shrieking now, wildly waving her arms, and running as if Satan were right behind her, as if Death himself were breathing down her neck.

Terence whooped and screamed, and whirled the sickle around and around, so that it whistled and whooped like he did.

'Emily! Wait up, Emily! You wait up, sweetheart!'

But Emily had scrambled down the crumbled, muddy embankment and reached the highway, and the people in the pick-up must have seen her, because they slewed to a stop, their windshield wipers flapping furiously from side to side. The driver's door opened up.

Terence came bounding over the last few furrows, slid down the bank, and stood in the road with his bloodied sickle in his hand, gasping and sweating and staring.

The car driver climbed out, and Emily almost collided with the door. He reached out his left hand, and pulled her in, pulled her in close, protectively.

He was a tall, thin, white-haired man in spectacles and a grey linen coat, the kind worn by watchmakers or french polishers. His wide grey trousers flapped in the wind. His hair blew wildly. He put his arm around Emily's shoulders, and as Terence approached him, Terence could see that he had a look on his face of plain determination, like Dr B.H. Keeby, the dentist who had posed for Grant Wood's painting, *American Gothic.* Pure Iowa – 'good and solid people'. As Terence came nearer, he could see the man's wife in the passenger seat, skinny and white-haired, waiting, as all such women wait, for the outcome of what their menfolk decide to do.

'You back off now!' the old man shouted. 'You hear me, mister? You back way off!'

Terence looked around him, left and right, even behind him, in mock bewilderment. His eyes were slitted against the rain. But all the time he was holding up the sickle rock-solid still, tight as tight, as if the sickle were magically nailed in mid-air and he were stuck to it.

'I don't know who you are, mister, or what you're trying to do!' the old man told him. 'But you'd better back off.'

'That's my daughter,' Terence shouted, coming nearer, one careful step at a time. 'That's my little girl.'

He spread his arms wide to emphasize his innocence, and to profess his lack of guile.

'I don't want to know the whos or the whys or the wherefors,' the old man replied. 'We can let the sheriff sort that out.'

'You take your hand off of my daughter,' Terence warned.

'No way, mister. This little lady's coming along with us.'

Terence shook his head, slow and wide. 'Hooh no,' he said, softly, so softly that the old man couldn't hear him at first. 'Hooh no, this little lady has to be saved.'

'Back off!' the old man snapped at him, and push-hustled Emily into the front seat of the pick-up. 'I'm warning you, mister, you keep your distance!'

Terence approached the old man, step by careful step, until he was standing only two feet away from him. Rain trickled down the sides of his face and hung like diamond earrings from his earlobes. He stared at the old man as if he had never seen anybody like him before. The old man gripped the top of his pick-up door and shivered, but he stared back with all the defiance of the truly frightened.

Terence tapped the blade of his sickle on the top of the door, tap, tap, tap, tap, and said clearly, 'That little lady is *my* little lady, mister, and if you try to take her away from me, you're going to be guilty of abduction. Worse than that, you're going to be guilty of sending her soul to hell itself, to stoke the fires for all eternity. Do you really want *that* on your conscience?'

'Abner,' called the old man's wife anxiously, from inside the automobile. 'Abner, we don't want to go upsetting nobody, on account of something that isn't our affair.'

Terence lifted the sickle and held it in front of the old man's face. 'That's right, Abner,' he said, his eyes staring. 'We don't want to go upsetting nobody, do we?'

He slowly lifted the point of the sickle and flicked off the raindrop that was dangling from the tip of the old man's nose. 'How about it, Abner? How would you care for some free cosmetic surgery? I can whip off that ugly old beezer of yours before you can say Jehoshophat.'

The wind squalled and the pick-up rocked on its worn-out suspension. The old man said: 'I don't want you to go threatening me like that, mister. I'm not going to say you ain't scaring me, because that would be telling a untruth. But daughter or not, I don't see how I can let you take this girl. You can see that, can't you? If anything should happen to her, she'd be setting on my conscience for the rest of my days.'

Terence lowered the sickle. 'Setting on your conscience?' he asked. 'That's what they call a *dye-lemmer*, then, ain't it? That's what they call your one hundred percentile drop-forged *dye-lemmer*.'

There was an odd, incomplete moment, when neither of them spoke, but the rain kept drumming against the sides of the pick-up, and the wind kept on blethering. The whole world was being blown apart, from Hawkeye Downs to Indian Creek. Over to the north-east, over Marion, lightning flickered behind the clouds, and there was a strong smell of ozone in the air, like freshly-opened graves.

Terence was about to say something more when he was interrupted by a loud, shrill screeching noise. His eyes widened, and he looked over the old man's shoulder towards the back of the pick-up.

'What the hell was that?' he wanted to know.

'Nothing. Nothing at all.'

' "Nothing" sure screams like the devil himself.'

The old man shrugged. 'It's pigs. Just a couple of Berkshire shoats I've been taking over to my cousin's place in Bertram. Believe me, mister – believe me, I don't want trouble. Please.'

Terence stared at him, not blinking, not moving, in spite of the rain that was trickling down his face. Then, keeping his sickle raised, he circled around the side of the pick-up and looked in the back. Two hefty young male piglets were tethered close to the back of the cab, on a bed of wet farmyard straw. One was blotchy pink-and-black, as if somebody had been shaking an inkpen at it; the other was pink as Spam. They snorted and grunted when they saw Terence approaching, and one of them began to squeal and thrash and kick frantically at the side of the truck.

Terence went right up to the truck and rested his elbows on it, holding the sickle up where the piglets could see it clearly. By now, both of them were in a state approaching hysteria, squealing and bellowing and yanking at their tethers.

'I spook 'em, don't I?' Terence said. He watched them squealing for a while. Then he returned to the old man's side, wiping the rain from his forehead with the back of his sickle-hand.

'Pigs!' the old man said, almost shouting against the wind. 'They're good judges of character! They're fellow mortals, same like us. They know what's what.'

'I've heard that,' said Terence. 'I've also heard it said that you can look in a pig's eye, and see how soon you're going to die.'

'Mister – please –' the old man's wife called out, from inside the pick-up. 'Your little girl's shivering in here fit to fly apart. Please let us go. We won't tell a soul what happened here, and that's a promise.'

Terence ignored her. 'Look in the pig's eye, Abner,' he told the old man.

'What?'

'Look in its eye, Abner. See when you're going to die.'

Abner hesitated. The wind began to rise even higher, and they were suddenly deafened by a huge thunderclap, right overhead, which made the roadway shake and the shoats scream out in terror. The rain hesitated for a moment, but then it began to pour down again, even more torrentially than it had before, and even more ghosts rose from the roadway.

'Mister, I'm getting soaked to the bone here, and I have the osteoarthritis.'

'Go on, Abner,' said Terence, prodding the old man in the chest with the point of his sickle. 'Look in its eye, I dare you!

Who has the need of a crystal ball, or tea leaves, Abner? Who has the need of a needle?'

The old man cautiously turned his head to the back of the pick-up. The shoats weren't squealing and kicking any longer, but they were still tugging at their tethers in a state of high anxiety. They smelled pungently of urine and fear.

In a tight, choked voice, the old man said, 'My Dorothy's telling you the truth, mister. We won't say a word to a single soul, and I swear it.'

'The eye, Abner,' Terence repeated.

The old man looked towards the nearer of the two piglets. The shoat stopped struggling, and stood quite still, even though its brother kept pushing against its side. It lifted its head, and stared up at the old man in – what? in sympathy? in grief? in bewilderment? After all, like the old man had said, they were fellow mortals.

The shoat's eyelashes were white and prickly, but its eye was liquid black. It reflected everything in curved and perfect detail – the side of the truck, the rain, the swiftly-moving sky, the thin round-shouldered figure of the old man who was searching inside his own reflection for some magical sign that he would be given mercy.

It reflected the bright hooked shine of Terence's sickle, like a new moon rising in a speeded-up film.

The old man glanced back at Terence a split second before Terence hit him, and jerked up his arm to protect himself. The sickle knocked all four fingers from his left hand, in a tumble of blood and bits of knuckle. It glanced across the left side of his face, slicing off the upper part of his ear, most of his cheek, and a fat crimson ribbon of lip.

The old man screamed, and fell heavily against the side of the pick-up. The shoats screamed too, and kicked and scrabbled in panic. Blood sprayed up against the pick-up's rear window, and across the driving seat. Emily screamed, as well.

Terence was in a rage now. This holy day was becoming a farce. This day of salvation was being ruined by meddlers and blasphemers and stupid pig-farmers and women.

Another ear-shattering rumble of thunder overwhelmed him as he stood over the old man and started hacking at him, again and again.

The old man screamed, and tried to get up. But his bloody hand slid down the pick-up's wet door, leaving a rain-streaked hieroglyph.

Inside the pick-up, the old woman was screaming, too, her face distorted behind the wet-speckled window. She struggled across the driver's seat and opened the door, but Terence violently slammed it shut again. He must have caught her fingers, because he heard her cry out like a trapped animal.

Terence hacked at the old man with grim-faced fury, his cuts falling in a herringbone pattern, first to the left, then to the right. The old man kept up a low, quavering howl, while Terence's sickle bit into his scalp and into his face and into his upraised arms.

Blood spattered everywhere. Terence had never seen so much blood, except in the slaughterhouse. He felt as if he were showering in it.

The sickle made a brisk, satisfying chopping sound, like somebody biting into an apple. It smacked off the old man's right hand at the wrist, and then his left forearm. It cut away most of his scalp, so that his hair hung down over his eyes in blood-sodden hanks. Lumps of flesh dropped all around him.

In a desperate attempt to protect himself, the old man crouched right down, with his face pressed against the rainwashed roadway, so Terence started hacking with terrible determination at his back and his shoulders. His linen coat was soaked black with blood.

In the back of the pick-up, the shoats kept up their hideous screeching; and kicked at the sides of the pick-up in mortal panic.

Terence lifted his sickle-arm to give the old man the *coup de grâce.* He could taste blood, he could taste rainwater. He wanted to cut this hayseed's head clean off his shoulder – even if it did mean that the interfering old fool would be saved just as surely as Lisa and George had been saved.

But as he tried to strike downwards, he felt his wrist seized by two bony claws. He turned around, furious, frustrated, his face measled with blood. The old man's wife Dorothy had let herself out of the pick-up, and come up behind him, and was clinging to his arm in fury.

'Stop it!' she screamed. 'Stop it! Stop it! You're killing him! He's my husband! What did he ever do to you?'

Terence wrenched his arm free, and stared at the woman. He was truly amazed that she should have intervened; truly. Look at her, she was tiny, white-haired, and as bony as a quail. You would have thought that the wind and the rain would have blown her away. She wore a red-checked shirt and jeans, and red plastic earrings. She was a hayseed's wife: the elderly spouse of an even more elderly hick.

'You're killing him!' she said, and her eyes were blurred with tears. 'He's my husband, and the father of my children, and you're killing him!'

Terence looked down. Beside him, on the gleaming wet tar of the road, the old man was bent double, the stumps of his hands clutched tight to his chest. He was groaning like a rusty door, *eerrggghhhh, errrggghhh,* and shuddering. Blood dripped from his mouth, and a wide wash of blood ran out from underneath him, and mingled with the rain.

'I ain't killed him yet,' Terence replied, in a quiet, faraway tone of voice. 'It ain't for want of trying, though . . . you have to give me that much credit. I've cut off just about everything that got in the way. 'Cepting his head, of course, and I was just getting to that.'

'You leave him be,' the old woman commanded. She took off her spectacles because of the rain, but she kept her eyes on Terence all the time. 'He's my husband. You leave him be.'

Terence half-turned away. He rubbed his right elbow, as if all that sickle-cutting had strained it. The shoats had settled down a little since Terence had stopped hacking, but as he turned back towards them, they started up squealing again in renewed panic.

He turned back to the old woman, and as he did so his right arm curled back behind him, right back, with all the fluency of a good tennis player, and the sickle flashed around and around, building up momentum, and then *whack!* and her head bounced clear off her shoulders, emptying out blood like a tipped-over bucket, and dropped with a heavy thud into the back of the pick-up and rolled to the tailgate and stopped. Her face ended up staring open-eyed at the straw, like a woman who has never seen straw before.

Her body stood squirting out blood, a high pulsing fountain of it, fifteen or sixteen inches into the air, out of her severed neck. Terence still stared at her. It was incredible that her body could stand by itself for so long, as if still believed that it could go on living, without a head. He almost expected her to take a step, or to reach out for him. But then a sharp squall caught her, and her knees suddenly buckled. She pirouetted sideways, and dropped down onto the bloody roadway next to her husband. One foot twitched in its cheap canvas lace-up, twitched and then finally stopped twitching.

Terence hacked into the old man's shoulder yet again – more out of pique than any genuine desire to hurt him. This time the old man accepted the blow without complaint. He was too agonized to do anything but die.

'Why don't you kill me?' he sobbed. 'Why don't you kill me?'

'Because you're dead already!' Terence shouted at him, so that the old man was sure to hear him over the storm. 'We're *all* dead. What difference does it make? We're all travellers, all of us. We're all taking a ride on the road of no return.'

The old man said, 'Fuck you,' and it was quite apparent from the way in which he said it that he had never sworn at anybody, ever, in the whole of his life, man or boy, right back to the days of Amos'n'Andy and Jack Armstrong and the Ralston Straight Shooters. Sober, modest and chapel-going. That was the kind of man that Terence was hacking to death.

He fell at last; and Terence, tired and distracted, *bored* even, stood up straight.

'Couldn't just die, could you?' he told the old man's body. 'Couldn't just *die*? You had to make a performance out of it. Had to curse. A minute and a half shy of heaven, and you had to curse.'

The storm was almost laughably wild. The rain was crossing the fields at a high diagonal, and drumming on the sides of the pick-up. The blood that Terence had spilled was whorled and marbled and washed into the ditches, mingling with the mud.

Holding up his hand to protect his face from the rain, Terence stalked to the open driver's door of the pick-up and checked inside. The passenger door was open, too. The seats were spotted with blood and rain, and there was a worn-out, beige leather purse and a shopping bag and a folded pile of pale blue knitting: a sweater, maybe, or a child's matinée jacket. Whatever it was, it would never be finished now. But there was no sign of Emily. Just the passenger door creaking in the wind and the rain trickling jerkily down the window.

Terence stood up, and looked around, sniffing, blinking, shielding his eyes with his hands. The rain was falling so hard that the fields were covered in a fine, silvery mist, and it was impossible for him to see more than two or three hundred feet.

'God damn it, I have to save her,' he whispered. 'This is the day; this is the very, very day. I have to save her. Can't let her down now.'

He circled around the front of the pick-up, walking erratically, as if somebody had hit him. Rain poured down the back of his neck, and streamed from the end of his nose. He scanned the edge of the highway for footprints, but it was raining so furiously that the ditches and verges had been turned into foaming pools of ochre dirt. Dear God in heaven, he felt as if he were drowning. His jeans clung wetly to his thighs, and the back of his shirt drooped down. And still the wind was rising, so that the shoats in the back of the pick-up stopped their squealing and started to moan in desperation, the way that humans moan when they're convinced that they're going to die.

'Emily!' Terence bellowed. 'Where are you, Emily?'

He narrowed his eyes and peered into the rain. At first, he couldn't see anything at all. But then – what was that? A flower, bobbing in the gloom? A flower, a shrub, or a little girl in a too-tight floral frock, a little girl with rain-blurred spectacles, running for her life?

Terence loped and squelched into the fields. He flung his hair back with his hand, his sickle-hand, and he started to run. His shoes and his jean-bottoms were heavy with mud, but he kept on running, harder and harder. His legs hurt; his arms hurt. His lungs were blocked with phlegm. But he threw back his head and closed his eyes tight and he swore to the Lord God that he would save his Emily from all of this, he would save her, he would save her. Ahead of him, he was sure he could see that floral dress bobbing, and he knew what it was, that it was Emily.

He was far too winded to call her name, but he closed his eyes tight again and he said a prayer for her, and he promised, he *promised* to save her, no matter what it took, no matter how far he had to run.

He would run and run till the sun came up, but he would save her.

Up ahead of him, only three hundred feet up ahead of him, Emily was crying and running at the same time. She knew that Daddy was after her, although she hadn't once turned back to look. She couldn't have seen him, even if she had. It was raining so hard that she had taken off her glasses, and she was carrying them in her hand. She was exhausted and she was soaked right through to her undervest, but she knew that she couldn't stop. She hadn't seen Abner die, she hadn't seen Dorothy die, but she had heard the piglets screaming and she had seen blood spraying up against the pick-up's rear window; and she knew that she had to run and run.

She didn't know where she was going. She didn't even know where she was.

The rain began to ease just a little. Terence could feel it easing, and the wind dying down. He could see Emily clearly now, and he knew for sure that it was Emily. He could see her frock. He could see her pale muddy legs running.

He gave a wet, catarrhal grunt of triumph. This would soon be over, and the Lord would soon be served. He whipped his sickle around and around, so that it whirred in the rain, and he knew that the Lord was with him. If he hadn't been so breathless, if his chest and his lungs hadn't been so congested, he would have cried out, '*Halleluja!*' The end of the bad blood.

Now there was only a hundred feet between them. The field

was so wet and the mud was so thick that Emily could barely manage more than a stumbling jog. Behind her, Daddy was keeping up a steady, pounding trot; and she could hear his feet plod-plod-plodding through the furrows. She turned around; and he was so close now that even without her spectacles she could see his unfocused outline. A tall, distorted figure, like half-melted shadow, with a bright curved blade in his hand.

And he kept on coming, dogged and determined. Not calling; not speaking; but slowly whirling that blade around his head, around and around, and keeping up that steady, pounding trot.

She managed another two hundred feet, and then it all became too much for her. The shock of what had happened; the blood; and the rain; and the screeching shoats. She tripped and fell into the mud, and lay there weeping and winded and exhausted, so that Daddy was able to ease off down to a walk, and approach her slowly, with his sickle lowered, wiping the rain from his face, sodden and winded but still compassionate.

She opened her eyes and saw his muddy shoes and muddy jeans; but she didn't have the courage to look up any further.

He sat down beside her, right in the mud, and dropped his head between his knees. His heart felt as if it were made of solid pumice stone and was scouring his chest cavity with every beat. He was soaked with rain and soaked with sweat, stinking and blood-soaked and almost finished. But he had sinned; and the Lord had sent him to atone for his sins; and to save Emily was the very last act he had to perform, before his place in heaven was assured.

'Emily?' he said at last, still panting.

Emily stared at him, too winded and terrified to reply. She could feel the mud and the whiskery young winter wheat against her cheek.

'I have to tell you, Emily, you gave me a run for my money there, you surely did.'

He hawked, and coughed, and then spat into the rain.

'I'll tell you something, sweetheart, you almost killed me, running the way you did. Almost sent me to meet my Maker before you did.'

He was silent for a while, trying to catch his breath, and then he said, 'I love you, Emily, I want you to know that. I love you the same way I love Lisa and George. Love you dearly, love you dearly. And this is why. You won't blame me, will you, for what I had to do today? You won't judge me for it? This is all for the best, believe me, sweetheart. This is what they mean by atonement, by making amends. This is what they mean by saying sorry, Lord, I sinned – I sinned real bad – and now I'm apologizing to you for what I did, in the only way I know how.'

Emily swallowed. It hurt to swallow. 'Don't kill me,' she begged him.

He sniffed, and frowned, and shook his head.

'Please, don't kill me,' said Emily. She kept her voice toneless, in the way that most victims do, in case they provoke their would-be murderers. The rain kept on lashing against their faces. They were so wet and muddy now that they were scarcely distinguishable from stacks of stubble, or bulldozed mud. They had become one with the Iowa landscape.

Terence eased himself onto his feet. He wiped his sickle on his muddy sleeve. 'You'll have to sit up, sweetheart. I can't take your head off cleanly, else.'

Emily stayed where she was, lying on her side in a furrow. Her eyes were open but they were completely unfocused. She was breathing through her mouth.

Terence leaned over her, and tapped her arm with the point of his sickle. 'Emily . . .' he coaxed her. 'You have to sit up.'

Emily said, flatly, 'Jesus wants me for a sunbeam.'

Terence grinned, and nodded, with a thin trail of snot

hanging from his nose. 'That's right, Emily, that's absolutely right. Jesus wants you for a sunbeam.'

Emily, at last, sat up, propping herself up on one arm. Terence paced around her, jerky as a marionette, seething with righteousness, oblivious to the rain, oblivious to the storm, thinking only of what he could do for her. He could save her! He could send her to heaven! Right out of this wet and windswept field, right up to heaven, where it was warm and golden and bathed in sunshine!

'Are you ready?' he asked her.

Emily looked dazed. Emily *felt* dazed. All she could think of was Momma, and bed, and ham for supper. Her legs ached from running and she hated being wet. She hoped that dying wouldn't hurt.

Terence bent over her, so that his nose was only two or three inches away from hers. 'I'm going to save you, Emily. It's going to be great! You're going to meet Jesus and John the Baptist and all of God's angels. No more bad blood, Emily. No more bad blood.'

Emily narrowed her eyes. Over Daddy's shoulder, through the mist, she thought she could see a blue light flashing. It vanished for a moment, and she thought that she must have imagined it, or maybe it was distant lightning. But then she saw it again, distinctly – a blue light, and then a red light, too.

'Come on, now, sweetheart, let's get this over with,' said Terence. 'There's a time to live and a time to die; and now is your time to die.'

Emily deliberately looked away from the flashing lights. She was terrified that Daddy might see them, too, and hit her with the sickle before she had a chance to get away. 'Could I clean my glasses first?' she asked him. It was all she could think of. 'I want to see the world properly, just one last time.'

'You want to clean your glasses?' he demanded, as if she had asked for something totally absurd, like a knickerbocker glory or a Big Mac or a last toboggan run at Jones Park. But then he thought: why not? Why not let her see the world for what it is – miserable, desolate and swept with storms? She'll be glad to leave it.

'For sure,' he said. 'Whatever. But don't take all day.'

He stood close beside her with his eyes closed and his head raised, so that he could feel the rainstorm pelting into his face. Apocalypse! Kingdom come!

Emily sat in the mud beside him, persistently trying to clean her glasses with the hem of her dress. When she put them on, they were still smeary, but she knew that she was saved. She knew that God had taken care of her, after all.

Slowly jostling toward them across the field, blurred by the rain, she could now see clearly what her daddy couldn't see, which was the flickering red-and-blue lights of two police patrol cars.

They stopped, both of them, less than fifty feet away. Doors opened, and officers climbed out, and unholstered guns. The rain fell between them in heavy curtains.

Emily said nervously, 'Daddy?'

Terence didn't hear her at first. 'Daddy?' she repeated, a little higher. She was ready to get up and run if he tried to hit her with the sickle.

Terence opened his eyes, his arms held out, like Christ on the cross.

'Freeze!' one of the officers yelled at him. Terence quarter-turned, but then the officer yelled '*Freeze!*' a second time, and Terence froze.

'Drop that sickle!' the officer ordered.

For one long second, Emily thought that he wasn't going to drop it, that he was going to try to hit her with it. But then, without even looking down at her, he let the sickle fall from his fingers. It stuck in the ground, handle uppermost.

'Now, flat on your face!' the officer shouted. Terence

lowered himself onto his knees, and then spreadeagled himself in the winter wheat.

A young officer with a black moustache came running forward. He lifted Emily out of the mud, and jogged back to his patrol car, carrying her in his arms. His coat felt damp and rough and his badge scratched her arm.

'How bad is she hurt?' she heard one of the officers asking.

'Cut on the shoulder, that's about it. She's probably shocked. Get her over to the Mercy Trauma Center pronto.'

Emily was wrapped up in a blanket and lowered into the back seat of the car. The car smelled of disinfectant and vinyl and stale cigars. The last she saw of her daddy, he was still lying spreadeagled on the ground, with two officers standing over him. In the far distance, she could see the dark corkscrew of a rising tornado, and she remembered what her daddy had told her, every time they saw a tornado: 'It's the devil, dancing on God's good earth.'

The patrol car jounced back onto the highway, and headed towards Cedar Rapids, with its siren whooping and spray rising up behind it.

It passed the bronze El Camino pick-up, and as it passed, a huge man in a sodden sheriff's hat and a voluminous grey plastic raincoat gave it a cursory wave.

A deputy came around the front of the pick-up, his collar turned up. In spite of the gloom, he was still wearing sunglasses with amber lenses.

'Can't find her head over there!' he shouted.

The sheriff looked exasperated. 'He didn't have it with him, did he?'

The deputy shook his head.

'Shit,' said the sheriff. 'This is all I need. And right in the middle of a storm, too.'

The deputy bent down and looked under the pick-up's seats. Then he circled around the back. The shoats squealed at him angrily, and he backed away.

'Jesus, those pigs are sure touchy.'

The sheriff walked over to the pick-up and peered into the back. One of the shoats started shrilling at him, too, but he held his ground and said, 'Shut your snout, bacon-face.'

Although the first shoat kept on squealing, the second was too preoccupied with snuffling around amongst the straw. Underneath the straw, two of the channels in the metal floor were brimming with red-stained rainwater, and the shoat was greedily lapping it up.

Blood? Now where the hell was that coming from?

The sheriff peered towards the back of the vehicle, and it was then that he saw what he was looking for: the old woman's face, staring at him coyly from underneath the straw, as if he had caught her playing hide-and-seek.

'My God,' he shuddered. It looked almost as if the old woman were smiling at him. Then, 'Henry!' he called. 'You can stop looking now! We got ourselves a head!'

Two

When the sheriff arrived at the Pearson house, Mrs Pearson was sitting in the kitchen, still wearing her blue floral apron. She was a thin, tired, quite pretty-looking woman of thirty-six or thirty-seven, with an angular Katherine Hepburn type of face and greying blonde hair and eyes the colour of cornflowers that had been pressed between the pages of a book, and faded.

She wore silver pendant earrings, with black onyxes in

them. The kind of earrings that she might have bought years ago, when she was young.

The kitchen was well-fitted but curiously dated, like the kitchen in *The Lucy Show.* There was a 1960s Westinghouse refrigeratator with blue and pink doors, a stainless-steel Robbiari espresso-maker, and a titanic cream stove, the top of which was crowded with saucepans. The oven had been turned off now, but the kitchen was still warm and steamy and smelled strongly of baking ham.

Sitting with Mrs Pearson was deputy Edna Bulowski (she of the braided brown hair and the steel glasses and the hairy mole). She gave the sheriff a look which meant 'better go easy'.

'Mrs Pearson – Iris –' she said.

Mrs Pearson looked up, distractedly. She was clearly in shock. She wasn't crying, but she was twisting a handkerchief in her hands, around and around, and she looked as if she could break down at any moment.

'Iris, this is Sheriff Friend. He wants to ask you one or two questions.'

The sheriff took off his damp scout hat and set it down on the table. 'Hallo, Iris. Why don't you call me Luke?'

Iris gave him a faint acknowledging nod. Luke dragged out a chair and asked, 'Mind if I sit down? I promise you I won't break it. Any coffee in that pot, deputy? I've been standing out on 151 for the past three hours with the heavens stuck on "open".'

Luke was huge, bull-shouldered, well over six feet, with cropped brown hair and a wide, Slavic-looking face. This morning his bathroom scale had told him that he weighed 304 lb – and that was after losing 11 lb on a 'no-cookies-no-potatoes-and-absolutely-no-Snickers' diet. He had always been big, ever since he was a kid. It may have been hormones, it may have been his mother's cooking. When he was a boy, the Friend family never got up from the table until everybody had cleared their plates of pork chops, stuffing, sweet potatoes and sweet biscuits, followed by ice-cream and gateaux, and all sluiced down with gallons of cold milk.

Luke was big, but he was remarkably agile for a man of his bulk. He took judo classes most weekends, swam whenever he could, and didn't work out enough at New Life Fitness World on 3rd Avenue.

'Iris,' he said, taking hold of Mrs Pearson's hands. 'The first thing I want to do is to tell you how sorry we are, the whole sheriff's department. This is a terrible tragedy. This is the kind of thing that should never happen to no one. The worst part about it is, it's happened to you.'

'Thank you,' Iris whispered. Her eyes darted, unfocused, from side to side. 'Everybody's been so kind.'

'I called the trauma centre on my way here. Emily's fine. She didn't even need stitches. She should be able to come home tomorrow.'

Iris nodded. 'Thank you.'

Edna Bulowski passed Luke a cup of black coffee. He took a tube of Sweetex out of one of the bullet-loops in his belt, and clicked five sweeteners into it. He paused, and then clicked in another one.

'Iris,' he said, 'I know it's real upsetting, after everything that's happened today, but the quicker I can find out why Terence did what he did, the better.'

Iris shook her head. 'I never knew why,' she replied.

Luke was vigorously stirring his coffee. 'You *never* knew why?'

'No,' she whispered. 'Never.'

Luke thought about that. Then he said, 'When you say you *never* knew why, that implies some kind of ongoing situation . . . like he threatened to do this before?'

'No,' said Iris.

'So he never threatened to do anything like this before? You were totally taken by surprise when he did it?'

'He never threatened before and he didn't threaten today. He just did it, without telling me. He took my children away and he killed them, without even telling me.'

'But you said you *never* knew why.'

She shrugged. Her eyes were beginning to fill up with tears. 'That's because I never did. All that talk about the Bible, and bad blood. He never stopped talking about it, never. Not a single day went by without him mentioning bad blood. I never understood what he was trying to tell me. I asked him to explain. You don't know how many times I asked him to explain. But all he ever said was, "It's private, it's shameful, and nobody should know".'

Luke sipped his coffee and then carefully replaced the cup on its saucer. 'How long has this kind of talk been going on for?'

'Ever since we got married, that was twelve years ago last Labor Day. Everything seemed to be fine for the first couple of months. Everything was wonderful! But then he took me to stay with his father in Des Moines, and after that he changed, totally, without any warning. He started worrying, he started having nightmares, he started talking about the Bible. He kept on and on about bad blood.'

'Did you seek any kind of professional help?' asked Luke. 'You know – a shrink, maybe, or a priest?'

Iris shook her head again. 'He said he was fine. So long as we didn't have children, so long as we didn't tempt fate, he said that everything was going to work out perfect.'

'So long as you didn't have children?'

'That's correct.'

'But you did have children,' said Luke. 'You had three of them.'

Iris lowered her gaze. 'Yes,' she whispered. 'Three of them.'

'Why was that, if he had specifically warned you not to?'

'I don't know. I guess it just happened. Emily came first. Emily was an accident. I told Terry that I'd have her terminated, if he really wanted me to, but he couldn't bear it. He said it was meant to happen, whether it was good or bad. I thought he was pleased. I thought he was really pleased. But when Emily was born he shut himself up in his room for nearly four whole days, and he came out looking so awful. Like a skeleton, almost. Thin, wild, I don't know.'

'Did he tell you why?'

'No,' Iris said, reflectively. 'No . . . he never told me why.'

'Weren't you the least bit curious, as to why?'

She lowered her eyes and they roamed around the floor, as if she were still looking for something that she had dropped, the back of an earring or a screw from the Robbiari coffee machine.

'Oh, for sure, I was curious. But Terry isn't the kind of man you can ask too many questions of. He's a good father, don't get me wrong.' She paused, twisting her handkerchief tighter and tighter. 'He *was* a good father – before this, before today. The children adored him and he seemed to adore them, too. I thought he did. I honestly thought he did. Otherwise I wouldn't have let him take them out. I would have kept them home and *never* let him touch them.'

Luke watched her for a while, his hands folded over his stomach. He liked to watch people. He could often tell more about a person from five minutes of watching than he could from five hours of interrogation. Their gestures; their unexpected smiles. The way they sat still, or the way they twitched. People who are telling the truth don't bite their nails after every sentence. People who are telling the truth never look up at the ceiling. Ever.

Eventually, he said, 'What was going on here, Iris? I need to know. You don't have to worry about Terry, about him hurting you or nothing, if you tell. We caught him right in the act. He's going to spend the rest of his natural-born days in Fort Madison, no question of that. You don't have nothing to be feared of.'

Iris stared back at him with those faded, heartbreak eyes. She opened her mouth as if she were about to say something, but then she didn't.

Luke heaved himself out of his chair, and walked around the table. He stood by the sink looking out through the window. The lower half of the window was curtained in cheery red-checked cotton, but through the top half he could see the black thunderclouds lowering over the buildings of downtown Cedar Rapids, and the rain falling from the upper atmosphere in grey, funereal curtains. The storm had mostly passed through the S W district now, but it was still raining, and the gutters still gurgled.

'Mind if I help myself to one of these cookies?' he asked Iris, opening up the lid of a porcelain cookie-jar in the shape of a small barrel filled with flowers. It was marked 'Czech Village, Cedar Rapids, IA'.

Iris said nothing so Luke took out three pecan cookies and started to munch them, standing right behind her so that he could see her face reflected in the glass of the kitchen cabinet.

'These are good,' he said. 'I shouldn't eat them, but I'm weak.'

'Me too,' said Iris, in a dull voice.

'What makes you say that?'

There was a pause, and then she said, 'I guess I always knew that he would do something terrible, one day. I could feel it building up and building up.'

'Iris,' said Luke, watching the expression on her reflected face. 'It's not your fault. It's nobody's fault, except for Terry, and Terry's locked up. You couldn't have done anything. You couldn't.'

'I could have told them not to go!' Iris burst out tearfully, twisting around in her chair.

'Hey,' Luke reassured her, and stroked her hair. 'You could have done, sure. But why *would* you have done? You had no good cause to, did you?'

'But there was always the room. I should have guessed that something was going to go wrong, one day. Normal men don't have a room.'

'What are you talking about?' asked Luke. 'What room?'

Iris wiped her eyes. 'Terry has a room. It's upstairs, in back. He always keeps it locked, and he never lets me in there.'

'Never once?'

'Never.'

Luke swallowed his last cookie and brushed the crumbs from his shirt. 'What do you think he keeps in there?'

'I don't know. I used to try to guess. At first I thought – well, dirty magazines, or something like that. Then I thought no . . . we have a good sex life, why should he lock himself into his room with dirty magazines? Then I thought he was meditating, kind of dropping out of daily life, trying to recharge his batteries, you know? Then I stopped trying to think, because I couldn't work out *what* he was keeping in that room, or why he spent so long in there. I just grew to accept the fact that he did, and that I'd never know.'

Luke lifted up the lid of the biggest saucepan. 'Corn, huh? I've always been a corn-o-maniac.'

Iris glanced up at him. 'Why don't you have some? I'm not going to eat, not now.'

'Unh-hunh . . . don't tempt me,' he said. Apart from Iris's cookies, he hadn't eaten since breakfast. But he could no more have touched this family's uneaten supper than eaten dead crow or roast rat. The family had been butchered to pieces, by fate, by madness, and the two littlest ones wouldn't be needing supper where they were going.

He lifted up another lid, and then another. Summer squash, carrots and red cabbage. Poor Lisa, he thought. Poor George.

Luke had seen the medical examiner lifting a plastic bag out of the undergrowth, silvery with moisture and splotched with blood – a plastic bag containing George's head. Luke had seen some bad things in his fourteen years as sheriff of Linn County; but he had never seen anything as bad as that. He knew when he saw it that he was destined to have terrible dreams about it, probably for the rest of his life.

'It was going to be ham tonight, then?' said Luke. He was trying to keep the conversation low-key, undramatic, but at the same time facing up to the reality of what had happened.

Iris said, regretfully, 'Yes, that's right. We always have ham Saturday nights. Ham is Emily's favourite.'

Luke nodded, and smiled. 'Do you think I could see Terry's room?' he asked, as offhandedly as he could.

'What do you mean?'

'I mean his private room. The one he always keeps locked.'

Iris stared up at him and bit her lip. 'I don't have the key! And in any case, Terry wouldn't like it at all! He could easily –'

'He could easily *what*, Iris?' asked Luke. 'He could easily get angry? He could easily start beating up on you?'

'He didn't beat up on me,' said Iris. 'He never beat up on me once.'

'No,' Luke agreed. 'I don't think he had to, did he?'

He walked back around the kitchen table and faced her. Far away, lightning flickered, and the overhead lights stuttered and dimmed. 'Terry's behind bars, Iris,' Luke reminded her. 'Terry's behind bars and he's not coming out. You don't have to be feared of him any longer . . . I promise.'

Iris sat thinking for almost half a minute, her eyes still darting around the floor. Then she suddenly looked up, and said, 'All right. You can take a look. You *should* take a look.'

She stood up, and brushed down her apron. 'Come on,' she said.

Edna Bulowski had been waiting outside the door, and had to step promptly back as Iris and Luke came out.

'We're just checking out the second floor,' said Luke, smiling fatly at her.

'Iris – you're sure you're okay?' Edna asked her.

Iris made a face that was made up of nine different expressions at once. Numbness, indifference, pain and despair, and a whole lot more besides. 'I'm fine,' she said, although she clearly wasn't.

Edna said, 'Sheriff – can you talk to Rick Smith from the *Gazette*?'

Luke shook his head. 'Tell him I love him like a brother and that I'll see him in twenty minutes. Come on, Iris, let's take a look at that room.'

Iris climbed the steep, flowery-carpeted stairs. The staircase was decorated with anaemic beige wallpaper with bamboo patterns on it, and hung with six or seven family photographs. Luke glanced uncomfortably at a picture of George in his baby-buggy, and thought of George's bagged-up head, and his little fallen body. It wasn't often that Luke wished that Iowa had the death penalty, but he would be delighted to see Terence Pearson pay for what he had done with his own miserable life. Guillotined, preferably.

They crossed the landing, and past the half-open doors of the children's bedrooms. Luke saw a white-painted rocking horse in George's room, and a large scrawly drawing of a house standing in a bright blue garden, with bright blue bushes and bright blue trees. In Lisa's room, a Cabbage Patch doll lay on its back on the floor, one leg raised, just where Lisa had dropped it.

Terence's private room was right at the end of the upstairs

corridor. Iris reached up and took down the key from the top of the architrave.

'You knew where the key was?' asked Luke, in surprise.

She turned around. 'Of course. He didn't hide it.'

'You knew where the key was and you still didn't go in there? *Ever?*'

'Terence said he would always know if I had been in there.'

Luke was about to say something, but then he decided not to. There was no accounting for the way that people lived. Only a couple of weeks ago, he had broken into an apartment in the Roman building on 2nd Avenue because the neighbours had complained of constant barking – only to find a naked man shuffling around on his hands and knees wearing a dog collar, while his wife sat watching *The Price Is Right* and occasionally tossing him dog biscuits.

Iris unlocked the door.

'Do you think we should?' she asked, nervously.

'You want me to come back with a warrant?' asked Luke.

'No,' said Iris. 'You don't have to do that.'

They stepped inside and Iris switched on the light. The room was quite small, only about nine by seven. Its single window was covered with a thick net curtain, which was grey with grime. The left-hand wall was completely filled with wooden bookshelves, which sagged under the weight of scores of books, some of them bound in cracked black leather, others covered with tattered paper jackets. The whole room smelled of stale books – sourish and dusty – and something else, besides. A smell like very old pot-pourri.

The right-hand wall was covered in sheaves of maps and astrological diagrams and newspaper cuttings, some of which were amber with age. Luke crossed over and took a look at some of the cuttings. Most of them came from the *Cedar Rapids Gazette* and the weekly *Marion Times*, although there were some from as far away as Wichita, Kansas, and Omaha, Nebraska.

Luke peered closely at one or two of them, expecting to see stories about murder or human sacrifice or some such, but every article was all about soybean yields and corn production and hog rearing. EAST AMANA FARMER'S RECORD-BREAKING SOYBEAN CROP. SWINE FEVER DECIMATES HAWKEYE HERD. BROCCOLI PRICES WAVER. The diagrams mostly showed sections of the Midwest, with shaded areas to indicate weather conditions – rainfall, storm activity and areas of unexpected drought.

Two of the astrological diagrams had been heavily marked with red felt-tip pen. There were three thick underscorings of Virgo, and a thick line connecting them with Aries. On the bottom of one of the diagrams, Terence had written in block letters, *JIG!!!*

'Do you know what any of this means?' Luke asked Iris.

Iris was standing in the doorway, nervously cradling herself in her arms. She shook her head.

'Is Terry particularly interested in agriculture? In crops?'

'He works in feed.'

'Yes,' said Luke. 'He told us. Indian Creek Livestock Supplies. What about stars?'

'Stars?' asked Iris, bewildered.

'Stars . . . you know. Astrology.'

'He was never interested in stars that I knew of. I mean he never read his horoscope, or anything like that.'

Luke looked over the cuttings and diagrams and didn't know what the hell to think. What kind of a man keeps track of crop yields and weather reports and astrological movements; and in such obsessive detail?

'He didn't talk about his work much,' Iris volunteered. 'He said it wasn't too interesting.'

'Then what *did* he talk about?'

'Not very much, I guess, apart from bad blood. Sometimes, when he was very angry, he wouldn't stop talking about bad blood for hours on end, and how we shouldn't have had children, because we were passing it on. He talked about the Bible, too, and God, and we always went to church on Sundays, and he would talk about the sermon, and usually say how bad it was.'

She lowered her eyes again. 'I guess you could say that he wasn't at peace with himself. I guess you could say that he wasn't at peace with anybody.'

Beneath the window stood a second-hand pine desk: it was too cheap and battered to qualify as an antique. There was a black-painted bentwood chair drawn up close to it, and it was strewn with open books and yellow notepads and dozens of pencils – literally dozens of them, a whole forest of pencils, all of differing lengths and various degrees of sharpness. Beside them rested a huge Bowie knife, with a rusted blade and its handle bound round with string. Luke picked it up and hefted it in his hand and tested the edge. It may have been rusty, but it was almost preternaturally sharp.

Terence had obviously used it to keep his pencils pointed. There was a wastebasket underneath the desk almost quarter-filled with aromatic cedar shavings.

He had used it for whittling, too. The right-hand edge of the desk had been scratched and scored, and the corner had been carved with an angry-looking man's face.

'Must've taken him hours to carve that,' Luke remarked.

'He was up here for hours,' said Iris.

Pinned to the wall beside the window was a large black and white engraving, about twenty inches by twelve, printed on heavy cartridge paper. It had obviously been folded and unfolded many times, and it had been foxed and faded by sunlight and damp. It showed a strange smiling man walking through the wavy grass of a stylized field. On one side of the field the sun was shining brightly. On the other, storm clouds were gathering. The man was dressed in a cloak made entirely of bay leaves, and tied with streamers. On his head he wore a conical hat, also made out of leaves. He carried a staff in his hand, cut from a flowering tree.

The engraving was crowded with hundreds of surrealistic little details. In one corner, a group of black rats were playing dice. In another, a naked girl was thrusting her arm into a rabbit's ear, right up to the elbow. Luke lifted the bottom of the engraving away from the wall, so that he could read the caption. It said simply *Mummer, K. Bulstrode fecit.*

'Do you know anything about this?' Luke asked Iris.

'Never saw it before.'

'It doesn't have a date on it. Looks pretty old, though, doesn't it?'

'Terry doesn't usually care for pictures, excepting for family photographs. I tried to hang up one of my mother's old pictures once, and he practically threw a fit.'

'Did he now?'

'It wasn't a picture of anything special. Just trees.'

Luke picked up one of the books. *Climatic Extremes and Their Effects on Agriculture,* by Dr Nils Thorson, of the University of Iowa. Then another: *May Day: The Cultural Significance of the Spring Festival* by Janacek Hubry. And another: *Pagan Fertility Rites and Other Folk Rituals.*

He put down the books and picked up Terence's notepad. It was written in a tiny, even hand, page after page of closely-spaced writing. But it was all in a foreign language, crowded with accents and diacritics.

'Terry speak any other language?' asked Luke.

'Not to me,' said Iris.

'This looks like Czech. Did Terry know Czech?'

Iris shook her head.

Luke ran his fingertip across the books on the bookshelves. All of the titles evinced the same kind of interests as the books on the desk. Agriculture. Astrology. Folk-ritual. And religion. The bottom three shelves were packed with bibles. There must have been forty or fifty of them, of varying ages and varying origins. Some of them were cheap Gideon editions, the kind you find in hotel rooms. Others were bound in worn black leather, with heavy gilt stamping. There were bibles in French, bibles in German, bibles in Polish, bibles in Spanish.

'He's pretty religious, then?' asked Luke.

'We go to church, if that's what you mean.' She paused, and then she said, 'We *went* to church.'

'Catholic?'

'Terry is. Not me. But we go to the same church.'

'Which one's that?'

'The Immaculate Conception. Terry doesn't much like Father Wozniak – says he betrays the Bible, whatever he means by that. But he likes the name of the church, Immaculate Conception. He's always telling people that's where we go, Immaculate Conception, as if he's really proud of it.'

'Well . . . does no harm to be proud of your church.'

'I don't know. Terry's pride wasn't your usual kind of pride. Terry's pride was almost like gloating.'

Luke held up Terence's notepad. 'Do you mind if I take this, Iris? Have it translated? Maybe it'll give us some kind of a clue about what was happening in Terry's head.'

'Go ahead. Please. I don't want it.'

Luke gave the room one last careful inspection. He was trying to sense what Terence Pearson actually did when he locked himself away from his family and sharpened his pencils and wrote all these pages of minuscule notes. He heard the faraway grumbling of thunder, and rain sprinkled against the window, soft and quick, as if a frightened priest had stood in the yard and hurriedly sprinkled it with holy water.

He found his attention drawn back to the strange smiling

man in the engraving. The man smiled at him from underneath his ridiculous leafy hat, and his look was deeply mocking. *Who am I?* he seemed to be asking. *And why am I dressed up like a walking bush?* For some reason, Luke felt as if he were missing something here, something fundamental but very weird indeed, and it made him feel deeply uneasy.

'Okay, thanks,' he said, at last, and they left the room. Iris locked it behind them, returning the key to the top of the architrave.

As they went back downstairs, she said, 'I won't have to see Terry again, will I?'

'You may be called to give evidence, when he goes to trial.'

'But he really won't get out?'

Luke laid his hand on her shoulder. 'They'll send him to Fort Madison, no question about it. Nobody gets out of Fort Madison.'

They reached the hall. Edna Bulowski was still waiting for them, looking tired and anxious.

'How are you feeling, Iris?' she wanted to know, pointedly ignoring Luke. The implication being that Luke shouldn't have subjected her to questioning while she was still in shock.

'Oh . . . I'm fine,' said Iris. 'I guess I'll have to clear away supper, now that the children aren't coming home.'

'Iris – you don't have to do anything except rest up,' said Luke.

Edna put her arm around her and led her back towards the kitchen.

'Is she going to be all right?' asked Luke.

'Dr Mayhew gave her a sedative. I'll give her another in a half-hour or so, and a mug of warm milk. Her sister's coming over from Dubuque.'

'Thank you, deputy,' said Luke. He picked up his hat from the kitchen table, and then he took hold of Iris's hand, and squeezed it. 'Thanks for talking to me, Iris. I appreciate it. I know this has been the worst day of your life, bar none. I guess that all I can say is: grieve for Lisa, and grieve for little George. But don't forget to grieve for yourself, too.'

Iris nodded wordlessly.

Luke went back to the front door, and Edna followed him. 'I talked to Rick Clark. He says that you can love him like a *sister* if you want to, but he can't wait one minute longer. He has a deadline to meet. And you have Joyce Leibold from WMT 600 waiting to talk to you, too.'

'Fame at last,' said Luke.

He opened the door onto Vernon Drive. The wet night was spangled with flashing red and blue lights, and the floodlights of local television crews. The storm had mostly passed over now, heading east towards Illinois, and a warm, drying wind was blowing. There had been some tornado damage in the Amana Colonies: the general store had lost part of its roof, and one of the chimneys at the woollen mill had collapsed. Near Kalona, six or seven hogs had been killed when they were caught in the open, and during the worst of the storm the Cedar Rapids Municipal Airport had been closed for two and a half hours. But that was about the length and the breadth of it. Just another late-summer tornado.

Deputy Norman Gorman had been keeping his post by the Pearsons' front door. He was short and stocky, built like a French Revival chest-of-drawers. He trained with weights in a fruitless and never-ending effort to increase his height: Luke had once found him hanging by his hands from his office doorway, with 50-lb weights attached to each ankle. Deputy Norman Gorman had a huge sense of humour about everything except how tall he wasn't.

Short as he was, though, he had emotional brown eyes and a heavy black moustache which seemed to appeal to all kinds of girls, both virginal and blowzy, and Norman was rarely short of female company.

'How is she?' he asked, nodding his head towards the front door.

Luke adjusted his damp, shapeless hat. 'Bearing up. But it hasn't really hit her yet. She's going to be pretty bad tomorrow, when the sedative wears off.'

'Shit – how could anybody do that?' asked Norman. 'Execute their own goddamned children.'

'He was a psycho,' said Luke. 'I just hope the jury don't accept a plea of psycho, that's all.'

'We should have shot him on the spot,' said Norman. 'We should have put him down, then and there, like a goddamned rabid dog.'

Rick Clark came hurrying up the pathway, the shoulders of his white trenchcoat soaked dark with rain, and his collar turned up.

'Sheriff?' he asked. 'You want to tell me how she took it?'

'Hey, asswipe, how would *you* take it, if *your* kids' heads were cut off?' Norman retorted.

'Norman,' said Rick. 'Why did your parents call you Norman, Norman?'

'They were poets, Rick, that's why,' Norman retaliated. 'They wanted to give me a name that rhymed with Gorman, just like your parents wanted to give you a name that rhymed with prick.'

Back in his office on the Third Avenue Bridge, Luke called home. His six-year-old daughter Nancy answered.

'Honey, can I talk to your mom?'

'Mom's in the shower. Are you going to be late?'

'That's right. I'm going to be late. I don't know *how* late. What's been happening today?'

'Nothing, except for Randy Stahmer wet himself in class.'

'Poor old Randy. What else?'

'Mom put my red socks into the wash with your blue polo shirt.'

'Oh, great. Now I have a purple polo shirt.'

'No, you don't. Mom tried to bleach it and now you have a tie-dye polo shirt.'

'Excellent. Even better. Have you been a good girl today?'

'Mrs Heslop was angry with me because I spat out my greens.'

'You know you're supposed to eat your greens. They're good for you. They make you – I don't know, charismatic or something.'

'I hate greens. I never want to see greens again as long as I live. I never even want to see the *colour* green.'

Luke bantered with Nancy for a little while longer, and then blew her a kiss goodnight and put down the phone. But afterwards, he leaned against his chill, air-conditioned window for a long, long time. His hand was pressed over his mouth, as if he were forbidding himself from speaking, and his eyes were serious and tired.

This was a Saturday night like any other Saturday night. Beneath his window, the Cedar River churned under the curved concrete spans of the Third Avenue Bridge, reflecting the jazzy broken-up lights of downtown Cedar Rapids and the stop–start flow of traffic on 1st Street.

But for no special reason that he could think of, Luke felt tonight that he had been doing this same job for far too long. He felt that he had come around the same curve so many times that he was no longer capable of approaching it any differently. The Pearson homicides had been so stark and terrible that they deserved original thinking. They deserved *rage.* Yet all Luke could feel was an overwhelming sense that he had been living and working in this city for most of his life; and that all those years had amounted to nothing very much.

A hill of beans? He should be so lucky. Lisa and little George had died, Abner and Dorothy Loftus had died. Young and old; both defenceless. The very people that Luke had promised to protect with all of his heart and all of his ingenuity. He felt that he had failed them all. He felt that he had cut off their heads just as surely as Terence Pearson had cut off their heads.

Maybe the Pearson killings were just one atrocity too many. The past four or five years had seen the comfortable well-being of Cedar Rapids beginning to sag and fray at the edges, like a worn-out mattress, like a well-loved family house falling into disrepair. On a rainy afternoon in March last year, Luke had been called to investigate Cedar Rapids' first drive-by shooting. Now he had mothers regularly complaining that they were picking up dirty syringes out of their back yards; and that they had to teach their children that bullets don't know your name. Long before they were taught addition and subtraction, grade school pupils were being drilled that when they heard the first shot, they needed to hit the ground as quickly as possible.

Now, routinely, Luke and his deputies had to break up suburban riots of car-smashing, fist-fighting and flying bullets; and try to catch eleven-year-old schoolkids running errands with mobile phones and bags of crack cocaine.

Last year, he had thought that he had seen the worst, when the medical examiner had rolled out the body of 17-year-old Destiny Wright, and showed him her seventeen stab wounds, one for every year of her life.

But now there was this. The ritualistic beheading of Lisa and George Pearson, and the frenzied killing of Abner and Dorothy Loftus. And Luke didn't know what to do. He had arrested Terence Pearson, yes, and Terence Pearson had freely confessed. But Luke didn't know what to do.

He was still leaning against the window when Norman Gorman came in.

'Sheriff? I found us a Czech translator.'

Luke turned around, and tried to smile. Standing a little

too close behind Norman was a thin, cadaverous old man, with a large nose and sunken cheeks and wriggles of veins across his forehead. He was dressed in a light brown herringbone suit that looked as if he wore it every day of his adult life.

'Sheriff, this is Mr Leos Ponican. He teaches ESL at Jefferson.'

'Glad you could come, Mr Ponican,' said Luke. 'Has officer Gorman told you what we want you to do?'

Mr Ponican nodded. 'Translate from Czech, yes?'

Luke picked up a sheaf of photocopies of Terence's pad, and handed it over. Mr Ponican produced a pair of wire-rimmed glasses from the breast pocket of his suit, put them on, and scanned the first page very slowly.

'Well?' asked Luke, after more than a minute.

'It is difficult,' said Mr Ponican. He looked very unhappy.

'What do you mean by "difficult"?'

'To start with, it is written very small.'

'That's correct, yes. It's written very small. In fact, I would go so far as to say that it's written very, very small.'

Mr Ponican stuck out his bottom lip and scanned the first page yet again. 'It is also . . . not very right.'

'Not very right? What does that mean? It's full of mistakes?'

Mr Ponican repeatedly snapped his finger on the corner of the pad. 'It is not like usual writing. It is . . . mad writing.'

'Oh, I see. Mad writing. In what sense is it mad writing?'

'Can I sit?' asked Mr Ponican. Luke nodded, and Norman pulled a chair across. Mr Ponican sat down and laid the photocopies on his lap. He traced the writing word by word, with his finger.

' "He comes with his three friends at the time of winter. They hit the door." That is, they knock at the door. "He hits and he hits but when the people inside cry out and say 'Who is it? Who is hitting our door?' he says no word at all. He does not speak. But he will hit the door for all time if the people inside do not open it and let him inside.

' "When he comes inside, he will stand with his three friends and say nothing. They do not speak. This why they are called –" I do not know this word in English. But it means people who do not speak.'

'Mutes?' asked Luke.

'No, not exactly mutes. The meaning is not physiological. The meaning is, they do not speak by choice. It is like they stay silent for the purpose of entertainment.'

'You mean mimes?' said Norman.

'Well, again, not exactly mimes. A mime tries to explain what he is doing by gesture and movement. These people arrive and stay silent. They have no explanation.'

'Trappists?' Norman suggested.

'For Christ's sake,' said Luke. But he suddenly thought of the engraving pinned to the wall of Terence's private room. The man dressed in leaves, with the mocking smile. What had it said at the bottom of it? *Mummer.* A man with a mask who never speaks. A man who stays mum.

He was about to say something but then he decided not to. He allowed Mr Ponican to continue.

' "He sits at the table. He expects wine and something else . . ." I don't know what this is. It sounds a little like *hovesy maso,* which is a beef stew. "He and his friends will bring out dices, and they will play until the fire dies down. This will only happen at a particular time of the year, and not every person is honoured by this visit. He travels many miles but nobody sees him travelling. In some towns that he has not visited before, the people pray for him to come. But in those towns that he has visited, they refuse to speak his name, just as he has never spoken theirs." '

Mr Ponican put down the page with a slightly-shaking hand,

and took off his glasses. 'The rest of it is all the same. All about people who come to visit and say nothing. They play dice, they leave gifts. They leave many different gifts. Each of them wears a different costume. I do not know whether this is supposed to be a story, or what it is.'

'Will you take it home and translate it for me?' asked Luke. 'I'd like to know what it says in full.'

Mr Ponican leafed through the photocopies, nineteen pages in tiny writing. 'It will take me a little time.'

'I can pay you quite a few extra korunas for doing it extra-quick.'

'Well – in that case, very well. I could maybe have this translated in two days.'

'How about thirty-six hours?'

'I will try my very best, Sheriff Friend.'

He left, taking the photocopies with him, and Luke eased himself back in his Western-style chair, stacking his feet on the desk.

Norman said, 'Pretty screwball stuff, hunh?'

'I don't know . . . I think we should reserve judgement until we see the full translation.'

'I think your first instinct was right. Pearson's out of his tree.'

'Norman – it doesn't really matter whether he's crazy or whether he's sane. Four totally innocent people got themselves killed. In Cedar Rapids, for Christ's sake. It makes me feel – I don't know – it makes me feel like we're reaching the end of the world. Apocalypse.'

He shook his head. 'My daddy used to think that beer and rock'n'roll and heavy petting were just about the greatest evils that Satan could think up. I'm almost glad that he's dead and gone.'

Norman checked his watch. 'Are you going to talk to Pearson now?'

Luke nodded. 'Then you and me can call it a night. It's going to be a long, long day tomorrow.'

Terence was standing in his cell with his back to the bars. Luke approached him and stood watching him for a while. Terence must have realized that Luke was there, but he didn't move and didn't say anything. Even his turned back communicated huge tension.

The cell block was down in the basement. The walls were painted in two shades of grey and the bars were painted grey, too. It was overheated and the air smelled of Lysol and vomit and cheesy feet. There were three drunks and a crack-runner locked up here, too, although the night was still very young and by the small hours of the morning there would be probably be standing room only.

One of the drunks was singing, 'Don't you break my heart . . . my achy, breaky heart . . .' Another was sobbing.

A young black officer was standing outside Terence's cell on special guard detail. Three years ago, Luke wouldn't have bothered with a special guard. But then a middle-aged homicide suspect had managed to hang himself with the sleeve of his shirt only a half-hour after Luke had arrested him. And less than a week later, a 17-year-old detainee had killed himself by pushing two pencils up his nose, lacing his fingers behind his head, and slamming his face against the fold-down table. Luke couldn't afford to have Terence Pearson going the same way.

'Pearson?' he said, tersely.

The young black officer said, 'He ain't scarcely opened his mouth in three hours. Only to ask for a Diet Coke, and what time it is.'

'Pearson?' Luke repeated. 'This is Sheriff Friend.'

'I know that,' said Terence. 'What do you want?'

'A little discussion, maybe.'

'Oh yes? I know what kind of discussion you want. A one-sided discussion in which I do all of the discussing. Like, I discuss what it is that leads a father to execute his own kids?'

Luke shrugged, coughed. 'That would be a start.'

Terence still didn't turn around. 'You have to understand one thing, sheriff, or else you're going to understand nothing at all. I wasn't executing them. I was saving them.'

'Saving them? Saving them from what?'

Terence paused for a while. Then he said, 'You wouldn't understand it, sheriff. You wouldn't understand it at all.'

'You could try me.'

Terence shook his head.

Luke stood outside the cell for almost a minute and still Terence didn't speak. The young black officer said, 'That's the most he's spoke since he's been here. Asked for the time once, that's all, that was 6.47; and once for a Diet Coke.'

Luke said, 'If you thought that you were saving them, Terence, you must have thought that what you were saving them from was worse than having their heads cut off. That sounds like logic, doesn't it?'

Terence still didn't reply, but his anguish was so great that he was giving off a smell, like the scorched hemp smell of overstretched ropes.

'All I have to work out now is: what could be worse than having your head cut off?'

Terence said baldly, 'You think I'm insane.'

'I don't know what to think, less'n you tell me what it is you were saving them from.'

'You couldn't even begin to –'

'What about the mummer, Pearson? Does the mummer have anything to do with it?'

Terence visibly quaked. His hands slowly squeezed into the tightest of fists. Still he didn't turn around.

'Come on, Pearson,' Luke cajoled him. 'I'm a pretty understanding kind of sheriff. Tell me what the mummer has to do with it. And all of those bibles. Greek, Japanese, you've got the whole works, don't you?'

'You've been in my room,' said Terence, his voice like a slowly-moving landslide.

'That's right, Pearson. I've been in your room. And it was the weirdest goddamned room that I ever clapped eyes on.'

Terence snapped around. His angular face was ashen, and his eyes were scarlet-rimmed. '*You had no right! You had no goddamned right at all!*'

'Calm down, Pearson. Your wife invited me to take a look.'

'*She had no right! I told her never to go in there! Never! And you had no right, neither!*'

'Oh, I had plenty of right,' Luke told him. 'I had a right in law and I had a moral right, too. A man who's done what you've done, he loses just about everything. His privacy, his dignity, everything. The only privilege that you have left is the privilege of being given a fair trial, and that's a hell of a lot more than you deserve.'

'You had no right to go into my room,' Terence repeated. Flecks of spit flew from his lips. 'I promise you, *I promise you*, you'll pay for doing that.'

There was a long, grating silence. Terence kept on staring at Luke and twitching with fury and Luke looked steadily back at him and wondered what kind of man he could possibly be. At last, Luke laid his hand briefly on the shoulder of Terence's guard, and said, 'Take good care of him, officer, he's bad people,' and left.

He was shrugging on his coat when Norman came up to him, smoking and carrying a blue manila folder. 'We've had trouble from our friend Terence Pearson before,' he said. 'Sergeant Mullally just pulled this jacket.'

'Oh, yes?'

'Remember that incident last fall, when somebody's dog had its head chopped off?'

'Yes, I remember. Hound Found Headless.'

'The dog belonged to Terence Pearson's nextdoor neighbour, and the neighbour actually accused Pearson of having killed it. It wasn't one of your cheap neighbourhood mutts, either. It was a Belgian Tervuren, couple of thousand dollars' worth of pure pedigree.'

'What happened?' asked Luke.

'Nothing, in the end. Pearson was questioned but nobody could prove that he'd done it, so they had to let it drop. Mind you, Pearson and his neighbour had just had the mother of all domestic disputes.'

'What about?'

'You're never going to believe it. Pearson objected to the colour they painted their back fence.' He opened the file, and said, 'The neighbour's exact words were, "Pearson came home from work. He saw my fence. He took a deep breath. Then he went totally berserk. He was screaming at us like a maniac. He said if we didn't paint it over right that minute, he'd kill us." '

'Holy shit. What colour did they paint it, pink with purple spots?'

'Unh-hunh. They painted it green. Good old regular garden green.'

Outside on the steps, the press and the TV cameras were waiting for him. The evening wind was warm and fresh, and he had to hold the brim of his hat to keep it from blowing away. He stood in the glare of the halogen lights, and said, 'I don't have anything to add to what I said earlier on. Terence James Pearson is being held on suspicion of multiple homicide in the first degree. We're not looking for anybody else in connection with these particular killings, although we would like to hear from anybody who might have seen Pearson and his children any time during the afternoon immediately prior to the killings. I've had a preliminary meeting with the county attorney, and Mr Dillard and I will be meeting again in the morning. Pearson has been advised of his rights, but so far he has declined to talk to a lawyer. Our investigations are continuing and I'll be calling a full press conference tomorrow. That's all, folks.'

'Sheriff – were these ritual killings?' asked one of the TV reporters.

Luke shook his head. 'I honestly can't tell you. Terence Pearson has certain unusual interests and we're looking into them now. They may or may not have any bearing on the killings.'

'What unusual interests? Satanism? Human sacrifice? Black magic? Or what?'

'He appears to be interested in farming, meteorology and bible studies. That's all I can tell you.'

One reporter snorted in amusement. 'Show me just one man in eastern Iowa who *isn't* interested in farming, meteorology and bible studies!'

'Sure. But maybe not in the way that Terence Pearson was interested in them.'

'What way was that, sheriff?'

'Aw, come on, sheriff, what way was that?'

At last Luke managed to reach his parking space, and climb into his big white Buick Park Avenue. He started up the engine, but Rick Clark rapped on his window, and mouthed something. Luke put down the window and said, 'Come on, Rick, I'm bushed.'

'Give me a break, sheriff. Do you have any theories at all why Pearson might have killed his kids?'

'Not so far. Let me ask you something: do you have any theories at all why somebody might go crazy whenever they see the colour green?'

'The colour green?' Rick frowned. 'I don't follow you.'

Luke shifted the Buick into gear. 'I don't follow me, either. But when we understand the answer to one of those questions, maybe we'll understand the answers to the other.'

Green, thought Luke, as he drove home northwards on 380. Why should Terence Pearson have been so enraged by the colour green?

He thought of his daughter Nancy, telling him how much she hated greens. *I never even want to see the colour green.* Then, he began to think about the Pearson house. Was there anything green in the Pearson house?

There were no houseplants, that was for sure. No green wallpaper. No green rugs. No green drapes. And hadn't Iris Pearson told him that Terence wouldn't let her hang up a painting that she had been given by her mother – a painting of trees? And that nursery-school picture in little George's bedroom – there was grass in it, for sure, but the grass was *blue*.

He remembered the Pearsons' supper. Squash, corn, red cabbage, but no greens. What good Iowa mother served up a roast ham supper without peas or beans or a dishful of greens?

Then he thought about the mummer, the sly smiling man in the leafy hat and the leafy cloak, and the more he thought about the mummer, and Terence Pearson's apparent aversion to the colour green, the more uneasy he became.

He switched on the radio, and caught Tom Jones right in the middle of 'The Green Green Grass of Home'.

Three

The two-lane highway reflected the sun so brightly that Nathan overshot the narrow side-road, and had to back up fifty feet, his transmission whining.

'What's wrong?' asked David, from beneath the brim of his bright red Kernels baseball cap. 'Why aren't you driving forward any more?'

'I missed the turnoff, that's all.'

He reached the intersection and checked the curled-up sketch-map that Dr Matthews had faxed him. 'See, he says a big green barn and a white-painted fence – and there, look, a sign saying Amana Nature Preserve.'

'No it doesn't. It says Aman Natu eserve.'

Nathan gave him an Oliver Hardy stare of long-suffering disapproval. 'Stop acting like a thirteen-year-old. It doesn't suit you.'

'I *am* a thirteen-year-old. Of course it suits me.'

It had taken Nathan over twenty minutes longer to get here than he had bargained for. First he had been caught up in a charity marathon on Diagonal Drive, thousands of bobbing people in gym vests and trainers, and then he had been forced to leave Williams Boulevard at Edgewood Road because a tractor-trailer full of live chickens had jacknifed across the highway, and the detour had taken him almost as far as the airport.

But now they drove with the windows open through the rolling Amana farmland, warm summer wind and the smell of ripe manure flowing into the car, past farms and fields and silos, and herds of black and white Friesians waiting patiently to be milked, like half-finished black and white jigsaws. A man on a ladder stopped hammering the shingles on the roof of his barn and shaded his eyes with his hand so that he could watch them drive by. It was probably the most exciting thing that had happened to him all day.

'Jeez, look at the size of that cow,' said David. 'It looks like a blimp.'

'She's probably pregnant.'

'Urgh! That means she's *done* it! Even if I was a bull, I wouldn't be turned on by cows.'

'Oh yes? So what would turn you on?'

'Sharon Stone and Ms Keppelmeyer in that order.'

'What makes you think that Sharon Stone would want to go out with a bull? What makes you think that Ms Keppelmeyer would want to go out with a bull? On second thought, what the hell am I talking about?'

This was about the fourth time today that Nathan had become entangled in one of David's surrealistic schoolboy conversations. He switched on the radio to listen to the news.

'*. . . average jobless rates in Iowa fell to 4.3 per cent this summer . . . although Clarke County, at 11 per cent, is still reeling from the closure of the Jimmy Dean meat plant . . .*'

In spite of the way in which they endlessly ribbed each other, Nathan and David had a close and unusually emotional relationship. People saw it in the way they constantly touched, the way they always looked out for each other. They resembled each other in every possible way. Nathan was lean and dark, with curly hair and a thin face that always reminded people of a young Elliott Gould. David was just as dark and pipestem skinny, with curly hair and a thin face that always reminded people of a very young Elliott Gould.

They spoke alike. They used the same gestures: particularly that way of knocking their foreheads with the heels of their hands whenever they made a mistake. They both had a passion for the Cedar Rapids Kernels that was way out of proportion to the team's success, and held season tickets at Veterans' Memorial Stadium. They both ate cookies-and-cream ice-cream as if Haagen-Dazs were on the edge of bankruptcy. What else? They both liked *Arsenio* – Nathan because he thought the show was witty, David because it meant staying up so late to watch it.

But only their closest friends knew of the tragedy that had led Nathan and David to depend on each other so much, and to mirror each other so exactly. David had been born a twin, one of two little boys who had looked like 'everything heavenly and lovable' when they were tiny – 'like puppies and sunlight', according to their grandmother. But six years ago, one stormy August afternoon, David's twin Aaron had gone into convulsions. Panicking, their mother Susan had left David with the nextdoor neighbour and driven Aaron to St Luke's Emergency/Trauma Center.

Coming off 380 at 8th Avenue, her station wagon's wheels had locked, and she had rear-ended a scaffolding truck at nearly 40 miles an hour. The hospital hadn't allowed Nathan to look at the bodies, but at the inquest, he had heard that a thirty-foot scaffolding pole had been driven directly through the station wagon's windshield into Susan's face. Two more had impaled Aaron in his baby-seat.

Nathan could never forget a pretty brown-eyed girl with a talent for giggling. David could never forget a brother who had been half of his identity. That was why they copied each other, and teased each other and clung so close.

'. . . hog market is still holding up despite Zapf-Cady being approved by Congress . . . estimated receipts at Iowa hog-buying stations 95,000 . . . US 1 back fat thickness .50 inch to .79 inch . . . sows uneven, generally steady . . . slaughter boars $2.50 to $3 higher . . .'

They passed a chain of lakes, dark-watered but glittering so brightly in the sunlight that they could scarcely look at them. The surfaces were ruffled by the breeze and by buoyant flocks of bafflehead ducks.

Nathan said, 'We should be there by now. You wait till you see this hog.'

'Dad, we live in Iowa. I've seen millions of hogs. I was all hogged out by the time I was three.'

'You wait till you see this one.'

A quarter-mile further on, Nathan found the small stencilled sign that read SIGS, and turned left down a single-track asphalt road. Long grass rustled and tapped against the sides of his car, and the suspension squeaked and jostled. Nathan had to drive so slowly that he was reminded of that Lawrence Ferlinghetti poem about 'the orangecrate train . . . creaking on so slowly that . . . butterflies . . . blew in and out'.

They passed under the branches of sheltering oaks. For five or ten minutes, they seemed to have entered a private world – cool, aromatic, lit only by emerald spangles, completely secluded from the rest of the planet. But then they were out on a dry, grassy stretch of ground, in brilliant sunlight, and the rest of the planet seemed to have arrived here in force.

A high razor-wire fence crossed the fields at a sharp diagonal. The roadway itself was barred by high metal gates. Outside the gates a motley assembly of vans and Jeeps and pick-ups was parked at all angles, as well as six or seven patrol cars from the Linn County Sheriff's Department with their lights flashing.

David sat up in excitement. 'Look, Dad, a riot!'

'Put up your window,' said Nathan. 'Come on, David – put it up, now.'

It wasn't exactly a riot. About a hundred demonstrators were milling around outside the gates, most of them young, most of them toting banners that said STOP ANIMAL EXPERIMENTS NOW. MURDERERS! NO MORE SADISM FOR SCIENCE. PIGS ARE

MORTAL, TOO. They were chanting and singing, while twenty or thirty uniformed officers were standing guard in front of the gates, some of them holding clubs and CS guns, most of them chewing gum, and all of them wearing amber sunglasses and looking bored. Their unusually large presence was probably explained by the van from Channel 7 news which was parked not far away in the shade of some tall yellow buckeyes.

Nathan drove slowly through the demonstrators, gently bipping his horn a couple of times to encourage them to clear the roadway.

'What are they doing, Dad?' David asked him. He smiled and waved at a grey-bearded man who had a picture of a crucified pig on his T-shirt, and the slogan, DON'T FORGIVE THEM, BECAUSE THE BASTARDS KNOW EXACTLY WHAT THEY DO'.

'They don't like scientists using living animals for experiments,' Nathan replied. 'They say it's cruel, and that animals have just the same rights as humans.'

'But we eat them for breakfast.'

'These people don't. Some of these people have never even eaten an egg.'

'I wouldn't mind if I never ate eggs. I hate eggs.'

'You like French toast.'

'French toast is different. French toast isn't proper eggs. It's mushed eggs.'

'Swede is still proper swede, even if it's mushed swede. Eggs are still eggs, even if they're mushed eggs. Jesus Christ, what the hell am I talking about?'

He had almost reached the gates when a very tall blonde woman approached and tapped on his window. At first he was reluctant to put it down, but she smiled, and tapped again, and mouthed something, and so he risked it.

The first thing he noticed about her was her teeth. They were large, carnivorous and startlingly white. The next thing he noticed about her was her eyes. They were large and droopy-lidded, and the most extraordinary smoky-purple colour; as if she had been born in a tornado, and looked up, and her eyes had caught the colour of the sky. She had a high forehead and a broad jaw and a short, straight chiselled nose. Her blonde hair blew across her face, and she had to sweep it away with her hand.

He also noticed her figure. He couldn't help it, because she was leaning over the car. She was wearing a plain white T-shirt that did nothing but emphasize her huge rounded breasts. A heavy silver crucifix dangled in her darkly-tanned cleavage; and her nipples must have been darkly tanned, too, because he could see them clearly through the white cotton. She was wearing faded blue shorts with ragged hems, and scuffy tan cowboy boots, and her legs were long and double-jointed and skinny as a stork's.

He thought to himself wryly that he could well be persuaded to join the animal activist movement – at least as an associate member.

'Sorry to trouble you,' the woman grinned. 'Do you work here, or are you just visiting?' She had a distinctive Missouri accent, and the slightest of lisps, which Nathan found surprisingly attractive.

'I'm just visiting,' Nathan told her. 'I have friends here.'

'So you know what they do here?'

'Yes, I do. They breed pigs.'

'But you must you know why they breed pigs?'

'For sure, and I happen to approve of it.'

The woman had been joined by four or five other young people also in jeans and T-shirts, who leaned on the car and listened in what could only be described as a passively threatening way. All wore lapel pins with the initials AHR2 – Animals Have Rights Too. One of them, a moon-faced young man with wire-rimmed glasses, kept on rhythmically smacking an axe-handle into the palm of his hand.

'How can you approve of animals deliberately being bred so that they can be cut up while they're still alive?' the woman demanded.

'My father nearly died of nephritis, that's how. Two pigs' kidneys kept him going while he was waiting for a human transplant.'

'So you believe that it's right to kill the animal in order to save the man? You approve of brutally sacrificing one mortal in order to preserve the life of another, just because it happens to be a so-called inferior species? Don't you think we were put on this planet to take care of our fellow creatures, rather than to slaughter them and torture them and exploit them?'

'He was my father.'

'And is he proud to call you his son?'

'Listen,' said Nathan. 'I'm just visiting a friend, if that's okay with you.'

'How can you be friends with a murderer?'

Nathan put up the window an inch or two, forcing the woman to release her grip on it. 'If you'll excuse me . . .'

'Sadist!' shouted the young man with the axe-handle, and beat it on the roof of Nathan's car. 'Flesh-eating fucker!' Immediately, the rest of them started to thunder on the roof with their fists, and to kick at the doors and the panelling. Although there were only a few of them, the noise inside the vehicle was deafening, and David clapped his hands over his ears and cowered in his seat.

Nathan gunned the Chevrolet's engine, but three of the protestors stood in front of him and blocked his way. He started to nudge at them with the front bumper, but they pummelled even harder on the hood, and he knew that he would in serious trouble if he injured any of them, or knocked any of them down.

'Sadist!' a young girl screeched at him, and spat against the windshield, so that spittle trickled down in front of his face.

'Torturer!' a man roared, and started to beat at the side of the car with a length of iron piping.

It was their faces that frightened Nathan the most. He had never in his life seen faces contorted into such expressions of hatred. They crowded against the car windows in hideous animated death-masks, like the zombies in *Day of the Dead.* More and more of them surrounded the car, screaming and whooping, and bouncing it up and down on its suspension. David started to sob, and Nathan blew his horn, again and again, and shouted, 'Let me through! Let me through! Get away, you bastards, you're scaring my kid!'

One of the protestors climbed onto the front bumper, and for one moment Nathan thought they they were going to be completely overwhelmed. But then the protestors suddenly began to scatter; and the young man on the hood was thrown off sideways as if he had been hit by an oncoming truck. One of the girls beat at the car window with her fist and screamed, 'We'll remember you – you sadist!' But then she was yanked out of Nathan's sight.

Twenty or thirty police officers were forcing their way into the mob with billyclubs and pickaxe handles. Leading the wedge was the bulky figure of Sheriff Luke Friend, his eyes hidden behind piggy little sunglasses, his stomach undulating like a waterbed underneath his sharply-pressed khaki shirt. Nathan had never seen him in person before but he recognized him from his election posters. Luke was breezily swinging a spring-loaded club from side to side as if he were conducting a barbershop concert by the Cedar Rapids Harmony Hawks.

A long-haired protestor tried to dodge past him, but Luke whacked him on the right knee with a nonchalant but deadly-accurate blow, and the protestor screamed like a run-over rabbit and dropped into the grass, clutching his leg and rolling over and over.

As the protestors noisily retreated, Nathan glimpsed the

blonde woman with the white T-shirt and the long legs. She was turning away, closely protected on all sides by some of the more threatening-looking activists, cadaverous men with ponytails and earrings. She caught Nathan's eye, and gave him a quick, suggestive grin that he couldn't interpret. What was she trying to tell him? I'll get you next time? I think you're a wimp? I like the way your hair curls?

Luke came up to the car window and indicated to Nathan with a downward flap of his hand that he should open it.

'Sorry about that momentary lapse in protection and service there, friend,' he said. 'These animal-lovers have a way of flaring up without warning. One minute they're all peace and love and let's not be mean to the poor dumb animals. The next minute they're acting so crazy that even hell wouldn't have them.'

'Thanks, sheriff,' said Nathan. He took out his handkerchief and gave it to David to wipe his eyes. 'For one moment there, I thought they were going to turn the whole damned car over.'

'Oh, I've seen them do worse,' said Luke, sniffing and taking off his sunglasses. 'Couple of months back they blinded a woman from Marion with bleach, just because she worked for Perrystone Pharmaceuticals, testing eye-liner on rabbits. And they firebombed two meat counters at Econofoods in Cedar Rapids, and burned one poor guy so bad that he's going to look like his own Grade-A hamburger meat for the rest of his life.'

'Well . . . we're a little shaken up, but I think we're okay,' said Nathan.

Luke stood up straight, and examined the Chevrolet from one end to the other. 'Car's not too badly beat up, neither. Few dents, here and there. Hope you're insured against being Watusied on.'

'Can I go in now?' Nathan asked.

'Oh, for sure. So long as I can see some ID, and a letter of invitation.'

Nathan reached into his shirt pocket, took out his identity wallet and the letter that Garth had sent him. Luke opened them up and frowned at them. 'Dr Nathan H. Greene, from Mercy Medical Center? Surprised I haven't met you before.'

'I'm an assistant pathologist,' Nathan explained. 'I work in the spare-parts section, lowly of the low. Kind of an Igor, if you know what I mean. The pathologist says "Bring me the brain, Igor", and I say "Yes, master", and scurry off and bring back the brain. What you'd call a backroom boy.'

Luke folded up the letter and closed the ID wallet and handed them back, with a smile. 'That all looks in order to me, Dr Greene. I hope you enjoy your visit.'

'Thanks,' said Nathan. He shifted into gear. 'By the way,' he said, 'who's the blonde in the white T-shirt and the cowboy boots?'

Luke didn't even have to turn around and look to know who Nathan was talking about. 'You don't recognize her? It's Lily Monarch. She's been on TV almost every week since Zapf-Cady was first drafted. She's Senator Bryan Cady's right-hand man – if "man" is what you'd call a looker like her. She's something, isn't she? President of Animal Activists, founder-member of Women Versus Fur, federal coordinator of BEAF – you know, Ban Eating All Flesh – vegetarian, agitator, one-time swimsuit model, occasional freebaser and all-round pain-in-the-seating-area.'

Nathan could just glimpse her hurrying away, tightly hedged in by her bodyguards. 'I thought she looked familiar. She looks a whole lot better in the flesh.'

'Dream on, Dr Greene. That woman only mingles with the mighty. And the vegetarian mighty, at that. You might stand a chance if you have the President's ear, twenty million dollars in the bank, and you never eat nothing but broccoli. Otherwise, forget it.'

Nathan drove towards the high metal gates, and a deputy opened them up and allowed him through. Inside, there was a security booth from which a bored black man in a peaked cap demanded that he show his ID and his letter of invitation once again.

'I showed them already.'

'Not to me, you didn't.'

Nathan's voice was trembling and over-adrenalized. 'One day Ice-T is going to write a rap about what we should do to security guards.'

The man looked back at him with huge contempt. 'One day, doctor, all men are going to be brothers. Straight ahead, straight through the trees. Pass the lake on your left. Then it's your third building on the right. Dr Matthews is going to be expecting you.'

They drove across a wide stretch of long wild grass, so dry that it was honey-coloured. Then they found themselves plunged into the shadow of some deep, cool oaks. Eventually, they emerged into the sunshine again, beside a small circular lake, its banks overgrown with rushes. Ahead of them stood the neat glass-and-brick buildings of the Spellman Institute of Genetic Research, with neat rows of automobiles parked outside, and neat green bushes in neat ceramic pots. Nathan pulled in beside the sign marked Visitors, and climbed out of the car.

Almost immediately, the glass door of the building opened and Dr Garth Matthews came hurrying down the steps, his hand already extended in greeting. He was a handsome, fortyish, broad-headed man, with smartly-brushed chestnut hair and a little clipped toothbrush moustache. He wore a blue lab coat, underneath which he was dressed in a blue shirt and tan slacks, and highly-polished brown Oxfords.

'Nathan . . . security told me you had some trouble.'

They clasped hands. Nathan said, 'We just experienced a little animal activism, that's all.'

'Those goddamned irresponsible carrot-chewing freaks. If

they had any idea how many human lives they put at risk, every time they stop us trying out some new genetic procedure.' Garth gripped Nathan's shoulder, and gave him an affectionate shake. 'You're okay, though? They didn't do too much damage?'

'They scared David. They scared me, too, to tell you the truth. They spat on the windows. They jumped on the hood. That's two or three hundred bucks' worth of damage.'

'It's okay . . . send me the bill and the Institute will pay. Just so long as you and David didn't get yourselves hurt.'

David climbed shyly out of the car.

'Is this David?' Garth enthused. 'Hey . . . I can't believe it! How are you doing, tiger? You've grown – what – about six inches since I last saw you. You're going to be taller than your dad, 'way taller. How about it, Nathan? Your own son is going to make you look like a shortass. That's the joy of genetics for you.'

An anxious thought suddenly struck him, and he turned to Nathan and said, 'The sample wasn't compromised?'

'Unh-hunh, not a chance,' Nathan reassured him. He couldn't resist a surge of guilty excitement. 'It's in the trunk; and it's too securely packed.'

'Well, that's another relief. Listen – how about we take it inside? Then I can give it straight to Raoul for DNA analysis. Bet you could use a drink, too.'

'You bet.' Nathan opened the Chevrolet's trunk and lifted out a machined-aluminum box, about the size of a videocamera case. He handed it carefully to Garth, who grasped it in both hands and gave an irrepressible grin of satisfaction.

'At last! You don't know how much this is going to help us. If this works out, this is the next giant leap for mankind. Or should I say swinekind.'

'I sure hope so,' said Nathan. 'After what you did for my dad –'

'Oh, come on, Nathan. Stop being so serious, you embarrass me. That was already a tried-and-tested surgical procedure. We would have given the same priority to anybody else, friend or no friend. Your dad didn't survive just because we both play golf at Elmcrest.'

'That doesn't stop me from owing you a favour.'

Garth patted the aluminum box. 'If this all works out, we're going to be more than quits, believe me.'

They climbed the steps, and David opened the tinted glass doors so that Garth could carry the box inside. They entered a chilly air-conditioned reception area, its floor tiled in polished marble. In the centre stood a modern abstract fountain, tastefully draped with designer ivy. Garth led them across to the reception desk, where a beige-suited brunette with scarlet lips and wide blue eyes and perfect bone structure said, 'Welcome to Spellman this morning!' She handed Nathan and David a security tag each, and gave David a Spellman Institute ballpen and a Spellman Institute keyring, too.

'You enjoy your visit, now,' she smiled. Garth gave her a wink and said, 'Thanks, Meg.' Nathan briefly wondered what it would be like to take such an immaculate girl to bed. Would she want to hang up her skirt first, and make sure that her pantyhose weren't inside-out? What would come first? Foreplay, or fingernail-laquering?

Garth must have read his mind. 'Beautiful girl, grrff!' he said, as he led them across the reception area. 'Sexy as hell. But what's the point? She has the IQ of a day-old Dunkin' Donut. She thought that Inuits were the opposite of exits.'

He led them across to an oak-panelled door at the back of the reception area, which carried a small but emphatic notice: *Unauthorized Personnel Totally Forbidden From Passing This Point. Absolutely No Exceptions.*

'Come on in,' said Garth.

They walked along a polished, antiseptic-smelling corridor,

painted mushroom grey. David found that he could squeak his sneakers very annoyingly on the vinyl-tiled floor. 'How's Deanna?' asked Nathan.

Garth rolled up his eyes in a 'don't-ask' look. 'She says she still hasn't come to terms with me leaving her. Financially, yes. But then she knows that she's bled me white. But emotionally, forget it. She's still so jealous, she calls me every morning before I leave for work, can you believe it, telling me not to forget my lunch, because Kayley is *sure* to have forgotten my lunch.'

'And does Kayley forget your lunch?' Nathan teased him.

'I wouldn't care if Kayley forgot my *name*. But as a matter of fact she doesn't. And she puts in pastrami with lots of mustard instead of that freaking tofu that Deanna used to give me.'

'Well, you know what they say about the way to a man's heart.'

'It's the way to a man's liver and a man's kidneys that I'm really concerned with.'

In some ways, Nathan and Garth were an ill-matched pair to be such good friends. Nathan had an introverted, serious turn of mind, and spent a lot of his spare time reading Noam Chomsky and Saul Bellow and trying to work out how it was that human beings were so much more than the sum of their spare parts. On the other hand, he had a slightly surreal sense of humour, like most pathologists. You can't handle spleens all day unless you can see the funny side of it. He also had a weakness for very heavy rock music. He thought that the Velvet Underground were 'twenty years too old, and twenty times too cheerful'. Maybe he listened to music like that to block out the world.

Garth was garrulous and sociable and flirtatious. He never stopped talking while he worked, and he never stopped talking after work. He was furiously untidy, in spite of his polished appearance. He read *Playboy* and *Practical Mechanics* and science journals. The September issue of *Genetic Engineering News* had described him as 'one of the most daring and innovative geneticists in the United States; and probably the world'.

His ex-wife Deanna called him 'a psychopathic eight-year-old in 38-year-old's clothing'.

Nathan and Garth had become friends seven and a half years ago, when they had casually started talking together at the bar of the Elmcrest Country Club. Nathan was there on sufferance: his senior pathologist had invited him along to play golf, and Susan had been convinced that it would be a good career move. Garth was a member. He was a moderate-to-accidentally-brilliant golfer, but most of the time he preferred to sit in the bar drinking old-fashioneds and flirting with other members' wives. Anything was better than going home to Deanna and her tofu.

Susan was dead now. Nathan had no more career ambitions. But he and Garth had remained friends; and while Garth had helped Nathan to grieve for Susan and Aaron, Nathan had helped Garth to extricate himself from his nightmarish marriage.

Then, of course, there was the matter of Nathan's father. They didn't talk about it very often; but it remained an undiscussed topic every time they met. It hung, pending, over everything they did and everything they said.

Two years ago, Garth had arranged for an experimental animal at the Spellman Institute to be slaughtered at less than an hour's notice, and two 'humanized' pig's kidneys to be rushed to Mercy Medical Center to save Nathan's father from imminent kidney failure. Nathan had never asked how many strings Garth had needed to pull, nor how many hundreds of thousands of dollars his action had cost, and who had paid for it, and Garth had never told him. Maybe it had knocked their friendship slightly out of true. Maybe it had strengthened it. Either way, it had subtly and permanently changed the balance between them.

They entered the large bright main laboratory. Along one wall were rows of microscopes, where three blue-coated researchers were bent like watchmakers, studying genetic samples. In the centre of the room were three workbenches cluttered with slides and test-tubes and books, as well as a half-eaten avocado-and-alfalfa sandwich and a dog-eared copy of *Tales of Power* by Carlos Castaneda. On the far wall there were nine Sperry-Rand computers and printers, and a special computer system designed for analysing DNA.

As they came in, they were greeted by a tall gangling black man with a thin curved nose and a narrow Ethiopian-looking face. He could have been an Olympic runner or a star basketball player. The security tag on his lab coat identified him as Raoul Lacouture.

'Raoul . . .' said Garth. 'This is my buddy Dr Nathan Greene, from the spare-parts department at Mercy. You name it – a leg, an arm, half a pancreas, a Hurst competition linkage for a '64 Barracuda – this man can get it for you.'

'Pleased to know you,' grinned Raoul. 'You're not this man's *friend*, are you?'

'Something funny in that?' asked Nathan.

'Not at all, Dr Greene. Just makes you unique.'

Garth cleared away the sandwich and carefully set the aluminium box down on the workbench. He picked up the book and looked at the cover. 'You're not turning hippie on me, are you, Raoul?'

'That's Jenny's. She says it's time she got spiritual.'

'How can she get spiritual when she's never been physical?'

'You wish.'

Garth opened up the catches at the side of the box. 'In spite of his merry banter, Nathan, Raoul happens to be the very best xenogeneticist there is. He studied in Amsterdam, Paris and the National Institute for Medical Research in London, England. His knowledge of pig genetics, if placed end to end, would reach from here to the Spam plant and back again.'

He lifted the lid of the box and Raoul peered inside. His breath smoked because of the chill-packs that had kept the sample's temperature down to 5°C. The sample wasn't much to look at: a translucent flower-shaped tracery of crimson and beige tissue, sandwiched between two gelatin slides like a pressed chrysanthemum. A micro-thin brain section.

'Who did you say who the donor was?' asked Raoul.

'I didn't,' said Nathan. 'Garth will tell you that one of the conditions that Mercy placed on this arrangement was that the origin of the section should remain unidentified, apart from its catalogue number.'

'It's definitely from a child, though, isn't it?' Garth put in.

Nathan flushed. 'Yes, I'm sorry to say that it is. A three-year-old boy who died no more than three days ago.'

'No brain damage?'

'None whatsoever.'

'No evidence of brain disorder or epilepsy?'

'None that we can determine. He died instantly of a single massive injury.'

'Well, this is just what we've been looking for,' said Garth. 'How would you like to run it through analysis, Raoul, and then we can think about getting Captain Black all prepped for surgery?'

Raoul closed the box. He looked at Nathan and Garth, and then across at David. His eyes were gentle and sad. 'You know something, I've been doing this kind of work ever since college, and I still can't forget that somebody had to die to make this possible. A three-year-old boy! All those days of sunlight he never saw.'

'Amen to that,' said Garth, uncomfortably.

Raoul carried the sample across to the far side of the laboratory, where there were gas and adsorption chromotographs set up, as well as spectrographs and two DNA analysers.

'How about that drink?' Garth asked Nathan. 'Raoul . . . why don't you show David how that analyzer works?'

He took Garth through to his office. It had been furnished and decorated at visible expense in a high-tech minimalist style. Garth's desk was nothing more than a perspex table, with a steel-and-leather chair, and the only other furniture was a curved leather sofa and a perspex coffee table. A grey and white abstract painting hung on one wall, and a spindly Giacometti-style sculpture stood in the corner.

The minimalist effect had been severely compromised, however, by Garth's spectacular untidiness. The perspex desk had been buried under heaps of reports and magazines and folders and books. Graphs and diagrams were arranged in fan patterns all over the floor – along with randomly-arranged golf shoes, pizza boxes, newspapers and shopping bags. Even the telephone was on the floor. The coffee table was awash with pages of scribbled notes and equations, as well as empty cans of caffeine-free Coke and half-finished cups of oily-surfaced coffee.

The sculpture had been crowned with a bright red golfing cap, and hung with a label which said 'The Anorexic Caddy'.

Nathan hopscotched his way over the papers and the graphs to the huge picture window which looked out over the Institute's central courtyard. A large bronze sculpture stood in the centre of the courtyard – a naked man standing between a trusting pig and a benevolent-looking cow. Garth opened up his icebox, produced two bottles of Schlitz and said, 'That one I call *Eleven O'Clock.*'

'Why's that?'

'Because the man is halfway between breakfast and lunch.'

Nathan took the beer bottle, swigged it, and wiped his mouth. 'You're a cynic, do you know that?'

'No, I'm not,' said Garth. 'Thick-skinned, maybe. Single-minded, yes. But when you're dealing with xenogenetics, you're dealing with moral and ethical dilemmas that most people have never even thought about. I mean – is it *really* justifiable to breed animals with human DNA, solely for the purpose of creating more acceptable transplant organs? If a pig had a wallet, would it carry a donor card? Would it have a pigskin wallet, or would it stick to vinyl? I'm not a cynic, Nathan, I'm simply doing something because it's possible and because it's legal – so far, anyway, unless Zapf-Cady gets through.'

'That would affect you, too?'

'Of course. Clause 23 specifically prohibits the use of living animals for any kind of scientific or commercial experimentation. If Zapf-Cady gets through, we'll have to close down our xenogenetics division altogether.'

'It's not likely to get through, though, is it? The farmers and the meat-packers are far too powerful, aren't they? And what about the public? You can't force a whole nation to turn vegetarian.'

Garth shrugged. 'Who knows? We forced a whole nation to go dry, didn't we? In those days, the bigots behind Prohibition were religious. These days, they're politically-correct, but they're still bigots, just the same. Zapf-Cady is nothing more or less than Volstead and his anti-booze Act made flesh.'

David came bursting in. 'Do you know something, that man let me look at my own hair through the microscope! It was like a tree, with branches, and everything!'

'Any monkeys swinging in it?' asked Nathan.

Garth said, 'How about a Coke? Yes? Then let's take a stroll around to the pigpens. You ought to take a look at Captain Black before we operate on him.'

They left Garth's office through a door which led them into the hot, bright, courtyard. On all four sides there were gleaming new laboratory buildings, in which they could see men and women working on every kind of genetic experiment from developing a faster-growing soybean to breeding bigger, leaner, disease-resistant cattle.

'Spellman is financed entirely by private industry,' said Garth. 'We have a research budget of well over one hundred and seventy million dollars a year, but it's money well-spent. Kettner Pharmaceuticals reckon that they've already made their money back three times over.'

'Kettner Pharmaceuticals?'

'Among other things, they produce Plasynth-10. Most surgeons tell their patients that it's a totally-synthetic blood plasma. In fact, it's blood plasma from genetically-engineered hogs. It's the same with insulin and a whole range of hormones – they're all derived from pigs. What most people don't know is that after meat medical uses rank a pretty close second in a pig's commercial value.'

'Luggage?'

'That comes way down the list.'

They left the courtyard through a tunnel between the buildings, and came out on a high, sloping field, where the dry grass blew in the wind in whispering waves, and daisies danced. At the top of the field stood two low brick buildings; and the wind brought from these buildings the ripe, unmistakable smell of pigs.

Garth said, 'People don't like to admit it, but pigs are much closer to humans than any other animal – physically and mentally. We've been using pigskin for years in human skin grafts, as well as pigs' heart valves for people with cardiac disease. I'll tell you something else: pigs are also the only animal which will drink hard liquor voluntarily. We did some tests on alcoholism for the Sedlacek Treatment Center, by giving pigs whisky and vodka. We had one Berkshire called Dino who drank a quart of Smirnoff every day. You couldn't go near him in the mornings. Grunted at everybody.'

They reached the pigpens. The buildings were new and smartly-painted, with air-conditioning plant buzzing busily outside. Garth unlocked the door of the nearer building, and they stepped inside. It was dimly lit, and the smell of pigs was much stronger.

Nathan peered into the gloom. The building was at least two hundred feet long, with a low ceiling and fluorescent lights. On either side, there were perspex-fronted pens, numbered 1 to 40, and each with a stencilled name. Daisy. Charlie. Whitney. Big Bill. Zoot. Einstein.

'Who gives them their names?' asked David.

Garth locked the door behind them. 'Look at their faces. They name themselves. See here, this one's called Lionel, after Lionel Richie. If he could speak he wouldn't speak, he'd be singing "Dancing on the Ceiling".'

He led them the length of the building, pointing out pig after pig – Hampshires, Berkshires, Durocs, Chester Whites, Yorkshires, Landraces – most of the classic American farm pigs.

'We've even been working on their sexual urges. That's because most farmers like their domestic sows to farrow two litters a year, of eight to ten piglets each, after a pregnancy of three months, three weeks and three days. In the wild, of course, pigs are like humans. They feel like nookie all the year round. They have a very, very powerful sex drive.

'You see this gilt here? A gilt is a female pig who hasn't produced her first litter yet. She's almost the perfect farm pig – strong, wonderfully proportioned, wide in the chest and rump, with very accessible nipples. She's almost 56 per cent leaner than the pigs we used to breed in the 1960s, and she's going to pass that on to her litter. She should take the sash for Miss Cholesterol-Free Bacon.'

At last they reached the end of the building. Here was a special pen that took up the width of the entire floor. It, too, was perspex-fronted, but the inside of the perspex had been deeply scored and scratched, and splattered with slobber, so that it was impossible to tell if there was anything inside it or not. On the left-hand side of the pen there was a metal door, with the number 20 stencilled on it and, underneath, 'Capt Black'.

Nathan approached the perspex and peered into the foggy interior of the pen. He could just about make out the straw that covered the floor, and the wallowing pool in the right-hand corner. All of the pens had a water-filled wallowing pool, because pigs have no sweat glands and need to wallow from time to time to keep cool. But this pool was three times larger than any of the others, and its water was dipping and slapping as if something huge had just climbed out of it.

'We bred Captain Black five years ago,' Garth explained, sorting out the key to the pen. 'He was one of our first experiments in humanization, and one of our most significant steps forward. Genetically speaking, Captain Black is so similar to a human being that you could use every organ in his body for surgical transplant . . . heart, lungs, liver, kidneys . . . provided, of course, the tissues matched.'

'Where's he hiding?' asked Nathan, cupping his hands around his face so that he could see more clearly into the pigpen.

'He's there all right. He probably heard us coming. He's docile enough, don't worry. In fact he's shy. Let's go in and take a look at him.'

'Go in?' asked Nathan, with a sudden surge of anxiety that took him by surprise.

'Nathan, he's only a pig. A big pig, I grant you. A very big pig. But you can feed him corn right out of your hand. You can sit on his back and ride him around the field. He loves human company. He'd hang out in singles bars if we let him.'

Nathan looked at the scratches and gouges on the perspex. Some of them were higher than ten feet up; and some of them were so deep that they had almost cut all the way through.

'He gets lonesome, that's all,' said Garth, when he realized what Nathan was looking at. 'He tries to get out, so that he can come join us down at the lab.'

'He's never succeeded, I hope?'

'He did once, a couple of years ago. In those days we used to have an ordinary mortice latch on the door. But Captain Black discovered that if he stood real close to the door when we penned him in, so that we had to press against it to close it, the catch wouldn't fully engage, and two or three kicks would open it. I came back from a meeting at Iowa University to find him wallowing down in the lake. We had to tranquillize him to get him back into his pen, because he sure wasn't going voluntarily. You think mules are stubborn? You wait until you square off with a hog.'

Garth unlocked the metal door, and opened it. 'Captain Black?' he called out. 'Are you in there, Captain Black? I brought some nice folks to meet you.'

There was a moment's silence – then a heavy rustling in the straw, followed by a deep, aggressive grunt. In fact it was more like a roar than a grunt.

'Jesus,' Nathan whispered, under his breath.

'Captain Black, are you going to be a good boy today?' asked Garth. 'We don't want any of those tantrums, do we?'

There was another shuffle, and a harsh scratching noise. Then something enormous collided with the back of the door, and Garth had to stagger back.

'You're not seriously suggesting we go in there with that?' Nathan appealed.

'He's okay, he's okay . . . he's probably feeling the heat. Come on, I promise you. He wouldn't hurt a fly.'

'I don't care how many flies he hurts. I just don't want him having a go at *me*.'

Garth heaved against the door. 'Come on, now, Captain Black, for Christ's sake! Get your ham area out of the way!' He pushed again. 'Come on, you stubborn bastard! I'll huff and I'll puff and I'll blow your freaking house down!' This amused David enormously, and he squeaked out, 'Not by the hair on my chinny-chin-chin!'

Garth strained with all of his strength to open the door, and Nathan joined him. For almost a minute they grunted and pushed, and grunted and pushed; and Captain Black grunted and remained exactly where he was.

'Captain Black!' David piped up. 'Open the door, Captain Black, I want to see you!'

The hog gave a roaring grunt that ended in a high, harsh scream. Then – almost miraculously, he stepped away from the door.

'Seems like you've got the touch,' said Garth, turning around to David with a grin. 'The boy who could speak Piglish.'

He pushed the door wide open. Then he put his arm around David's shoulders, and said, 'Come in and meet him. Don't be frightened. He's big, I'm warning you. He's also awkward and very opinionated. In fact he probably thinks that he's human, just like us, so what is *he* doing in here while we're allowed to go anyplace we want. But if you're good to him and you show him that you're not afraid, well, he'll be good to you back.'

He guided David into the pen, and Nathan cautiously followed.

The stench hit Nathan first. This wasn't ordinary hog-smell. This was a sour, musky, virile odour – an overpowering mixture of urine and pheromones and *beast.* But there was something else, too: the pungent glandular undertones of something that was very much more than beast.

The pen was so dark and Captain Black was hidden so deeply in the shadows that Nathan didn't realize at first how huge he was. All he could see were two glittering black eyes, and the black wetness of a twitching snout. But then Captain Black took two or three steps towards them, into the smeary light that fell through the window. Nathan said, 'Holy Moses,' and took or three steps back.

Captain Black stood over five feet high and nine and a half feet long. His body was covered in coarse black hair, and he was the size and shape of a massive 500-gallon oil drum resting on a trestle. He was so enormous that Nathan could hardly believe he was real. But his huge black ears occasionally twitched, and he kept on stepping forwards, a few inches at a time, so that his trotters clicked and scuffed on the concrete floor.

His body was awesome enough, but his face made Nathan swallow in discomfort. It was more like the face of a giant werewolf than a hog: it was covered all over in thick glossy black hair, with a hideously flattened snout. Two curved incisors rose from his lower jaw, and strings of drool swung with every step he took.

His eyes were black, too – bright gleaming black, intelligent black, black like liquid tar, not dead black like the eyes of a shark. He was staring at Nathan without blinking, and there was some terrible disturbing quality in the way he was staring that made Nathan think that he was capable of rational thought, that he could have spoken, if only his vocal cords could have formed the words.

It was almost like looking into the eyes of a man who had been trapped by some dreadful enchantment inside an animal's body.

'That's some hog,' Nathan said, respectfully.

'Biggest living hog in America,' said Garth, without making any attempt to conceal his pride and his satisfaction. 'He's a Poland China hog, five years two months old. He stands fifteen and a half hands high, nine feet seven inches from snout to tail. Last time we weighed him, he came in at two thousand nine hundred and seven pounds. That's well over one and a quarter tons. Same as a Volkswagen Beetle.'

'I'm impressed,' said Nathan; and he was.

David had been standing staring at Captain Black for a long time without saying a word. Then, gradually, he approached him, a step at a time, until he was close enough to touch him.

David –' Nathan warned. But Garth said, 'Hey, it's okay. He's perfectly tame. Just let him know you like him and he'll like you back.'

David reached out his hand and patted Captain Black between his floppy black-mottled ears. Captain Black half-rolled his head away, and did a nervous little two-step, but he didn't seem to find David threatening.

Garth said, 'He likes his ears massaged, that's what I've heard.'

David lifted up one of Captain Black's ears and rolled it gently between the palms of his hands, as if it were pastry. 'It's so soft,' he said. 'Everything else is so bristly, but his ears are really soft.'

Captain Black may have been enjoying David's ear massage, but he didn't once take his eyes away from Nathan. After a while, Nathan half-shielded his face with his hand, because he found the hog's stare so unsettling.

A man, enchanted, in a hog's body.

'He's phenomenal,' he said.

'Phenomenal is right,' said Garth. 'I mean, this guy isn't just the biggest hog in America . . . he's also the most genetically close to a human being.'

'So where does my brain-section come into this?' asked Nathan. 'You said in your letter that you wanted it for genetic analysis. How are you going to apply that to Captain Black here?'

'It's highly experimental. But once we've analysed the genetic coding in the brain-section, we believe that we can use it to biochemically alter Captain Black's thought processes. The theory is that if we can use genetic coding to give him a humanized liver and a humanized heart – why not use a similar technique to give him a humanized personality?'

Nathan stared at him. 'Garth – you can't turn a pig into a person.'

'Of course not. That's not what we're trying to do. We're trying to prove that you can alter somebody's personality by genetically recoding their brain – just like rewriting a computer program. The medical possibilities are infinite. Think what we can do to help schizophrenics and depressives and epileptics and old people suffering from Alzheimer's. No more senility. No more mad people. In ten years' time, we may even be able to recode brains to lift people out of comas.'

Nathan lowered his hand and looked cautiously at Captain Black.

Captain Black, unwavering, stared back.

'Is that why you wanted such a young brain-section?' asked Nathan. 'So that it wasn't too educated; or too sophisticated?'

'Got it in one, *mon ami*. We needed a brain that had already acquired language skills and coherent visualization processes, but a brain that was reasonably free from prejudice and misinformation. In other words, not a totally clean slate, but a cleanish one.'

David started to massage Captain Black's other ear. He turned to Nathan and smiled in triumph. 'You see, Dad, he really likes me!' Captain Black grunted and snuffled, and his huge belly swung from side to side.

'So, after you've operated on him, Captain Black will have the same personality as the boy whose brain-section I've brought you?'

'Very roughly speaking, yes – although he won't lose his own essential *hogness*, if you understand what I mean. He'll still be a hog. The only difference is, he'll know he's a hog.'

'Will he know the difference between right and wrong?'

'There's no reason to suppose that he won't.'

'And he'll have an imagination?'

'Possibly – although we don't yet have any way of finding out what he might be imagining. Not unless he finds a way of telling us.'

'What about a sense of humour? What about a conscience?'

'Who knows? It's an experiment, that's all.'

Nathan slowly shook his head. 'I don't know, Garth. All I can say is, I hope you know what you're letting yourself in for.'

Captain Black let out a sudden screech, which made them all jump back, David included.

'Come on,' said Garth. 'I can't take much more of this stink. Sometimes I have to spend the whole morning in here, and then even my lunch tastes of hog.'

David gave Captain Black one last cautious scratch between the ears.

'So long, Captain Black. I'll come back and see you soon.'

They left the pigpen and Garth locked the door. Captain Black did nothing but snuffle and grunt. As they walked back along the length of the building, however, they heard a violent thumping sound, followed by a tortured squeak of hog's trotter on plastic that set their teeth on edge.

Captain Black was standing on his hind legs, up to his full height, a massive black shadow behind the blurred, slobbery perspex of his pen. He threw his head back and let out a roar that had them all walking away more quickly, in spite of themselves.

'That's one domestic animal that I wouldn't relish meeting on a dark night,' said Nathan, as they stepped out into the sunshine.

'He's *cool*,' said David. 'He's really cool. I love him. He's better than a dinosaur. I mean, he's like a monster, only he's *real*.'

Four

Emily sat at the kitchen table eating her chicken soup and watching *Getting By* on television. Occasionally, she glanced around at her mother, who was sitting in the living-room sewing. Iris had done nothing but sew since Emily had come home from hospital. Emily kind of understood. There was something in the neat, painstaking mindlessness of it that must be helping her to come to terms with her grief.

Emily hadn't yet started to grieve. She still couldn't believe what had happened. She thought about Saturday afternoon over and over and over, and she found it almost impossible to think about anything else. The station wagon stopping at a tilt. The wind whistling, and the storm getting up. The clouds as dark as Daddy's eyes.

She thought about running, most of all, running in the rain, with the wheat whipping her legs. She thought about her father, lifting his sickle – and blood, splattering the windows of the Loftus's pick-up.

What was really strange, though, was that she was completely unable to visualize her father's face. She could see his clothes as clear as day. She could see his hands and his hair and everything. But where his face should have been, all she could imagine was a smudgy white blur, as if somebody had drawn his face in pencil and then rubbed it out with a soft plastic eraser.

She dawdled over her soup. It was only Campbell's Cream of Chicken, which she didn't like very much; and in any case she wanted to see what happened to Marcus in *Getting By*.

At last, however, her mother put down her sewing and came into the kitchen and stood beside her.

'Don't you want any more of that?'

Emily put down her spoon. 'I'm not too hungry.'

Iris glanced at the television. 'I don't know how you can watch something like that, after what's happened.'

'Oh, Momma, don't turn it off. It's Lisa's favourite.'

Iris hesitated for a moment, and then said, 'All right . . . I understand.'

She drew up a chair and sat down. 'I had a call from Father Wozniak this afternoon. The funeral's arranged for Tuesday morning.'

Emily stared at her, and swallowed. 'Not until Tuesday?'

Iris took hold of her hand. 'That's the earliest he could do. Besides, we have all the arrangements to make. Your grandpa will want to come, won't he; and your cousins from Kansas City, Missouri; and all of Lisa's friends.'

'But Tuesday . . .'

'What's the matter, sweetheart? Why not Tuesday?'

'They'll go bad by then!'

Iris closed her eyes for a moment, to contain the pain. Then she opened them again, and said, 'It's all right, Emily. The people in the funeral home have ways to keep them fresh.'

Just then, the kitchen door opened and Iris's sister Mary came in, carrying armfuls of groceries. Emily jumped up to help her, while Iris cleared away Emily's soupbowl.

Mary was two years older than Iris – recognizably Iris's sister, but shorter and plumper. When they were little girls, Iris had always thought that Mary was far prettier than her. But time had not been very kind to Mary's looks. In childhood her face had always been so angelically chubby, but now it looked oval and dull and disproportionately big. Iris, however, who had always looked so pinched and peaky, now looked handsome and clearly defined – though tired, of course, and sad.

Both sisters were dressed in black: but Mary puffed and panted and bustled about so much that she might just as well have dressed in purple with crimson zigzags. 'I couldn't get that Meadow Gold ice-cream you wanted; you know, the fat-free. But I got that no-cholesterol mayonnaise. Oh – and Emily, I found those hair-grips you asked me for.'

'Thanks, Aunt Mary.'

Mary said, 'Now, I'm going to cook tomorrow. I don't want any ifs or buts. You two guys haven't eaten properly for two days now, and you're going to need your strength.'

'Mary, that's sweet of you,' said Iris. 'But I really couldn't.'

'What are you telling me? That you're never going to eat again? Listen, Iris, I know you don't have an appetite, but you have to keep yourself healthy, for Emily's sake. All I was planning on cooking was a chicken pie – tasty, light and easy to swallow.'

Iris had tears in her eyes. She couldn't stand it, the way that she suddenly started weeping, without any warning. She clamped her hand over her mouth to stop herself from sobbing, and nodded yes.

'So, I bought the chicken quarters,' said Mary, lifting them out of the shopping bag. 'I bought the bacon, the onions, the cream . . . and some fresh broccoli, too.'

She put the broccoli down on the table, big dark-green florets, tinged with purple. Emily stared at it in horror. She opened her mouth and then closed it again, and then turned to Iris, wide-eyed. 'Momma?' she said, in the tightest of whispers.

Iris slowly took her hand away from her mouth. She stared

down at the broccoli, too, nervously biting her lip.

Mary had been delving into her shopping, and hadn't noticed. But suddenly she became conscious of the silence, and lifted her head, and said, 'What?'

'It's nothing – honestly,' said Iris, shakily.

Mary looked from Iris to Emily and back again. 'What do you mean "it's nothing". Look at the two of you. You look like you've seen a ghost.'

'Mary, really, it's nothing.'

'Who are you trying to kid? I'm your sister. Tell me what's wrong. Did I buy something wrong? Did I upset you? Listen, if I bought something wrong, George's favourite cookies or something, you're just going to have to forgive me.'

'Forget it, please,' Iris insisted.

Mary planted her fists on her hips. 'No, I won't forget it. I came here to help, Iris. I left a perfectly good husband back in Dubuque living off Hungry Man dinners and washing his own socks, and the least you can do is tell me what's wrong.'

Iris took a deep breath. Then she said, 'It's the – ah – broccoli.'

'The *broccoli*?'

'It's – well, we don't eat broccoli.'

Mary's face went through five different expressions of disbelief. 'So?' she said. 'You don't eat broccoli. Leave it on the side of your plate. I'm not going to take it personally. Jesus! You and me fell out over Mom's sapphire necklace, sure, but I hope we're not going to fall out over what vegetables we eat.'

She picked up the broccoli, opened up the refrigerator, and was just about to drop it into the vegetable compartment when Emily said, in a high, fearful voice, 'We don't have broccoli in the house.'

Mary slowly stood straight. 'Now, wait a minute. You don't have broccoli in the house? You mean, *ever*? Is there some superstition about broccoli I never heard of?'

Emily furiously shook her head. 'We don't have beans or peas or bell peppers, either.'

Iris took a deep breath. 'You may as well know it, Mary. Terry wouldn't allow anything green in the house. Anything at all.'

Mary slowly looked around the kitchen. Iris was right. There were no green pictures, no green houseplants, no green dishcloths, no green herbs.

Without saying a word, she walked through to the living-room, still carrying the broccoli, and looked around there, too. She came back with a look on her face of total perplexity.

'You're right,' she said. 'I never noticed before. You don't have anything green.'

'It's just a thing of Terry's, that's all.'

Mary said, 'It's just a *thing*? He won't have anything green in the house, he won't let you eat green vegetables, and that's just a *thing*? Oh, Iris, you should have got help with Terry years ago. You should have *left* him years ago. Allen always said that he was a whacko.'

'All the same,' said Iris. 'Could you . . .' she waved toward the broccoli.

'Could I what? You mean, could I throw it away?'

'Well, yes, please,' said Iris, with an edgy smile that wasn't really a smile at all. 'It would make me feel more comfortable.'

'Iris, what do you think is going to happen to you if you have broccoli in the house? Or anything green?'

'I don't know – I just – Terry's always so insistent about it. I mean more than insistent. He gets into such a temper if there's green in the house. The nextdoor neighbours painted their fence green and he was ready to kill them.'

'Did he ever tell you why?' asked Mary, in gradually rising astonishment.

Iris said, 'No. Not really. Terry didn't like to explain what he did. He said actions speak louder than words.'

'It was the Green Traveller,' put in Emily.

'Ssh!' snapped Iris. 'That's nonsense!'

'But it was. Daddy always said that Momma should never open the door to the Green Traveller, *ever*, no matter how long he knocked.'

'Emily, that's enough!' Iris insisted.

But Emily persisted. 'If you don't have anything green in your house, then the Green Traveller can't come in. He has to knock and knock until you open the door.'

Mary looked down at the broccoli she was holding; then at Iris. 'Surely you don't believe that – ?'

'Well, no, no, of course not, it's just a story,' Iris flustered. 'Terry used to say all kinds of things to frighten me. It was just his way.'

'But you still want me to throw away the broccoli?'

Iris nodded, embarrassed but quite emphatic.

'I'll tell you what I'm going to do,' said Mary. 'I'm *not* going to throw it away. It was 59c a pound and it's good for you and I'm not going to throw it away just because of some ridiculous superstition. Terry's in jail now, sweetheart, and he's going to be staying in jail for the rest of his life, so you don't have anything to be frightened of.'

She dropped the broccoli into the icebox and closed the door. Then she said, 'Tomorrow, I'm going to buy some green apples and some green onions and some green tea towels. Then we'll see about this Green Traveller.'

Emily stood staring at the icebox as if she were willing it to open and the offending broccoli to come flying out of it. But Mary said, 'You go take a bath, young Emily. I'll come up in a while to scrub your back. If you're ready by nine, you can watch some TV for a while.'

Emily looked towards her mother, but Iris said, 'Go on, Emily. Do what Aunt Mary tells you.'

When she had left, Mary rummaged in one of her shopping bags and came up with a bottle of Tanqueray and a jar of pimento-stuffed olives.

'How about I make us a very dry martini?'

'Mary –'

'Come on, Iris, it'll do you good to get smashed. Married to Terry for all those years, you deserve it. And what a way for it to end – losing Lisa, and losing George. I'll never forget Allen telling me, the first time we visited: "That man's a whacko. That man's a whacko, and one day he's going to do something seriously whacky".'

Iris sat down. 'He did, didn't he? He did do something seriously whacky.' Her eyes looked glazed, because of all the sedatives that she had been taking.

Mary went to the cupboard and took down two mismatched martini glasses. 'You want to tell me about this Green Traveller thing?'

'There isn't much to tell. Sometimes, when Terry got mad, or when he got drunk, he used to go all around the house, shuttering the windows and locking the doors, and saying that the Green Traveller would find us one day, because of what we'd done; and that when the Green Traveller found us, our lives wouldn't be worth living. He said that dying of stomach cancer would be nothing, compared with what the Green Traveller would do to us. He said that he would rather have his arms and legs cut off, without any anaesthetic. He would rather be burned all over naked with a blowtorch. He used to scare me so much I could hardly breathe.'

Mary took a water jug to the freezer compartment, and noisily filled it with crescents of ice.

'Terry was *disturbed*, Iris. That's about the kindest way I can put it. There's no such thing as the Green Traveller, whatever the Green Traveller was supposed to be, any more than there's Bigfoot or Dracula or Frankenstein's monster.'

She gurgled the whole bottle of Tanqueray into the jug, and then added the slighest splash of dry vermouth. 'Where's your strainer? You do have a strainer?'

She poured Iris a drink, and then popped an olive into it. 'There!' she said, pleased with herself.

Iris stared at the drink unhappily.

'Come on,' said Mary, holding up her own glass. 'Bottoms up!'

'I don't know,' said Iris.

'Oh, for goodness' sake!' said Mary. 'What can it hurt?'

'It's *green*,' Iris explained, in desperation. 'The olive . . . it's *green*.'

Luke returned to his office a few minutes after nine o'clock. His air-conditioning was on the fritz for the second time that month, and the temperature was well over 75°. He stood over his desk, mopping his face and his neck with his handkerchief, leafing quickly through his messages. Outside, the river continued to glitter, and the traffic continued to flow.

There was nothing urgent on his desk, for a change. Two black folders contained the post-mortem reports on Lisa and George Pearson, and he glanced through both of them. No traces of alcohol, drugs or other toxic substances in the bloodstream, no sign of physical beating or sexual molestation. The only act of abuse that Terence Pearson had committed against his children was to cut off their heads.

There was a two-inch-thick report on drug abuse in major centres of population in the Midwest; plus an assessment on electronic signalling devices for tracking stolen vehicles. There were two messages from Sally-Ann, asking him to bring home milk, and not to forget the church social tomorrow evening.

He blew his nose, and then thrust his handkerchief back in his pocket. He buzzed Norman's intercom.

'Norman? Good, glad I caught you. Where's that translation?'

'I'm sorry, sheriff. Ponican didn't show.'

'Did you call him?'

'For sure. But he didn't answer.'

'Shit, Norman, I wanted that translation today.'

'I know that, sheriff. I'll keep on calling.'

'Where does he live?'

'The Pepperwood Apartments on 34th Street, NE, apartment 603.'

'That's on my way home, more or less. Try calling him one more time. If he doesn't answer, I'll drop by his house and pay him a personal visit.'

'Whatever you say, sheriff.'

Luke finished going through his mail. Invitations, advertisements, circulars, that was all. Then he switched off his desklamp and stood in the darkness and stretched. He had been feeling a little more cheerful today. He had cleared over three hundred demonstrators away from the Spellman Institute without any serious casualties, and Gina Ramirez of Channel 7 news had called him 'the Gentle Giant'. She must have failed to see him forcing one struggling young student face-down onto the ground, and standing on the back of his head. Either that, or she had deliberately directed the cameras in the opposite direction. Popular opinion in Linn County wasn't much in favour of animal rights activists: apart from people who worked for giant corporations like Amana Refrigeration and Quaker Oats, almost a third of the population was connected in one way or another with hog-rearing, and those who didn't rear hogs themselves were largely dependent on the spending money of those who did.

More good news: two of Luke's deputies had at last managed to collar a pair of teenage joyriders who had been terrorizing Hiawatha for the past three months, stealing

Mustangs and Camaros and doing high-speed 'smokies' around the four crescents that led off Northbrook Drive, as if they were looping the loop. One of the joyriders had somersaulted his Firebird into somebody's front yard and ended up in hospital with a broken neck, a quadraplegic for life.

Best of all, though, Luke had talked to the county attorney over strong coffee and eggs benedict at the Collins Plaza, and it looked like a 90 per cent certainty that Terence Pearson could be arraigned for homicide in the first degree. All the county was looking for was hard, irrefutable evidence that Pearson's beheadings were premeditated. Luke needed to be able to prove without question that Pearson had planned in advance to 'save' Lisa and George from a fate worse than death: that was why he was counting on Mr Ponican's translation of Terence Pearson's notes. All he needed to find in those miniature scribblings was *one* mention that Pearson intended to 'save' his children – or, better still, that he was going to execute them – and Pearson would be going down for life.

Well, more than life. Luke had a pretty graphic idea of what Pearson's fellow inmates would do to him, when he reached Fort Madison. The last child-killer who had been sent there, a 55-year-old Methodist priest named Herbert Kent, had been nailed to a wooden chair with four three-inch nails, one through each testicle, and two through his penis. He had been forced to shuffle the length of a seventy-foot corridor to get help.

Ten days later he had committed suicide, slashed his wrists with an open bean can.

Luke's intercom warbled. 'Sheriff? It's Norman. Ponican still isn't picking up.'

'Okay . . . I'll get on round there. I'll see you tomorrow.'

The night was still warm when Luke left the office, although there were distant flickers of lightning. The weather forecast hadn't predicted rain, but late-summer weather was always unstable. There was a feeling in the air that things were going to change; that something strange and inexplicable was about to happen.

Luke unlocked the door of his Buick, but he paused for a moment, smelling the wind. He hadn't felt like this since he was at summer camp, at the age of 15. He could remember one night when the air had smelled just like this: taut with static electricity, loaded with tension. They had all slept badly that night. In the morning, Luke had walked down to the lakeshore under a beating summer heat to find his best friend Michael hanging from the flagpole at the end of the jetty. Luke had stared up at him, almost expecting him to speak, to thumb his nose and say 'Fooled you, Luke!' But the early-morning fish crows had already pecked out his eyes, and his tongue was hanging out like a grey dishrag that had been used for mopping up blood.

Luke climbed into his car, slammed the door, and drove out of the parking lot. Milk, milk, he mustn't forget milk. There was a store on the corner of 34th Street, he could get some there. He switched on the car radio, and listened to Sonny Landreth singing 'Outward Bound'. '*Two doors open . . . one in and one out . . .*'

He joined in, singing, '*Two steps taken . . . one back and one forth . . . love in both directions . . . for richer or poorer?*'

He drove up 3rd Avenue as far as 12th Street and then headed due north on Oakland Road. Although it was only a Monday night, traffic was clogged up, and he was stopping and starting all the way. A black Corvette drew up alongside him at the 29th Street stop signal, throbbing with bass from a U2 record. A pretty blonde girl with train-track orthodontic braces and a red Hawkeye cap gave Luke a finger-wave and revved up her engine until it screamed. Luke tiredly took his badge out of his shirt pocket and pressed it against the window so that the girl could see it. When the signal changed to green, he drove away sedately at 30 m.p.h. and, equally sedately, the Corvette followed him.

There were times when it was good to be sheriff, just for the pleasure of screwing up other people's fun.

He stopped outside the store on 34th Street and bought a quart of milk and (guiltily) some cherry Danishes. He crammed one Danish into his mouth, and stuffed the rest of them into the glove-box. He hadn't had a cherry Danish for over nine weeks, and after what he had achieved today, he reckoned he deserved one. The Gentle Giant, right? He would probably use that in his next election campaign.

It took him a further five minutes to reach the Pepperwood Apartments. They were a drab, E-shaped block of yellowish concrete, with a small parking lot out front, and a row of dusty, stunted fir trees on either side (described in the letting agent's brochure as 'mature natural landscaping'). Luke parked in the street and walked across the parking lot to the porch. The glass door was on a powerful spring, and after he had passed through it and let it go, it went *joink–joink–joink* backwards and forwards.

The porch was tiled in swirly yellow and black vinyl tiles, and there was a 1960s 'contemporary' table against the wall, with metal legs and ball feet. There must have been a mural on the wall years ago, but all that was left now was a grubby rectangular mark and six rusty screws. The porch hadn't even been swept: the floor was strewn with dried-up bay leaves.

There was a smell of Johnson's Wax and stale meals.

Luke pressed the elevator button, and eventually the elevator came whining down to ground level, hesitating for a moment before it finally came to rest, and then dropping the last two inches with a loud bang.

On the left-hand side of the elevator door, there was a small circular window, and Luke was startled to see a pale oval-shaped face peering out of it. The face was peculiarly masklike and androgynous, and its eyes shone like blackbeetles. As the elevator door slid open, Luke stepped away. There was a heartbeat's pause, and then a tall man swathed in a rustling white summer raincoat swept out of the elevator, and across the porch.

Luke frowned, and turned around. There was something unsettling about the man, something that caught Luke's attention and made him turn around. The man looked inexplicably *blurry* and out of focus, as if Luke were looking at him through Vaseline-smeared glass.

As he approached the door, it appeared to swing open before he had reached it, *joink–joink–joink*, and to start swinging shut again before he had passed through it. Yet he did pass through it, and then he was nothing but a white shape in the parking lot, and then he was gone.

Luke stared after him. Maybe he was overtired. Maybe he needed glasses. But he was convinced that the man had actually opened the door without touching it, and walked through it while it was half-closed.

He stepped thoughtfully into the elevator and pressed 6. The door juddered shut, and the elevator cranked itself upward. Through the window he could see the passing floors. He smelled chili con carne, and heard a woman playing 'Stand By Your Man' at top volume, and singing along, off key. On the next floor he heard a man and a woman arguing. '*You're crazy! You know that? You're a crazy person!*' On the floor above, he heard gales of laughter from a TV game show.

The elevator slowed down and crept the last few inches to the sixth floor, as if it were afraid that there might not be a sixth floor, after all. Luke waited and waited, and at last the doors slid open. This floor was totally silent, and the single fluorescent tube that lit the corridor was flickering and stuttering, so that it was quite difficult for Luke to make out the names and numbers on the doors.

Apt. 601: E. Salzgaber. Luke walked on, his thick shoes squelching on the tiles. Apt. 602: Sy W. Moline. He turned a corner, where it was gloomier still, and there was Apt. 603: L.R. Ponican. He pressed the doorbell, and waited.

A long, long minute went by. Luke pressed the doorbell again, and called out, 'Mr Ponican? You home?'

Still there was no reply. Luke was growing increasingly impatient. Where the hell could Ponican be? He had promised his translation within thirty-six hours, dammit, and if there was any evidence in it that Terence Pearson had been planning his children's 'salvation' *before* Saturday afternoon, Luke needed it now.

He pressed the doorbell and kept his hand on it for almost half a minute. He could hear the bell shrilling inside the apartment, and he knew that Ponican wasn't there, but he kept on ringing just to vent his irritation.

He was still ringing when the next apartment suddenly opened, and a very tall, broad-shouldered woman stepped out. She had a huge beehive of bouffant black hair and lips the colour of smashed raspberries. She was all dressed up in an electric-blue satin blouse and a black micro-skirt and fishnet pantyhose. She was wearing the same perfume that Sally-Ann's mother had given her for Christmas, Poison, and lots of it.

'Pardon me – do you happen to know the guy who lives here?' Luke asked her.

The woman batted her eyelashes. 'Sure, of course I do. We've been neighbours for nearly five years. More than neighbours: soulmates. Two lonely spirits in a lonely town.'

'Have you seen him this evening?'

'No, I haven't. But he should be home: Monday is his evening off. I'd keep on ringing, if I were you. He's probably asleep.'

'Asleep?'

'He has three jobs, you know. Poor Leos! He teaches English as a second language at Jefferson during the day, then he waits table at Flamingo's chicken diner during weekday evenings; then weekends he gives guided tours at the National Czech and Slovak Museum.' She patted her hair. 'It's a very good tour: you really ought to go.'

'So, Leos is a pretty busy man, huh? No wonder he sleeps on his evening off.'

'Well . . . to be truthful, he does like an occasional drink. He's probably been celebrating Dvorak's birthday or Dubcek's wedding anniversary or something like that. He's always celebrating something. With slivovitz. He gave me some once, and goodness! Bottled Amnesia, that's what I call it.'

The fluorescent tube suddenly flickered more brightly, illuminating the woman's cheek. It was thickly covered with foundation – not only to mask the pimples and acne craters, but the unmistakable blueness of a six o'clock shadow.

Luke stepped out of the woman's way. 'Thanks for your help, miss,' he said, touching the brim of his hat. 'It's appreciated.'

'Any time. It's good to meet a man-sized man for a change. No, really, I'm being serious. If you *do* manage to wake Leos up, could you tell him that I'll feed Skoda for him?'

'Skoda?'

'His cat. He did ask.'

'For sure,' said Luke, and watched her teeter off down the hallway. She pressed the button for the elevator, turned, and blew him a little kiss. Jesus, thought Luke. Ogled by a 6ft 1in cross-dresser. Thank God Norman isn't around: I'd never hear the end of it.

He pressed Leos Ponican's doorbell again, and called out, 'Leos! Mr Ponican! It's Sheriff Friend here! I need you to open the door! Come on, Mr Ponican, wake up! This is urgent!'

There was still no answer. Either Leos Ponican was so drunk that he wouldn't have woken up for the end of the world, or else his flirtatious nextdoor neighbour had been mistaken. Luke pencilled himself a note to call Flamingo's when he got home, to see if Leos had decided to work.

He gave it one last try: thumping on the door with his fist and shouting: 'Leos! Come on, now, Leos – wake up!'

He had thumped only two or three times when the door unexpectedly shuddered open by itself. It hadn't been locked. It hadn't even been properly closed. Luke found himself peering into a narrow, shadowy hallway, where a homburg hat hung on a hatstand over a long brown double-breasted raincoat, and an Austrian wallclock ticked a slow and secretive tick, and where scores of faded watercolours and photographs cluttered the walls.

To the right, there was a closed door, but chinks of light shone all around it. Luke guessed that if Leos Ponican had gone out, he probably hadn't been gone very long, because the sun hadn't set until 9.17, and he wouldn't have switched on his lamps until then. Maybe he had gone out to eat, or to buy more slivovitz. Maybe he hadn't even left the building, but had gone to visit somebody else in another apartment. That could account for him leaving the door unlocked.

'Mr Ponican?' Luke called again, stepping into the hallway. He peered at one or two of the pictures. A painting of the Vltava River, frozen in winter; and another painting of the Forest of Bohemia. The photographs were mostly solemn, formal groups of men and women in black overcoats. The only exception was a portrait of an exquisitely beautiful young girl, in a traditional Czech bonnet decorated with feathers and flowers and pearls. She had one of those haunting faces that you can fall in love with even when you realize (as Luke realized, when he looked at the date on the bottom of the photograph) that they have probably been dead and buried for more than fifty years.

The caption said simply 'Karolina, Prague, 1941'. What pale, melting eyes she had! During the war, Luke's father had served in Czechoslovakia in Patton's 50th Division, and had told Luke again and again about the way that they had stopped advancing on 6 May 1945, after they had reached Plzen, even though they were less than 80 km away from Prague, and could have easily taken it. Roosevelt and Churchill and Stalin had already decided what the zones of occupation were going to be, and Patton had to stop. The result was that Czechoslovakia was closed behind the Iron Curtain for the next forty years – and Karolina with it, if she was still alive (which she probably wasn't).

Luke's father used to say: 'Those bastards. We could've been driving through the city centre by lunchtime.'

Luke rapped at the closed door. 'Mr Ponican? You in there? This is Sheriff Friend.'

He waited three or four heartbeats, and then he opened it. This was Leos Ponican's living-room: brown and drably furnished with a worn-out couch and two mismatched armchairs. The drapes were drawn, and a single table lamp was lit. In the far corner stood a glass-fronted display cabinet containing a set of crimson Bohemian punch glasses, two porcelain fruit bowls, a metal model of St Vitus cathedral, and china statuettes of Jesus and the Virgin Mary. A brown and cream plastic portable television stood on a stack of Czech-language encyclopedias that had been partially concealed with an embroidered tablecloth. Luke laid his hand on it, and the television was still warm.

The room smelled musty, as if it needed dusting and airing. It smelled of meals-for-one, and loneliness, and fly-spray.

Another doorway presumably led to the kitchen. The door was wide open and a light was shining in the kitchen, too. For a man who needed three jobs to stay solvent, Leos Ponican was pretty lavish with his electricity.

Luke walked across the living-room and into the kitchen. It was then that he shouted out '*Ah!*' in shock, and took an involuntary step back, so that his shoulder collided with the doorframe.

Leos Ponican was standing with his back turned, over the sink. He was wearing a white shirt with the sleeves rolled up and the same brown trousers that he had been wearing when he had visited Luke's office. What had made Luke jump so much was the *way* in which he was standing, with his head bowed and his hips slouching to one side. He had never seen anybody standing that way before. In fact, it didn't seem possible for anybody to stand like that.

There was a smell in the kitchen: a strong, ripe, sweet smell, like shit and rotten pears and gone-off chicken, all mashed together.

'Mr Ponican?' said Luke, softly. 'Mr Ponican – is everything okay?'

He glanced quickly around the kitchen. It had been fitted out in the mid-1960s with green Formica-fronted cupboards and Formica worktops; and there was a cream Formica-topped table in the middle of the room, with four chairs. The table was littered with the photocopied pages of Terence Pearson's notepad. Some of them were crumpled up: others looked as if they had been crumpled up and then smoothed out again. Some of them were blotched with ink. A black Pelikan fountain pen lay on top of them, its top unscrewed. A Czech–English dictionary lay on the floor where it had obviously been dropped.

'Mr Ponican?' Luke repeated, and edged his way around the table.

As he came nearer, he knew that something hideous had happened. He could see now that the draining-boards on either side of the sink were splattered with blood; and the sink itself was actually coated in it, glutinous and congealing, like crimson nail varnish.

Luke came closer still. He opened his mouth to say 'Mr Ponican?' one more time, but he closed it again.

Leos Ponican's shirt front was unbuttoned, all the way down to his waistband. In his right hand, in the vicious clutch of rigor mortis, he was holding a large triangular-bladed cook's knife, the handle reversed, the point towards him, the blade lumpy with congealed blood. His stomach had been sliced open, from the left-hand side of his navel all the way up to his breastbone. The thick skin gaped apart like an unzipped white-rubber wetsuit. Most terrible of all, his intestines and his liver were hanging out, in garish glistening heaps, stringy and bloody and slippery with mucus. They were piled into the sink, and over half of the large intestine had been pushed down the Insinkerator. The disposal unit was still switched on, but too much intestine had been crammed down it, and it had jammed solid. It was only the tautened ropes of gut that were snagged in its blades that were keeping Leos Ponican upright.

Luke approached the sink with a feeling of freezing, prickling dread, the kind of dread that crawls back over your scalp and down your back. Leos's eyes were open, so that he appeared to be staring down disgustedly at his eviscerated stomach, and for one insane moment Luke was terrified that he was still alive, and that he was going to turn around and speak.

But then a thin web of blood slid from between Leos's lips, and dripped down into the sink, and Luke was sure that he was dead.

He edged closer. Leos's arms were hanging inside the sink, and left hand was buried deep in his guts. *Buried* in them, as if he himself had been lifting them out his abdomen. *Buried* in them, as if he himself had been pushing them down the sink-disposal. Jesus.

On the window-sill above the sink was a torn-off sheet of paper. In large, cursive letters was scrawled the message, *I fear the pain too greatly – L.P.*

The thick, excremental smell of a human being's freshly-opened body was overwhelming, and it tightened Luke's throat and brought tears to his eyes. It was foul, but it didn't make him feel queasy: he had smelled it too often before. At least, thank God, it was fresh. It was when they had to prise open the trunk of an abandoned car with a crowbar and lift out the month-old semi-liquefied remains of a homicide victim, that was when he felt queasy. Human *cioppino*, yuk.

All the same, he was more than glad that it wasn't his job to disentangle Leos's intestines from the sink-disposal.

He took his mobile phone out of his coat pocket and punched out 398-3521. 'Norman? I'm at Ponican's place. Yes, he's here all right. I guess he was here all the time, but he's bought the farm. I don't know yet. It's very messy: about 9½ on the Yuk Scale. It could be homicide, but it looks more like suicide. If it's homicide, we're looking for a psycho worse than Terence Pearson. If it's suicide, well, I never saw a suicide like this before. He cut himself open and pushed his guts down the Insinkerator. His own guts, yes. I'm not kidding, no. Come see for yourself. No, I'll call John Husband at C R P D. You call Dr Weitzman.'

He dropped his phone back in his pocket, and took a longer look around the kitchen. There were no signs of a tussle, no indications that anybody else had been here apart from Leos Ponican. A single porcelain coffee cup had been washed up and neatly placed upside-down on the end of the draining-board, balanced on its saucer. The blue woven drapes were drawn tight, and when Luke lifted them up to look behind them, he saw that the metal-framed windows were not only locked, but painted over. He left the note where it was, in case it bore any fingerprints apart from Leos Ponican's, but there was no doubt that it was in Leos' handwriting.

Out of the window, there was a view westward, over the twinkling lights of the north-east suburbs, as far as route 380. Luke could even see the seven-storey Collins Plaza Hotel, where he had breakfasted this morning with the county attorney.

He walked around the table and leaned over the papers that Leos Ponican had been working on. Almost completely hidden under one of the smoothed-out sheets of paper was a thick feint-ruled pad. Luke sniffed and took out his ballpen and lifted the sheets of paper away from it, so that he could read what Leos Ponican had been translating.

'The people who come in winter are four in number, sometimes five, sometimes seven. Their leader is a man all garbed in green, sometimes known as Restless Janek, or Janek-Who-Journeys, or simply Janek Green Man. There is always a swordsman with them, and there is always a doctor, and always a fool. Sometimes there is a leper, too; and the twins called Knife and Naked.

'Janek travels many miles and is rarely seen. In back days (olden days?) he travelled in a black carriage drawn by four black horses, with drapes of shroud-fabric tightly closed over the windows. From Janek's carriage came the myth of Count Dracula's carriage which appears in vampire movies! In Russia it was said that he traversed the snowbound tundra by night, in his own black locomotive without lights or windows. Even this day Russian mothers make a special sign when they hear a locomotive howling in the night and also clutch tight their children.

'In Czech and Slovak republics the same sign is made whenever a black carriage passes.

'There is a famous sighting of Janek and some of his friends in the winter of 1881 in Venice during the time of the European cholera epidemic. An Albanian doctor was visiting Venice and saw them one misty morning just before dawn on the Canale della Giudecca. They rowed in a black gondola, with a black flag hanging from its prow. Janek himself sat in the prow. The doctor ran to find witnesses but it was too early in the morning and nobody was about. When he returned the gondola had vanished. Perhaps into one of the many smaller canals. Perhaps into thin air.

'Janek comes with his three friends at the time of winter. They knock at the door. Janek knocks and knocks but when the people inside shout out, "Who is that, knocking at our door?" he says nothing. He will never speak. But he will go on knocking until doomsday if the people inside do not open the door and let him in.'

The lower half of the page had been torn off. Luke glanced at Leos Ponican again, and wished he could ask him what the hell this was all about. But Leos remained where he was, at that strange sideways angle, his head bowed over the sink.

Luke lifted the torn-off page with his ballpen and read what Leos had translated next.

'Open the door, and Janek will enter the house and seek hospitality. Once fed, he will play dice with his friends until the fire dies down (i.e. until it is very late). He will promise riches. He will promise great harvests. He seeks only one favour, to lie with the mistress of the house. He has a rod (a penis?) like thick braided stems. He is very persuasive. This is because of the locked swords. Those who refuse may end up looking at their feet.'

There was nothing more: or, if there was, Leos had crumpled it up and thrown it away. Luke let the pages drop back and stood in the kitchen staring at Leos and tapping his ballpen against his teeth.

Every time he came across an apparent suicide, he always asked himself three questions. Why had they done it? (Usually, a suicide note gave him the answer to that.) Then: why had they chosen to do it that particular way? (By hanging, or drowning, or taking an overdose.) And lastly: did the method correspond with the motive?

People who burned themselves alive were usually trying to make a religious or a political point. This was martyrdom: burning oneself at the stake. People who took an overdose of barbiturates either wanted to slide out of life as quietly as possible – to sleep and never to wake up – or else they hoped that they would be discovered at the last moment, and saved, and *then* wouldn't everybody feel sorry for them?

People who shut themselves in automobiles with garden hoses attached to the exhaust pipe were usually practical people who had simply had enough. Bankrupt businessmen, usually; or cancer sufferers; or middle-aged lovers caught up in inextricable triangles.

Young people hanged themselves – with belts, neckties, bathrobe cords. College students frightened of failure. Teenage offenders faced with jail.

But Leos Ponican? If Leos Ponican had killed himself, nothing seemed to fit, nothing seemed to add up. He had written *I fear the pain too greatly*, but if he was afraid of pain, why had he chosen what was probably the most painful way of killing himself that he could have thought of? Maybe – by killing himself as painfully as this, he must have wanted to punish himself. Maybe – by pushing his intestines down the sink-disposal unit, he had symbolically been trying to eliminate any trace of himself altogether.

It was possible that Leos had grown tired of being lonely. Maybe his doctor had told him he was terminally sick. Norman would have to check that. But if he were lonely or sick, he wouldn't have killed himself like *this*. Cut your own guts out, for Christ's sake! Hadn't he screamed? Hadn't anyone heard him?

Gutting yourself was a highly unusual form of suicide, except among Japanese, or Westerners who were obsessed with Japanese culture. The only case that Luke had come across in Linn County was six years ago, when an Oriental Studies student at Coe College had read too much Yukio Mishima and attempted to commit *seppuku* with a mail-order samurai sword, but he had lost his nerve at the last moment and survived with only one serious cut.

Luke let fall the sheet of paper he had been reading, and walked back around the kitchen table and stood as close to Leos as he could bear.

'What were you trying to do to yourself, you son-of-a-bitch?' he asked Leos, under his breath.

Inside the kitchen, there was silence. In the distance, Luke could hear the wailing and yipping of sirens. It sounded like Norman and Lieutenant Husband were on their way. In a few minutes, this apartment would become chaos. Lights, cameras, medical examiners, photographers.

'Were you trying to escape?' Luke asked Leos, in their last quiet time together. 'Or were you trying to punish yourself? What did you do, Leos, to deserve being punished like this?'

He paused, and looked down at the knife. 'Maybe somebody murdered you. Somebody who really didn't like you. Somebody who hated your guts so much they wanted to grind them down and flush them away.'

He thought about that, and then he turned round and looked at the crumpled-up papers on the table. 'Or maybe you found something out, something that scared you. Something that scared you so much that you wanted to disappear – physically, to disappear – rather than face it.'

There was a moment's pause, and then Leos suddenly turned on one heel. His head tipped back, and he stared Luke right in the eye, with the most intense expression of suffering that Luke had ever seen. For a fraction of a second, Luke thought: *he's still alive!* But then he saw that Leos' intestines were stretching and tearing apart, in webs and strands, and that he was simply collapsing, dead, onto the floor.

Luke made a half-hearted attempt to catch him. He caught at his sleeve, but all that did was to twist him around, and fling one of his arms up into the air, like a mock Hitler salute. He fell with a complicated thud onto his side, his nose pressed against the plinth of the kitchen cabinet.

Luke stepped back. He looked down at Leos and then he looked at the contents of the sink. Without warning, his stomach went into a tight, clutching spasm, and his mouth flooded with bitter-tasting bile and lumps of half-chewed Danish pastry.

He lumbered to the toilet and vomited. He stood with his hand on the cistern for a very long time until his stomach had settled down.

He was still standing there when he heard a soft, rattling sound close behind him. A sound like somebody trying to breathe through a throatful of blood.

He turned around, trying to wrench his gun out of its holster. Standing in the hallway, watching him with green and baleful eyes, was Leos Ponican's tortoiseshell cat, Skoda.

'Jesus,' said Luke. 'You were nearly an ex-cat there, friend.'

The cat stalked up to him and rubbed its head against his leg.

'You talk Czech, Skoda?' asked Luke. 'You talk any language, apart from cat? No, thought not. Guess I'm going to work out what happened here all for myself.'

Iris heard the clock in the hall strike midnight. She turned over in bed, and then turned over again. In spite of the sedatives that Dr Carter had given her, she still couldn't sleep.

She wasn't used to lying in this big oak bed alone. She wasn't used to having two of her bedrooms empty. The house seemed unbalanced, unsettled, as if it were waiting for something to happen.

She thought about her dear dead children, her dearest darlings, again and again. She tried to picture Lisa's face, and Lisa's hair, and what she felt like and what she smelled like. She tried to remember every day of Lisa's life. She wished that she had never turned her back on Lisa, ever, nor sent her off to play with friends, nor sent her up to bed early. She had missed so much of Lisa's life, missed so many precious moments.

She thought about George. She reached up into the darkness of her bedroom and tried to remember what it was like to hold his hand. She stroked the darkness and tried to imagine that she was stroking his hair. His dear, soft hair. She tried to hear him giggling. She tried to see him, marching across the yard, with a stick-rifle on his shoulder.

And the terrible thing was, she couldn't.

She couldn't see either of them, Lisa or George. She couldn't feel them, she couldn't smell them. She remembered broken bits and pieces – moments of brightness, like the sun glittering off the sea, but that was all. She couldn't even remember what they had looked like. Not really. Not exactly.

She lay on her back and the hot tears streamed uncontrollably down the sides of her face, and she couldn't believe that it was possible for a human being to experience such misery.

She wept for nearly twenty minutes. But then, without expecting it, she fell asleep. After the shock of Saturday, and a weekend of grieving, she was too exhausted to stay awake any longer. The tears dried on her face. One hand rested, open, on her chest, as if she were expecting something to fall into it while she slept – something soft and imaginary, like a ball from one of George's baby games.

She dreamed, but she didn't dream about the children. Instead she imagined that she was still lying on her bed, wide awake, not weeping any more, but fully alert. Outside, she could hear a dog barking, and the sweeping spectral sound of automobiles passing along the street. She wondered where she was, what house this was. This wasn't her house, surely? It looked the same, superficially, but there was something very different about it, something disturbing.

There was something green in it.

She sat up in bed. It was a warm, oppressive night, but she shivered. 'Someone's cutting the rock to make your headstone,' that's what her grandmother used to say, whenever she shivered like that.

She thought she could hear noises in the yard below their bedroom. Rustling noises, and the low murmuring of unfamiliar voices. She glided across the bedroom rug and went to the window. She parted the thin blue and white striped cotton drapes an inch or two, no more, and peered cautiously down into the yard.

To her surprise, she saw Emily there, wearing nothing but her long white nightgown. The nightgown flapped in the wind in an oddly-jerky way, as if Iris were watching it in an old-fashioned black and white movie. Emily had her back to the house, so Iris couldn't see her face. She said, '*Emily*,' under her breath, even though she knew that Emily couldn't possibly hear her. She thought of opening the curtains wide, and banging on the window. But then Emily started to make a beckoning gesture to somebody who was out of Iris's line of sight, behind the shed; and for some reason Iris thought it would be wiser if she kept the curtains closely drawn together.

She watched with mounting alarm as the yard gate swung open, and a tall figure in a white raincoat appeared. She had never seen him before: she didn't know who he could be. But he stood in front of Emily and started to talk to her as if he knew her well; and Emily nodded and gestured in reply.

Every now and then, Emily raised her left hand, and pointed back to the house, and the figure in the white raincoat would look up in Iris's direction. She tugged the edges of the curtains as close together as she could, but all the same she had the unnerving feeling that he knew that she was there.

He turned away – stopped, said something more to Emily – then turned away again. Emily began to walk back towards the house.

Iris called out, 'Emily! *Emily!*' But this was only a dream, and no matter how loud she screamed, no sound came out of her mouth. She tried to open the window, but it was jammed fast, and the handle seemed to be made out of some soft and crumbly alloy, more like marzipan than metal.

She was ready to beat on the window with her fist when she saw the gate swing open a second time. Nobody came in but a burst of leaves scurried into the yard, and the rotary washing line starting slowly to turn, with the dishcloths flapping on it. The wind was up, all of a sudden, as if a summer storm were imminent.

Something was coming.

Iris heard the kitchen door slamming, as Emily came into the house. Was this really a dream? It seemed far too realistic to be a dream. She was just about to run downstairs and see if Emily was all right, but for some reason she hesitated. It was the leaves: they made her afraid. It was Emily, too: Emily made her afraid.

At first, there was little more than a scattering of leaves, dancing and chattering on the concrete path. But then more and more of them blew across the yard, catching in everything – the steps, the flowerbeds, the trashcans, the spokes of Emily's bicycle wheels.

Maybe this was a dream, but Iris was sure that she could

hear the leaves quite distinctly. More and more of them, thicker and thicker.

She thought to herself: maybe this is a dream, but who can say whose dream it is, or if it isn't more real than reality? It sure feels real, with all of this wind and all of this weather, and all of these leaves, still pouring ceaselessly into my yard and piling up everywhere, every corner and crevice. Look at them! It's going to take me hours to sweep all of those up, and you can bet your life that Emily's going to help me.

Emily should never have opened the gate. *She shouldn't have opened the gate.* He can never come in – not unless you open the gate for him. Terry had repeated that warning, over and over, every time the kids left the yard gate ajar. He had never said, 'Don't leave the gate open because your baby brother might run into the road and get hit by a truck.' No, he had always said, 'Don't leave the gate open, because he'll come in otherwise, you mark my words, and then we'll all be skinned like rabbits.'

He had never explained who 'he' might be – this 'he' who would tug off their skins. But Iris always conjured up a vivid picture of rabbits' pelts being dragged inch by inch off their bare mauve babylike bodies, and that frightened her badly. She was a Christian: she wasn't afraid of sudden death. But she was afraid of pain, and she was afraid that if somebody ever tortured her, she would renounce everything that she had ever held dear, just to save herself from any more agony.

She had asked Terry time and time again, 'Who *is* he?' But Terry had always lost his temper. He had slammed the gate so hard that the catch had jumped out of its screws, and then gone up to his room and brooded – or whatever it was that he did in his room.

Fear, uncertainty and weirdness – that was all Iris could remember from her marriage. Terry was always giving them warnings, wildly irrational warnings, endlessly repeated, until even she began to believe them. 'Never bring green into your house, anything green, anything. Green belongs outside.' 'Never pray for a good harvest, never. If the weather holds, you'll have a good harvest. If it doesn't, you won't. Don't tempt God by asking him to give you the crop that you deserve: it's just possible that he might oblige.'

She heard Emily coming up the stairs. Then she saw that the dried-up leaves were surging into the yard in a floodtide. They made a thick, rushing, high-pitched noise that was almost overwhelming, like standing too close to a steam locomotive; and they heaped themselves up in greenish-silvery drifts. It was like fall, like every fall that ever was, piled together.

Something's coming. Something dreadful. First the leaves, first the wind. Then the thing that nobody can ever summon up enough courage to confront face to face.

Her bedroom door burst open. She woke up instantly, with a dislocating jolt. She wasn't standing by the window, she was still lying in bed. Mary stumbled across the room and snatched at her arm and screamed out, '*Iris! Iris! There's someone in the house!*'

Iris sat up, stunned.

'*Don't you understand?*' Mary screeched at her. '*There's someone in the house!*'

Iris turned towards the window. Lights were flickering somewhere outside, and a strong wind was blowing. She could hear the rushing of dried leaves – and another sound, the sound of a door banging, again and again, as if it had been left open, or somebody was banging at it so that Iris would let them in.

'Oh God I'm frightened,' said Mary.

Iris stood up. 'Where's Emily?' she asked.

'In bed, of course, where else would she be?'

'I don't know. I just have a feeling. Can you go check up on her?'

'*Me?*' asked Mary, aghast. 'But supposing there's – *something?*'

Iris went to the window and looked down into the yard. It looked exactly like her dream. The gate was wide open, and a floodtide of leaves was pouring in. She stood watching it, completely unsure of what she should do.

She was no longer sure which was dream and which was reality. Was she still dreaming, or had been she been awake before, and had only just started to dream?

'What is it?' asked Mary, coming up close behind her. 'What does it mean?'

'I don't know,' said Iris. 'Maybe it's a storm.'

The door banged, and banged again.

'What are we going to do?' asked Mary.

Iris said, 'Close the door, for beginners.'

'Don't you think we should call the police?'

'I don't know. What was it you heard?'

'I heard the door banging, and the door wouldn't have banged if somebody hadn't opened it, and if somebody opened it – that means that somebody's –'

Iris walked around the bed, and picked up the baseball bat that Terry had always kept hidden underneath it.

'What are you going to do with that?' Mary wanted to know, her face white with night cream, and fright. 'Supposing he has a gun. What good is a baseball bat going to do you then?'

'Mary, will you go check on Emily? That's all I want you to do.'

'All right, all right. But this is crazy. You should call the police.'

Without another word, Iris stepped out of her bedroom onto the landing, with Mary close behind her. She reached the top of the stairs, and there she stopped, listening for any suspicious noises.

'Can you hear anything?' Mary hissed.

Iris listened a little longer, and then shook her head. 'Only the wind; and that damned door.'

'Iris, listen to me. I'm begging you: call the police.'

Iris tugged her arm free from Mary's anxious grip. 'It's my house, Mary. Lisa's dead; George's dead. I'm protecting my own.'

'What are you trying to say to me? You've got nothing left to live for, is that it, so you want to commit suicide?'

Iris didn't answer. It was possible that Mary was right. What did it really matter, if she lived or died? Mary would bring up Emily, bring her up like her own dear daughter. Without a family, what kind of a woman was she now? She might just as well be dead.

At least, when she was dead, nobody could hurt her any more.

She started edging her way downstairs, past the rows of family photographs. White faces watched her from every side – the white faces of memory. Lisa riding her first two-wheeled bicycle. George sitting in a field of oxeye daisies. The fourth stair creaked, and she froze for a while, listening. But all she could hear was those cascading leaves. They were so deep now that they had begun to sound like a bus driving through winter slush. All she could hear was the bang–pause–bang of a downstairs door.

She turned the half-landing, and crept her way down the flight that led to the hall. She stopped for a moment, and looked back up at Mary. 'Mary – go check Emily, for God's sakes.'

'Okay, Iris, but *please* be careful. *Please.* You don't have any idea of who might be down there; or *what.*'

Iris had almost reached the hall when Emily suddenly

appeared out of the dining-room doorway, and stood right at the bottom of the stairs, staring up at her. Emily was wearing her long white nightgown and it flapped in the draught in an oddly-jerky way, as if Iris were watching it in an old black and white movie, thirty-five frames per second. Her face looked very pale, the palest ivory colour, and her eyes were glittering and black, like jets from a funeral necklace. She was smiling sweetly. Such a sweet smile! And yet the intense sweetness of it made Iris stop where she was, one hand clutching the banister rail, the other clutching Terry's baseball bat, feeling suspicious and alarmed and *cold*.

'Momma,' said Emily. A few stray leaves scurried across the shiny woodblock floor, hesitated, and then scurried again. They made a rattling sound like somebody drawing their last breath.

'Emily . . . you're supposed to be in bed.'

'Not tonight, Momma. Tonight's the night.'

Iris stared at her narrowly. Was she sleepwalking? Was she drugged? A dreadful thought struck her: maybe Emily had discovered her sedatives, and had swallowed some, thinking they were candies. Her voice sounded so strange, as if she were clogged up with phlegm, or speaking from another room.

'Emily, what's wrong?' Iris asked her.

'Nothing's wrong, Momma. Everything's fine and dandy.'

'Don't you know what time it is? Go back to your room and get into bed.'

Emily shook her head. 'It's too late for that, Momma.'

She looked down the corridor that led to the kitchen, and the door that led out to the yard. 'You can come in now,' she said, speaking higher and sharper, as if she were talking to somebody who was standing outside.

A sudden burst of dried leaves came rushing along the corridor, and tumbled around Emily's ankles. 'You can come in now!' she called out. 'Everything's fine and dandy now, you're welcome to come in!'

Iris stared at her. 'Who are you talking to? Emily! *Who are you talking to?*'

But Emily didn't answer. She didn't even look up. She just continued to beckon, and to give encouraging little nods of her head.

Iris rushed down the last few stairs, and seized hold of Emily's shoulder. 'Emily! Who are you talking to?'

Emily said, 'Ow,' and tried to twist herself free. But Iris kept a tight grip on her, and turned around to see who it was that Emily had been beckoning.

The corridor was dark, the kitchen was dark, but the yard outside was bright with moonlight. Iris saw the drifts of greenish-silvery leaves, some of them dancing and whirling in the wind, but she saw something else, too. Something huge and shadowy, right in the middle of the yard. Something that shuffled. She didn't know if it was a bush or a gigantic heap of leaves, or a man who was cloaked in leaves.

Whatever it was, it terrified her, and it was approaching the house at a measured, stilted pace, as if it could go faster if it really wanted to, but would rather observe some obscure but age-honoured ritual, like a priest walking up to the altar, or an executioner walking up to the block.

'Emily!' Iris screamed. 'Emily, what is it?'

'I've invited him in,' said Emily, in a wobbly, transparent voice.

'You've *what?*'

'He's holy. He's Daddy's father. I've invited him in.'

'*No!*' said Iris. Even if she didn't know what or who this heap of leaves actually was, she knew for certain that she didn't want it in the house. She let go of Emily, and hurried to the kitchen door, jarring her thigh on the edge of the kitchen table as she did so.

Dark and formless as it was, the heap of leaves must have had some consciousness, because it instantly reacted by rushing furiously towards her. Iris managed to slam the door shut and twist the lock, but she was only just in time. The leaves collided against the door with a heavy, splintering bang, and one of the windows shattered, so that broken glass and dried leaves blizzarded onto the kitchen floor.

'Mary!' Iris shrieked. 'Mary! Call the police!'

Emily ran into the kitchen. Her face was white and her eyes were staring.

'Open the door!' she cried. 'You have to let him in!'

The leaves collided with the door yet again. This time the wood frame splintered, and one of the hinges popped. Iris pressed her shoulder against it, but Emily kept tugging at her wrist and screaming, 'Let him in! Let him in! You have to let him in!'

The leaves crashed against the door again, and yet again, and yet again. Iris's shoulder was badly jarred, and she felt as if her neck had been whiplashed. But her whole system was flooded with terror and adrenaline, and she knew that she had to keep this thing from out of her house.

Terry had warned her: the Green Traveller will come knocking at your door, and he will knock and knock and go on knocking until somebody lets him in. And then God help you.

And then God help you.

The door shivered one more time, and the second window broke.

'Mary!' shouted Iris. 'Mary, call the police!'

Emily kept on snatching and scratching and tugging at her, and in the end Iris swung back her free left arm and smacked her across the side of the head. 'Stay away, Emily! Stay away!'

But Emily continued to pull at her; and tore the sleeve of her nightgown.

Iris tried to smack at her again, but at that instant the door crashed open. Iris and Emily both lost their balance and fell onto the floor, with the broken door on top of them. Emily screamed; but Iris didn't have the breath to do anything but gasp. The door was pressing against her cheekbone and her chest and she thought she was going to be crushed. She dropped the baseball bat and placed the flat of her hands against the splintered woodwork and pushed upward. There was a moment when she thought her wrists were going to break. But then the door tilted, and half-swivelled off her. Panting, coughing, she was able to struggle free, although her right ankle bone was caught against the broken hinge, and painfully grazed. She thrashed and heaved herself back across the floor, and then climbed onto her feet – straight into a hurricane of stinging leaves.

She took two blinded steps backwards, and tripped over the leg of a fallen chair. She went down as hard as if somebody had punched her: rolling across the floor on a noisy carpet of prickly leaves and shattered glass. She heard a noise like something falling from a great height, like a bomb falling, and lifted her arm to protect her face. The huge leaf-shape surged dark and boiling into the house, over the smashed-down door, and in the middle of its darkness she thought she saw *eyes* glaring at her, eyes as glittery-black as Emily's had been.

'Oh God no God *please* God no.'

On all fours, like a frenzied animal, she scrambled across the floor to the hall doorway. Fragments of glass dug into her knees and lacerated her shins. Her lower legs were plastered in blood, but she felt nothing at all, only panic. She managed to climb to her feet, and to turn back to the kitchen, with her eyes narrowly slitted against the wind and the grit and the hurtling leaves.

'Emily!' she screamed. She clung tightly to the door-frame

to keep herself upright. She felt as if she were standing on the deck of a schooner, in a force-nine gale. '*Emily*!'

There was no reply. But just as she was about to step back into the kitchen, she heard the sharp rustle of leaves, so close that it made her shout out. Her arm was snatched by something that felt like a thin-fingered, broken-clawed hand, incredibly strong, and she was swung violently against the wall.

'*Get off me!*'

She fought back, wildly and hysterically, even though she had no idea what she was fighting against. She flailed with her fists into the darkness, and struck leaves and branches and prickles. It was like fighting a bramble bush. Her hands were ripped, her fingernails were broken, even her hair was tangled up in the branches.

Somehow, she managed to tear herself free. Her nightgown was torn away from her shoulder, baring her breasts and lacerating her back. She ran along the corridor into the hallway, and then started to scale the stairs, two at a time.

This is a dream, she kept telling herself. *This is a dream.*

But then she turned the corner in the staircase and there he was: standing right in front of her. She froze, and took one step down, and then another.

He was dimly illuminated by the reflected light from Mary's bedroom, on the landing above. His face was pale and his raincoat was white and his expression was totally emotionless, as if he had never been able to feel anything in his life. He was carrying Mary in his arms; poor dangling Mary, one arm swinging, the other arm crooked, her face turned aside. Her stomach had been torn open, and pillaged for its contents, and her intestines hung down in elaborate bloody festoons, a terrible festival of reds and purples.

'Oh God,' Iris said. 'Oh God, this can't be real.'

But then she heard the rustling of leaves close behind her,

and turned, and saw what it was; and knew for sure that it was real.

Five

In the Presidential Suite of the Collins Plaza Hotel on Collins Avenue, Senator Bryan Cady sat back in his huge gilt rococo armchair with his eyes half-closed, watching the morning sunlight blur through his eyelashes, thinking of nothing.

In front of him knelt a startling-looking black girl with short-cropped hair, crimson collagen-injected lips and a criminally short black dress. Bryan Cady's right foot was buried in her lap, and she was using a chamois pad to polish up his toenails. She was perfumed strongly with Giorgio Red.

Bryan Cady's feet, of course, were bare; but otherwise he was dressed up like a fashion-conscious mortician. Grey Armani slacks and a black silk Armani shirt, with a black Cerruti necktie. He was smoking a torpedo-shaped Elegante cigar, which he had just relit, so that when Lily came into the room his head was momentarily masked in smoke, as if it had just exploded, like the villain in *Scanners.*

Bryan's personal assistant, Carl Drimmer, was standing by the window with Bryan's black silk socks draped carefully over his arm.

Lily strode across the thick eau-de-nil carpet and kissed Bryan on top of his reappeared head. He reached up his hand and possessively took hold of her wrist.

'Lily! That was some interview! You shone, as usual, you *coruscated*! How come you always manage to look so edible on television?'

'I live clean and I think clean,' Lily retorted. 'And I don't smoke those disgusting cigars, like you do.'

With her fingers, she combed back her blonde rough-cut hair. Unlike the T-shirt and denim shorts in which Nathan had seen her when she was demonstrating outside the Spellman Institute, she was dressed this morning in an expensive grey silk Yves St Laurent suit with deep lapels and loose, flowing sleeves. She levered off her slingback shoes with her finger and kicked them lightly across the floor.

'You coruscated,' Bryan repeated. 'You gave them all kinds of grief. Especially that guy from the Spellman Institute.'

'Garth Matthews? *Him.* He's a psychopath. He's not content with cutting up live pigs and stealing their internal organs. Oh, no, he's got to give them a psyche, too, so they'll *know* that he's going to steal their internal organs, and how much it's going to hurt, and *why.*'

Bryan's cigar went out again. He took out a solid gold Dunhill lighter and studiously relit it.

'Do you *have* to?' Lily demanded.

Bryan drew on his cigar very slowly, with pursed, wet lips. 'This is my only vice, Lily, apart from you. A hand-rolled Elegante, colorado maduro, its wrapper moistened with the vaginal secretions of the specially-trained Dominican novices who made it.'

Lily wrinkled up her nose. 'You're kidding.'

Bryan gave a thick chuckle. 'Yes, I am. Some toothless old bastard in a sweaty vest probably rolled it in his armpit and stuck it together with spit.'

Lily said, 'I need a drink. Those TV studios always make me so dehydrated. I mean, emotionally, too. I can't *believe* that Garth Matthews. He's the *definition* of sadist. He talks about vivisection as if it really turns him on, as if he really relishes every moment he's causing those animals pain. Do you know what he told me? He said he never hides their eyes, when he's operating on them. No wonder he wants to give them human consciousness. He'll probably be walking around with a permanent boner.'

Bryan hesitated for a moment, as if he were thinking about the idea of a permanent boner, and didn't altogether disapprove. Then he snapped his fingers, and said. 'Carl . . . get Lily a drink, would you? What do you want, sweetheart? The mango or the cucumber?'

'Water . . . that'll do. Ramlosa. I don't like Perrier any more, that last bottle was so lacking in spirituality, I couldn't believe it.'

'Perhaps you should try a shot of vodka in it,' said Carl.

Lily ignored him, and perched herself on the edge of the sofa as close to Bryan as she could. He changed hands with his cigar so that the smoke wouldn't trail in her face. The black manicurist glanced up at her, but didn't stop pedicuring Bryan's toenails. There was something very possessive about the way she did it, about the way she was holding his bare foot so deep between her thighs, but Lily knew that it was ridiculous to feel jealous. All the same, she found after a few moments that she was too irritated to watch the intimate way in which the girl held Bryan's bare heel in the palm of her hand and pushed his cuticles back with her orange-stick.

'I just hope I did some good today, that's all,' she said, restlessly.

'Don't fret so much,' said Bryan, patting Lily's hand. 'I had a call from Duncan White as soon as the show was over. He's prepared to reconsider his vote if we can guarantee that extra soybean subsidy. By the end of next month, this country will legally be vegetarian, I promise you. In five years' time, vegan.'

Lily kissed Bryan's cheek. Her eyes brimmed with admiration. 'You're amazing,' she said. 'I always dreamed about saving the animals, but I never believed that it could ever come true.'

'Hey . . . I can't take *all* the credit,' said Bryan. 'It never could have come true, if a majority of Americans hadn't wanted it to come true.'

'All the same –'

'No, these days, Americans are looking for new ideals. And what's more idealistic than turning vegetarian, and saving animals from so much suffering? Your average Americans are healthier, wealthier and better educated, they're politically sensitive to the pain of others . . . and that doesn't just mean ethnic minorities or sexual groupings or people who are differently abled. That means other mortals, too. Cows, pigs, sheep . . . whatever. You know what the song says.'

'Yes,' smiled Lily. ' "Whoever we are, whatever we are, we all come from Earth" '.

Carl came in with Lily's glass of water. Bryan watched her while she thirstily drank it, one of her hands cupped lightly over her left breast, her Adam's apple surging up and down. The black manicurist dug sharply into the corner of his big toe with her pointed orange-stick.

'Aren't you done yet, Ticia?' Senator Cady asked her, irritably. 'My feet are beginning to feel real fussed-over.'

'Just buffing now, sir,' said the manicurist.

'Well, forget it for now. You can buff tomorrow. I don't know: buff Wednesday.'

There was a tight pause. Then, 'Yes, sir, senator.'

Lily edgily sipped her water while the manicurist put away her scissors and her emery boards and her bottles of polish. When the manicurist had eventually closed the door behind her, Lily smiled and relaxed more, and sprawled across the arm of Senator Cady's chair.

'You should let me do that for you.'

'Polish my toenails? You're a major socio-political force. You're a *Zeitgeist. Zeitgeists* don't polish people's toenails.'

'You really think that Zapf-Cady has a serious chance?'

Bryan made a complicated kind of a face, as if to indicate

that he was mentally running through dozens of different options. 'I won't try to deceive you, Lily: it's going to be *this* close. But it's such a now issue, and right at the moment Congress is desperate to show the President that they can be just as *now* as he is.'

'Pfff,' put in Carl, without making any attempt to conceal his derision. 'You may get all the now promises now, but what about the now votes tomorrow?'

'Like I said, it's going to be close,' Bryan retorted. 'But the Vice-President will give it his casting vote, if he's called to. He's a vegan himself – and what's more, his wife's in remission from stomach cancer, so all she can eat is grits and strained spinach. Jesus. Socks, please, Carl.'

Carl handed back Bryan's socks with an Oscar-winning performance of high disdain. 'I don't know, Senator,' he said. 'When it comes to the moment of truth, what do you think those able, learned and distinguished colleagues of yours in the Senate are going to put first? Nutritional correctness; or rare filet steaks at the Rib Room at the Mayflower?'

He paused. 'Personally, I think they're going to vote with their appetites.'

'You're a cynic, Carl,' Bryan told him.

'Of course I'm a cynic. I've been your personal assistant for eleven and a half years: who wouldn't be? I've seen you pork-barrelling, Bryan. I've seen you wheeling and dealing. Sometimes I've disagreed with your methods but I've never disagreed with your political agenda. Not until now. This Zapf-Cady bill is nothing short of bizarre: political correctness gone mad. Zapf-Cady isn't now. It isn't even *then*.'

Bryan lifted his cigar. 'You're so wrong, Carl: do you know that? This bill is the future. We're talking about global survival, we're talking soya protein and hydroponics. We're talking about *everybody* eating: not just the pampered, high-protein minority in the West. We're talking about a whole new view of the Earth we live on, and the mortals who share it with us.'

'Well,' said Carl, sniffily, 'I got my first-ever job at McDonald's, that's all; and I'm just wondering how many millions of people Zapf-Cady is going to put out of work? Hormel alone sell 140 million cans of Spam every year. If Zapf-Cady is ratified, who are they going to sell *those* to? Not Israel, for sure.'

Bryan shook his head, with the smiling dismissiveness of the true evangelist. 'Zapf-Cady has the most progressive compensation structure of any prohibitory measure in US agricultural history. No farmer or breeder or meat-packer is going to lose money. Jobs are going to be relocated, for sure, from livestock to vegetables, but not lost, not to any substantial degree.'

'What about people like me, who simply don't want to give up eating meat?'

'We'll be doing you the greatest favour that anybody ever did you. You won't even know yourself. You'll feel pure, you'll feel sexy. Do you have any idea what animal fats can do to your arteries? Do you know how many hormones there are, in your average supermarket chicken? Do you know what hotdogs are made out of? Jesus, Carl, eat a lettuce instead of a steak and set yourself free. Your whole charisma is weighed down with saturates. You might even stop being such a goddamned depressive.'

Bryan stood up. He was a small, rather Italianate-looking man, only a shade over 5ft 7in, very lean, with thin wrists and ankles and narrow, almost spidery fingers and toes. He was also remarkably handsome. His hair was soft, you could see how soft it was even without touching it, and a natural shade of very dark brown, almost black, with silver-grey highlights, the colour of an Indian ink drawing that has been hung in a hallway in very strong sunlight. His face was sharply cut, like a half-starved angel, with hooded brown eyes and a perfect nose and lips that always looked as if they were about to say something alluring but cruel.

His vanity and his ego were so powerful that they were almost visible, like the heat from a sunbaked highway. At 51, he was one of the youngest chairmen ever of the Senate Committee of Agriculture, Nutrition and Forestry. It was hard to think that he had once helped to feed the pigs on his father's farm in East Pleasant Plain, Jefferson County, Iowa; and that he had told his school careers teacher that his greatest ambition was to produce 'dry-cure bacon that gets well-respected, statewide'.

Something had happened to Bryan Cady in his twenty-second year. He had met the beautiful, wild, discontented wife of Senator William Olsen, quite by accident, at the St Nikulas Day celebrations at the Czech Village on 16th Avenue S W, in Cedar Rapids. Four months later she had telephoned him, panting, drunk, in urgent need of sex, and they had started an irrational but absolutely incandescent affair. She had taken him everywhere – Washington, New York, San Francisco, London – and introduced him to everybody. By the time he was 23, he had seen enough of wealth and political influence to know exactly what he wanted to be. He didn't want to produce dry-cure bacon any more, no matter how well-respected it was. He wanted to be rich, famous and powerful.

Two years later, after returning from a Kernels ballgame, Senator William Olsen had been paralysed by a massive stroke. He had been forced to retire from politics, but his mind had stayed as abrasive as ever, and his hunger for high office was unabated. He had chosen young Bryan Cady as his proxy – not only in bed with his wife, but as his political proxy, too – supporting him with all of the wealth and all of the political influence at his disposal, which were huge.

At the age of 27, Bryan had been elected to Congress as a Republican representative for the state of Iowa. Nine years later – when he was a year younger than John F. Kennedy had been when he became senator for Massachusetts – Bryan had been elected to the Senate. William Olsen had continued to bankroll him, and to use all of his political power to drive him ever upward.

William Olsen wanted to be President: in fact, if not in name.

William Olsen wanted to control a world that had robbed him of his manliness, and taken away his mobility. Bryan Cady was going to be the man who would do it for him.

Carl said, 'Senator, don't forget that you have that presentation lunch with the Chamber of Commerce at 12.30; and that we're meeting with Cargill at three.'

Bryan ignored him, and ran his hand into Lily's hair, and looked into her eyes with the same slow-burning look that had first set Nina Olsen on fire. 'Are you coming back to Washington with me?' he asked her.

'Tonight, Bryan? Well, no, I don't think so. I've been trying to arrange a meeting with the Spellman Institute, to see if we can't persuade them to abandon this xenografting project. All the signs are that we've put them under so much media pressure these past couple of weeks, they might agree voluntarily to postpone it, at least. If I come back to Washington now, this whole thing is going to lose so much momentum.'

'Momentum?' said Bryan. 'I don't know why you're wasting your time. The only thing that will ever budge the Spellman Institute is the law. Once Zapf-Cady is ratified, they'll have to quit experimenting, and then you won't have to worry *what* they think. Killing any kind of animal for any reason will rate as murder. The Spellman Institute will have to shut down, just like every other place where animals are killed or mistreated. There won't be a slaughter-house standing from one side of this country of ours to the other. Nor a meat-processing plant, nor a cosmetic-testing laboratory, nor any place at all where animals have to suffer for the sake of human comfort.'

Lily took hold of Bryan's hands and drew him close and kissed him. She was at least two inches taller than he was, even without her shoes, but Bryan didn't care that he was shorter. What he lacked in height, he more than made up for in money and aura and sheer power.

'I don't like you having your nails done,' she breathed in his face.

He studied her thunderstorm eyes. 'You want me to cut you to ribbons when we're making love?'

'You're the lover. You should know what I want. But what I mean is – *I* could do them.'

Bryan touched his forehead with one finger as if he had only just thought of something important.

'What is it?' asked Lily.

'We're having lunch with the Cedar Rapids Chamber of Commerce, right?' Bryan asked.

'Right,' said Carl.

'Did you bring my suit from the cleaners?'

Carl frowned at him. He always reminded Bryan of a Madison Avenue type from a 1960s *New Yorker* drawing: neurotic and buttoned-down and eternally pessimistic, and able to laugh at nothing but the mediocrity of other people. The kind of man who would move to the neighbouring state if they brought the taxes down, and move back again if the same thing happened in reverse. He was blondish-grey, pale as suet, with a slight cast in his right eye. Once he had left the room, Bryan could never remember exactly what he looked like.

'I'll go bring your suit from the cleaners,' he said, dully. He waited for a moment longer than was either polite or necessary, and then left.

Lily kissed Bryan again and again, holding him close. Her breasts were squashed close to his Armani shirt. She breathed, 'Carl gives me the heebie-jeebies, he really does.'

'That's why I like to have him around.'

'Just to give me the heebie-jeebies?'

'No, because he disagrees with everything I say and everything I do. He believes in wearing fur and eating pork chops and keeping women out of politics. He hates blacks. He hates Koreans. He hates every ethnic minority you can think of. Jesus, he hates *Tibetans.* He hates the way I dress, he hates the way I talk, he hates the way I think. Can you imagine anybody more suited to keeping my feet on the ground?

'Let me tell you something, Lily, I will never, ever believe the shit that my publicists put out about me. Ever. The day you believe your own publicity, that's the day your career starts to dematerialize. Me – I keep people like Carl around me, and that's why I'm going to turn this country into a land fit for all mortals to live in, humans and animals in peaceful coexistence, and that's why I'm going to be President.'

He kissed her, sliding his tongue in between her lips. Then he licked the tip of her nose, and smiled at her, and said, 'Don't forget . . . you heard it here.'

She needed something very different when it came to sex. She had told him about it the very first time he had taken her to bed, at the Hotel Bristol in Warsaw, where they had both been attending last year's World Conservation Conference. They had sat together in the mellow afternoon light of the Cafe Bristol, drinking coffee and eating pastries, and she had laid her hand on top of his, and said, 'I have one special need.'

He had looked at her through the rising steam from his espresso. He had said nothing. He had been Nina Olsen's lover; and the lover of many other wealthy and powerful women besides. He knew something of special needs.

He took her hand now and led her into the bedroom. Outside the window there was a wide view southward, to downtown Cedar Rapids, where traffic sparkled, and the Cedar River gleamed like a stream of molten brass.

He didn't draw the drapes, however. Apart from the fact that the Presidential Suite was too high up for anybody to be able to see inside it, Bryan would be obscuring the light in a different way.

Lily said, 'How long will it take Carl to fetch your suit?'

'There is no suit.'

'Then –'

He kissed her, and kissed her again, and unbuttoned her jacket. 'There is no suit,' he repeated.

He slid the jacket off her shoulders. Underneath she wore a simple but expensive white silk T-shirt with a deeply scooped neckline. Her cleavage was very deep and it gave off the warm aroma of body-heated perfume. She was wearing a white lace quarter-cup bra which supported her breasts without restricting any of their bounce or their fluidity, and which left her nipples uncovered. Without taking his eyes away from hers, Bryan lifted his two middle fingers, and circled each of her nipples through the thin slippery silk, hardly touching them, around and around, sometimes not touching them at all, until they stiffened, and he was able gently to tug at them, and twist them between his fingertips.

Lily continued to stare at him, scarcely blinking, her lips slightly parted, her breath rising in soft, patient gasps.

'You coruscated,' Bryan assured her, and smiled. 'You were like the sun's halo around the moon. You made me hard inside my pants, just watching you; and so jealous. I wanted to burst into that TV studio and fuck you on screen, live, in front of all of those millions of people.'

He lifted her T-shirt. It lifted her breasts, too, for just a moment; but then they slid out of the silk, and were bared in front of him, with tightened nipples and wide pink areolas, the colour of fallen rose petals. He kissed each nipple and she watched him kissing them. Then he reached around her and unfastened her bra, so that her breasts dropped just a little, and swung in a heavy swing–*pause*–swing motion.

'I wanted the cameras to come up close, and show us kissing and licking each other,' he said. His voice was low and soft and breathy now, like somebody blowing across the neck of a bottle. 'I wanted to show everybody in this whole Godless country what they were missing; and why I adore you; and why I would rather eat you than let you leave me.'

He unfastened the buttons and hooks around her waistband, and his fingers slid down the zipper of her skirt like a surgeon making his first incision. Her skirt whispered and rustled to the floor, and she stood in front of him wearing nothing now but the tiniest of white lace panties, embroidered with lilies. He cupped his hand over the front of her panties and at the same time he kissed her, his tongue seeking every detail of her teeth, every ridge and every whorl of her inner gums, like a blind urgent predatory sea-creature. She felt breathless; she felt frightened. She always did when Bryan made love to her.

Outside the window, Bryan could see the needle-sharp sparkle of a Northwest Airlink airplane lifting off from Cedar Rapids Municipal Airport, more than eight miles away. He thought it was extraordinary that people were flying and talking and drinking cocktails while he was breathing in the fragrance of a near-naked woman, all this distance away. Lily said, 'Bryan . . .' as if she were trying to attract his attention; but apart from that her lovemaking was completely passive.

He tugged down the thin elastic of her panties. '. . . they could see you naked . . .' he told her, continuing his tele-play. '. . . millions of men, staring at your cunt, wanting it, needing it, and none of them could have it but me . . .'

She lifted each leg with all the elegance of a well-trained horse, so that he could pull her panties over her right foot, and then her left foot. He crushed her panties in his hand as if he were crushing pot-pourri, and held them for a while in his tightly-closed fist, to ensure that he crushed out of them all the distinctive aromas which they held, nervous sweat and urine and sex. Then he buried his nose in them, inhaling deeply. '. . . and none of them can share the *smell* of you, either . . .'

He touched her lower stomach with infinite gentleness, the tip of his middle finger resting in her navel, the tip of his little finger stroking her mound of Venus; enough to rouse only the softest tingling of her nerve-endings. He kissed her again, slid and swam and hunted through her mouth, demanding information and submission. 'Bryan,' she repeated, with her eyes closed, waiting patiently for what she really wanted. Perhaps he wouldn't give it to her: perhaps he would make her wait longer than she could bear.

Her vulva was covered with only the finest of newly-grown hairs, almost invisible, like a ripe peach. His middle finger explored her slit – parting her slippery lips, sliding down gently, so gently that she could hardly feel him, the fingertip slipping inside her vagina for just a second, no time even to squeeze her muscles so that she could really feel it, then touching her perineum, and circling just once between the rounded cheeks of her bottom, teasing her anus, but she couldn't have that, either, because his finger had gone by then, and was trailing slowly, slowly down the back of her naked thigh, like a spider lowering itself on its spiderweb.

'Bryan,' her voice was becoming anxious now, deeper into her throat.

He kissed her again, he slid his fingers down her bare back. He cupped her heavy breasts.

'*Bryan* –' She tried to seize his wrist, to cram his hand between her legs. But he gripped her wrist in return, and held her implacably tight, so that she shuddered and struggled but couldn't get free. Another plane winked in the distance. It was like a heliograph message from a distant butte.

Gradually, Bryan forced Lily down so that she was sitting on the end of the kingsize bed. Her eyes were still closed. He knelt between her legs, gripping her left wrist so fiercely that she couldn't even move her fingers. With his own left hand, he pushed her back so that she was lying on the bedspread, with her thighs wide apart. Her huge breasts fell either side of her chest, nipples erect. The skin of her breasts was almost luminous, and mapped with veins.

He lowered his head between her legs and used the tip of his tongue to open up her inner lips. They parted stickily, like the wings of a newly-emerged butterfly. His tongue-tip lingered around her clitoris, circling, circling, until the nerves in his tongue-tip could feel the nerves in her clitoris responding, and her clitoris swelling and stiffening.

His licking slid downward, momentarily probing her urethra, which made her shiver. In response, his hand gripped her wrist more tightly, as if to remind her that *she* was his mistress; and that *he* would decide when she could respond. At last – after a pause so long that it almost suffocated her, holding her breath – his tongue slid into her open vagina, and curled, and licked. He hotly breathed into her, and then retreated.

This was the Sniffing, this was the Tasting. Now came the Rutting; and Lily could hardly contain her trembling. She shook like a woman with a fever. All of her movements were uncoordinated and uncontrolled. She started to whimper; and to let out little high grunts through her nose. Her whole body went into spasm. Her fingers clawed at the bedspread, and Bryan's shirt; and she would have scratched his face, too, if he hadn't quickly ducked and circled his head.

He didn't talk to her any more. This part of the ritual was silent, except for Lily's grunting and gasping. This was no longer two human beings making love. This was an animal encounter: voracious and fierce.

Bryan reached beneath the bed, and pulled out two white silk scarves. Then he stood up, and twisted Lily over, forcing her face-down onto the bed. She struggled and kicked and thrashed at him, but he twisted her left arm right up between her shoulder-blades, and then he slapped her bare bottom – once, twice, three times – leaving bright red fingermarks on her luminous white skin.

She tried to struggle free, but he pushed her even harder onto the bed, squashing her breasts against the brocade. Then he climbed astride her back, and pulled back her head, and tied one of the white silk scarves around her eyes, and knotted it tight, so that she was completely blinded.

She screamed and grunted more; but now he dragged her right arm behind her, too, and used the second silk scarf to bind her wrists. She kicked at him, but he slapped her bottom again, sharp stinging smacks, and she pulled her knees up underneath her, and crouched on the bed, quivering.

Bryan stood up. Unhurriedly, he tugged his necktie free, unbuttoned his shirt, and unbuckled his pants. Lily remained where she was, naked, blindfolded, cowering on the bed, her hands tied up behind her.

Her sex was completely exposed to him; and, as he undressed, he never took his eyes away from it, relishing the sight of those pink glistening lips, and the way in which her muscles occasionally winced.

Naked, he was lean, wiry, and whorled in black hair. His cock stuck out, fully hard, its glans as purple as a fresh eggplant. It softly throbbed in time to his circulation. His balls hung heavy between his thighs, looking as if they might hatch at any moment.

Lily whimpered and snorted and thrashed her head from side to side, an animal in panic. Bryan knelt up on the bed, and parted the cheeks of her bottom with his thumbs, as wide as he could. Blinded by one scarf, bound by another, Lily started to scream. But Bryan leaned forward with all the calmness in the world, so slowly that he could have been living in a quarter-speed nature movie, his tongue extended like a chameleon reaching for a sweet-tasting treat, and touched her exposed anus with the very tip of it.

Then, with a huge smile of satisfaction, he took hold of his erection in his hand, and forced its swollen head deep between Lily's legs, sliding, sliding, right up to his joggling balls, until she looked as if she had grown black public hair, too.

He fucked her quickly and angrily. His cock thumped into her again and again, and she lay face downward on the bed with her eyes blindfolded and her wrists tied behind her back, her teeth gritted in ecstasy and need and painful fulfilment.

She said, 'Bryan, Bryan, Bryan,' under her breath, but he didn't hear her. His blood was thundering in his eardrums and the sticky slippery sounds of intercourse were all that penetrated his concentration.

It didn't take long before he cried out, 'Shit, I'm coming, shit!' and bent forward onto Lily's back, his face reddened, his eyes squeezed tight, his whole being concentrating not on Capitol Hill or fooling the electors or successful TV soundbites, but on squirting a teaspoonful of sperm into the open vagina of a girl who needed to have sex like a hogtied animal.

There was a moment's panting; a moment's intense hotness; a moment's intense relief. These were the moments when Bryan knew that he didn't really love her; that he couldn't take any more of this blindfolding ritual, not until the next time, anyway. These were the moments when he felt most like himself: and saw himself for what he was. But moments like these were too few and far between for him to think about change. Whatever happened, win or lose, Zapf-Cady was political dynamite, and if this was the way to make the most political capital out of it, then bring on the scarves, bring on the whips, bring on the handcuffs; whatever Lily wanted, Lily could have.

Bryan, soft, drew himself out of her. For an instant, a thin shivering web of sperm connected them, then broke. She said, hoarsely, 'Untie me,' and he untied her, as she always trusted him to. He took off her blindfold.

'You were sensational,' he said. 'You excelled.'

'I was lost,' she replied. Her voice was tiny – childlike, pathetic and bleak.

'Lost?' said Bryan. 'What do you mean by lost?'

'I was lost in the field, but Momma came looking for me.'

Bryan flopped back on the bed beside her, and reached for his quarter-smoked Elegante. 'Childhood memory, that's all. They can come to plague you when you least expect it.'

He paused for a while, to find his lighter. Then he added, 'You never talked about your mom before.'

'I never knew her.'

'She rescued you when you were lost in the field.'

'Oh, sure, that, but that wasn't really my mom.'

Bryan lit up his cigar. 'You don't have to explain. I don't expect a life history.'

She lay in his arms, very close. Her skin felt cold and occasionally she shivered. He asked her if she wanted him to turn up the air-conditioning but she said no, she liked it chilly. She could feel his wetness between her legs when it was chilly, and she liked that, it made her feel taken.

He said, 'I don't understand you sometimes, the way you phrase things. You know, like "taken".'

She reached across and held his softened penis in her hand and squeezed it. 'I don't understand you, either – some of the words you use.'

'Hey, I was self-educated. I like people who are self-educated. They're originals.'

She slipped down the bed and took his penis in her mouth,

sucking it and rotating it, probing it with her tongue and gently chewing it. While she did so, Bryan stared at the reflections that danced on the ceiling of the Presidential Suite and marvelled at the way in which political expediency could bring enemies and lovers together; and create metaphysical conundrums which were almost impossible for anybody to solve.

Luke arrived at the Pearson house a few minutes shy of eleven o'clock. The street was cluttered with police cars and press vehicles and station wagons from the Cedar Rapids coroner's office. The morning was hot and blurry, and turkey vultures were circling lazily around in the middle-distance. As well they might. There was carrion here.

Chief Husband was standing in the front yard chewing gum. He was a stocky, muscular man, handsome in a bullish way, with short-cropped grey hair and the clearest blue eyes that Luke had ever seen on anybody; as if he could see through locked doors; as if he could see through solid steel. Luke approached him in the way that their personal protocol demanded, kind of sideways, a sort of mating dance. All of this was unbalanced by the fact that, spectacularly drunk, Chief Husband had once taken down his pants and shown Luke the terrible bullet-wound in his groin, the tentacled squid-like scar tissue, the single testicle, the patchy pubic hair, and the way his penis hung so crooked.

'Hallo, Luke,' said John, still chewing. Close-up, he smelled strongly of Old Spice shower gel.

Luke gave him a cautious smack on the shoulder. 'How're you doing, John. What's the picture?'

'One middle-aged married white female not just dead but extremely dead. One middle-aged married white female assaulted with cuts, bruises and lacerations, and severe shock. One eleven-year-old white female with no discernible injuries and no immediate indications of shock: she probably didn't witness what happened.'

'The woman who died? That was Iris Pearson's sister, wasn't it? The one who came from Dubuque, to help her get over her kids being killed.'

'That's right. Mrs Mary van Bogan, 5537 Asbury Drive, Dubuque. Her husband's flying here now.'

'And Iris?'

John shook his head. 'How would *you* feel, if your husband executed your kids, and then two days later your home was broken into, your sister was gutted and you were whipped, scratched and beaten every colour of the rainbow?'

'Any ideas at all?'

'I don't know. It beats the hell out of me. I want to talk to Terence Pearson, though: you can count on that.'

'You can be my guest. They've appointed Wendy Candelaria to represent him.'

John Husband reached into the breast pocket of his coat and took out his gum wrapper. He carefully spat his gum into it, and folded it up. 'One less black blob on the sidewalk,' he said.

Luke didn't know what to say. He felt hot and prickly and irritable, and he dragged out his handkerchief to mop his face. John had a way of making him feel very much bigger and messier than he normally felt, and 82° F didn't help.

'Take a look inside,' said John, beckoning him in through the front door. Two police photographers and a fingerprint-duster stood back respectfully. Luke said, 'How're you doing?' to the fingerprint-duster and the man gave him a weak smile and an even weaker shrug.

'Pretty disgusting, hunh?'

'Prints aren't looking too hopeful, neither. Whoever did this was wearing gloves. Either that, or they didn't have no fingerprints.'

Luke stepped into the hallway. The lower flight of stairs was draped entirely in blue waterproof sheeting, as if it were still under construction and the builders wanted to protect it from the rain. But it bulged and snaked here and there, in shapes that were hideously suggestive of what lay beneath. Luke also noticed the fine spray of blood that marked the wallpaper all the way down from the second-storey landing, speckles and squiggles and exclamation-points. One hook-shaped drop of blood had congealed on a photograph of Terence Pearson, so that it looked as if his left eye were bleeding. He was smiling blandly at nothing at all.

One of the MEs was standing twitchily in the kitchen, waiting for John to give the order for Mary's remains to be cleared up and taken away. Luke smiled at him, but he didn't smile back: all he did was take off his half-rimmed glasses and polish them busily on the end of his necktie.

Luke approached the staircase with a slow, cautious tread. The floor was strewn with pale dried-up leaves, and his feet crunched with every step.

'What the hell are all these leaves?'

'Bay leaves,' said the medical examiner, returning his glasses to his snippy little nose. '*Laurus nobilis*, of the family Lauraceae.' He bent down and picked up one of the leaves, turning it from side to side between his finger and thumb. 'It used to be the victor's laurel of ancient times. Nowadays we dry the leaves for cooking and the berries for veterinary purposes.'

Luke looked around. 'I didn't notice a bay tree in the yard before. And in any case, what are all these leaves doing in the house?'

'Good question,' said John. 'Because you're right – there is no bay tree in the yard. Besides that, our friend here tells me that the bay is evergreen, so it doesn't shed its leaves in fall, besides which it isn't even fall yet.'

'Besides which,' the medical examiner put in, letting the dry leaf zigzag back to the floor, 'this particular bay is native to southern Europe, and not to the United States; and we're too far north for red bays or swamp bays or loblolly bays, which *are*.'

John said: 'The logical conclusion has to be that these leaves were brought here deliberately or accidentally by the assailant or assailants.'

Luke refolded his handkerchief and dabbed more sweat. 'That might be the logical conclusion, but what would they logically do that for? Or even illogically? Couldn't Iris Pearson have been using them for flower-arranging, or drying them for cookery, or something like that, and they just got scattered in the struggle?'

'Unh-hunh,' said John. 'You haven't seen the back yard. There are heaps of them. Heaps and heaps. I've got four officers bagging them up now, so that we can sift through them back at headquarters. If Iris Pearson was going to use them for a flower-arrangement, it was going to take up the whole damn living-room.'

A blowfly settled on the blue waterproof sheet, rubbing its probosces together. Luke flicked at it, but it stayed where it was. That was a bad sign, in Luke's experience. It meant that the fly's attraction to what was underneath the sheet was far greater than its fear of being swatted.

'Well,' he said at last. 'You'd better show me the worst.'

The medical examiner stepped forward and fastidiously drew back the sheet. It made a slithery, rustling sound, and four or five bloated-looking flies came fizzling out. It took Luke a moment or two to understand what he was looking at, because Mary's head was hanging back at an awkward angle over the tread of the second-to-bottom stair, staring open-eyed at his shins, while her thorax and abdomen had been so comprehensively cut open that her body no longer had any coherent human shape.

'The bloodstains in the spare bedroom indicate that the victim was cut open during a forcible struggle on the bed. The wounds were inflicted with a long sword-like instrument, very sharp. There are severe cuts on the victim's left hand and forearm, as well as bruising around her right wrist consistent with being relentlessly gripped. This is pretty conclusive evidence that the assailant was right-handed.'

Luke craned his head sideways like a man browsing in a library, trying to make more sense of her abdomen. He saw ribs chopped short like ribs ready for a barbecue. He saw backbone. But all he could see was bone and muscle. No internal organs, nothing soft. None of those glistening bladdery things that he always hated so much, when human beings lost their external integrity. He lifted the sheet a little further so that he could look up the bloodstained stairs. Nothing up there: no tissue, no flesh, no strings of repulsive things.

'What's the matter?' asked the medical examiner.

'She doesn't have any . . . viscera.'

'No insides, no. No stomach, liver, kidneys, pancreas, lungs or intestines, apart from a shredded section of lower bowel approximately eighteen inches in length. No heart, either. To all intents and purposes, sheriff, this woman is empty.'

Luke took a long last look, pressing his handkerchief hard to the back of his neck. Then he said, 'Okay, that's all I need to see.' The ME let the sheet slither back. He gave Luke an odd, almost prissy look, as if he was the proprietor of a terrible freak show – as if he understood only too well the petty courtesies with which people disguised their shameful urge to stare at mutilation and death.

'Come check out the yard,' said John, taking hold of Luke's elbow. What he really meant was: let's get some fresh air. He, too, had been trying to get some fresh air when Luke had first arrived here; breathing extra-deeply and chewing spearmint-flavoured gum to take the stench of rapidly-decomposing body out of his sinuses.

In the yard, a red-faced shirtsleeved police officer was shovelling the last of the bay leaves into a sack. Seven other bags were neatly stacked along the picket fence. Luke walked to the end of the yard, lifting up the clothes line so that he could duck his head underneath it, and then stood for a while, breathing, sweating, resting his hand on the roof of the kennel, and looking at John with the look of a man who really needs an answer.

'I don't have any more theories, any more than you do,' said John. 'Cigarette?'

'Quit.' He was silent for a while, and then he said, 'You talked to Iris Pearson? What'd she say?'

'She said that a man dressed in white came down the stairs carrying her sister, and that her sister had been all cut open. It wasn't easy to get any of the details out of her, but it sounded like her sister was all hanging out. You know what I mean? Her –'

'Viscera,' said Luke.

'That's it, viscera.'

'Hmm,' said Luke, and looked around. 'Where's little Emily right now?'

'Across the street, a neighbour's taking care of her.'

'Did you talk to her, too?'

John pulled a face. 'She didn't see nothing. She was sleeping when it happened. Just as well.'

'That's what she told you? She was sleeping? When did she wake up?'

'Her mother woke her up, that's what she said. Her mother woke her up and told her that something bad had happened and that she should stay where she was, in her bedroom. So that's what she did, she stayed there, until the first patrol car arrived.'

Luke inspected the bags of leaves, prodding some of them, kicking others, opening two of them up and rummaging inside. The red-faced police officer looked at his boss in desperate, mute appeal; but John tersely shook his head. You could call Sheriff Luke Friend a sloppy administrator and a bully ('Gentle Giant'? My ass!). But you could never call him anything less than professional, or hard-headed, or capable of doing the kind of job that too many American sheriffs had long since forgotten how to do.

'What time was that?' asked Luke.

'Four-oh-seven.'

'Emily was in her bedroom and Mary was dead on the staircase and Iris was where?'

'Iris was in the living-room, lying on the floor.'

'What state was she in?'

'Naked, bruised and lacerated, like somebody had been whipping her with barbed wire.'

'Mary was lying dead and gutted all down the lower part of the staircase, but Iris managed to climb up that same staircase, naked and whipped to ribbons, just to tell Emily to stay in her bedroom? Then she went back down the same staircase so that she could lie on the living-room floor, and wait for the patrol car to show up?'

John reached into his pocket and took out another piece of spearmint chewing-gum. 'That's the logical conclusion you'd arrive at, if you talked to Emily.'

'Maybe Emily got it wrong.'

'She's an eleven-year-old kid, Luke! She's just been traumatized by one killing, now she's witnessed another, even worse!'

'That still doesn't explain why her mother behaved that way. You have a brother, don't you?'

John blinked. 'You know I do, my brother Tom.'

'If Tom were lying filleted on the stairs of your house, would you tromp up through his blood and his guts, just to tell your kid to stay in bed, and then tromp down again? Come on, John, you wouldn't be able to do it, even if you hadn't been beaten and bruised. The girl's not telling it the way it was: she couldn't be.'

'Why should she lie? She's eleven years old, she's lost her brother and her sister and her aunt. Her father's in the slammer and her mother's practically a basket-case. Why should she lie?'

'I don't know,' said Luke, thrusting his hands into the tight pockets of his trousers, and looking around at the swept-up yard. 'But let's start thinking about this case, John. Why did Terence Pearson execute his children? Why did Leos Ponican push his guts down the sink-disposal, after translating Terence Pearson's diary? Who came to this house last night and disembowelled Terence Pearson's sister, and beat up Terence Pearson's wife, and how come Terence Pearson's daughter has invented some totally unbelievable account about it?'

John looked as if he were about to answer for a moment. His mouth was pursed, his eyes were bulging. But then all he could do was shrug, and say, 'Pfff,' and then, 'Jesus, Luke, I don't know. We're going to have to wait on forensics.'

'And all these leaves!' Luke shouted, kicking at one of the sacks. 'All these fucking leaves! Where did all these leaves come from?'

He stopped; and was silent; and pressed his hand against his mouth. Then, without saying anything more, he went back into the house, leaving John standing bewildered in the yard. John looked at the officer who had been sweeping up the leaves, and made a *moue*, and the officer shrugged back at him, and said, 'Beats me.'

Luke crossed the street, mopping his neck and his face yet again and cursing the heat. He made his way up the sloping concrete driveway of No. 1224, a neat small house with a red permanent-shingle roof and white aluminum sidings, and a shiny silver Toyota parked outside.

The lady of the house must have seen him coming, because she opened the door just before he managed to press the doorbell, and startled him. She was a plump, pale woman in her late fifties, with an odd mannishness about her face which was emphasized by her complete lack of make-up and her short, pot-scourer hair.

She wore a ribbed purple sweater and beige stretch ski-pants, with loops under the feet.

'Mrs Terpstra?'

'That's me. You'll be wanting to talk to Emily.'

'How is she?'

'Cool as a cucumber.'

'No tears? No shock?'

'You heard me: cool as a cucumber.'

'That's kind of surprising, all things considered,' said Luke, taking off his hat and wiping the sweatband.

Mrs Terpstra twitched her head in the direction of the Pearson house. 'Nothing surprises me about that family.'

'Oh, yes? What makes you say that?'

'That Terence Pearson, there was always something crazy about him. We always knew that something bad was going to happen, the way he used to rail at everybody. Iris was a lovely girl, God bless her, but what could she do, married to a creature like that? She used to come over for coffee, now and again, when Terence was at work, but she was always nervous, because he used to call her unexpected, just to make sure she was home.'

'Jealous type of guy, then?'

Mrs Terpstra pursed her lips. 'I don't know about jealous. He was always asking her if anybody had paid her a visit.'

'Anybody in particular or just anybody?'

'Somebody in particular, that's the way it sounded. Once he asked Leland – that's my husband – "Did you see anybody in the neighbourhood today?" Leland was out front, cutting the grass, and of course he'd seen all kinds of folks, the mailman, neighbours, everybody, and he said "Anybody special?" And Terence Pearson said, "A man in white, a man in colours and a man in green." '

Luke frowned. 'Did he say who these people might be?'

Mrs Terpstra shook her head, so that her double chin wobbled. 'He was touched in the head, if you ask me.'

'Last night – when Mrs Pearson's sister was killed – did you see anything or hear anything? Anything at all?'

She continued to shake her head. 'Chief Husband asked me that. I was awake, round about the time it happened, because it was so warm, and because I heard the wind getting up, and the neighbours' screen door banging. But that was all.'

At that moment, a thin balding man with a mottled face appeared in the doorway, right behind Mrs Terpstra, and laid his hand on her shoulder. 'I saw something,' he said.

'You're Mr Terpstra?' asked Luke.

'If he isn't, I'd like to know what he was doing in my bed last night,' Mrs Terpstra put in.

'What did you see, Mr Terpstra?' Luke asked him. He wasn't in the mood for wisecracks.

Mr Terpstra said, 'I went to the bathroom round about four ... I've been taking medication on account of my skin allergy and it makes me need to go.'

'Three or four times every night,' Mrs Terpstra confirmed.

Mr Terpstra closed his eyes for a moment, as if this were the way he always dealt with his wife's interruptions. Then he said, 'On the way back, I looked out the window and across the street, because I could see leaves blowing all across the yards and the sidewalks.'

'Yeah, leaves,' Luke repeated, without much patience. 'I saw those, too.'

'But not just leaves. I seen a light flashing in one of the upstairs windows in the Pearson house. Only an instant. Blink and you could of missed her.'

'What kind of a light? Like somebody switching the light on and off, real quick?'

'Oh no, no. It was like a reflection, like something shiny. A mirror, maybe, or metal.' He described a pattern in the air with his finger. 'Criss-cross, like this, or more like a Star of David.'

Luke took out his notepad and a rollerball pen. 'You want to try sketching that for me? That'd be helpful.'

'Come on inside,' said Mrs Terpstra. 'Leland can do your drawing for you, and you can talk to Emily.'

The house was small inside and excruciatingly neat. There were china figurines everywhere: dogs and ballet dancers and balloon sellers and soulful orphans. There was also a small shrine in one corner, with the pennant of Cornell College and the crest of the US Marines, and a colour photograph of a young man with a crewcut and heavy glasses. Underneath, a gold scroll said 'David Kirkwood Terpstra 1966–1989 – *Semper Fidelis*'.

Emily was sitting in the family-room watching *Teenage Mutant Ninja Turtles.* Her hair was neatly brushed, and she was wearing a clean T-shirt and shorts. A sprig of feathery-looking evergreen leaves was safety-pinned to her sleeve. She didn't turn around when Luke came into the house.

'Let me see now, let me get this right . . .' said Leland Terpstra, taking his glasses out of his shirt pocket and sitting down at the dining-table.

Luke approached Emily and crouched down beside her. Still she didn't turn around.

'Emily?' said Luke, at last.

'I'm okay, I'm fine,' said Emily, her eyes fixed on the TV screen.

'You want to talk about what happened?'

'There's nothing to say. I didn't see anything. I didn't hear anything.'

'You said your mom came up to your room, to tell you to stay in bed, and not to move.'

'That's right, and so I didn't move. I stayed in bed like she told me.'

'Did you see or hear anybody else in the house, apart from your mom and your Aunt Mary?'

'I was asleep. The first thing I knew was, momma opening my bedroom door and saying don't move.'

Luke nodded, and watched Michaelangelo and Donatello leaping over a warehouse roof. Then he said, 'When your mom came into your room, what was she wearing?'

At last Emily turned her head and stared at him. There was something about her expression that he found unsettling – almost as if she could read exactly what he was thinking. 'You don't believe me, do you?' she asked.

'Hey . . . I just want to understand exactly what happened, that's all.'

'I don't *know* what happened. My momma told me to stay in bed and so that's what I did.'

Luke said, 'When your momma came into your room, was she upset or crying or anything? Was her nightgown torn?'

'I didn't really see her, you know. I just heard her.'

There was a curiously aloof quality about the way she said 'you know', almost as if she were scolding him. She stared at him for one drawn-out moment longer, and then turned back to the television.

'What's that pinned on your sleeve?' asked Luke, touching the sprig of leaves on her T-shirt.

'Yew,' she said.

'I didn't know that any yew trees grew hereabouts.'

'It's the tree of death,' said Emily.

'Oh, yes? Who told you that?'

'Everybody knows that the yew is the tree of death. They plant them in graveyards, and the roots spread out and every root goes into the mouth of somebody buried.'

Luke folded and refolded his damp handkerchief. 'That's kind of a grim idea.'

Emily glanced at him, 'Life is grim.'

'You're eleven, and you think that life is grim?'

'My sister's dead and my brother's dead.'

'Your aunt, too.'

'My aunt wasn't the same at all.' Reflections of Mutant Turtles danced and flickered in her eyes. She gave off such an atmosphere of mockery and indifference that Luke, in spite of himself, shivered. He couldn't understand her. He had thought that by squatting next to her and chatting to her – well, he could establish some rapport, the way he always did with kids. Kids liked cheerful fat men, especially cheerful fat men in uniform. But Emily was giving him nothing. Sitting down next to Emily was like sitting down next to an open freezer.

He had the feeling that she actually despised him.

'Sweetheart,' he said, 'we have to catch the people who killed your aunt. They hurt your momma bad, too.'

'I didn't see anybody. I promise.'

'Why don't you think about it? You could give me a call, if you want to. Here's my private number at work.'

'I didn't see anybody. Besides, everybody needs to feed.'

Luke stared at her. 'What? What did you say?'

'I didn't say anything.'

Luke waited for a long, long time, but he knew that he wasn't going to get any more out of her. He eased himself up, and turned to face Mr and Mrs Terpstra. Mrs Terpstra gave him a look that meant 'I told you so – she's cool as a cucumber'.

Mr Terpstra came up with his drawing. 'Here, this is it. This is exactly the shape I saw. Like a light, if you understand what I mean. Like a reflection.'

Luke took it and held it up. It was more like a pentagram than a criss-cross diagram.

'Okay, Mr Terpstra, thanks. I don't know what this is, but it could be useful evidence.'

With a sudden inspiration, he turned his notebook around and held the diagram in front of Emily. 'Look at this, Emily. This is what Mr Terpstra saw, shining out of your house last night. Did you ever see anything like this before?'

Emily stiffened. '*Take it away,*' she said, in a childish growl.

'Come on, Emily. Maybe this will jog your memory.'

Emily's head turned towards him with a harsh, crunching sound, as if her neck were broken and bones were grating against bones. Her pupils were dilated, and her whole face had been dragged back over her skull. Luke couldn't help himself: he jumped back nervously, a single clumsy jump, and dropped his notebook, and said, 'Chrissakes, Emily, what's wrong?'

She said nothing, but beckoned him closer. At first he didn't want to go, but then she beckoned him again.

He looked at Mrs Terpstra, but all Mrs Terpstra could say was, 'She's only a child, sheriff. She's only eleven years old.'

Luke leaned closer; but Emily beckoned him closer still. She gave off the strangest odour. She smelled like fresh-cut grass, but the freshness was underlaid with the sweetness of decomposing grass, too.

'What?' he asked her, nervously.

'Closer,' she whispered. 'Come closer and I'll tell you.'

He looked into those dead, tightly focused, calculating eyes. He looked at that luminous skin, dragged tight back across those sharply-defined cheekbones. He felt like Ulysses in the presence of the Sirens. He felt as if Death were seductively licking the tip of its wet, mauvish tongue around his ear.

'What?' he repeated.

'My friends are walking the land again,' she whispered.

He leaned back, bewildered. But she seized his necktie and twisted it around her fingers. 'My friends are walking the land again, and so much the better for the land. The Witness is walking the land, the Surgeon is walking the land, the Green Man is walking the land. They, and others, the festival's coming. The festival's here already!'

'Emily,' he said, trying to talk to her as if she were an eleven-year-old girl. 'Emily, this has all been terrible . . . but you have to keep yourself together. Mrs Terpstra is going to take care of you for an hour or two, and then somebody from City Hall is going to come around and find you somewhere safe to stay.'

'You don't understand, do you?' she whispered.

'What?' he said. He could hardly hear her.

'My friends are walking the land again.'

Luke stared into her eyes from less than four inches away. What did she want? What was she trying to say to him? Her breath smelled appalling: in fact it stank. Maybe she hadn't eaten. Maybe the shock had upset her digestive system. But how could she smell so strongly of rotten vegetation and stale saliva and that sweet, cloying stench that he could only associate with piss?

He swallowed. 'Tell me who your friends are.'

'I've told you. The Witness, the Surgeon, the Green Man.'

'And others, you said.'

'Yes, others.'

Leland Terpstra interrupted, 'You want to take a look at this schematic now, sheriff? It's as close as I can get it.'

Luke lifted his right hand to indicate that he had heard, but he didn't take his eyes away from Emily, nor she from him.

'Who are they?' Luke insisted; even though he knew that it was totally wrong to press a juvenile witness so hard, and that whatever she said would be inadmissible. 'Come on, Emily, your friends, who are they?'

Emily's mouth widened in the slowest smile. Her face expressed glee, but her eyes were as dead as stones. Luke felt the sweat rolling off the back of his neck and into the collar of his shirt. *What?* he kept thinking. *What the hell is she trying to say to me? This is totally unbalanced: totally crazy.*

Emily opened her mouth wider and wider, as if she were about to take a bite out of an apple. Luke thought: *she's yawning – what the hell is she doing, she's yawning.*

But then her tongue seemed to swell, fat and crimson, and slide out from between her lips. In total shock, total disgust, he realized that it wasn't a tongue at all, but a man's penis, glistening with saliva, shiny and distended, with its foreskin rolled right back. A thin web of mucus trailed from the penis's opening, and dripped down Emily's chin.

There was a split second when their eyes made intense contact and he knew what she was saying to him. She was saying: this is what my friends are, this is what my friends can do, and this is more than you can begin to comprehend, fat man. The penis reared totally rigid, almost an inch proud of her wide-open lips. Then it slid back inside, the rim catching slightly on her upper teeth; and she swallowed hard, and it was gone.

Luke turned to the Terpstras in horror, but Mrs Terpstra was fussily rearranging her figurines and Leland Terpstra was still smiling at him helpfully and holding out his diagram. Obviously, neither of them had seen the obscene thing that had slithered out of Emily's mouth.

Luke knelt down beside Emily and seized her arms. 'Open your mouth,' he insisted.

'What for?' she said, feigning innocence.

'Open your mouth, Emily!'

'No!' she struggled. 'Get away from me!'

'Open your goddamned mouth!' Luke barked at her. He

tried to take hold of her jaw and force it open, but Emily clamped her lips tight shut and twisted her head from side to side.

'Here now, what are you trying to do to her, sheriff?' asked Leland Terpstra.

'I think she's swallowed something,' said Luke. 'I just want to take a look.'

'No!' protested Emily, hitting out at him. 'No! Leave me alone!'

Luke let go of her, and stood up. Emily stared up at him, her eyes black with triumph and hatred.

Mrs Terpstra came up and laid her hand gently on Emily's head. 'Come on now, sugar: what was it you swallowed?'

'Nothing,' said Emily. 'I didn't swallow anything.'

'Well, then, you won't mind opening up your mouth and letting Sheriff Friend here take a look, will you?'

Emily hesitated for a moment, then smiled and stuck out her tongue.

'There, you must of made a mistake,' grinned Leland Terpstra. 'Maybe she was just funning.'

Luke swallowed. He was breathless and trembling, and all the sweat down the back of his shirt had suddenly chilled.

'Sure,' he said. 'Maybe she was just funning.'

Leland Terpstra said, 'Are you feeling all right, sheriff? You're looking kind of pale.'

'Pale,' Luke repeated. He looked down at Emily, he looked at the Terpstras, he looked at his watch. He looked down at Emily again, sitting so sweet and composed, cool as a cucumber, watching the Turtles.

'Sheriff?' Leland Terpstra repeated.

'I'm fine,' Luke assured him. 'I'm fine.'

And it was then that Emily gave a creaky, sly little giggle; more like an old woman than an eleven-year-old girl.

Six

Captain Black came out of surgery shortly after 3 p.m., following nine hours of gruelling teamwork by three different surgeons and eighteen neurologists, biochemists, veterinary anaesthetists and assistants.

Draped with a large green surgical sheet, he was wheeled huge and slumbering on a flatbed trolley to the laboratory in the north-east wing of the Spellman Institute. Here, under minute-by-minute supervision, he would recover from the anaesthetic and recuperate from his surgery. The chart on the end of his trolley was stencilled with the name *Black, Capt.* It was a joke, but the staff at Spellman regarded their single most important patient with deep respect. This animal, this mortal, had gained a human personality, and everybody knew it.

Still wearing their green surgical gowns and green surgical boots, Garth and Raoul retreated to Garth's office, gave each other a weary high five, and then opened up a bottle of Chandon Brut. 'Here's to Captain Black,' said Garth. 'If this works, he's going to be the first side of bacon to *know* that he's a side of bacon.'

Raoul tossed a heap of papers onto the floor and collapsed into an armchair. 'Eat your heart out, Porky Pig.'

Garth lit a cigarette, and blew smoke out of his nostrils. 'You were brilliant, Raoul. Absolutely fucking brilliant.'

Raoul waved his hand dismissively. 'I'm just naturally good at micro-surgery, that's all. It's my genetically-inherited sense of rhythm.'

'Bullshit. You were brilliant.'

Raoul shook his head, and smiled, and said, 'Wow, that was

some operation, wasn't it?' He swallowed more champagne. 'I just wonder how he's going to feel.'

'What do you mean?'

'When he wakes up, and knows he's a pig, what's he going to feel?'

Garth made a face. 'I can't imagine. It depends how well the implantation went. In any case, we won't know until he develops some way of telling us.'

'Do you really think he'll be able to?'

'Sure he will,' said Garth. 'I don't have any doubts about it at all. If everything works out the way we planned it, I think he'll have the potential for quite sophisticated communication.'

'The potential, maybe,' Raoul agreed. 'But will he have the capability? I'm not too happy with the animal communication systems we've managed to develop so far. So Remo the chimpanzee can type "banana please". So a dog can bring us a picture of a tree. One's hungry, the other wants to go for a walk. That's not what I call sophisticated communication.'

'I know college graduates who communicate less clearly than that,' said Garth. 'But this is something I want to discuss with the whole team. I know we've developed the Xeno-symbol system and the word-recognition system, but I think it's time we re-addressed the whole issue. Captain Black won't be able to talk. He doesn't have the larynx to articulate anything resembling human speech. But I still think that we should be exploring the possibility of *some* kind of language.'

'I don't think the director is particularly keen on that avenue of research,' said Raoul. 'He told me a couple of days ago that he didn't relish the idea of the staff speaking in grunts and squeals.'

'So why did he employ Meg in reception?' asked Garth.

'Hey, be fair, she's a good girl, Meg. Besides, we got talking pigs already.'

'Oh, yes?'

Raoul set down his glass and tossed across that day's copy of the Cedar Rapids *Gazette.* 'Oh yes, we got talking pigs all right. They're called senators.'

Garth opened the paper. On the front page, there was a large photograph of Senators Doreen Zapf and Bryan Cady with their fists triumphantly raised above their heads. The headline read 'ZAPF, CADY CONFIDENT OF VEGETARIAN VOTE'.

Garth read the first few paragraphs and then dropped the paper onto the floor. 'You don't seriously think they're going to approve Zapf-Cady, do you?'

'I don't know,' said Raoul. 'It seems to me that it's one of those ideas that's caught the country's mood, do you know what I mean? Everybody's struggling to be holier than thou.'

'Nobody has to struggle to be holier than me,' said Garth. He looked down at the fallen newspaper. 'Did they mention me?'

'They called you "vivisectionist Dr Garth Matthews, 49".'

'The bastards.'

'I know. You're not a vivisectionist, you're a research pathologist.'

'It's worse than that, I'm 46, not 49.'

'Come on, Garth,' said Raoul, seriously. 'It's going to stop us dead in the water if Zapf-Cady does get through. Quite apart from any other consequence, you and me are going to be out of a job.'

Garth thought about it for a moment, smoking, drinking, and then said, 'Nah. It won't be passed, take my word for it. It's just a political food-fad. Like macrobiotics; or nouvelle cuisine. Do they really think that they're going to be able to stop Americans from eating meat? The South will rise again!'

'I don't know,' said Raoul. 'I have a bad feeling about it.'

'How can you? Who's going to give up hamburgers, and steaks, and fried chicken, and bacon, and babyback ribs?'

'I have a bad feeling, that's all.'

'Raoul – even if they do pass it, which they won't, it involves a three-year phasing-out period. There has to be, doesn't there – or else how are farmers going to dispose of their existing stocks? How is the federal government going to pay them compensation? Jesus, you should have heard what that guy from the Department of Agriculture was telling me yesterday, at the TV studio. There are more than a hundred million cattle in the continental US alone; not to mention fifty-five million pigs and ten million sheep. That's more than the population of Japan. It's a nation within a nation.'

Raoul said, 'That's why people are starting to question the morality of eating them, isn't it? They may be cows, they may be pigs, they may be sheep. But people are starting to look them in the eye and say, "Hold up here, this is another *being* I'm about to put in my mouth!" '

'Jesus,' said Garth. 'You're beginning to sound like Lily Monarch and all the rest of those crackpots! Don't you like fried chicken?'

Raoul thought about it, and then he said, 'No, I don't, as a matter of fact. The only tasty part is the skin, and I hate the skin.'

Garth crushed out his cigarette. 'I give up,' he said.

'You may have to,' said Raoul. 'The phasing-out period is for farm animals only. Animal research is going to be stopped as soon as Zapf-Cady is signed. Likewise the fur trade.'

'Let me make you a promise,' said Garth. He reached across and clinked his glass against Raoul's. 'Zapf-Cady will die a death. Ham-hocks for ever!'

'Better not let Captain Black hear you say that. He may take it personally.'

They were both tense: they were both tired. The conversation turned back to the operation they had just performed. It had taken them over nine years to prepare for it, and nine hours to complete. Garth didn't know whether he felt elated or depressed or simply numb. He felt as if his whole career had reached its point of maximum focus. For those nine hours, all of the disparate skills and inspirations that he been given through all of his life by his parents and his professors and his colleagues had been concentrated into one unwavering beam of total energy, like concentrating the sun's rays through a magnifying glass. *This is my destiny, being acted out, right in front of my eyes. This is what I was born for.*

He had taken precisely-selected genes from the vertical brain section that Nathan had brought him from Mercy Medical Center. The section had been microscopically thin, thinner than tissue paper, but it had contained genetic material from all sections of the brain, from the parietal lobe to the lateral sulcus.

It had contained all of its donor's personality: his intellect, his imagination, his sexuality and his emotions. Raoul had implanted it in all the critical areas of Captain Black's brain, using a technique that bypassed his original brain functions, rather like electrical wiring bypassing a faulty junction-box. Anatomically, Captain Black was still a hog, but psychologically he was now a human boy. At least, that was what Garth's nine years of research had led him to expect. He would only know for sure when Captain Black woke up.

He would *think* human: and that was the reason why Garth had insisted so vehemently that the brain donor should be young, and healthy and free of prejudice. When Captain Black awoke from his anaesthetic, the last thing that Garth wanted on his hands was a creature with the brain of a psychopath and a body the size of a small family car.

Raoul said, 'If the do-gooders leave us alone, Garth, this is just the beginning. Think of what we can do. We can change people's behaviour. We can cure Down's syndrome. We can cure schizophrenia.'

Garth lifted his glass. 'We can operate on politicians, and make them kind and sensible.'

'We can operate on gays, and make them straight. We can operate on straights, and make them gay.'

'Brain transplants?' Garth suggested, over the rim of his glass.

Raoul puffed out his cheeks. 'Why not, my man? Fifty years ago, if you had suggested kidney transplants, they would have thought you were crazy. What's so crazy about brain transplants?'

Garth finished his wine. Suddenly, he began to look grey. 'I don't know. Maybe I'm tired.'

'Take a shower, then. Get some sleep. I'll look in on Captain Black.'

'Oh . . . don't worry. I'll come with you. I feel like I'm almost his daddy now.'

They were still laughing and drinking when Jenny Hennings, Raoul's senior assistant, came quickly into the office without knocking.

'Jenny?' asked Raoul. 'What's wrong?'

'It's the captain,' she said. She was small and dark and pretty and flustered. 'He's coming around.'

'Already?' said Garth. 'I expected him to sleep for at least five hours.'

'It's not only that. He's screaming.'

'He's what?'

'He's screaming, Garth. He's screaming like he's totally gone crazy.'

They ran along the corridor, and at every turn they were joined by other members of staff. The alarm siren was dolefully whooping, *bllaarrrp, bllaarrp, bllaarrp.* One of the veterinary anaesthetists stumbled bleary-eyed into Garth's shoulder, and said, 'What? What's happening? I just woke up.'

'He's awake!' said Jenny. 'Captain Black's awake!'

'He's awake? You're out of your mind! I gave him enough methoxyflurane to put him out for a week!'

'He's awake!' Jenny repeated; and that was all she needed to say. The anaesthetist ran after them; and they collided together through the swing doors that led to the north-east wing.

They could hear the hog screaming all the way down the corridor. It was the most terrible sound that Garth had ever heard: an agonized, long-drawn-out screeching, mingled with roars of rage and confusion; and a thick, sticky gargling, like a throatful of thickly-liquefied phlegm.

Garth reached the laboratory door just as one of his juniors came out, white-faced and bleeding.

'Peter, what the hell's going on? Have you been hurt?'

'He caught my hand, that's all. We were trying to restrain him.'

'How long has he been awake?'

'Two or three minutes, but that's enough. He's not listening to anything or anybody. If you ask me, he's totally out of his skull.'

As if to emphasize the point, Captain Black let out a scream that had them paralysed, right where they were.

'He's not in pain, is he?' asked Garth.

'No reason why he should be. The operation went like a dream.'

Garth eased a nurse out of his way and reached the open door of the recovery room. Inside, there were overturned trolleys, scalpels and tongs and cotton scattered everywhere. Torn blue curtains hung from half-collapsed rails. Three Honeywell monitors were smashed, and the floor was a bright, crunchy carpet of broken glass. The alarm kept on repeating *bllaarrrp, bllaarrp*, and a red light kept flashing on and off. Two security guards were edging their way back towards the door. One of them had his handgun raised, although he holstered it immediately Garth and Raoul appeared.

'Dr Matthews! Thank God you didn't leave yet.'

'It's okay, Steve. You don't have to be frightened. The captain makes a lot of noise, and he looks scary. But he never hurt anybody; and he's not going to start hurting people now. We've given him the mind of a three-year-old kid, that's all. He's scared and he's hurt and he's probably hollering for his momma.'

Captain Black must have rolled off the trolley on which he had been resting after his operation. The green sheet had slithered onto the floor, and was twisted around one of his front trotters. He was standing on the far side of the room, huge, black, pungent with the smell of animals and anaesthetic and dried blood. His head was wrapped in bandages, which obviously annoyed him, because he kept trying to shake them loose, or to run them up against the cupboards.

His eyes were filled with blood and rage and a total lack of comprehension. Whatever they had managed to do, inside of his mind, he looked stunned and very angry about it.

'Captain Black!' Garth called out. 'Come on, now, Captain Black . . . everything's going to be fine.'

Captain Black threw back his head and bared his yellowed teeth and let out another hair-raising scream. Even Garth backed away. Raoul said, 'Come on, Garth, there's no use in trying to humour him. He needs a sedative, and fast. He looks like he's suffering bad.'

Garth quickly smoothed back his hair. 'Yeah . . . maybe you're right.' He turned to the anaesthetist. 'What can we give him that won't cause too many side-effects?'

I'll fix you something,' said the anaesthetist. 'We're going to have to inject it by dart, though. There's no way that I can give him a shot manually. Even so, it's going to have to be point-blank, pretty much.'

'Okay . . . make it pronto, hunh?'

Captain Black quietened down. He stood staring at Garth, his huge flanks heaving as he breathed, saliva dripping from his hairy lower lip. Garth could sense that he had changed; and that it wasn't just the pain he was suffering that had changed him. He had never stared with such concentration before. He had never watched Garth with such intensity. He was obviously still stupefied with anaesthetic, but all the same he breathed and watched, and Garth believed that he was *thinking.*

Raoul said, very softly, 'I think we've done it.'

'Kind of early to tell,' Garth replied.

'Look at his expression, though. I'm sure we've done it.'

'Nobel prizes all around?'

'Could be, my man. Certainly could be.'

Jenny said, 'It's frightening. I keep trying to imagine what's going on in his head.'

'One monster headache, I imagine,' said Garth.

'It must be like – I don't know, being *born,* almost. Or waking up after an accident.'

Captain Black began to scrape fretfully at the floor with his front trotters. He looked grotesque in his head bandages, almost ludicrous, as if a small girl had been trying to dress him up as an Indian in a turban. But Garth knew that there was nothing ludicrous about his strength, or his stubbornness, or his ability to create more mayhem than the Spellman Institute's security staff could possibly handle.

The methoxyflurane which had been used to put him under before his operation was still making him woozy and unbalanced. He staggered to one side, and his back legs dropped, so that he was sitting. But even when he was sitting, he was an impressive and alarming sight, a fetid black mountain of thickly-haired flesh, capable of crushing a man to death, or of biting through a three-inch steel pipe. Everybody remained crowded in the doorway, giving Captain Black the whole laboratory to himself, and there was no doubt that if he had taken two or three steps towards the doorway the corridor outside would have rapidly emptied, too.

'Shit! He must have been under-anaesthetized,' said Raoul. 'I told you we should have gone for halothane.'

'Unh-hunh. Couldn't risk damaging his liver,' said Garth.

'We're going to lose more than his liver if we can't control him now.'

Captain Black rolled his head around, as if he were in pain. Then suddenly, he lurched towards the door, colliding with a trolley full of test-tubes and instruments, and scattering them everywhere. Jenny Hennings took hold of Garth's arm, and clutched it tight; and Garth glanced at Raoul; and Raoul made a face which meant 'she's getting physical at last'.

The anaesthetist came back, red-faced and panting, with one of the long-barrelled dart-guns which they used to deal with escaped or berserk animals. 'Okay . . . this is loaded with enough methohexitone to stop a Mercedes-Benz. It'll knock him out just long enough for us to get him back on the trolley and make him secure.'

Captain Black was standing in the middle of the laboratory now: with the afternoon sunlight shining through the window behind him, so that he looked prehistoric and pagan, as if his hair were on fire. His eyes smouldered crimson with bafflement and pain. As the anaesthetist stepped carefully into the room, the dart-gun raised in front of him, Captain Black let out a low and rumbling growl, which suddenly raised itself into a horrendous, twisted squeal.

The anaesthetist took one careful step nearer; then another. Captain Black's skin was thicker than a pigskin suitcase, and if the anaesthetist he had any chance of penetrating it, he was going to have to shoot him from less than six inches away.

A third step; and a fourth. Captain Black slowly rotated his huge bandaged head towards the anaesthetist, and a foot-long rope of thick saliva swung from his lips. With an off-key scraping noise, like a knife scraping a dinner plate, he began to paw at the laboratory floor. Garth called out to the anaesthetist, 'Be careful, Jack . . . he's feeling real irritated, I can read his body-language. Just do it quick and get it over with.'

The anaesthetist edged closer and closer, until the gun barrel was almost touching Captain Black's deeply-heaving flank. Although he was way back by the door, and although the laboratory was sharply antiseptic, Garth could smell the rich, fetid odour of Captain Black's masculinity. This was a hog, baited and challenged by men. This was the largest hog in America. But this was something else, too, something more than a hog. This was a hog that could understand its limitations, and also its strengths.

There was a moment's silence. Captain Black stopped scraping his trotters and stayed unnervingly silent, unnervingly still. The anaesthetist pressed the gun muzzle against his right upper shoulder, against the meaty section that a butcher would have described as a Boston butt.

Raoul said urgently, 'Come on, Jack, don't piss around, drop him!'

The anaesthetist pressed the muzzle even deeper into Captain Black's shoulder. But as he did so, Captain Black twisted around, like a boiling black river of hair turning around, and caught the anaesthetist's left forearm between his jaws. There was a crunching sound like wine glasses being broken inside a sack. The man threw back his head and stretched open his mouth and screamed. He tried to pull his arm out of Captain Black's mouth but the hog had clamped his jaws together with enough pounds-per-square-inch to jack up a truck.

Raoul shouted, 'Hold on, Jack! Hold on!' and dodged into the laboratory. He picked up a fallen shelf of broken test-tubes, and whacked Captain Black on the shoulder with it, once, twice, three times.

Garth said, 'Not his head, Raoul! Not his head!'

'He's killing him, for Christ's sake!' Raoul shouted back.

Raoul pushed his shoulder against Captain Black's shoulder, and thrust his fingers in between the hog's teeth, deep in slobber and pumping blood, and tried to prise Captain Black's jaws open. Captain Black irritably shook his head, and grunted deep in his throat, and Raoul was forced to let go.

Close behind Garth, one of the security men unholstered his gun again and said, 'Stand clear, here! Let me take a shot at him!'

'No!' said Garth. 'You won't drop him, you'll just make things worse!'

'But if I hit him in the head –'

'*No! And that's an order!*'

Raoul picked up the shelf again, and forced the end of it into the side of Captain Black's mouth. Splinters of laminate cut into Captain Black's lips and gums, and he roared with fury, but he still wouldn't release his grip on the arm. The anaesthetist stopped screaming, and collapsed. His face had drained from lightly-browned pink to the colour of sun-faded paper. He wasn't even standing on his own feet: all that was keeping him upright was Captain Black's relentless grip on his badly-mangled arm. Blood spattered in fanlike patterns from one side of the laboratory to the other, and Garth raised his hand to stop it from flying in his eyes.

'Call 911!' he ordered the security guard.

'What?' asked the security guard, aghast.

'Call 911 *now*!'

Jenny Hennings said, in anguish, 'Raoul! Raoul! For God's sake, be careful!'

The anaesthetist's feet were dragging on the floor from one side to the other, in a bloody-streaked semi-circle. His shoes made a tumbling sound, like dice. His unfired dart-gun dropped to the floor, and skated away. Raoul hit Captain Black again and again with the shelf, and then threw it to one side, and kicked Captain Black on the shoulder.

Garth should have remembered. When he was a boy, and a pig was running towards him, his father had told him to kick it in the shoulder. That was the way to stop a pig. You might end up with a broken leg; but you would have stopped the pig in mid-charge.

Captain Black stopped, too, and aggressively shook his bandaged head, and dripped blood. Slowly, he opened his jaws, and the crushed arm of the anaesthetist dropped out, his fingers trailing down Captain Black's long wet purple tongue in a grotesque caress. The anaesthetist dropped flat on his back on the floor, shuddering, his brightly-polished shoe-heels drumming on the vinyl in a lightly-syncopated pattern of agony.

Raoul backed away, but now Captain Black was after him, too.

Garth shouted, 'Captain Black! Come on now, Captain Black! Cut that out!'

But while Captain Black might have heeded Garth before, when he was nothing but animal, he ignored him now. He limped and trotted and barged after Raoul, unbalanced, out of control, and Raoul had to dodge around the banks of monitoring equipment so that the hog couldn't get him.

Garth hesitated. The anaesthetist was seriously hurt. In fact, he was probably dying. He was pumping glossy arterial blood all over the floor in an ever-widening lake, and his twitching was becoming more jerky. He said, 'Mom?' in the faintest of voices, and a clear bubble of blood burst on his lips.

Garth took two or three steps into the laboratory, with the intention of dragging the man back to safety. He managed to kneel down, and twist his hands around his lapels, but then Captain Black abruptly turned and half-staggered towards him. The hog collided with Garth's shoulder, his full weight, bristly and black, and Garth was slammed back against the door-frame. He lay on his side, stunned and numb. He felt as if he had been knocked down by an automobile. Captain Black stood and watched him for a while, with a look that meant 'stay away'. Then he turned back to Raoul, which allowed Jenny Hennings and the Spellman security guard to help Garth onto his feet.

Raoul called, 'I'll distract him, okay? I'll distract him! Then you can pull Jack out!'

'Raoul – the dart-gun!' called Jenny.

Raoul skirted around the far end of the monitoring equipment. He didn't take his eyes off Captain Black, who kept edging and trotting and staggering towards him.

'Raoul – the gun! It's under the table!'

Raoul ducked his head like a basketball player. 'I don't see it!'

'Over to your left, that's it, a little more!'

Raoul ducked his head again. 'That's cool, I see it now!'

The anaesthetist groaned, and bubbled more blood, and then suddenly opened his eyes and said, 'Calvary! I can see Calvary!' Garth glanced uncomfortably at Jenny; and in the distance they heard sirens. Police, and ambulance, and he prayed to God they wouldn't be too late.

Raoul said, 'Okay, okay . . . why don't you jump into the room, man, and shout and clap your hands, then I can slide under the table for the dart-gun, and shoot him at point-blank range?'

'Fine, sure, fine,' said Garth, although he was sweating and nervously trembling.

'When I say three, you jump into the room and shout and clap your hands, okay?'

'Okay, when you say three.'

Captain Black lowered his snout and began to push against the bank of monitoring instruments that should have been charting his gradual recovery from methoxyflurane. A respiration monitor toppled over with a shattering crash; then an EKG-meter; then a toxicometer.

'Captain Black!' Garth called him. 'Captain Black! You hold up now! You stay where you are, and don't you do no more damage!'

Captain Black replied by twisting his head around and screeching like nine varieties of devil, all at once. His breath reeked of anaesthetic and blood.

'I don't believe this,' said the security guard. 'How are we ever going to get rid of a thing like this?'

'We use our heads, that's what we do,' Garth told him. 'If I can distract him long enough for Raoul to pick up the dart-gun . . . then we're home free.'

'I'll go fix another dart-gun,' Jenny suggested.

'You're a junior geneticist. What do you know about methohexitone?'

'About as much as I know about male superiority.'

'In that case, *don't* go fix another dart-gun. Raoul can handle himself.'

Raoul was edging his way along the far wall of the laboratory, one hand held behind him to guide himself, his fingertips sensing the lines of air-conditioners. He never once took his eyes away from Captain Black; and he never blinked. He had seen something in Captain Black's face that Garth hadn't yet seen, and it frightened him. Garth had seen the first rudiments of human consciousness. Raoul had glimpsed whose consciousness it was. This wasn't an innocent three-year-old boy who was after him. This was somebody who knew how to taunt, who knew how to play. This was somebody dark-minded and highly sophisticated.

Garth shouted, 'I'm going to jump into the room now, okay? On the count of three!'

He stood crouched in the doorway for as long as he could; and when he was fairly sure that Captain Black wasn't looking, he bounded into the laboratory – long, noisy steps, and clapped his hands, and shrieked out, 'Wayyyhooooo . . .! I'm right here, Captain, you come get me! Come on, Captain Black, you want human for supper, you don't have to look any further than here!'

He couldn't have felt more foolish. Captain Black didn't even turn to look at him. Captain Black clumsily turned towards Raoul, as Raoul dived beneath the table for the dart-gun. The table tipped over with an ear-splitting bang, but Raoul managed to twist himself around and seize the dart-gun's handle in his left hand. He dropped it, but picked it up again, just as Captain Black stepped on his stomach with the full weight of his right front trotter.

Raoul didn't cry out. He *couldn't* cry out. Captain Black had pinned him down with over a third of a ton of weight concentrated into an area that was smaller and sharper than a garden trowel. The trotter pierced his skin, pierced his muscles, pierced his subcutaneous fat. It punctured his stomach lining so that thick porridgey food flooded warm and acidic into his abdomen. It pinned him to the floor. The next thing he knew, Captain Black was lowering over him, with foul, furnace-hot breath, and chilly strings of thick saliva were being draped across his cheeks. He tried to cry out, but couldn't work out how it was done. There was no breath left in his body; nothing but pain and shock and utter paralysis. He didn't realize that Captain Black's trotter, apart from piercing his stomach, had severed his spinal cord.

Captain Black dipped his head down and blotted out Raoul's vision. Raoul couldn't understand what was happening at first, and there was a moment in which he felt that he was saved, that it was night-time, that the worst was over. He closed his eyes and said the prayer that his mother had taught him when he was little. '*Cher Jesu, la nuit est si profonde, aidez-moi.*'

But then Captain Black took two or three steps backward, and he looked up and saw Garth and Jenny and the Spellman security guard.

'Raoul!' shouted Garth. 'Raoul! Shoot him!'

Raoul twisted his neck and saw that he was still holding the dart-gun. At that moment, Captain Black dipped his head again and seized Raoul's thigh between his jaws. Raoul couldn't feel it, but he could hear it. A deep, gristly crunching noise, and the high-pitched tearing of skin.

Captain Black shook his head violently, and tore off more muscle. Then he sank his teeth deep between Raoul's legs, snapping one side of his pelvis, and penetrating his right buttock with a triangular tooth that was more than four inches long. At last Raoul managed to drag air into his lungs. He choked for a second, gargled, then he screamed a bubbling scream that sprayed his own face with blood, and tried to pull himself free, but he was paralysed from the mid-back downward, and Captain Black's jaw muscles were locked into his pelvis with all the power of a hydraulic jack.

The security guard stepped into the laboratory, holding up his .38. He kicked one of the fallen chairs out of the way, and then he climbed over the fallen table, and pointed his gun directly at Captain Black's bandaged head.

But Raoul screamed out, 'No! No! Don't hurt him! Don't hurt him!'

The security guard didn't understand, although he held his fire.

'Don't hurt him!' Raoul repeated, in a weaker voice, though just as panicky. 'Don't hurt him, for God's sake don't hurt him. He's my life's work.'

Captain Black growled and grunted, and furiously shook his head from side to side.

'Oh, God,' said Raoul; and then the hog lifted his head up, his jaws dripping with all the bloodied components of Raoul's ravaged groin. Raoul stared into the hog's eyes, and his eyes were black and glittering, like funeral jewellery, like polished black granite.

He lifted the dart-gun. For one wavering moment he pointed it at Captain Black. But then he took the barrel in his right hand, and aimed the muzzle directly under his own chin. Before the security guard could stop him, he had fired – a sharp, pneumatic crack – and the dart had burst through his lower jaw, right through his tongue and the roof of his mouth, and blasted directly into his brain. Even if it hadn't been loaded with a massive dose of methohexitone, it would have killed him instantly. He turned his head to one side, and dropped the dart-gun, and his eyes stared at nothing at all.

Garth shouted out to the guard, 'Get back here! Don't shoot him! Get back here! We're going to lock him in for a while, see if we can calm him down!'

The guard didn't need a second telling. He came scrambling back over the furniture as fast as he could. Captain Black didn't attempt to chase him, though: he remained where he was, slowly chewing the flesh of one of the men who had helped to make him what he was. He wasn't expressionless any more, though. Garth was sure that he could see contempt on his werewolf-like face; contempt and derision.

Maybe pigs were naturally contemptuous and derisive: and this was the first time that a pig had been able to show it.

More likely, however, Captain Black had acquired contempt and derision from his genetic donor.

But were these the feelings of a three-year-old boy? What kind of three-year-old boy harbours such sneering hatred of his fellow human beings?

Garth, shaking, closed the laboratory door, and locked it. He peered through the reinforced-glass window at the dark, motionless bulk of Captain Black. He could just see one of Raoul's feet, at an awkward angle.

Jenny was silently sobbing, her hand pressed over her mouth. The security guard held his arm around her. 'What do we do now, doctor?' he asked Garth, and there was a rising hint of insubordination in his voice. 'You should have let me waste him while I had the chance.'

Garth's reply was sharp, although his throat was clogged, and it sounded a little off-key. 'Captain Black is the result of nine years of highly-advanced genetic research and more millions of dollars than you could count in a lifetime. Not only that, he is everything that Dr Lacouture ever worked for.'

The guard didn't flinch. 'Excuse me, but Captain Black is also an ornery hog who just took the arm off of one man and killed another. I should have wasted him, then and there.'

'You did what you could. You don't have to worry about that.'

'Dr Matthews, when humans get eaten by their own breakfast, that worries me.'

They heard ambulance and police sirens arriving outside. Garth took hold of Jenny's hand and said, 'Come on . . . there's nothing more that you can do here.'

To the security guard he said, 'Watch the door. Make sure that Captain Black doesn't try to get out.'

The guard holstered his gun and folded his arms. He didn't say anything, but the expression on his face told it all.

In the bright Italian-tiled conservatory of his house in Georgetown, Washington, William Olsen was feeding his pet raven with tiny scraps of chopped-up chicken. The bird was huge and glossy, with plumage like a 19th-century funeral hat. It was chained by the leg to a T-shaped chrome-plated perch, which was placed sufficiently close to William Olsen's basket chair for him to be able to feed it with his one good hand.

Bryan Cady sat with his back half-turned. His natural fastidiousness was offended by the sight of the raven pecking and choking down fragments of stringy chicken-skin. Apart from that, he preferred not to watch William Olsen when he was trying to express delight. His leonine, once-handsome face twisted into an extraordinary snarl, and his tongue lolled out.

Bryan was dressed as usual in greys and blacks, and a snowy white shirt. William Olsen wore a maroon dressing-gown with his intertwined initials embroidered in gold on the breast pocket, and a yellow cravat, which Nina had tied for him.

'Goldberg called me this morning,' said Bryan. 'He's a definite maybe.'

'I thought he'd come around,' said William, in his throaty, swallowing voice. He always sounded like somebody trying to lick a Popsicle and talk at the same time. 'He's a professional straw-in-the-wind.'

'If the meat lobby doesn't change his mind, I think we have a better than even chance of winning,' Bryan affirmed. 'The country's in the mood for it. There's a definite feeling of dietary saintliness in the air.'

'And how long do you think they can hold out, before they start missing their Big Macs?'

'It doesn't matter if Zapf-Cady is repealed in a year. We'll still get everything out of it that we planned to get out of it.'

William Olsen tossed another piece of chicken to his raven, which snatched it in mid-air. 'You see that?' he said gleefully. 'A true predator. He doesn't even hesitate for an instant: he takes what he wants without even thinking about it. That's the same quality that I admire in you, Bryan. You and Pallas here, you're two of a kind.'

Bryan looked uncomfortable. He always enjoyed acclaim, and fame, but he didn't like personal compliments: they embarrassed him. 'We've gone about as far as we can go,' he told William. 'Everything's ready – all we need now is the vote.'

'Which we'll probably win,' William reassured him.

'I don't know . . . it's that "probably" I still don't like. There's so much riding on it, William. Everything else has worked out so good, I think I'd have to shoot myself if we lost.'

'We'll *win*,' William insisted.

'We better had, considering we've bought a 60 per cent interest in Continental Soybeans; and 53 per cent of Farmland.'

'Stop being so paranoid,' William chided him. 'We'll win.'

Bryan took out a cigar, and held it to his nose, and breathed its aroma. He was feeling edgy today. He was confident that the House of Representatives would vote for Zapf-Cady: there was such a strong majority of young, politically-correct Democrats, eager to show that they were radical and caring and modern-minded. He was almost confident that the upper house would vote for it, too. But it was still too close to be sure, and some senators were refusing to commit themselves until they saw which way the political wind was blowing.

It had been Lily Monarch who had inspired Bryan to think up Zapf-Cady. She had approached him at a fund-raising festival at the U of I two years ago and brazenly asked him if he had ever thought of the suffering that people inflicted on animals. If it had been anybody else, he would have put on his plaster-cast senatorial smile and given her the usual platitudes about economic necessity and painless slaughtering and live-and-let-live. But it hadn't been anybody else: it had been Lily Monarch, long-legged, touzle-haired, big-breasted, and electrically-charged with youth and beauty and clear-eyed crusading innocence.

Bryan had invited her for dinner at Hemingway's that weekend, and he had sat back for three hours and listened without interrupting her while she enthused about a world in which animals were treated as fellow mortals. She hadn't been your usual dour, dismissive vegetarian – the sort who say, 'I never eat anything that had a face' or, 'I never eat anything that had a mother.' She truly believed that we share the Earth with animals; and that animals share the Earth with us; and that a cow is not a *thing*, to be reared and slaughtered and eaten, but a member of another race. 'If we kill and eat our fellow mortals on Earth, then we're guilty of cannibalism. There's no other way of looking at it.'

Bryan had listened and tried to stay calm and detached. He had wanted to take her to bed that very first evening, but he had told himself (vehemently, in the mirror in the men's room) *back off, Bryan, and stay backed off.* He had wanted to win her trust first, and to find out more about her beliefs. He sensed that she personified a coming change in American popular thinking: slow-moving, perhaps, almost glacially slow, but very, very deep.

Three days later, he had called Senator Doreen Zapf, a notoriously vociferous campaigner for animal rights, and asked her if she was interested in jointly putting forward a bill to end 'all rearing and slaughtering of all sentient species for the purpose of human consumption'. The press response had been sensational. Lily Monarch had called Bryan in the middle of the night, ecstatic. Zapf-Cady had been born.

But Bryan was neither idealistic nor vegetarian nor stupid. He had seen in Zapf-Cady not just the opportunity for political sainthood but the chance for enormous profit and enormous power. Before he had announced it to the media, he had set up a holding company and acquired a majority interest in Continental Soybeans, a huge but ailing co-operative which controlled the larger part of soya bean production and processing in Kansas, Iowa and Missouri.

After Zapf-Cady had been announced, and meat prices had taken a sudden dive, he had acquired a large share in Farmland Industries, Inc., of Kansas City, the nation's largest agricultural co-operative. Farmland had recently started vertical integration in the Iowa pork industry, involving itself in everything from owning and feeding to processing and packing.

If Zapf-Cady was ratified, Bryan's interest in Continental Soybeans would be worth millions more, as the production of soya protein was stepped up to meet the demand that could no longer be satisfied by animal products. Soy steaks, soyburgers – even soy chicken-breasts. If and when Zapf-Cady was eventually repealed (which he expected it would be) Bryan would have a substantial interest in a newly-booming meat co-operative.

Between ratification and repeal, Bryan was also sure that there would be a steady demand for black-market meat (what he liked to call 'bootleg bacon'). He would be ready to meet that demand, too, for highly-inflated prices.

William Olsen had financed Bryan's acquisitions in Continental Soybeans and Farmland Industries, but Bryan was confident that he could make plenty of profit of his own out of Zapf-Cady; and eventually tell William Olsen just where he could stuff his raven.

All this, he thought, and Lily Monarch, too. To her, he was almost a god. She had called him the only honest and dedicated politician that she had ever met. And she would never need to know any different.

William Olsen finished feeding Pallas and wiped his hands on a damp facecloth. 'Will you be staying tonight, Bryan?' he asked, trying to sound matter-of-fact.

'I don't know. I don't think so. I have an early start tomorrow.'

'Nina was asking.'

'I don't know. I have to take the seven o'clock flight to Kansas City, Missouri. I have an eight o'clock breakfast with Dudley Cambridge.'

William drummed his fingers lightly on the arm of his basket chair. 'I think Nina would appreciate it if you stayed. She says you seem to be more and more distant lately.'

Bryan looked at William over his shoulder. 'Distant? No, just busy.'

'We have a deal, Bryan. You know that. It may not be engraved in stone, but it's damn well suggested in blood.'

He paused, and then he said, with infinite coldness, 'You also know that if I got my health back – today, now, I'd kill you. I wouldn't even think twice.'

Bryan stood up, and walked across to William's chair. Pallas the raven shifted uneasily on its perch, its claws clicking on the chrome. Bryan reached out and stroked William's wiry, greying hair, as gently as if William were a woman.

William said, 'Don't do that!'

But Bryan carried on: and smiled at William beatifically.

'Don't do that, for fuck's sake!'

'William,' said Bryan, 'I will probably be President, one day soon, and I will owe it all to you. Everything you want to see enacted, I will enact. Every bastard you want to see ground down, I will grind down for you. Every snivelling grafter who ever did you a favour, I will give him an office, and a secretary, and a limo, and half a million dollars per annum. I will give your wife orgasms and then some.

'I'm beholden to you, William. I know that, and you will get more than your money's worth. But I have to be in Kansas City, Missouri, for breakfast with Dudley Cambridge, which is important, and I don't feel like fucking your wife tonight. Is that okay?'

William noisily swallowed. 'Just stop stroking my hair, all right? Nina thinks she's being neglected. She gets angry when she feels neglected. She starts taking it out on me.'

Bryan said nothing, although he did stop stroking William's hair.

'She insults me,' said William. He swallowed again, and tried to lick his sagging lips. 'She humiliates me. She says that I'm not a man any more.'

He took a deep breath, and then he said, 'Sometimes she hits me.'

Bryan said, 'I'm sorry. I didn't know.'

'It's not the kind of thing that a man normally admits to, is it?'

'No . . . I guess not.'

'I know plenty of able-bodied men whose wives hit them. You remember Jack Walters? His wife hit him in the face with a skillet when he was asleep. Some joke, hunh? When he came back to the office, he said he broke his nose skiing. But he was crying when he told me.'

He took another deep breath. 'Sometimes, I cry too.'

The conservatory door opened. A plump, blonde, fortyish woman stepped in, her shoes clicking on the tiled floor. She was highly groomed, in a slightly dated Midwesternish way, like Doris Day or Grace Kelly. She wore a navy blue Chanel jacket with gold buttons and a gold spray brooch, and a taupe skirt that was just about half an inch too short for her. She was slightly too sunburned, too.

She moved one of the conservatory chairs to one side, its legs scraping on the floor. She was the kind of woman who couldn't do anything without making a noise.

'Bryan . . .' she said, and took hold of his arms and kissed him loudly on the lips. 'We're having sautéed sea squab for supper tonight . . . your favourite.'

Even if she hadn't been serving sea squab, the succulent meat from the backbone of the blowfish, almost impossible to find these days, Bryan had a compelling reason to stay. He had taken everything that William had been able to offer him: his wife, his money, his political career. He had to give something in return.

He looked at William and tried to smile. 'Thanks, Nina . . . you coruscate.'

'You use such words,' she said, linking arms with him, and pulling him possessively close. William looked away, and Pallas the raven ruffled his oil-black feathers.

'Coruscate, that means to glitter,' said Bryan.

Nina giggled, and kissed him. 'I'll bet you say that to all the girls.'

Deputy Norman Gorman was driving east on 51st St NE playing 'Annie, I'm Not Your Daddy' on the car stereo and doing all the bottom-rotating and finger-popping that went with it. This afternoon, when he was questioning some of the people who claimed to have seen Terence Pearson and his children in the last hours before their murder, he had struck it very lucky with a lush Hispanic girl who had glimpsed their station wagon on 7th Avenue, heading west.

The girl's information was of no practical use whatsoever; but that hadn't stopped Norman from requesting a further interview over dinner. The girl had fluttered her eyelashes and said, 'Of course, anything to help the law.'

Norman liked girls like that. They were useless as witnesses, but they asked no questions and they told no lies. All they wanted was a man in a smartly-pressed uniform: a man who hung his shoulder holster over the back of their bedroom chair, so that they could ogle his greasy loaded gun while he was strenuously humping them.

Norman was off-duty: driving his own metallic-blue Regal Grand National back to his apartment on 42nd St. His blue fluffy dice swung from the rearview mirror. He was feeling tired and sweaty, but a hot shower and a long, tall, cold drink would soon put that right. He had arranged to meet the lush Hispanic girl at seven at Huckleberry's, so that he could feed her, fill her with cocktails, and then drive her back to the

Gorman establishment for a night of Afro-Cubano records, more cocktails, and a little shoulder-holster-hanging. Her name was Vella. *La Bella Vella.*

He wasn't usually so tired, but the Almighty Luke Friend had decided to get the sheriff's department all tangled up in the killing of Iris Pearson's sister Mary, even though the Cedar Rapids police were quite capable of handling it themselves (in Norman's opinion, anyway). At Luke's behest, Norman had been doggedly interviewing potential witnesses all day, and asking all kinds of questions, such as 'Do you own or have you ever owned a European-type bay tree?' and 'Did you ever hear the word "mummers"?' and (wackiest of all) 'Do you have any kind of aversion to the colour green – and if so, why?'

On the whole, the answers to those questions had been 'Huh?' or 'What's it to you?' Norman hadn't been surprised. But who was he to argue? If the Almighty Luke Friend told him to go out and ask the questions, he went out and asked the questions.

Norman fondled his moustache as he drove. He wondered if he should trim it before he went out tonight. There was nothing that girls like better than a well-trimmed, glossy moustache. Norman didn't have any illusions about it. All that girls could think about when they saw a well-trimmed moustache was having their pubic mounds swept, from side to side, like leafy sidewalks.

'Oh Annie . . .' he sang, 'I'm not your daddy . . .'

He had just passed Econofoods East when a huge black Chevrolet van sped out of Pat McGrath Chevrolet with its suspension bouncing and its four tyres shrieking. It U-turned in front of the supermarket and headed west at high speed, leaving a blue cloud of smoke behind it.

Norman said, '*Jesus.*'

This wasn't any ordinary van. This was a six-wheel customized job with lowered suspension and a turbocharged engine.

Its windows were blacked out, and it was thickly streaked with mud. Mud and grass hung from its underside like the fringes of a funeral-shawl.

Cursing under his breath, Norman spun the steering-wheel flat-handed and turned the Buick around, its aged shock-absorbers banging. He snatched up the handset that was dangling below the dash and called out, 'Sheriff's department, this is deputy Gorman! In pursuit of a black Chevy van repeat burr-lack Chevy van headed west from 1600 51st St.'

'Ten-four, deputy,' replied a crackly girl's voice. 'Do you have a *crackle-crackle* plate?'

Norman peered up ahead of him, at the swiftly-bouncing van. Its rear windows were mirrored and it was filthy and black and that was all. 'No licence plate.'

'We read you, deputy Gorman . . . how far west are you now?'

'Almost to Center Point Road. I can see the traffic signals.'

'What's your estimated speed?'

'Sixty, I don't know! Seventy! Jesus – he went through the lights! Jesus – he almost hit that camper! Jesus – get me some back-up, why don't you?'

'Back-up's on the way, deputy Gorman.'

The black van was bucking along 51st Street at over 80 m.p.h. Norman slammed down his foot on his rubberless gas pedal, and the Buick did everything it could to give him a surge of speed. Ten years ago, this had been a 'T-package' sports model, but 74,000 miles and Norman's carelessness about regular servicing had taken the guts out of it. It gave him plenty of smoke and some frenzied exhaust-pipe rattling, but that was about all. The black van began to pull way ahead, ignoring all traffic signals, ignoring the wailing protests from other cars, weaving in and out of the traffic like a hearse hellbent on getting to the crematorium, no matter what.

'You bastard,' Norman breathed to himself, as the two vehicles screeched southwards on Center Point Road. 'You don't get away from me.' He shifted down to 2 on the automatic gearbox and stamped on the gas, and the Buick gave him a sloppy, half-hearted response; then did nothing but whine because he was holding it back. He shifted down to 1, so that it roared and screamed, but then he shifted back to Drive again, and tried to keep up with the black van with skill and dexterity, rather than speed.

The black van was being driven with consummate nervelessness: as if the driver didn't really care whether he lived or died. You can never compete with people like that, as Norman knew from his own experience. There had been several occasions when he had given up close pursuits, because he knew exactly what would happen if he carried on. He had seen too many overturned automobiles, smashed-up bodies, blood spattered as black as photographic developer.

They were driving in the downtown direction now, with route 380 glittering on their left. They passed Texas, Hollywood, Arizona and Richmond Avenues. The sky was quite clear this afternoon, clear as melted glass, with that faint hint of violet that suggests that it's harvest time, and that Labor Day isn't too far away; then fall, then winter.

Dying time, thought Norman, as he edged sideways to overtake an old, slow-moving Cadillac. The Cadillac driver was a white-haired black man, who stared at Norman balefully, his spectacle lenses reflecting the sky. Norman tried to give him a reassuring smile, but he was much too tense.

When he looked up ahead again, the black van had vanished.

He strained his eyes. This was crazy. There were no right-hand turns until 32nd Street, and the van would have had to be travelling at well over 100 to have reached that intersection by now. There were plenty of stores and gas stations and restaurants, of course, but Norman was sure that he would have seen the van slowing down and turning off: he had averted his eyes for only a split second, just long enough to smile.

He slowed down, and crept along the right-hand lane, looking into every parking lot and side-alley. He covered over a mile, but he couldn't see the van anywhere. He picked up his intercom and said, 'Deputy Gorman here . . . cancel that back-up. I've lost him.'

He was just about to turn around and head back home when he thought he glimpsed the rear end of a black van behind the Hot Turkey Family Restaurant. He braked sharply – to the annoyance of an old woman who had been tailgating him for the last three blocks – and then backed up. He was right: the van was parked in the otherwise empty lot at the back of the restaurant, next to the trash cans and the stacks of Coca-Cola crates.

Same van, all right. Blacked-out windows, no licence plate.

Norman watched it for a while. Up above him, on a 50-ft brown-painted pole, a huge brown-painted roast turkey slowly rotated. Norman considered making another call for back-up, but then decided against it. After all, the van driver had committed nothing worse than a traffic misdemeanour. He waited for almost a minute, until the Kid Creole tape came to an end and there was nothing but a soft sizzling sound coming out of his stereo speakers. Then he climbed out of his car, and locked it, and walked across the sidewalk and around the side of the restaurant. He could hear the clattering of dishes from the kitchen, and somebody singing 'It's Now or Never'.

He approached the van cautiously. Its engine was switched off, and its closed windows were blacked-out so completely that all Norman could see was his own reflection, in his crumpled beige cotton windbreaker and his pink flowery shirt. He circled the van once, then he walked up to the front and laid his hand on the radiator grille, to make sure that it was warm.

He went round to the driver's door. He took out his deputy's badge and held it up in full sight of the window, and knocked at the panelling with his knuckle. 'Would you step out of your vehicle, please? Police.'

There was no reply. The dishes continued to clatter, the baritone continued to sing. Norman knocked a second time, and called, 'If there's anybody in there, would they step out of the vehicle, please?'

Still no answer. Norman bit his lip. He could walk away, report the vehicle to traffic, and forget about it. After all, if he stayed around much longer, he was going to be late for his date with the gorgeous Vella, and Vella might not take too kindly to being kept waiting. She had Hershey-brown eyes and breasts like the front bumpers of a '59 Sedan de Ville.

He tapped on the van one last time, using his brass death's-head ring. 'Hallo in there! This is your last warning. This is the sheriff's department. Come out of your vehicle and show yourself.'

A whole minute went past. Traffic rushed past on highway 380, just behind him; music played; children laughed in the yard next to the parking lot. Norman watched the huge roast turkey going around and around, and worked out that it took twenty-two seconds to turn a complete circle.

He reached out with his left hand and tried the door handle. It was *cold*, the door handle, so cold that the chrome looked dull and breathed-over. Norman was almost relieved to find that it was locked. The van was empty, right? Locked and empty. The driver must have abandoned it. Maybe he had stolen it in the first place. He would drive back to Pat McGrath Chevrolet and see if it had been hijacked from there.

He was already walking away when he heard a scratching, rustling sound from inside the van. He hesitated. He could keep on walking, pretend he hadn't heard it. For some reason he couldn't quite articulate, this van gave him a particularly bad vibration – 'street voodoo' one of the black deputies always called it, making a cross with his fingers.

This was one of those situations that really frightened him, because there was nothing obvious happening here, nothing that could be categorized – if there was anything happening at all. From Norman's experience, it was always the non-obvious situations that turned out to be dangerous, if not fatal. The smiling old geriatric who suddenly pulled a gun on you. The kid who gave you a high five and a low five and then stabbed you in the lungs with a sharpened screwdriver the second you turned your back.

But he heard that scraping sound again, and the van squeaked just a little on its suspension, and Norman was sure that it rocked from side to side. There was somebody hiding inside it, no doubt about it. What Norman was going to do about it was something else altogether.

He walked back and stood on tippy-toe and peered into the back of the van. At first he couldn't see anything at all, because of the sky reflected in the darkened glass. But then he cupped his hands around his face, and pressed his nose right up against the window.

He saw dark, mauvish shadows, one leaning to the left, one leaning to the right, then separating. He saw another outline, darker, much more hunched, and then a flailing brushlike shape.

He stepped back, then stepped back again, his heart galloping, his stomach tightening up with alarm. What the hell was going on here? He reached into his windbreaker and unfastened his holster. He wasn't yet sure whether to pull out his gun or not. He wasn't even sure if he was going to take this investigation any further. This was seriously strange stuff.

He turned around and started walking back to his car. He wasn't going to do anything at all without back-up. Whoever it was who was shuffling around inside that van – drug-dealers, mafiosi, or some gun-toting religious cult – the probability was that he was massively outgunned.

He was passing the kitchen when he heard one of the van doors opening. He spun around, almost lost his balance, and threw himself back against the plastic crates of Coca-Cola, his gun raised in both hands.

A tall pale-faced man in a white raincoat was standing at the back of the van, his hands in his pockets, staring at him. He didn't say anything, he didn't move. He stayed where he was, his lips slightly pursed, his eyes as dark as cigarette burns.

The afternoon light was dying, but the man's raincoat was so white that it was dazzling. Norman fumbled in his windbreaker with his left hand and lifted out his badge. 'Sheriff's deputy,' he called. 'Stand away from the vehicle, please, and place your hands on your head.'

The man remained where he was, his hands still thrust in his pockets. Norman left the shelter of the Coca-Cola crates and came a little closer. 'Step away from the vehicle, sir.'

The man neither moved nor spoke. It was quite obvious to Norman that he was completely unafraid, too. It was every deputy's nightmare: the suspect who didn't care if you pointed a gun at him or not. It was becoming more and more common, with crackheads and psychotics and other assorted malcontents. But this man didn't look like a crackhead, and he didn't look as if he had been 'released into the care of the community', either. He looked like a mean, calculating, intelligent son of a bitch who simply wasn't afraid that Norman was pointing a gun at him.

Norman came up close. The man watched him with an expression that bordered on contempt. He had a strange, oval-shaped face, with grey, brushed-back hair. His skin was luminous but faintly cratered. A face from the surface of the moon.

'Are you the owner of this vehicle?' Norman asked him.

The man gave him an infinitesimal shrug. He didn't even blink, not once.

'You speak English? You understand what I'm saying?'

The man nodded.

'All right, then. Are you the owner of this vehicle? Comprendo? Does – this – van – belong – to – you?'

The man steepled his hands, and then made an odd triangular chopping gesture, the edge of each hand chopped in turn against the edge of the other.

'I don't know what you're trying to tell me,' said Norman.

The man repeated the gesture, chopping his hands one way, and then the other.

'Okay . . .' said Norman impatiently. 'I've had enough of this. I'm calling for back-up, you got me? I'm calling another police car. This police car will take you downtown to the Cedar Rapids police department, you understand what I'm saying? They will check your documents and check your vehicle, and ascertain what the fuck you're doing here, and why you've been driving like a crazy person. All right?'

Norman was about to turn back to his car when the man suddenly let out an extraordinary half-strangled cry.

'What did you say?'

'Ernhhh,' the man insisted. 'Ernhhh! Ernhhh!' He pointed towards the back of the van, almost in panic.

'What's the matter?' asked Norman. 'You can't talk, what? You're a mute? Why didn't you say so?'

He walked two or three steps to the back of the van, and opened the left-hand door.

In his very last instant of sight, he saw something that frightened him so much that his bowels released themselves in a thick, hot gush. He didn't even scream – couldn't.

A man burst out of the back of the van but the man was leaves and branches as well as a man. His eyes were dark and hollow and his face was entangled with wriggling roots and fibrous branches, and his arms flailed with brambles and creepers. He lashed Norman across the side of the face, right, then left, with thorns and spines, ripping the skin away from Norman's cheeks, snatching flesh from the side of his nose. Norman staggered back, stumbled, and fell, knocking his head on the concrete. The man leaned over him and lashed him again, tearing his face apart, lashing and lashing and never giving Norman the chance to get away.

The last two lashes caught him across the eyes. He felt them rip through his lids, right, then left. He opened his eyes, he tried to open his eyes, but everything was darkness. He was blind.

He eased himself back on the concrete. His face raged with pain, as if it had been set on fire. It hurt so much that he didn't even dare to touch it. He heard a brittle rustling noise, and the sound of feet. He heard metal sliding, and the sound of something sharp. He heard the man in white saying, 'Ernhhh! Ernhhh!'

The van started up. Norman lay on his back and dreamed of better times. Any time was better than this, with all this pain. He felt the late-afternoon breeze playing over his lacerated cheeks; he felt the blood congealing stiffly around his shirt collar. He wondered what Vella would think, if she could see him now. She couldn't, of course, and she wouldn't. She was probably getting herself ready for their date at Huckleberry's, painting her face and wiggling her butt and making herself look totally sexy.

While he lay blind and bleeding in a Hot Turkey Family Restaurant parking lot, waiting for help that would never come.

The van backed up. He could smell the exhaust, only inches away.

You bastards, he thought. *I'll kill you for this.*

They couldn't have read his mind, or maybe they could. But

they backed the van right up to his legs, so that he could feel the rear tyres dragging at his jeans.

'Get off of my legs!' he screamed at them. Or thought he did, his mouth was so ruined.

But they continued to back up, infinitely slowly, so that the van's rear wheel mounted his leg just above his left kneecap, fracturing his thighbone and crushing his muscle. He had been shot in the shoulder once (albeit by a .22), and knifed. But he had never experienced a pain like this. This pain was black and scarlet and shrieking. He would gladly have died, right this instant, rather than suffer this pain. But it went on, and on, and on, as the van inched back over his left leg, and then his right leg. He forgot about his blindness. He forgot about his face. He dug his fingernails into the concrete and screamed so loud that he deafened himself.

He heard voices, shouting. A blurt of sirens. The van suddenly roared, and took off, its rear wheels spinning on top of his ravaged thighs. Rubber burned, denim burned, flesh burned, nerves burned.

Norman shrieked, 'God in heaven, save me!'

He didn't hear the van snaking into the street. He didn't hear the police cars arriving. He lay back on the concrete thinking of nothing at all, except that it was probably over, his face screeching, his world collapsing.

'Oh, Mom,' he whispered, not caring any longer that his mother had died of cancer seven years ago. 'Oh, Mom, please help me.'

His mom didn't come to help him, but after a long, long time, Luke Friend came to save him, running across the parking lot in those big squodgy-soled boots of his, and kneeling down beside him.

'Norman? Norman? Jesus, Norman, It's Luke!'

Norman dropped into limbo. His afternoon vanished, just like the van had vanished. Luke stayed kneeling beside him while the paramedics came rattling across the parking lot with a shiny chrome stretcher trolley.

'Holy shit!' said one of them, nasally. 'What happened to him?'

Luke swallowed, shrugged, couldn't say anything at all. The paramedics opened up their medical cases, unwrapped their crinkly space-blankets. 'What's his name?' asked one of them.

'Norman,' Luke told them. 'He's one of us.'

'Norman, can you hear me, Norman?' called the other paramedic, without much enthusiasm.

'He's one of us, for Christ's sake!' Luke shouted at him. 'He's one of us!'

The first paramedic reached across and touched Luke's forearm. Crowds were beginning to gather; sirens were whooping toward them from all directions. 'We'll take care of him, okay? I promise you.'

Luke nodded, and shrugged, and hoarsely managed to say, 'Okay.'

But as he knelt there in the dying afternoon, he noticed two or three dried-up bay leaves tumbling across the parking lot, and catching in the chicken wire that fenced it off from the yard next door.

He stood up slowly, and walked across to the fence, and picked one of them up, and crushed it in his hand, and sniffed it. Bay leaves, no question about it.

He was sure now that he was looking for somebody who was very strange and very frightening. He was looking for somebody who was much more ruthless than a crack-dealer or a gang-leader; and very much crueller, too. He was looking for somebody whose motives had some kind of pattern to them, but not the kind of pattern that made any kind of street-sense.

He was looking for somebody who gutted women, for God's sake, and blinded men, and left *leaves* behind him.

Terence Pearson had given him enough clues. *The Green*

Traveller, for Christ's sake. Leos Ponican, too. *Janek-in-Green.*

These were supposed to be folk stories, weren't they? Myths and mummers; people who didn't speak. Sheriff Luke Friend, 37 years old, wasn't supposed to believe in people like that. But inside of Sheriff Luke Friend, 37 years old, there was still a seven-year-old boy from Marion who had been wakened one August night by the sound of a child sobbing. High-pitched sobbing, heartbreakingly sad. He had seen a boy in a dirty flannel nightshirt standing in the corner of his bedroom, his face to the wall, crying.

He had sat up in bed, shivering with dread. 'Who are you?' he had whispered. 'Why are you crying?'

The boy had turned around for a moment, and his eyes had glittered as black as shrimps' eyes, in a transparent face. Then he had faded away – faded, and vanished, as if he had never existed. Luke had run to the wall and clapped his hands against it in fear and astonishment. The wall had felt chilled, and the wallpaper had felt damp.

But that was all. The boy had gone.

Over twelve years later, Luke had discovered from sheriff's department records that a drunken auto-mechanic called Jack Breen had kept his stepson Jamie locked in this same room for over a month, feeding him nothing but candlewax and saucers of rainwater and little plates of cat's excrement. The boy had died there; but Luke had seen him. Luke had *seen* him, and he believed. Even after all these years of robbery and domestic violence and drunken drivers, he still believed that there were people who weren't like the rest of us, maybe not ghosts, maybe not even zombies, but people who didn't obey the normal rules of human existence, people who lived for hundreds of years, giants, dwarfs, people who could pass through walls, or float in and out of upstairs windows.

It was all mad; all irrational. But Luke had seen Jamie Breen, that August night, he had seen him for real. He didn't know whether that made him a better sheriff or a worse sheriff: but he had the sense today that something similar was stirring up, something deeply weird, and he knew that he had to be ready for it.

The paramedics wheeled Norman past him. One of them wore mirror sunglasses, and a neat-clipped moustache. He said, 'We'll take him to Mercy, sheriff. You can check on him there.'

'You take care of him,' said Luke, with a very dry throat.

'You bet,' said the paramedic.

Chief of Police John Husband arrived, wearing a loose-weave cream-coloured sports coat and pale blue golfing slacks. 'What happened?' he wanted to know. 'I heard on the r/t that Norman got hurt.'

Luke looked left; and then he looked right. 'He's been blinded,' he managed to say. He was silent for a long time, swallowing, while John Husband patiently waited for him to speak. 'I don't know,' he said, and this time he couldn't hold back his tears. 'Did you ever feel that it's time to call it a day?'

Seven

Garth was waiting at his table outside of the Original Rag-Top Diner when Nathan and David arrived. It was a warm, overcast day. Nathan wouldn't have minded driving out to the Spellman Institute, but Garth had insisted on meeting somewhere else. The Institute was in a state of shock: all research work had been suspended for the day, except for critical ongoing experiments, and the whole building was crowded with reporters and sheriff's deputies and administrative busybodies.

Apart from that, Garth had something on his mind; something disturbing; and he didn't want to be seen talking to Nathan until he had sorted it out.

Nathan and David walked around the turquoise '55 Thunderbird that was parked on display outside the diner, and sat down at the table, under the black and white striped umbrella.

'That's some car, isn't it?' said Garth. 'My old man used to have one of those, in black and red. I used to hate it, because I was all squashed up in the back.'

'They don't make them like they used to,' said Nathan.

Uncharacteristically, Garth was wearing an open-necked polo shirt and slacks. He looked very tired, and Nathan knew why. He and Raoul had been more than colleagues, they had been fellow explorers. They had been like two men struggling through a complicated system of flooded potholes in total darkness, with only their companionship to keep up their courage. When a potholer drowns in a cave, his fellow explorer doesn't blame the cave – any more than Garth blamed Captain Black for killing Raoul. It was one of the risks. But Garth was grieving, all the same.

'Are you eating?' asked Nathan.

Garth shook his head. 'Don't let me stop you, though.'

A waitress came up, and said perkily, 'What can I get you? Our special today is chicken croissant with a cup of soup, $4.25, and our soups are vegetable, beef and clam chowder.'

'Can I have a cheeseburger?' asked David.

'For sure,' said Nathan. 'And I'll have a vodka-tonic on the rocks.'

Garth was silent for a long time. He swirled his drink around, and then tipped back the last of it. 'I don't know what I'm going to do without Raoul. I feel – lost. Totally lost. Like I've lost my brother or something.'

'I don't know what to say,' Nathan told him. 'I was never really close to anybody like that, not at work, anyway.'

'What's happened to Captain Black?' asked David. He asked it very gently, with all the special sensitivity that children can bring to moments of grief. His eyes were very serious; his face was pale.

'Well, he calmed down after a while, and we managed to break open a window at the back of the lab, and shoot him full of tranquillizers. He's back in his pen, under close observation. The last time I saw him, he was sleeping.'

'You're not going to put him down, are you?'

Garth said, 'No, we're not going to put him down. If you want to know the truth, we can't afford to put him down. He's cost us $18.5 million, and nine years of research, and it wouldn't matter if he killed twenty people, we still wouldn't put him down?'

He put down his glass, and gave David a bittersweet smile. 'Let's put it this way: if we turned Captain Black into bacon, he'd cost you twenty big ones a rasher.'

'Have you any idea what happened?' asked Nathan.

'He woke up,' said Garth. 'He was supposed to be heavily anaesthetized, but he woke up.'

'But why did he go berserk?'

'That's one of the reasons I wanted to talk to you.'

Nathan frowned. 'I don't understand. How should I know why he went berserk?'

The waitress came out with Nathan's vodka-tonic, and Garth ordered another Jack Daniel's. Garth said, 'This is strictly unethical, Nathan, and under any other circumstances, I wouldn't even dream of asking you. But where did that brain-section come from? Whose brain was it?'

Nathan looked at Garth and didn't know what to say. Ever since Garth had called him this morning, he had guessed that Garth might ask him about the sample. Indirectly, maybe. A casual remark like 'He was all right, wasn't he, the child you took that brain-section from?' But this was an out-and-out demand; and this was an out-and-out demand from the man who had saved his father's life, at unimaginable expense.

This was an obligation that had come home to roost, like *The Raven*; and could never be dislodged.

'Garth . . .' he began, trying to think of a way to say 'no'.

'Nathan, let's lay it out country-simple. I saved your father's life. I've never asked you for anything and I've never expected anything. But now I am. I need to know who that brain-section came from.'

'Garth –'

'Captain Black was always stubborn and self-willed but he was never violent. We always knew that his own personality would be subjugated by the new brain-material we implanted in him. A human personality will also dominate a hog's personality. That's why I asked you for a three-year-old, or even younger. We wanted a personality that was innocent, gentle, unwritten-on.'

'I believed that was what I was giving you, Garth,' said Nathan.

'Well, okay . . . there's a remote possibility that the brain-section had nothing whatever to do with the way that Captain Black behaved. He could have been suffering from intense synaptic pain. He could have been suffering from post-operative trauma or God knows what. But the likelihood is that the brain-section was the source of the violence.'

Nathan stirred the ice in his drink and said nothing.

David said, 'Can I see Captain Black again? I mean, when he's better? I've told all my friends about him.'

'You might have to wait awhile,' said Garth, gently; although he didn't take his eyes away from Nathan.

Nathan said, 'Shit. Yes, you saved my father's life. That's how you got the brain-section in the first place.'

'What do you mean?'

Nathan took a deep breath. 'I mean that Mercy are not in

the habit of donating the brain-sections of recently-deceased patients for the purposes of advanced genetic research.'

Garth stared at him. 'You're trying to tell me that this wasn't authorized?'

'That's exactly what I'm telling you. I said that I could pull strings but the fact was that I couldn't. I asked the board if Spellman could use one of our brain-sections and they flatly refused.'

'I hope you're kidding me.'

Nathan said, 'No, I'm not kidding you. They said absolutely not. Even if the victim's next-of-kin said yes, they didn't want to have anything to do with it. Believe me, Mercy have ethics that make the Ten Commandments look like ten things a boy should do at summer camp.'

Garth steepled his hands in front of his face and had a long think. In the meantime, the waitress brought David's cheeseburger, and David blobbed it enthusiastically with ketchup and started to eat.

'Okay, let's get this straight,' said Garth. 'You felt that you owed me a favour, because of what I did for your father. So when I asked you for a brain-section, you took one out of the Mercy mortuary without permission.'

'That's right.'

'But you had all the paperwork, for Christ's sake. You had a letter from the Head of Pathology.'

'I'm afraid that it only *looked* like a letter from the Head of Pathology.'

'Jesus Christ, Nathan!' Garth breathed.

'I'm sorry. I just wanted to help.'

Garth couldn't even begin to think of the legal and ethical complications of what had happened. At last he said, 'Do you know whose brain-section it was?'

'Yes, I do.'

'Then I really think that you have a duty to tell me.'

Nathan pressed his fingertips against his forehead, as if a migraine were coming on. 'Garth, if this gets out, you realize that I'm probably going to lose my job?'

'For Christ's sake – Raoul lost his life!'

'You're not trying to say that I'm responsible, are you?'

'I don't know. I don't know what the hell happened. I apologize, I didn't mean to snap at you. But, I can't believe you did that. I really can't.'

Nathan reached into the breast pocket of his green checkered shirt and took out a neatly-folded piece of paper. 'I had an idea this was what you were going to ask me. The brain-section came from a Caucasian boy called George Shephard Pearson, aged three years and seven months.'

Garth took the paper, unfolded it and read it. Nathan watched him with a mounting feeling of embarrassment and misery. Next to them, a girl laughed loudly. The diner wasn't too busy at this time of the morning, but there were half a dozen young people sitting at nearby tables, jostling and chatting and enjoying the atmosphere 'Where '50s Fun Lasts For Ever'. Nathan would have done anything at that moment to go back to June 1980, when he had first walked into the Dairy Queen Brazier with his long hippie curls and his skin-tight jeans, and seen Susan sitting at the table with strawberry yoghurt all around her mouth, her spoon poised in mid-air.

He would have done anything, rather than be here, today, without her; and with this black obligation perched over him.

'George Pearson?' asked Garth. 'Why does that name ring a bell?'

'You probably heard about him on television. He was the boy who had his head chopped off. Him and his sister.'

Garth said, 'God, Nathan, this is one hell of a mess. You took a post-mortem sample from a homicide victim, without authority, and you gave it to Spellman as a genetic implant donation? What the hell were you thinking about?'

Nathan shrugged, coughed, looked away. 'It's common practice. We take all kinds of glands and tissues from deceased patients without asking permission. Besides, I was thinking about my father, what you did for him.'

'But what I did for your father, that was just as valuable to our research as it was to you. I didn't expect anything in return. Especially not this!'

'I'm sorry.'

'You're *sorry*? Raoul Lacouture is lying in the funeral home this morning, and Jack Lezard has lost his right arm; and you're *sorry*?'

'Hold up, wait a minute,' Nathan interrupted. 'None of that is my fault. There's no direct evidence to suggest that Captain Black went berserk because you coded his brain with George Pearson's genes.'

'Medically, I think the conclusion is almost inescapable,' said Garth. 'Your Poland China hog is one of the most naturally docile beasts on the face of the earth. He very rarely attacks other hogs, let alone humans.'

'But George Pearson was only a three-year-old boy.'

'For sure, but he was a three-year-old boy who must have been severely traumatized by being killed. Just because he died, that doesn't mean the experience didn't make a permanent impression on his cerebral cortex. Jesus, Nathan. Don't you know what would happen if the press found out about this? What kind of a meal do you think Lily Monarch would make of it? And Senator Cady? They'd chew us up and spit us out!'

'I'm sorry,' said Nathan. He was quaking. 'You want it in blood? I'm sorry.'

Garth stood up. 'I'll have to have a long think about this, Nathan. Maybe I can call you later today.'

He was about to leave, but Nathan took hold of his arm, and held him back. 'Listen, Garth, don't let's fall out about this. I was wrong to take that section without authority, I know that. But it's not critical. It's nothing to do with Raoul getting killed, and nobody needs to know about it.'

Garth thought for a moment, and then he drew his arm away. 'I'm not about to tell anybody, Nathan. Not yet, anyway – not until I've done a whole lot more tests on Captain Black. If there's even the slightest indication that he was affected by little George Pearson's personality – or by the trauma he experienced when he was murdered – well, that's going to be the end of my career, too. Raoul's family will have us bankrupted before you can say liability action.'

'We've been friends, Garth,' said Nathan. 'Friends make mistakes. That doesn't mean they stop being friends.'

Garth shrugged, and clapped him on the back. 'Okay, old buddy. Sorry if I lost my temper.'

David said, 'When can I see Captain Black?'

'Give it a week. Then ask your pa to drive you over.'

'Thank you, sir!'

'Be seeing you,' said Garth, and left the diner, without even pausing to look at the '55 Thunderbird, or the girls who were clustered around it.

Nathan finished his drink and ordered another. David said, 'Are you in trouble?'

'Kind of. But don't you worry.'

'You gave him a piece of that murdered boy's brain, and you weren't supposed to.'

'That just about sums it up, yes.'

'But he was *dead*, that boy. What difference could it make?'

Nathan ruffled David's hair. 'I made a mistake. I shouldn't have done it. The next thing I know, they're going to start calling me a bodysnatcher.'

'What's a bodysnatcher?'

'Back in the old days, when surgeons needed dead bodies to cut up, so that they could find out what people's anatomy was like, there used to be guys who would dig up people's graves and steal their bodies. Strictly for profit, of course.'

'But you didn't do it for profit.'

Nathan shrugged. 'I did, in a way. I did it to pay him back for saving Grandpa's life.'

David said, 'I don't think you were wrong.'

'They gave that boy's personality to Captain Black; and Captain Black went crazy. He killed Dr Lacouture; and he practically bit the arm off one of their lab workers.'

'But Dad, that wasn't the boy, was it? Three-year-old boys don't kill people!'

'You don't think so? Well, maybe this one would. This one had an awful lot to feel sore about.'

They sat together for a very long time, holding hands. Eventually, David said, 'You've done everything right, Dad. You always have. It wasn't your fault that Mom died and Aaron died. This isn't your fault, either. Please, Dad, you don't have to *try* so hard. You don't always have to say sorry.'

Nathan looked at David and it was like looking at himself, the way that he had always wanted to be. He suddenly thought: I brought you up right. I taught you understanding and I taught you good values. And God knows how I managed to do that, because my own mother taught me nothing except guilt, and shame, and responsibility for everything: 'I wanted a doctor for a son. What did I get? A pathologist. Your father's sick, what can you do? You can't even cure him.'

Nathan *had* cured his father – with faith, with dedication and by knowing Garth Matthews. But he hadn't managed to cure him before his mother had died – quite suddenly, quite soundlessly, while walking across the ice of Seminole Pond on a February afternoon, under a dim orange sun, slipped, fallen, and lain in her furs with her eyes open and her mouth open, as if she were just about to speak.

It was that moment, more than any other, that had decided

Nathan to give George Pearson's brain-section to the Spellman Institute, ethics or not. He had been showing his mother that he could save people, that he was a proper doctor, that he could change people's lives.

David said, 'You mustn't cry.'

'Who's crying?' he asked.

'You,' said David.

He smeared his cheeks with his hand. 'Flies in my eyes, that's all.'

Luke gave himself a couple of hours off that afternoon and went shopping at Econofoods with Sally-Ann and Nancy. He liked to shop when he was worried or annoyed: the mindlessness of walking up and down the aisles always settled him down and helped him to straighten out his thinking. Here was a bright, cheerful world of Lucky Charms and Ballpark Franks and giant pepperoni pizzas. For a while he didn't have to worry about Leos Ponican, gutted and tilting. He didn't have to worry about Norman Gorman, blinded, crippled, and fighting for his life in Mercy. He didn't have to worry about bay leaves that filled up yards where no bay trees grew, or about butchered women, or grinning men who dressed up like bushes.

Sally-Ann linked arms with him for a moment, and smiled up at him, and Luke smiled back. He had never believed that he would marry. He had always been so big, so clumsy, so thick-fingered, every girl's pal but no woman's lover. When he was 21, he had dated an intense, fat girl called Marlene, and for a month or two he had been under the impression that this was the real thing. 'You're Scorpio, I'm Leo, it's perfect,' she kept telling him; and she had adored cunnilingus, hours of it. He couldn't remember how many sunny days had darkened into twilight while he laboriously licked her until he was out of breath – and she lay back with her eyes tight shut, uttering self-indulgent little twitters that sounded like phoebe song. But then she had told him that she couldn't consider a serious relationship with anybody involved in law enforcement. All of her friends smoked illegal substances and believed in 'freedom of self', whatever that was. His efforts to explain that nobody could really be free without law enforcement had fallen on deaf ears: or ears that no longer loved him, or never had.

He had met Sally-Ann by accident: while arresting a dog-handler at the German Shorthaired Pointer Club of Eastern Iowa's licensed field trial, at the Crumbacker Wildlife Area. There had been an argument over the winner in the Open Puppy class, and somebody had started waving a shotgun around. That somebody had been Sally-Ann's boyfriend; and Sally-Ann had loyally accompanied him to headquarters.

While Sally-Ann's boyfriend had been cooling off in a holding cell, Luke and Sally-Ann had got to talking, and discovered that they had hardly anything at all in common.

Who could say why they sparked together? Physically, he was far too big for her. She was neat to the point of prissiness: petite and blonde with tip-tilted nose and more dazzling white teeth than anybody had a right to. She was the outdoors type, a farmer's daughter from Swisher, with a passion for riding and dogs. Luke liked her dogs (two over-enthusiastic pointers) but he had never tried riding – 'I don't dislike any horse enough to sit on it.'

'Do you want to try this new low-cal Cajun dressing?' Sally-Ann asked him.

'Sure . . . anything to stop lettuce tasting like lettuce.'

'You shouldn't grumble so much, sweetheart. You're looking so much trimmer.'

'Trimmer? I'd commit genocide for one of those cinnamon doughnuts.'

Little Nancy was skipping from aisle to aisle in her OshKosh overalls and her blue floppy denim hat. 'Think about it,' said Sally-Ann, linking arms with him. 'The trimmer you are, the longer you'll live. You want to see your grandchildren, don't you?'

'You bet I do,' he grinned, and kissed her on top of the head; although what he was really thinking was what he always thought. Why should I deprive myself of cinnamon doughnuts when I could walk into a bullet tomorrow? What am I trying to do – make life easier for the pallbearers? But he never said things like that aloud. Sally-Ann was anxious enough about what he did for a living, without him making her feel worse.

They passed the books and magazines. The latest copy of the *Gazette* was on the stands, with a photograph of a large Poland China hog like Captain Black and the banner headline BIGGEST HOG KILLS ANIMAL BOFFIN.

'Wasn't that awful?' said Sally-Ann. 'My dad used to keep a big Polish boar, and when I was little he used to scare me out of my wits. You'd only have to look at him and he'd come for you. I don't think most people realize how dangerous a pig can be.'

Luke glanced at the headline quickly. 'Yeah . . . I'm expecting a report on it later. Can you see this month's *Hot Bike* magazine?'

'They'll have to put it down, won't they?'

'Put what down?'

'The pig. The one that killed that scientist.'

Luke shook his head. 'I doubt it. It happened in the lab, when they were operating on it. It's not like somebody's pit bull biting somebody's kid. Besides, it's worth a fortune, from what Mike was telling me.'

Nancy came up and took hold of his hand. 'Are you coming to the barbecue Sunday?' she asked him. She was petite and skinny-wristed and small, like her mother, thank God. He hated to think what a girl who inherited his looks would have had to suffer.

'Sure I'm coming, sweetheart. I wouldn't miss it for worlds.'

'You said that the last time,' Nancy rebuked him.

'Well, last time I got all snarled up in a whole lot of pretty serious work.'

'You're all snarled up in some pretty serious work now, aren't you?'

'I'm still coming to the barbecue. Sheriff's honour.'

'Cross your heart and cut out your guts and hide from the horny hedge?'

Luke laughed out loud. '*What* did you say?'

Sally-Ann said, 'Nancy, baby! That's not very nice!'

Nancy went pink, and looked upset. But Luke said, 'No, no, it's okay, it's okay. Tell me that again.'

Nancy shook her head.

'It's just awful,' put in Sally-Ann. 'Don't make her say it again.'

'Nancy, please sweetheart,' Luke cajoled her. 'I really want to hear that again.'

Nancy looked down at the floor and scuffed the sole of her shoes. 'Cross your heart.'

'Yes, go on.'

'Cut out your guts.'

'Yes.'

Long pause. Then, all in a rush, '*And-hide-from-the-horny-hedge!*'

Luke patted her on the shoulder. 'Good, you did good. You can have a sucker for that when we get to the checkout.'

'She certainly can't!' Sally-Ann protested. 'Not only is she saying the most disgusting things, she's being rewarded for it – and with sugar, too!'

Luke stayed patient. 'Is that something you learned from one of your friends?' he asked Nancy.

'All of the kids say it. It's just a craze.'

'But *I* never said anything like that, when I was a kid.'

'It's new, Jake Marek started it. He said his grandfather told it to him.'

'Czech,' said Luke.

'Check what?' asked Sally-Ann.

'Czech like in Czechoslovakia. Jake Marek, his parents are Czech.'

'I don't see what that has to do with it,' said Sally-Ann.

'It could have everything to do with it. Terence Pearson wrote about a man who went around dressed in green; and there was a picture on his wall of a man covered in leaves, like a bush. His notebooks were all written in Czech – which was why poor old Leos Ponican was translating them for us. And what happened to Leos Ponican? And to Terence Pearson's sister-in-law?'

'I hope you're not going to answer that question in front of Nancy,' said Sally-Ann.

'They had their guts cut out,' put in Nancy, brightly. 'Everybody's talking about it. That's why Jake started saying it.'

'Did he say anything else about it? Like what it was supposed to mean?'

Sally-Ann commandeered the shopping-cart, twisting it out of Luke's grip. 'Luke . . . we're supposed to be shopping, not carrying out a homicide investigation for the Linn County Sheriff's Department. You know how much I hate it when you do this.'

Luke said, 'I'm sorry. I'm truly sorry. But this could be critical.' He looked at his watch. 'Listen . . . I'm going to have to leave you. I hate to do this. But Nancy's kind of put my mind in gear.'

'Luke, we have all of this shopping to take home!'

'I'm sorry, sweetheart, this is 300 per cent important.'

He kissed Sally-Ann on the cheek, even though she snapped, 'Don't!' and tried to evade him. He kissed Nancy, too, and then he strode out of the store, his shoes squelching on the vinyl floor. He didn't look back. It burned him up, leaving them like this. But once his brain had started working and his adrenaline had begun to surge, there was no point in him trying to do anything mundane.

A skinny young cab driver was leaning against his car, talking to some toothless old Hawkeye boys outside Nelson's Sports Bar & Grill. Luke said, 'How about the Third Avenue Bridge, and quick?'

The cab driver looked him up and down. 'What's your rush, chunky?'

Luke produced his wallet and showed the cab driver his badge. 'I have to get to my office to make an urgent complaint to myself about unwilling and insulting cab drivers. I only hope that I'll take myself seriously, if you know what I mean.'

The cab driver lifted both hands in surrender. 'Okay, sir, sheriff, I'm sorry. I didn't mean nothing by it.'

Luke heaved himself into the back. 'You listen to me, punk,' he said, as the cab driver swerved away from the kerb. 'This city has a worldwide reputation for its courtesy, and that's the way it's going to stay.'

'Yessir, sheriff.'

There was a Dunkin' Donuts bag on the front passenger seat, which rustled from side to side as the driver took corners.

'You want a tip?' Luke asked.

'Well, sheriff, it's up to you.'

'The tip is: give me a donut, and I'll think about forgetting that complaint.'

'Hey,' said the driver. 'Take the whole bag.'

When he reached the office, deputy Bulowski was there, sitting at her desk, scowling at a page of reports as if she could scowl it into non-existence. Luke knocked loose-knuckled at her door, and smiled, but she scowled at him, too, as if she could scowl him into non-existence, too.

'How're you doing, Edna?' he greeted her. 'Did you heard any more from the hospital?'

'They called about a half-hour ago. Norman's making progress.'

'How much progress? How are his eyes?'

'The doctors think that he's permanently blinded. He may regain some minimal sight in his right eye, but that's an outside chance. He may have to have his left leg amputated, too. The knee was completely crushed.'

She paused, and then she added, with some cynicism, 'Apart from that, he's making progress.'

Luke said nothing. He'd already heard that Norman would lose his sight.

'Comes with the territory, hunh?' said Edna; being cynical, but sad, too.

Luke nodded, and nodded again, and then said, 'Edna, what did you make of the Pearson household? I mean, what do you think the hell was going on there?'

Edna Bulowski took off her glasses and rubbed her bulging eyes. 'I don't know, sheriff. Terence Pearson was obsessed; Iris Pearson was browbeaten. The kids were spoilt, but then they were killed.'

'But all of this folklore stuff that Terence Pearson was involved in. What do you make of that?'

'You mean the Green Traveller?'

'That's right. The Green Traveller, and all of those leaves.'

'If you ask me, sheriff, I think we have to be careful to be completely level-headed, and not to start seeing things from

Terence Pearson's p-o-v. I don't believe in all this stuff about solving crimes by trying to seeing things the way the criminal sees them. Criminals see things in a totally perverted and anti-social way, and Terence Pearson is a whole lot more perverted and anti-social than most.'

She replaced her glasses. 'If we start seeing things like him, we're going to lose sight of what we're really looking for. Facts, evidence. And proof.'

Luke didn't answer. He pretty much agreed with Edna when it came to fashionable police psychology. He, too, set very little store by the idea that it was essential to empathize with a killer before you could catch him. Screw empathy. What you needed was thorough, well-organized policework and reliable witnesses – not to mention all the fibres and fingerprints and matching DNA you could lay your hands on. But in this case, the strangeness of what was happening was extreme, and deeply unsettling. Day by day he was growing increasingly convinced that he would never get anywhere at all if he didn't have at least half an understanding of what Terence Pearson had been trying to do.

'Lookit,' he said, 'there's a clear connection between the homicides that Terence Pearson committed and the killings of Leos Ponican and Mary van Bogan. There's some evidence, too, that the same people who attacked Iris Pearson and Mary van Bogan, also attacked Norman – if a few dry bay leaves amount to evidence. The doctors are checking Iris Pearson's injuries and comparing them with Norman's. They both had serious facial lacerations. If they're the same, that's even more evidence. We're running a check on the tyre-tracks, too.

'So – we have obvious connections. Each homicide, each attack, one connects with the other. But so far, none of it makes any damned sense at all. They don't connect for any sensible reason. That's why I want to read the rest of Terence Pearson's notebooks. That's why I'm trying to follow up this folklore angle. Maybe there isn't a Green Traveller, or a Janek-the-Green, or whatever his name is. But the crucial element seems to be that Terence Pearson thought there was, and acted accordingly.'

'But Terence Pearson was in custody when Leos Ponican and Mary van Bogan were killed.'

'Of course he was. But maybe there are other citizens of Cedar Rapids who think there's such a person as the Green Traveller. Maybe there's a Green Traveller Fan Club, for Christ's sake.'

Deputy Bulowski's phone rang. She picked it up, and said, 'Bulowski.' Then, 'Yes, yes. He's here, as a matter of fact. Do you want to talk to him? Sure.'

She handed the phone over. It was Detective Mike Whipps, of the CRPD. 'Sheriff? I've just been given the results of the medical tests on Iris Pearson and Norman Gorman. I'll fax 'em to you, but I thought I'd talk to you first.'

'Go on.'

'According to Dr Schneebaum, both Iris Pearson and Norman Gorman suffered severe lacerations from the twigs of the same-type shrub or tree.'

'Same-*type*, or same?'

'Same-type: that's as close as he can say for now. He'll be running more tests later. Plant DNA, cellular structure, but they take time.'

Luke sighed, and said, 'Shit.' Then, 'Okay, Mike, thanks for calling.'

'One more thing, sheriff. Those Pearson notebooks you passed over to us, so that we could get Officer Hora to translate them for you? I'm sorry to tell you that Officer Hora has declined.'

'*Declined?*' Luke frowned. 'What do you mean, declined?'

'Sorry, sheriff. He wouldn't do it. First of all he said his Czech was too rusty, then he straight-out said that he wouldn't.'

'Did he give you any kind of reason?'

'He brought them back to Chief Husband, sir, and then he went home sick.'

'So what's happening to them now?'

'I'll be taking them round to Professor Mrstik at Kirkwood College, sir. He's a friend of Chief Husband's: they both belong to the same lodge. He's promised to translate them for us overnight, if he can do it.'

'Okay, then, very well. Keep me informed.'

Luke put down the phone. Deputy Bulowski looked up at him, blinking, trying to read what had happened in his face.

'Bad news?' she asked him, at last.

But all he said was, 'Cross your heart, cut out your guts, and hide from the horny hedge.'

A gritty wind was getting up when he arrived outside the Marek house, which was only four blocks away from his own. Although it was so close, the street was much shabbier. The porches were scabby with weathered paint, and the newest automobile parked at the kerb was an '86 Caprice with a ripped-up vinyl roof. Scraps of waste paper were tangled in the shrubs, and the whole neighbourhood looked exhausted. These were the homes of laid-off engineers, welders who had been forced to take pay cuts, junior teachers, mail carriers, clerical staff, all of those people whose pride and savings had gradually been worn down by years of recession.

The concrete path was cracked, but on the whole the Marek property was one of the best-kept. There were red roses around the latticed porch, and it had been recently repainted. Luke pressed the doorbell and it chimed 'The Bluebells of Scotland'. Pretty appropriate for a Czech family living in Iowa, he thought. A scruffy black dog came trotting around the side of the house and stared up at him with its tongue hanging out. It made him think of Emily Pearson's tongue, and he turned away. He still couldn't understand what had come sliding out of Emily's mouth, and he didn't want to think about it. He must have been stressed, that's all. Norman had sworn that he had once seen somebody sitting in the back seat of his patrol car but he had instantly stopped and searched the car and found nobody. Stress, it plays tricks with the eyes. Not that it would ever play tricks with Norman's eyes again.

Luke saw a dark shape moving behind the frosted glass panels of the door. Then he heard a thickly-accented voice call, 'I don't want none! Go away!'

'Mr Marek, Senior?' asked Luke. 'Is that Mr Marek, Senior? I'd like to talk to you, sir, if I could.'

'I don't need no auto shampoo! I don't got no auto! Go away!'

'Mr Marek, this is Sheriff Friend. I'd really like to talk to you, sir. I can show you my badge.'

The door opened about three inches. Luke saw black, glittering, suspicious eyes, like a cautious rat. He held up his badge and waited patiently. The wind made the brim of his hat flap up at the back. Eventually, the door opened wider, and a small, elderly man said, 'Okay. Better to come in.'

Mr Marek Senr. had white hair combed straight back from his forehead, an angular, fleshless face, and an upper lip stained sock-yellow from decades of smoking. His nose was curved like a hand-carved implement for opening soft-drink cans.

He wore a spotless white shirt, a red silk tie, and a red and yellow silk waistcoat. On his knobbly wrist he wore a heavy, plain stainless-steel watch, of the kind once issued by Soviet Railways.

'I don't know how to help you, sheriff,' he said, in a tobacco-thickened voice. 'I never did nothing and I never saw nothing.'

All the same, he took hold of Luke's elbow and ushered

him into the living-room. This was a large, gloomy L-shaped room with a television the size of a small cathedral and huge stained-oak furniture. An icon of St Wenceslas hung on the chimney-breast, and there were religious pictures everywhere. The house smelled of damp and stale cigarettes and sauerkraut.

He shook a Gauloise out of its blue paper pack and stuck it into the side of his mouth. 'Ten years ago, we never had no crime in this neighbourhood. Now what happens? The kids steal everything. They would come in when you were sleeping and steal your eyes, if your eyelids wasn't closed.'

He lit his cigarette with an old-fashioned brass gasoline lighter. 'Sit down,' he said. 'You want tea, maybe? Or how about vodka?'

'I'll pass,' said Luke, sitting on one end of the couch. The cushion let out a long, squalid farting noise.

'I don't get no visitors, usually,' Mr Marek Senr. explained, his cigarette waggling on his lower lip. 'I watch a little TV. I read the paper. Sometimes I take the dog for a walk. They say you shouldn't smoke, you'll die. What do I care, with a life like this?'

Luke leaned forward. 'Mr Marek . . . my daughter Nancy plays with your grandson Jake.'

'So? What's he been doing?'

'Oh . . . nothing bad, don't worry about that. No, it was something he's been saying that interests me. "Cross your heart, cut out your guts, and hide from the horny hedge".'

Mr Marek Senr. blinked and smoked and blinked. 'So?' he said, after a while.

'According to Nancy, you taught it to him.'

'That's right. I use to say it myself, when I was a kid. All of us kids used to say it. In Czech, of course.'

Luke said: 'I'm interested to know why you should have taught it to him now.'

Mr Marek Senr. blinked some more. 'Because of the murders,' he said, as if it were so obvious that he couldn't understand why Luke should even have bothered to ask him. 'The children, with their heads whopped off, yes? That one. Then the man from the Czech Museum with his guts out. Then the aunt of the children who had their heads whopped off.'

He blew out smoke, and made no further attempt to explain himself.

Luke said, 'What's the connection?'

'What connection?'

'The connection between the murders and the words that you taught your grandson?'

'I don't understand you. The words are what you always say when this thing happens. Like, what do you call it? . . . a hex.' He interlaced the index fingers and middle fingers of both hands in a criss-cross pattern and held it up. 'For keeping them away.'

'For keeping *who* away?' asked Luke, trying to be patient.

Mr Marek Senr. continued to hold up his fingers. 'To keep away the people who never speak, of course. Who else?'

'You mean the mummers?' asked Luke.

Mr Marek Senr. nodded. 'For sure. The mummers. The dice-players, that's what we called them in Klatovy, when I was a kid. Or else the dumb-people.'

'They were real people?'

'Depends what you mean by real people.'

'Did you ever see them?'

Mr Marek Senr. carefully peeled the wettened cigarette from his lower lip. 'Sure I seen them. But only once. My father told me look away, and made the same sign, and said the same words. "Dumb-people, dumb-people, promise you don't come knocking on my door. Cross your heart and cut out your guts and hide from the horny hedge".'

'How many dumb-people were there?'

'I don't know. I only saw four. Some people said there were more. They was all different, depending on their crafts, do you understand what I mean?'

'What about the Green Traveller, Janek-the-Green?'

'Sure. I saw Janek-the-Green. There was another rhyme about him. "All the country is filled up with bay, The bushy man is coming on his way." Something like that.'

Luke sat back and the couch made more puffing noises. He could sense that he was close to finding out more about Terence Pearson's obsession with the Green Traveller, but Mr Marek Senr. wasn't exactly making it easy for him. To Mr Marek Senr. the mummers were obviously so ordinary – so much a part of everyday life – that he couldn't understand why he had to explain them. It was like being asked to describe dogs, or fish, or the sky.

'Tell me about them, the dumb-people,' he said.

Mr Marek Senr. stared at him for a long time with one eye closed against the cigarette smoke. 'You want that vodka? A story like this needs vodka.'

'Okay, just this once, I'll have vodka.'

Mr Marek Senr. shuffled out and came back with two cloudy-looking tumblers and a half-empty bottle of bison-grass vodka. Luke hated bison-grass vodka: he thought that it tasted like distilled lawn-cuttings. But he tried to smile when Mr Marek Senr. passed him a brimming glassful, and said, '*Nazdravye*!' and tipped it back.

Mr Marek Senr. said, 'The story is, that for five years the harvest in Bohemia was so bad that everybody was starving. The sugar-beet was bad, the fruit in the river valleys was bad, the potatoes were blit.'

'Excuse me?'

'The potatoes were blit. Blit like in blight. Past tense. Light, lit. Blight, blit.'

'All right,' said Luke. 'Sorry to interrupt.'

Mr Marek Senr. said, 'This was way back – way, way back, we're talking 10th century here, just after St Wenceslas was killed by his brother Boleslav. Brothers, hunh? Who'd have them? I had a brother once. He didn't care for me none and I didn't care for him none.'

He smoked, and blinked, and then he said, 'All the farmers said what the hell are we going to do, we're all starving here. They'd been praying to God but God hadn't helped them. So they asked a Boii priest what should they do. The Boii people were the original Bohemians, right? Bohemia was named after the Boii. Most of them were killed around fifty years before Christ was born; but a few of them survived, and kept up the old magic ways. They were the kind of people who prayed to the land and prayed to the rivers and prayed to the skies.

'Anyway, the Boii priest said you should choose one of your farmers, and take him into the forest, and open up his guts, and plant a tree inside of his guts. Then the tree will grow in his guts, and soon you won't be able to tell which is tree and which is man. They'll grow together, you'll have yourselves a man-tree. Which is where the name of Janek-the-Green came from.

'Janek-the-Green will have the power to make things grow; to make the harvest good. All he has to do is travel from farm to farm, and knock at the door, and offer to make the harvest good. The only trouble is, the tree in Janek's guts will eat his guts and he'll keep on needing more guts just to stay human instead of tree. More guts! Doesn't matter where they're from, so long as he has them. He'll tell the farmer in dumb-show what he needs. Guts! That's what he needs, and he needs to eat them right out from the body! Can you imagine that? So the farmer has a choice: to give him guts in exchange for a good harvest, or to suffer another bad harvest.'

Luke took another sip of vodka, in the hope that hunger

and Mr Marek Senr.'s story might have given the flavour just a touch more piquancy. They hadn't. It still tasted like that thin yellowish-green liquid that drips out of compost heaps. He coughed and crossed his legs.

Mr Marek Senr. said, 'First of all, the farmer says no, I can't give you guts. Whose guts is he going to give him? His wife? His children? But Janek-the-Green sits and plays with the dice and says nothing and waits. For one life, you could have a good harvest. And the farmer thinks of all the people who die anyway, because of cold and hunger and working too hard, and he thinks what the hell, why not?

'Especially since Janek-the-Green tells him in dumb-show that he won't ask for the guts now, not for thirty-six long years, so long as he can go to bed with the farmer's wife. Just once, no more. That's all he asks. And outside, the fields is naked of crop, the wireworms just chomped the last of the sugar-beet, and winter is on the way. So what does the farmer say?'

'I guess yes,' said Luke, drily.

Mr Marek Senr. lifted a single finger. 'That's right. He thinks: thirty-six years, that is for ever, and Janek-the-Green will be dead and gone by then. After a while, the farmer – he persuades his wife to mate with the Green Traveller. Persuades her! He whispers to her, "It won't be so bad, what is this man, nothing but a tree-man?" And so the Green Traveller takes the farmer's wife into the woods and who knows what they do there, because none of the wives would ever talk about it later. But after that, you tell me, is everything blooming? The potatoes are the bigness of footballs, yes? The corn is enormous? Yes – yes, it is. Ah, yes, the Green Traveller, he has been walking the land, and everything bursts – wonderful, wonderful! He is fertility itself, fertility! And what else is bursting – yes, the farmer's wife, who is pregnant with a baby. Janek's baby.'

Luke said, 'How did he do it, this Janek-the-Green? How did he make the crops grow?'

Mr Marek Senr. took the cigarette out of his mouth and let smoke leak slowly out of his nose. 'Sheriff . . . if I knew such things, would I be sitting here now, in this house, telling you this story? I would be rich farmer, with Cadillac. But we all know of rainmakers; people who can change the weather. There are such people, yes? So maybe Janek-the-Green is one of those. I don't know. Maybe he is more. He is half of a plant himself. Maybe he knows how to speak to plants, and make them grow.'

He was silent for a short while, and then he said, 'The crops grow good. The baby gets born. But the farmer knows that this is not his baby. He *knows.* The baby has a look in his face that is not his, yes?'

'Yes,' said Luke, not quite sure where Mr Marek, Senr. was taking him.

'So . . . Janek's son grows up and marries, and has children of his own. But these children are also Janek's descendants . . . and, one day, when the thirty-six years have gone by, Janek comes knocking at the door, asking for the guts which he was promised. Yes? You understand this now? Thirty-six years is a long time, looking forward; but no time at all, when looking back. However long it is, the day comes around; and the day comes around when Janek expects his feast.

'It is like a deal with the devil. You know, like Dr Faustus, to sell your soul. But, we all know that God protects our souls, and that the devil is not true. And, besides, Janek is not interested in souls; if they exist at all. He wants our insides. Our actual flesh.'

'So Janek-the-Green knocks at the door?' Luke asked him. 'Then what happens?'

'He cannot enter the house unless he is invited. If he is not invited in, he must knock and knock until somebody grows tired of his knocking and says, "Oh, stop that knocking and come on in!" Usually, however, his grandchildren will invite him in. He is grandfather, after all: they do not know him, but they feel that he is part of them, and that they are part of him, and they will ask him in.'

'Then what?'

Mr Marek Senr. crushed out his cigarette. 'Then he will get the guts that he was promised, that's all. From his own son; and whoever else he can find. And he will feed.'

'On *guts*?'

'Living and raw, with the victim still alive. The worst death that anybody ever had to suffer, that's what they say.'

'I can imagine.'

Mr Marek Senr. tapped out another Gauloise. 'I don't think that you can imagine it, sheriff. Not for one moment. We are talking now about a very special kind of suffering, yes? Not many people have to bear such suffering. It is the kind of suffering you would kill yourself to escape it, or kill anybody else, even people you loved.'

'Your own children?' asked Luke.

'Anybody,' said Mr Marek Senr.

Eight

Luke said, 'There are other mummers, right? Janek-the-Green isn't alone.'

'Well, of course not,' said Mr Marek Senr. He was standing by the window now, with the net curtain raised in his right hand, smoking and looking out. It was almost six. The clock seemed to have jumped, the way it does after 4 p.m.

'A swordsman? A witness? A leper? And some twins called Knife and Naked?'

Mr Marek Senr. slowly turned towards him. 'You know more than you told me, sheriff.'

'No, I don't. Terence Pearson kept a kind of a diary, in Czech. We had part of it translated, and that's what it said.'

'What about the other part?'

'We should have that translated by tomorrow.'

'Well . . . good luck to you. You wouldn't have *me* to translate such a thing.'

'Oh, yes? And why not?'

Mr Marek Senr. made the same criss-cross sign with his fingers. 'Don't ask. It's bad enough I should speak Janek's name.'

'But that was back in Czechoslovakia, wasn't it? Years ago, before World War Two. Why should you worry?'

Mr Marek Senr. let the curtain fall back. 'Because Janek-the-Green is always travelling and looking for people's guts, for people to feed on. He is here now, which is why I teach Jake that little thing to say.'

'The same Janek-the-Green? After a thousand years?'

'The story says that he can live for ever. The story says that all the dumb-people can live for ever.'

'Tell me about the others.'

'The others? Each of them stands for a different craft, yes? A different skill. The swordsman he crosses his swords, like my fingers, see? And in the middle of his swords is your head. He says to you, stay still while they cut out your guts, or I will cut off your head. There is a way to unlock his swords, but most everyone is too frightened to find it. So they suffer.

'Or – if they say, it would be better for me if you cut off my head, then the swordsman will pull the handle of just one sword, and all the swords will shut together, *snikk!* like camera-shutter, and cut off their head. But the surgeon will put it back on, so that they can feel the pain when they cut out their guts.'

'Come on, now,' said Luke, growing more and more sceptical. 'The surgeon can sew on a severed head?'

'It's the same thing as what-do-you-call-it? . . . black people's magic.'

'Voodoo?'

'That's right, the same as voodoo. You know about voodoo? It's the very same thing. He doesn't sew the head back on, he puts it back on, and *whoof*, it's just *on*.'

'So next time I lose a shirt-button, I don't have to sew it on, I just put it on, and *whoof*, it's just *on*.'

'You would need the herbs. You would need the right prayers,' said Mr Marek Senr., and he wasn't even smiling.

Luke sat silent for a moment. He wasn't at all sure how to deal with any of this Janek-the-Green mythology: but in spite of that, it had given him the first and only explanation of what had been happening in and around the Pearson household since Saturday. And he couldn't forget that sly, smiling face on Terence Pearson's wall. That mummer, that sly-faced man, all dressed up in leaves.

Unless he *wasn't* dressed up.

Unless the leaves were him and he was the leaves, and you couldn't tell where tree ended and man began.

Which of course was impossible. USDA-quality bullshit, as Norman Gorman would have put it.

Mr Marek Senr. said, almost off-handedly, 'Janek will always rape his son's spouse, always. This is the way he makes quite sure that he will have guts to feed on, in future times. His son's spouse will have children; and those children will invite him into the house, to feed on his own son; and so on, and so on. One generation after another. And of course he has many, many sons. Wherever people want fatter crops, whenever people want something-for-nothing, Janek-the-Green is always there.

'When times are bad – when there are storms, or floods, there will always be farmers who will pray that Janek-the-Green will come knocking. They don't think of the cost. Only later, in thirty-six years' time, do they think of the cost. Then they start to watch the weather. They pray that the weather will stay fine, and that Janek-the-Green will be travelling elsewhere in the world. They pray that he will stay away, and maybe forget to visit them.

'Almost every country in the world has such a story of the dumb-people. In England he is Jack-in-the-Green, yes? and they still remember him. They have hotels and what-do-you-call-them? pubs, all called The Green Man, after Janek-the-Green. In the Sudentenland they used to call him Jan Baumkopf – Jack Tree-Head. And how many countries have stories about babies being born under bushes? Almost every one. That is where they came from: Janek-the-Green.'

Luke took out his handkerchief, folded it, and dabbed his forehead. Although it was windy outside, the Mareks' living-room was stuffy and very oppressive, and the bison-grass vodka hadn't helped.

'Listen,' he said. 'This is myth, right? Mythology.'

'I don't understand.'

'All this about Janek-the-Green, it's fiction? An old folk-story?'

'No, no. It's a – what do you call it? Documentary? Fact?'

'Some guy is half a man and half a tree, and he eats people's guts, and he's fact?'

Mr Marek Senr. stared at Luke, slowly running his hand through his hair. 'You don't believe me?'

'Let's put it this way, Mr Marek. I don't *disbelieve* you, but it's hard to come to terms with what you're saying.'

'You came here looking for this.'

'Excuse me?'

Mr Marek Senr. paused to light another cigarette. 'You came here looking for this. You came here looking for somebody to say that you were not crazy. Didn't you? You knew all about Janek-the-Green already. You couldn't believe it. So what did you do? You came here to find somebody else who knew about it, so that you could say, "Ho-ho, Janek-the-Green, this is crazy talk".'

'All right,' Luke retorted, 'so you're saying they're real, the Green Traveller and all his mummers. They're legendary, people have been telling stories about them for hundreds and hundreds of years, but they're really real?'

'Real, that's right. Just like a band of gypsies. *Hark, hark, the dogs do bark, the beggars are coming to town!* Remember that? The beggars in that song were Janek-the-Green and his mummers. *Some in rags, some in tags, and some in velvet gown.*'

'Oh, come on now, Mr Marek. They're real and they live for ever?'

Mr Marek Senr. stared at him hard through the trailing cigarette smoke. 'You believe it as well as I do.'

Luke said nothing for a long time. Then he slowly nodded. 'Yes, Mr Marek. I guess I do. I just can't get my head round it, that's all. I just can't understand what they are.'

'Gypsies, beggars, mummers. Travelling people, that's all.'

'Travelling people who live for ever?'

'Well, sheriff, like I said, there are two, maybe three different stories about that. One story says that Janek and the dumb-people are the same as vampires; that they are dead already and cannot rest. I don't know about that. I never believed in vampires. In any case, the most common story says that they were granted immortality by the Church in Rome.'

'By the Pope? Why would the Pope want to do that?'

'For the same reason that most popes used to do anything: for money. The story says that Janek-the-Green left Bohemia because of the cholera, and went to Tuscany. He went knocking on doors there, too, and made many farmers very rich. Olives, lemons, wheat – after Janek-the-Green had visited their farms, they could grow anything! But once they were wealthy they soon began to think that they did not wish to pay for their wealth with their children's lives. They found the Green Traveller and pled with him to have mercy.'

'Lead, led. Plead, pled,' Luke put in.

Mr Marek Senr. frowned at him. 'They pled, that's right. They pled! They pled so much that, in the end, Janek told them that he would spare their children if they could find a way to make himself and his followers live for a thousand years.

'The farmers did not know how to make anyone live for a thousand years. Well, do you? So they went off to the Pope and said, "Pope, tell us how to make somebody live for a thousand years and we will give you gold and money and promises of gold." The Pope needed money badly for fighting holy wars. Pope Formosus it was – one hundred and eleventh Pope. In return for all of this money and gold and promises of gold, he secretly took out of the vaults of the Vatican the thirty pieces of silver which Judas Iscariot had been given to betray Jesus.'

'The actual thirty pieces of silver? They had them there?'

'For sure. They got holy relics all kinds. The sponge that was soaked full of vinegar and passed up to Christ on the cross. The ashes of John the Baptist. The real ashes! And every single one of those thirty pieces of silver.

'I'll tell you something: lots of people have wondered over the years why Judas would have betrayed Jesus for such little money. Scholars, historians, they've all said, why? But what they didn't know was that these coins were not ordinary silver coins. They were special – very, very special, and that was why Judas wanted them so bad.'

Mr Marek Senr. coughed, and coughed again, and then started a prolonged coughing fit that Luke thought was never going to end. At last, however, he took a mouthful of vodka, swilled it from cheek to cheek and then noisily swallowed it.

'These coins – these thirty silver coins – the legend is that they were struck hundreds of years BC, by Persian thieves. The thieves had taken the silver from the courtyard of the actual tabernacle which Moses built for the ark of the holy-of-holies. If you read in the Bible, it says God insisted that the pillars in the courtyard was all banded with silver, and the silver that these coins were struck from, this was one of the actual bands. Each coin was stamped with the words *Zivot v Smrti*, which means Life Within Death.

'You have to carry five of these coins, right? One for the Father, one for the Son, one for the Holy Spirit, one for Jesus, one for the Virgin Mary. If you do, you'll always be a single heartbeat behind everybody else. In time, I mean. A single heartbeat in time. That was how God was going to protect the ark of the holy-of-holies, by making sure that it was visible, yes? By making sure that people could see it. But they could never damage it or destroy it because it simply didn't exist in present time. It was always in the past.

'That's how the Green Traveller and the dumb-people have stayed alive for so long. They have never, ever caught up with us. It's the day that they should they die? Never – they haven't quite reached it.'

'So the farmers gave the coins to Janek and his mummers?'

'That's right, five coins each, in leather purses, one for each of them.'

'So the mummers never died?'

'That's quite right.'

'And the Green Traveller spared the farmers' children?'

'Oh, no, you're joking! Spared them? Not Janek! He killed them anyway. He was not a fool. The farmers couldn't *prove* to Janek that the coins would make the mummers immortal, not for many years anyway, and Janek needed guts. Even immortals have to eat, sheriff. They may live for ever, but they are not invulnerable to hunger, or pain, or any of the physical troubles which beset the rest of us.'

'So they can be killed?'

'Of course, if you damage them physically. You would have to rob them of their coins to do that, so that they would catch up with you in time. But it is the same thing as killing Dracula with a stake through his heart, or shooting a werewolf with a silver bullet. Not that I believe in Dracula or werewolves, you understand.'

'But you do believe in the Green Traveller?'

'Without question. And so must you. You have the proof, after all. You have the leaves.'

'The leaves?' asked Luke.

'Seven bags of leaves, that's what it said in the newspapers. Where do you think they came from?'

Luke stood up. 'I think I'm going to have to think about all of this.'

'Janek-the-Green,' said Mr Marek Senr., hoarsely. 'That's where they came from. And until you believe me, you're going to be sweeping up plenty more. Not to mention more dead people. He's *here*, sheriff, with the rest of the dumb-people; and he wants what he wants.'

'Which is what?'

'Who knows? He always wants something. He's a greedy fellow! But when you find out what he wants, you'll catch him, that's for sure.'

Luke shook Mr Marek Senr.'s hand. 'I want to thank you, sir. You've been very public-spirited, very helpful.'

Mr Marek Senr. lit another Gauloise. 'Suicidal, more like.'

Garth walked the length of the pigpens until he reached the

very end, which was pen No. 20, Capt. Black.

Although the perspex windows were so scratched and lacerated, he could distinguish at once the huge black shape of America's biggest hog, lying in the far corner with his bandaged head. He stood looking at him for a long, long time, and he didn't know what to feel about him: pride, or anger, or hopelessness.

The board of directors of the Spellman Institute had insisted that the xenografting programme must continue without delay, and they had already promoted Garth to take over Raoul's job as chief of surgical research. But Raoul's death had knocked all of the stuffing out of him, he really didn't care any more. Apart from which, he was deeply suspicious of Captain Black. The giant hog had remained reasonably docile after his first outburst, but there was something very disturbing about him – about the way he stayed in his pen, brooding, about the way he looked at people with those glittering, unfeeling eyes.

He was still standing outside the pen when Jenny came up, wearing a blue lab overall and jeans, her dark hair pinned up in tortoiseshell slides.

'How is he?' she asked. There was a well-chewed pencil in the top of her clipboard. Her fingernails were bitten, too.

'I don't know. He looks the same as usual. I was just debating on whether I ought to risk going in and talking to him.'

'On your own?' Jenny had a tiny dark mole on her left cheekbone, just below her eye. He wondered why he hadn't noticed it before. Maybe he hadn't really looked at her at all.

'We can't go forward until we start communicating with him, can we?'

Jenny gave a wry smile. 'Maybe we should put in a loudspeaker system. It'd be safer.'

Garth said, 'No . . . he has to see us. He has to associate

words with physical gestures. You stay right here. If he starts getting touchy, I'll get out of there pronto, and you slam the door.'

'Is this authorized?' asked Jenny, nervously.

'Jenny, I'm the new chief of xenografting procedure. I can authorize it myself. As to whether it's a good idea or not . . . well, we'll have to see what happens.'

'I don't know. I think we ought to have someone else here. Someone with a gun.'

Garth shook his head. 'He's been sitting there quiet as a kitten ever since. We spent more than eighteen million dollars on this hog. We have to make some kind of a start somewhere.'

Jenny said, 'Well, okay. Remember what O. Henry said. "The true adventurer goes forth aimless and uncalculating to meet and greet unknown fate." '

'Too right,' Garth agreed. He approached the door to Captain Black's pen, and unlocked it. It swung open outwards; and at once Garth smelled the ripe, strong, fetid stench of pig. The stench was powerful enough to stop him for a moment. It was much more powerful than it had ever been before, and when he glanced across at Captain Black's wallowing pool he realized why. The pool was still clean, which meant that Captain Black hadn't been anywhere near it.

All hogs wallow, especially in the hot weather, but Captain Black hadn't.

Garth stepped into the pen. His heart *beat* – suspended – *beat*. The afternoon light was filtering dimly through the window, outlining the captain's curved and black, bristly back. His ears had flopped forward, although Garth could still see his eyes, watching him intently as he came nearer and nearer. His snout looked dry, and there were cracks in the leathery black skin around his nostrils. Drool hung from his lower jaw, and glistened as he slowly turned his head.

'How're you doing, old buddy?' asked Garth. 'Head still feeling sore?'

Captain Black grunted and whuffled, and his trotters scraped on the concrete floor.

'You've been a bad pig, Captain Black,' said Garth. 'Maybe it wasn't your fault, but you've been a bad pig, all the same. You killed Raoul, and Raoul loved you, old buddy. He loved you so much he wouldn't even let anybody hurt you, even when he knew that he was dying. Greater love hath no animal researcher.'

Captain Black tossed his head irritably. His bandages were grubby, even though the veterinary team had replaced them late last night when he was drowsy with methohexitone. His head would heal completely within a few days: the bandages were mainly for protection. During the operation, they had shaved his bristles, peeled back his scalp in a single large flap, and cut a section out of his skull that was almost two inches square. This had enabled them to access all the major synapses which they had wanted to recode. When they had finished, they had literally glued the 'trapdoor' back into position with a strong surgical adhesive, sewn back the flap of skin, and applied standard non-stick antiseptic dressings.

Garth approached the captain even closer. His heart continued to beat slow and irregular, and he could almost imagine the unsteady line it would make on an electrocardiogram monitor. *Blip – blippp – bleepp – blip.* He could hear the captain breathing now, whining in and out, the breath sticking slightly in his nostrils. He could smell the fetid air that blew out of the captain's lungs. It smelled like compost, and vinegar, and death. *Something's gone wrong here,* he told himself. *Something's gone badly wrong. I expected a willing and co-operative infant. Instead, I've got myself a brooding sociopath.*

He had said nothing yet to Spellman's board of directors. They still believed that the brain-section which Nathan had brought them was legal and authorized and all above board.

For his own part, Garth knew that Nathan would never have knowingly given him a brain-section that had shown any indications of abnormality. He had been angry at Nathan for not telling him what he had done. But he didn't seriously believe that Captain Black's behaviour had been Nathan's fault. He and Raoul had taken animal behavioural research to the very limits: to the very edge of possibility, and a little way beyond, and Raoul had paid the ultimate price.

'Come on now, boy,' Garth said, soothingly. 'Everything's fine now. You and me are going to get along good.'

Captain Black backed away; almost as if he were frightened.

'Come on, now,' Garth coaxed him. 'You're nothing but a kid, right? You're nothing but a child. I won't hurt you, I promise. Come on, now. I know this isn't easy. But all you have to do is to show me that you understand. If I say to you, "Is your name George?" – all you have to do is nod your head.

'Do you think you can do that?'

Captain Black shuffled and grunted. Garth had no idea whether the hog understood him or not. But he had to start trying to establish some form of communication with him: otherwise nine years of laborious and astronomically-expensive research work would prove quite valueless; and Garth's own career would end less violently and just as emphatically as Raoul's.

Captain Black watched him with glistening black eyes and yellow, upcurved tusks. For the first time in his life, Garth felt genuinely afraid. He had seen Captain Black tearing out Raoul's crotch, in one huge jawful, and he had been terrified ever since then that Captain Black would do the same to him. It wasn't so much the pain, because Raoul couldn't have felt much pain. It was the spectacle of seeing yourself emasculated, right in front of your eyes, and knowing that you were probably dead already – and that, if you weren't, you very shortly would be.

Captain Black shuffled further and further back into his darkest corner.

'Come on, old buddy, let's talk about this, yes? We can be friends. You know that, don't you? Whatever happened, it wasn't your fault. We can still be friends.'

Jenny called, 'Are you okay, Dr Matthews?'

'Fine so far,' said Garth. 'He's acting like a bashful kid. Which is exactly the way I'd expect him to act.'

'I'll call for security if you want me to.'

'Unh-hunh. No need.'

He walked right up to Captain Black and held out his right hand, palm forward, in a gesture of calmness and conciliation. Captain Black had never smelled so sour before. Garth could hardly breathe in without retching. But he knew that he had to make contact. Just one contact, to show that Raoul hadn't died for nothing. A deliberate and responsive nod of the head, a scratch of his trotter, anything.

'Tell me your name, then,' Garth coaxed him. 'Is your name Philip?'

He shook his own head slowly from side to side. 'No . . . your name isn't Philip. How about Ken? Is your name Ken?' Again he shook his head, and pulled a glum, disappointed face. 'No, your name isn't Ken.'

Captain Black was starting to grow fidgety. His sides were heaving in and out, and his breath was blasting warm and fetid out of his snout. Garth sensed that he had only a few seconds left before Captain Black lost patience with him. Captain Black might have the brain of an innocent three-year-old child, but he had sufficient physical bulk to turn a child's tantrum into a rampaging nightmare.

'How about *George*, then?' Garth suggested. 'Is your name George?'

He nodded his head up and down, to show Captain Black that his name was George.

Captain Black twitched his face a little, but made no attempt to copy him.

'Come on, George,' said Garth. 'Your name is George and you used to live with your daddy and mommy and your two sisters, didn't you? One sister was called Emily and one sister was called Lisa.'

Captain Black stayed quite motionless for a moment: then, unexpectedly, he lowered his head. His silky black ears flopped down over his eyes, and Garth was unable to see his eyes.

'There was Emily and Lisa and you, right? And you lived on Vernon Drive?'

As soon as Nathan had told him where the brain-section had come from, Garth had bought all of the back issues of the *Cedar Rapids Gazette* relating to the Pearson murders, and read them three or four times over. He knew everything about little George Pearson that the media had printed; and he intended to talk to the Pearsons' neighbours and schoolteachers and friends (if they had any friends). To all intents and purposes, Captain Black was now George Pearson, or a hog-like version of him, and the more Garth could find out about him, the easier it would be to communicate.

'George,' said Garth, very gently, approaching Captain Black so closely that he could feel his breath. 'I know that you were frightened . . . I know that you were hurt. But everything's okay now. You're different, you're going to feel different. But you're still George, whatever. You're still your mommy's little boy.'

He took hold of Captain Black's ear, and began to massage it between his fingers. 'You and me, we've been through a whole lot together, haven't we? I bred you, I raised you, I fed you. Now you've got yourself a soul, too. A human soul. I want you and me to get on together, to *talk* to each other. One day I want you to understand who it was you killed when you killed

Raoul Lacouture, and understand what he did for you, and what you did to him, and pay him your respects.'

He kept on stroking Captain Black's ear, but tears had filled his eyes, tears for Raoul, and he thought to himself, I hate this fucking pig. I wish I had the authority or the nerve to put it down. But then Raoul would never forgive him, Raoul would shake his head at him from beyond the grave, and say, 'What did I die for, man, if you destroyed my life's work?' And Garth would have no answer to that.

When he was very much younger, he had believed that xenogenetics would eventually yield up the Theory of Everything – the key to God, the key to the Universe, the answer to why we were here. Instead, he had found that the more he discovered, the less he knew. Xenogenetics was wonderland and looking-glass land joined together, a world in which everything was backwards, and the wrong way round; and the more you found out, the less you understood.

Last birthday, Raoul had given him a copy of one of Tenniel's illustrations from *Alice*, in which the baby that Alice is holding slowly metamorphoses into a pig. Underneath, Raoul had written, 'Beware of pigs who ain't what they seem to be.' At the time, it had been intended as an affectionate joke. It had turned out to be a bitter prediction of Raoul's own death.

As a state-of-the-art experiment in xenogenetics, Captain Black had turned out true to form: enigmatic, unpredictable, inexplicable and dangerous. And like every other groundbreaking experiment that Garth and Raoul had done together, Captain Black had raised moral issues that were almost unanswerable.

Yet somebody would have done it one day; and it was probably better that it was done by them, properly equipped, properly supervised, under strict federal guidelines.

This wasn't the first time that Garth wished he had done something completely different with his life. He should have run Doc Matthews' Bar, on an island in Polynesia, with the tropical rain drumming on the roof and beautiful flat-featured island girls gliding between the tables. But he had chosen this, and done it well, and he felt morally obliged to see it through. And now he had Raoul Lacouture's work to finish, too. It was the least he could do.

Captain Black lifted his head, tugging his ear out of Garth's grip. He stared at Garth with cold ferocity, and bared his teeth. Garth could see himself reflected in Captain Black's eyes. He felt a slowly-rising sense of fear, but he braced himself and stayed where he was. You should never show an angry boar that you're frightened of it, that's what his father had said. The boar won't give a shit one way or the other, but at least nobody will be able to accuse you of being a coward.

Captain Black circled his head around, so that he draped his drool over his own jaws, and let out a noise like somebody dragging a sofa across an uncarpeted floor.

'George,' breathed Garth. 'Listen to me, George, you're back with friends now. Everything's going to be fine. I know you got hurt. I know you got scared. But everything's going to work out fine.'

Captain Black growled again, thickly, deep in his throat.

'You're still alive, George, in another body,' Garth told him. 'The boy you were is something different . . . something very different. But you're still alive. You can see your mom again, and your sister, too. You can see Emily.'

Captain Black's reaction to that was volcanic and instantaneous. He let out a chilling shriek of rage, and charged at Garth with his black trotters clashing on the concrete floor. Garth tried to twist out of the way, but the hog's massive shoulder collided with his hip and sent him hurtling across the pen and into the wall.

Jenny called out, 'Garth! Garth! Go for the door!'

Stunned and winded, Garth tried to climb to his feet, but

Captain Black came after him again, and crushed him violently against his metal feeding trough. Garth felt one of his ribs crack, and he gasped with pain. He reached for the edge of the trough, trying once again to get to his feet, but Captain Black's bristly flank bumped against him like the side of a barge bumping into a dock, and he had to snatch his arm quickly out of the way to stop his fingers from being mangled. As he did so, his forearm snagged on the metal lip at the side of the trough, and his muscle was sliced open all the way from his wrist to his elbow, so deep that the bone was exposed. To Garth's surprise, he hardly felt anything: but blood welled up and filled the cut immediately, and he had to press his arm tightly against his chest to stop it from spraying everywhere.

Captain Black must have scented blood at once, because he turned around at the far end of the pen, and stopped completely still, his huge head lifted, his dry nostrils flaring, his eyes shining bright.

Garth shakily managed to stand up, his arm still pressed against his chest, a widening stain of blood turning the front of his shirt from dry blue to wet maroon. Captain Black was fifteen feet away from him: the open door was just about the same, off to his right. Jenny was standing in the doorway with her arm outstretched, beckoning him to make a run for it.

'Garth! Come on, Garth! You can make it easily!'

Garth took one unsteady step, then shouted out 'Aaah!' and dropped onto his right knee. His ankle felt as if it had exploded. It was either broken or badly twisted, and he couldn't put any weight on it at all.

Captain Black stood silently watching him. Even before his operation he had looked as if he had human understanding, but now he had a calculating, malevolent expression in his eyes, as if he were genuinely debating with himself what mischief he could do.

Jenny took two or three steps into the pen, with the intention of helping Garth up, but Captain Black instantly grunted at her, and scraped his trotters on the floor with a sound like knives scraping on plates.

'Jenny – don't. Stay back,' Garth warned her. 'Press the alarm button.'

'I already did. Security should be here any second.'

Even if there was a fire, the alarm didn't sound inside the pigpen itself, in case the pigs were panicked. But there was a direct link to the main institute building, and it took only minutes for the security guards to drive out to the farm area. The trouble was, Captain Black was already starting to advance on Garth, his jaws dripping with saliva, and minutes might be minutes too many.

Garth shuffled towards the door, one agonizing shuffle at a time. His shirt was soaked and blood was dripping from his elbow onto the floor. He was beginning to feel faint. The inside of the pen seemed to be blurred and echoing, and the stench of hog was so strong that he thought that he was going to pass out.

Captain Black trotted through his wallowing pool, and then stood between Garth and the door, watching him still, not moving.

It occured to Garth that Captain Black was going to kill him. Not because he was an animal, but because he was something very much more than an animal. Captain Black was going to kill him because Captain Black was angry; and he wanted his revenge for whatever it was that had made him so angry.

'George,' said Garth, 'think what you're doing. If you kill me, George, there'll be nobody left to take care of you. They'll kill *you*, George. No doubt about it. They could forgive one man dying but they won't forgive two.'

Captain Black tossed his head, and let out a series of deepening growls.

'Are you trying to tell me something?' Garth asked him. The blood that soaked his shirt was stickily beginning to congeal, and he was shivering with shock. 'Come on, George, are you trying to tell me something?'

Captain Black tossed his head again. A nod? thought Garth, dizzily. Was he really trying to nod?

He heard the far doors of the pigpens opening, and the sound of men shouting and feet running. Security had made it, thank God. He was almost ready to drop to the floor.

'Come on, George, tell me what upset you,' he said. 'I said "mom". Did that upset you?'

Captain Black continued to stare at him without moving.

'I said "Emily". Did "Emily" upset you?'

There was a second's pause, then Captain Black threw back his head and literally *screamed.* A security guard had arrived in the doorway, holding up a Mossberg 12-gauge pump-action shotgun, but even he jumped back in fright. 'Holy Ker-ist, what's got into *him*?!'

Garth raised his left arm warningly. 'Jim – don't shoot. Not unless you really have to. Did you bring a stun gun with you?'

A second security guard called out, 'Dr Goodman's here with the metho.'

Garth dragged himself a little nearer the door. 'George,' he said, 'I don't know why "Emily" upsets you, but I don't want to see you upset. How would you like it if I brought Emily to see you? What would you think about that?'

Captain Black started to growl again. For a moment, Garth thought that he had badly miscalculated. Maybe Captain Black wasn't capable of understanding him at all. Maybe George Pearson had been so traumatized by his murder that he was no longer rational.

Garth was now so close to Captain Black that if the hog decided to charge, the stun gun wouldn't be able to stop him in time. Only the security guard with the pump-action shotgun had any chance of saving Garth from being killed or seriously injured – by blowing Captain Black's head off.

The security guard was hidden from Garth by Captain Black's huge bristly bulk, but he heard him working the pump-action.

Garth said, more softly this time, 'I'll bring Emily to see you . . . how about that? Would that make you feel better?'

For one long-drawn-out moment, Garth was convinced that Captain Black was going to charge at him again. But he had no doubt that Captain Black was thinking, *thinking*, working things out in his mind, weighing up the odds.

The guard stood with his shotgun levelled at Captain Black's head, unwavering, and Garth knew that it needed just one threatening move towards him and Captain Black would be history.

Jenny tried to step into the pen, behind the guard's back, but the second guard caught hold of her arm and said quietly, '*Wait.*'

Captain Black twitched his ears. Then, very carefully, he stepped backwards, three or four steps, making it quite clear that he wasn't going to attack Garth again. He turned around, crossing his pen to the opposite corner, and stood with his back to them. He couldn't have communicated his decision to let Garth alone any more clearly if he had actually been able to say it out loud.

'That's it,' said the security guard. 'Go in and get him!'

He stood between Captain Black and Garth with his shotgun raised, while Jenny and the second guard ducked into the pen and dragged Garth to his feet. Garth's ankle bent beneath him at a hideous angle, and he shouted out loud with pain. But even then, Captain Black stayed where he was, showing no further signs of aggression. Jenny and the guard managed between them to heave Garth out through the door, while the other man gradually backed away from Captain Black, his shotgun still raised, until he, too, had stepped out of the pen, and slammed the door behind him.

Garth lay on the floor, shivering and trembling, while Dr Goodman gave him first aid. Dr Goodman was one of the institute's finest veterinary surgeons, and even if he wasn't a pig or a cow or a sheep, Garth knew that he was in more than capable hands. He lay back while Dr Goodman bandaged up his forearm, his bald head shining in the filtered daylight, his glasses occasionally flashing a message of reassurance.

'You were real lucky you didn't sever an artery,' said Dr Goodman. 'Another quarter-inch and we could have been calling for the coroner.'

'I'll be okay,' Garth told him, in a hoarse voice. 'I think one of my ribs is busted, but I'm so damn sore I don't know which one.'

'Just lie still,' said Dr Goodman. 'I don't know what you were doing in Captain Black's pen in the first place. Trying to get yourself killed?'

'I communicated with him,' said Garth. 'I actually got him to understand me. I know I did.'

Dr Goodman glanced up at Jenny, and then back down at Garth. 'You communicated with him? How do you know that?'

'Because of his reaction. He didn't go berserk until I mentioned his sister's name. I said "Emily", and it was like dropping nitric acid on phosphorus. He flared up, just like that, no warning at all.'

'You said "Emily"?' asked Dr Goodman, puzzled. 'How did you know his sister's name was Emily?'

Even in his shocked state, Garth realized that he had made a ridiculous mistake. He had been so fired up about communicating with Captain Black that he had totally forgotten that he wasn't supposed to know the identity of the brain-section donor at all.

'Jesus –' he winced, 'go easy with that ankle.'

'Oh, I'm sorry,' said Dr Goodman. 'Listen – the paramedics are almost here.'

Dr Goodman didn't mention Captain Black again, but it was clear from the expression on his face that he wasn't going to let the subject drop. If Garth Matthews knew the identity of the brain-section donor, how come nobody else on the research team knew what it was – and was there a reason for it?

Inside his pen, Captain Black roamed and grunted and collided aimlessly with the walls. Garth knew what he was waiting for, and that he would never settle now until Garth had arranged it for him. Captain Black wanted to see Emily.

As he was wheeled out of the pigpens Garth saw Dr Goodman talking confidentially to Jenny, with his hand covering his mouth. He saw Jenny nodding, and nodding again.

Behind them, however, rearing up on his hind legs, he saw the massive bulk of Captain Black, dark as a thundercloud, mysterious, strange and terrible, a creature of his own making, for whom he bore both responsibility and ultimate blame.

Luke sat next to Iris Pearson's hospital bed for almost twenty minutes before she woke up. When she did, she surprised him by smiling at him wanly, and saying, 'Hallo, sheriff. You're the last person I expected to see.'

'Thought I'd come by to see how you were.'

'That's very kind of you. Do you mind if you pass me a glass of water? I get an awful dry throat in here.'

Luke poured her a fresh glass and passed it to her. She drank a little and then gave it back to him. She looked terrible. Her face was still puffy and bruised, and her left cheek was badly lacerated. Her left eye was so swollen that it was almost closed. Her head was heavily bandaged and so was her right hand.

All the same, she still had that sharp, angular, Katherine

Hepburn attractiveness; wounded but emotionally wiry. In the end, Luke thought, you wouldn't wear down a woman like Iris Pearson until you stripped her flesh down to the bone.

'I'm feeling better,' she said. 'Still sore, though, like Brer Rabbit, thrown into the bramble-patch.'

'I thought Brer Rabbit got out of that bramble-patch without a scratch.'

'Well, maybe he did. But I didn't, did I? And Mary, poor Mary. It should have been me, not her. They couldn't have wanted her, could they?'

Luke cleared his throat. 'The way I understand it, they don't mind who they go for.'

She blinked at him with those swollen eyes. 'You know who they are?'

'I have a suspicion. The trouble is, I have to think about it, real hard; and I have to talk to you. It's not what we would normally categorize as a logical suspicion.'

'In what way, sheriff?' she asked him. Her voice was as light as water.

'I've been asking questions of folks in the Czech community, and the folks in the Czech community have some kind of myth, or legend. It's all about mummers . . . people who used to pay a visit to farm communities in Europe back in medieval times. They may date even further back than that. They were supposed to have the power to make things flourish, to make your corn grow fat and your wheat grow tall.

'But in return, they wanted people's lives. Kind of a human sacrifice, I guess.'

Iris was silent, biting her lip. She was searching Luke's face for the reality of what he was saying. Was he saying it to make her feel better; or was he saying it to trick her?

'You remember the picture on Terry's wall, don't you?' he said. 'The man all dressed up like a bush?'

She swallowed, and nodded.

'In my opinion, that was a pretty close representation of one of these mummers . . . their leader, I suspect. He has a whole lot of aliases, but the Czech people call him Janek-the-Green.'

'The Green Traveller,' Iris whispered.

'Yes,' said Luke; and now at last he knew that he was getting somewhere. 'That was why Terry had all of those crop charts and all of those weather maps pinned on the wall. When the weather's bad, and the crop yields look like they're going to be poor, that's when Janek-the-Green comes travelling around, knocking on doors, seeing if any local farm folk want to do a deal with him.'

Iris shuddered, *shuddered*, but said nothing.

Luke reached across the bed and took hold of her hand. 'I have to know what happened that night, Iris.'

'I talked to two detectives already,' she told him.

'I know you did. I saw their report. But I think something happened that you're keeping to yourself.'

Her eyes darted quickly from side to side. 'Why do you say that?'

'Because the folk-story says that Janek is half a man and half a kind of living tree. That sounds impossible, right? That sounds ridiculous. But police officers cleared seven bags of European bay leaves out of your yard, immediately after you and your sister were attacked. Seven bags – but there are no bay trees of that type in your yard, or in the yard next door, or anywhere in the neighbourhood. In fact, the closest bay tree of that type we've been able to locate is in Noelridge Park, on Collins Avenue.'

He paused, and squeezed her hand, trying to show her that she could trust him. 'The folk-story also says that because Janek is half-man, half-tree, he needs human insides to survive. Your poor Mary had her insides taken. Another man, a Czech translator who was working on Terry's notepads for me

. . . well, it looks like *he* took out his own insides, rather than let Janek get to them.'

Luke watched Iris's reaction minutely; every flicker of her eyes, every nervous lick of her lips. Anybody who hadn't seen for themselves that the legend of Janek-the-Green was more than a legend wouldn't have believed him for a second. But he was sure now that Iris had witnessed far more than she had told John Husband's detectives. All she had said was, 'It was dark . . . somebody hit me with a branch. The next thing I knew, the police had arrived.'

Luke said, 'I've been thinking about this long and hard, Iris. It's impossible, and yet it's happening. The weather's unstable, the crop predictions are way down. First Terry kills George and Lisa; then Leos Ponican kills himself; then your Mary gets herself killed. You've been attacked with some kind of bush, and so has one of my deputies.'

'One of your deputies, too?' asked Iris, her eyes widening.

'He was investigating a traffic misdemeanour. He was attacked by a tall pale guy in a white raincoat, and then lashed in the face with a bush or a branch. The doctors say that it was the same-type bush or branch that gave you your injuries, too.'

'Is he all right?' asked Iris.

'Lost his eyesight, I'm sorry to say.'

Iris said nothing for a long, long time, but Luke could tell that she was thinking hard.

'Iris,' he said, 'these guys are still out on the loose. Whatever they did to you and your sister, they're going to do the same thing to somebody else. We have to find them, whether they're real or mythical or who knows what.'

Iris swallowed dryly. Then she said, 'I told her not to bring that broccoli into the house.'

'Who? Who brought the broccoli into the house?'

'Mary – Mary brought it in.' In a sudden near-hysterical rush, she said, 'I told her we couldn't have anything green, but she said it didn't matter. She brought broccoli and olives and all kinds of stuff, and she didn't take the labels off any of the cans that had green on.'

'Tell me what difference that makes,' said Luke.

She stared at him desperately. 'It's the only way to keep him out, that's what Terry always said. That, and keeping the children quiet.'

'Keeping the children quiet? Is that what Terry said? You didn't mention that before.'

'I didn't think that it meant –'

She stopped. Obviously, she couldn't bring herself to say the words 'killing them'.

'But Terry definitely said that if the Green Traveller was coming, the only way to keep him out was to keep the children quiet? Those actual words?'

Iris nodded.

'Would you testify to that in court? Remember – you wouldn't be obliged to. A wife doesn't have to give evidence against her own husband.'

She nodded again. 'After what he did to Lisa and little George –'

Luke gave her hand another squeeze. 'There's something else I want to talk to you about, Iris. I went to see Emily round at the Terpstras' house, the morning after you and Mary were attacked. This is a difficult thing to put into words, but she didn't act the way I would have expected her to act. She didn't seem particularly shocked, or upset. In fact, I'd go so far as to say that she didn't really care what had happened to you.'

'I can't explain that,' said Iris.

'It could have been trauma. I talked to the child psychologist we use for juvenile cases, and she said that some kids keep their distress buried for weeks, if not months. Emily's been a witness to things that would have driven most adults half-crazy.

'On the other hand, having talked to her myself, I personally don't think so.'

Iris turned her head away. Beside the bed stood a tall vase of pale orange gladioli, and six or seven Get Well cards. There was also a black-edged card that said In Sympathy For Your Bereavement.

Luke said, 'Tell me what happened, Iris. I have to know.'

Iris said nothing for nearly half a minute, but Luke knew when to wait and to hold his tongue. Outside the hospital window, the clouds were heavy and grey and featureless. It was a day without shadows; and it would probably bring rain.

'Will Emily get into trouble?' asked Iris, at long last.

'Of course not. She's only eleven.'

'They won't try to take her away from me?'

'Why should they? You're her natural mother, right?'

She hesitated a moment longer, and then she said, 'If there's nothing green in the house, he can't come in, even if he knocks all night and all day. But if there *is* something green, then he can, provided he's invited.'

'You're trying to tell me that Emily invited him?'

'Yes,' said Iris.

Luke let out a noisy breath. 'I guessed she might have. Those Czech people I was talking to, they told me that Janek's grandchildren are usually the ones who ask him in.'

'You think that –?'

'You told me yourself that a couple of months after you were married, Terry took you to see his father in Des Moines. Isn't that right? After that, you said that he was different, that he kept talking about the Bible, and bad blood, and said that you oughtn't to have children. Now, why do you think he would have done that, if his father hadn't told him something that made him afraid of the consequences of having children?'

'I don't know. I just don't know.'

'You said you met his father. Did you ever meet his mother?'

'No, I never did. She died just before Terry and I first met.'

'Any idea how?'

Iris shook her head. 'Terry never said.'

Luke sat back. 'The night that Mary died . . . why don't you tell me what happened, Iris? All of it.'

In a hushed, hesitant voice, her eyes lowered, Iris told Luke how she thought that she was dreaming. She told him about the man in the white raincoat, standing in the yard. She told him about the wind getting up, and the leaves blowing. She told him how she had come downstairs to find Emily standing in the corridor; and how Emily had said, '*He's holy. He's Daddy's father. I've invited him in.*'

She told him how she had tried to escape. She told him how she had seen the man in the white raincoat carrying Mary down the stairs, Mary already disembowelled and dying.

And how the thing that was half-bush and wholly vicious had attacked her.

Luke listened without saying a word. After she had finished, he looked at her narrowly, watching her eyes, watching the way she fidgeted with her bedsheet. There was still one unanswered question, and it was the most important question of all.

'I'm real glad you came out and told me all of that, Iris,' he said. 'It's been a considerable help, and I appreciate it. I know that it wasn't easy for you.'

Iris swallowed, nodded, said, 'That's okay, sheriff.'

'Only one thing . . .' said Luke. 'Why didn't you tell us any of this before?'

'I didn't want you to know that Emily let them in.'

'Is that all?'

'I didn't want to believe it myself. It was too strange. It was too horrible. I think about it over and over and I can't believe it but I have to, because it really happened.'

Luke stood up, and laid his hand on her shoulder. 'You

should try to believe it, Iris, because I believe it, too, even if the rest of the world thinks that we're three sandwiches short of a picnic. And let me tell you, I'm going to find these guys. I'm going to find this Green Traveller of yours; and he's going to pay the price for what he's done.'

He picked his hat up off the nightstand, and walked around the bed towards the door. At the very last moment, however, he stopped.

'Just one little thing that's been exercising my mind,' he told Iris. 'Why do you think they didn't kill you, too?'

Iris was already pale, but now she went paler still. Her lips were so bloodless that they were almost blue.

'What do you mean?' she whispered.

'The folk-story says that Janek-the-Green takes all the insides he can lay his hands on. Yet he didn't take yours.'

'No. I don't know why.'

'Iris . . . do you mind if I ask you a real personal question? In the folk-story, Janek-the-Green keeps on trying to perpetuate his line, if you understand what I mean . . . he keeps on fathering more and more descendants, so there will always be grandchildren to open the door for him . . . always be people for him to feed on.'

'Is that right?' asked Iris, her face still white.

'That's what the folk-story says, and we've seen for ourselves that a whole lot of the folk-story could be more than just story, haven't we? So the real personal question I have to ask you, Iris, is: that night when your sister Mary was killed, were you interfered with in any way? Was there any attempt at indecency, or rape?

'I might be stepping out of line here, Iris, but I have to consider the possibility that Janek-the-Green might have spared you because he hoped you were going to have his baby.'

Iris didn't answer, didn't move. But clear sparkling tears

began to run down her white, bruised cheeks, and drip onto the bedsheet. At the same time, clear sparkling raindrops pattered against the window. More bad weather on the way: more crops flattened. More farmers willing to take a chance on any offer of help that might come knocking at their door.

Nine

Nathan put down the phone. His father, who was drying up dishes in the kitchen, called, 'Was that the garage? About time they finished that goddamned respray.'

Nathan said, 'No,' and came back into the kitchen looking grim. 'There's been another accident with that hog at the Spellman Institute. Garth's been injured.'

'Oh, God. Is it serious?'

'Pretty bad. He has a lacerated arm, broken rib, broken ankle, lots of bruises. He's conscious, though: and apparently he's going to be okay.'

'But you think that it's your fault? Is that it?'

Nathan looked at his father. Nobody who met him for the first time would think that this bright-eyed, sprightly, white-haired 72-year-old had nearly died on the operating table, and had only been saved by a hair-raisingly risky transplant operation. The only giveaways were his pot-belly, the sallowness of his skin, and the puffiness around his eyes, the side-effects of steroids.

Moses Greene had looked God right in the face, close enough to feel His breath: and he hadn't been afraid of Him. All the same, he gave thanks every day that his first audience with the Almighty had been postponed for a while, and that he had been spared to share a few more years with Nathan and David. He was needed here. That was why God had spared him. Nathan was still so vulnerable. He still blamed himself for Susan and Aaron; and he was quite ready to blame himself for what had happened to Dr Lacouture, even though there was no pathological or psychological evidence at all that little George Pearson's brain-section had been the cause of Captain Black going berserk.

Nathan had told his father all about it yesterday evening, after he had talked with Garth at the Rag-Top Diner. His father had gripped his wrist and said, 'Stop beating your breast, Nathan. You did what you thought was right. You're not to blame for everything tragic that happens in this world, even if you want to be.'

He had added, 'These guys, these scientists, they know the risks of what they're trying to do. You can't make an omelette unless you break some eggs.'

Nathan hadn't felt particularly reassured. When he was younger, his father had always brought him up to feel that a man was responsible for the consequences of everything he did. Now his father had changed his mind? When you cheated death, did that mean that you had to cheat on your principles, too?

'Listen,' said Moses Greene, hanging up his dishcloth, 'I'm sorry for Garth. I know he's your friend. But until they come out and say that they have scientific proof that it was your fault that this hog went crazy, stop feeling so sorry for yourself. Everybody's innocent until somebody can prove that they're guilty.'

Nathan shrugged, and said, 'Okay,' although he still felt bad. He looked around the narrow kitchen to make sure that all the dishes were cleared away. He made a point of keeping the house as clean as Susan had always kept it, always polishing, always buying fresh flowers. David may have lost his mother, but that didn't mean that he had to grow up in a dump.

Nathan switched off the light and they went through to the living-room, where David was lying on the floor watching a repeat of *Weird Science* on the television. There was still half a bottle of red wine left, and Nathan poured a glass for each of them, and sat down in one of the big brown leather armchairs that he and Susan had inherited from his father. The wallpaper was brown, too, intertwining patterns like barley sugar twists; and there was a brownish framed print of Jerusalem over the fireplace.

'You want to go see Garth?' asked Moses. 'I'll take care of David for you.'

'What's the matter with Garth?' David piped up.

'There's been another accident. Captain Black went wild again, and broke one of Garth's ribs.'

'Dad –' David began, but Nathan lifted his hand to silence him.

'You don't have to tell me. It's not my fault. I know. I'm just beginning to wish that I'd never had anything to do with it.'

'That's what I call sensible,' said Moses. 'So what do you want to do? You want to go see Garth or not?'

'Yes, I would,' said Nathan. 'How about you, David? You want to stay with grandpa, or come to the hospital, too?'

'Hey, I'll come,' said David. 'I've seen this movie about a grillion times already.'

Moses reached out and laid his hand on top of Nathan's hand. 'Let me tell you something. You're a man, that's all. You're a good man, you've taken care of your son, you've taken care of me, too. You don't have to be anything more. Leave the miracles to the people who deal in miracles.'

'Sure,' said Nathan, and got up to go.

Terence Pearson sat with his big, angular head resting against the wall of his cell, his eyes half-slitted, trying to sleep, trying not to sleep.

Since his arrest, he felt as if almost every light inside of his soul had flickered and died for want of attention. Yet a single last light remained, and he was determined to keep it burning as long as he could, like the last foolish virgin shielding her guttering lamp against the early-morning wind.

Emily had escaped, and Emily had to die, and since nobody would ever think of killing Emily but him, he had to survive, he had to stay alive. Even if it took for ever.

It showed on Terence's face how much the killing of his children had taken out of him. His face had always looked pallid and waxy: now it looked more like a death mask. His eyes were expressionless with exhaustion; and his gingery hair was greasy and stuck to his scalp. His chin was stubbly, and he knew that he smelled of stale sweat.

He didn't want to sleep because he was terrified that Janek-the-Green was going to come looking for him. He didn't want to stay awake because he couldn't come to terms with what he had done; what he had been duty-bound to do. He cursed God. He cursed Janek-the-Green.

Most of all, he cursed his own clumsiness in letting Emily get away. Emily was the oldest of the Green Traveller's grandchildren, the wiliest, the most articulate, the one he feared most. He cursed his legs for not having run faster. He cursed the rain and the wind and the weather for holding him back.

Now Janek-the-Green and his mummers would be after him, they would be sniffing the air for the subtle perfume of his terror. Even the thought of what they would do to him was enough to make his stomach contract and the palms of his hands crawl with nervous centipedes.

He kept trying to remember everything that he had learned from his books and bibles – everything that he had written in his diaries, all those complicated rules and observances by which Janek-the-Green was obliged to live. Janek-the-Green had been created at a time when heaven and hell were considered to be real; when God was the supreme arbiter of all natural law, and Satan was the architect of all evil. Terence couldn't believe that Janek had spared him out of kindness, because Janek knew no kindness whatsoever, just as the weather knows no kindness, nor flood, nor dust storm.

He knew for sure that Janek-the-Green found it difficult or even impossible to enter a house without being asked. He was a traveller, after all; a homeless wanderer, dependent on the hospitality of anybody who was greedy or gullible enough to let him in. He knew that Janek's difficulty in gaining entrance was greatly increased if there was nothing green in the house, especially anything *living* and green, like plants.

He knew that Janek's ability to be able to confer fertility on a farmer's crops was connected with his physical intertwining with trees and bushes. Janek possessed a similar kind of occult influence as corn dollies and other rural fetishes – but he possessed it to a huge degree. It was 'crop magic', the same supernatural force of Nature that farmers had invoked since pre-biblical times, but it was hair-raisingly powerful crop magic.

But Terence also knew that what gave Janek-the-Green his power was also his greatest weakness. He had no viscera of his own, only roots and tendrils, and he urgently needed to feed on his own descendants to keep whatever was left of his humanity. Without a constant diet of living lights, he would gradually be overwhelmed by the plants that were tangled into his being, and become nothing more than a tree with a human soul entrapped in it.

Even the ancient Greeks had known of beings like Janek-the-Green: hamadryads, who were human deities whose lives were indissolubly intertwined with a particular tree, and who died when their tree died.

Terence had read in one of the oldest books that he had discovered that '*ye Gryne Travelere in returns for hyss favores demands to lye with ye spouse of him who askes hyss help*'. He knew that the Green Traveller was so potent that the wife invariably became pregnant, and bore him a son, and that after '*thryce douzaine years*', when the son itself had children, the Green Traveller would eventually return to the family and devour them all – except for his son's wife, whom he would make pregnant, so that the whole grisly procedure could continue.

The 16th-century descriptions of death at the hands of the Green Traveller were more horrifying than anything that Terence could have imagined possible. '*Ye cuttynge-outte of ye liver beings ye grateste of agonyes & its devouring in fulle syte of ye dyinge victim, whose cries cause ye visible inflatynge and deflatynge of ye lungs.*'

The Green Traveller and his entourage didn't usually find it difficult to gain access to the house where his son and his family lived – except when they had acquainted themselves, as Terence had, with all of the myths and all of the legends, and had taken all the necessary precautions to keep him out.

All the same, the children of one of Janek's sons would have Janek's blood running through their veins, and when he came knocking they would always be tempted to invite him in; even though they, too, would be food for Janek's hideous appetite.

And he was one of Janek's sons.

He remembered the evening that his father had told him all about it. Pacing, smoking, trying his damnedest to make it seem real. The television had been flickering in the background, *The Mary Tyler Moore Show.* For some inexplicable reason, the normality of what was showing on television had helped to convince Terence completely that everything his father was telling him was true.

His life had split apart that evening, like a horse-chestnut casing, to reveal itself for what it was. Extraordinary, unthinkable, and terrible – doomed from the very beginning. His father had condemned him before he was even conceived. Not only him, but his own grandchildren, too, because the line of Janek-the-Green existed only to feed Janek-the-Green, him and his entourage – father to son, child after child.

As the years had passed by, Terence had grown increasingly frantic. He had subscribed to news-cutting services from Sausalito to Sarasota, from San Antonio to Niagara-on-the-Lake – always searching for items about unexpected crop yields, or sudden switches in the weather, micro-climates and flash floods. He had learned Czech (badly) through a Berlitz course, so that he could read about ancient Bohemia and all of the plagues and the famines that had ravaged Eastern Europe in the Middle Ages.

The evidence, mostly, had been very fragile, as thin sometimes as the streaks of gasoline in a roadside puddle. But Terence had painstakingly checked it all; and written it all down. On 8 March 1982, a farm family had been found disembowelled just outside of Pocatello, Idaho; and an eyewitness had spoken of 'three or four strangers, seen around the house, one hooded, one wearing a white coat, carrying a bush or a tree for some reason; although sometimes the bush seemed to move by itself'.

Sometimes the bush seemed to move by itself. That was the kind of evidence that had frightened Terence more than anything else. *Sometimes the bush seemed to move by itself.*

On 3 September 1987, a mother in Hardshell, in Breathitt County, Kentucky, had been found disembowelled in her house, the victim of a 'maniacal attack', although her six-year-old daughter had escaped without a scratch. The local newspaper reported that 'the woman was found lying on a bed of dry leaves', although no further attempt had apparently been made to find out why; or what it meant; or where these leaves might have come from. The newspaper's editor had laconically remarked that 'Some people were drawing comparisons between this particular homicide and the notorious murders committed in Victorian England by Jack the Ripper'. He had obviously been trying to suggest that the victim was a woman of loose morality; but Terence had seen his remarks very differently.

From folk-tales and newspaper stories, he had traced Janek-the-Green's progress across Europe year by year, century by century, from the Russian steppes to the plains of Poland and the High Tatra of what was now the Czech Republic. Janek had been seen in Northern France in February 1837; and then, in February of 1838, terrified Londoners had reported seeing a creature called 'Spring-heeled Jack', an alarming figure that flew through the air in great leaps and bounds.

A girl called Jane Alsop, from Bearhind Lane, Bow, was seized and clawed by a violent stranger, who seriously lacerated her face and neck. She didn't see her assailant clearly, but she did tell magistrates that she saw a man wearing 'a kind of helmet and a tight-fitting white costume like an oilskin. His face was hideous, his eyes were great balls of fire. His hands had great claws, and he vomited blue and white flames.'

For thirty years, 'Spring-heeled Jack' was hunted by police and soldiers all over England. Still in London, he sprang out on Lucy Scales, the 18-year-old daughter of a Limehouse butcher, while she was walking along Green Dragon Alley. He lacerated her face and blinded her. On 31 August 1888, a prostitute called Mary Ann Nicholls was approached by a man in Buck's Row, in the East End of London. Her throat was slit and she was hideously mutilated. Exactly a week later, the same murderer killed 'Dark Annie' Chapman, leaving her rings and a few coins carefully arranged at her feet. She had been completely disembowelled.

Terence knew the names of the victims by heart. 'Long Liz' Stride; Kate Eddowes, the most terribly mutilated of all; and Mary Kelly. He also knew who Scotland Yard had been looking for: an 'Eastern European' man – either a Russian doctor called Michael Ostrog, or a Polish Jew called Kosmanski, or a strange Czech actor called Janek Gryzn.

He knew, too, who was hunting for him. His real father: the creature to whom his mother's husband had sold his very viscera, before he was even conceived, for the sake of a single year's harvest.

He supposed that he had heard of worse atrocities between father and son. In Bosnia, in the fighting that had followed the collapse of communism, captured Moslems had been forced by Serbs to castrate their own sons with their teeth. Real facts, real people, recorded by UN observers. But that didn't make Terence feel any less horrified by Janek-the-Green. Because Janek-the-Green came by invitation, not by force; and came to everyone who wanted him; and the sacrifices that Janek-the-Green demanded were freely given.

He remembered his father sobbing, smearing his face with tears. '*I didn't imagine – after all this time –*'

He remembered sobbing himself, when Emily was born; and knowing what he might have to do to her, one day. But he had always held out hope. He had always believed that he could protect his family – with guile, with careful study, by reading the Bible and watching the weather.

It hadn't worked out that way. Perhaps it had always been far beyond his capabilities. But Terence had tried his best; and in the end he hadn't blamed anybody else but himself, not really, not in his heart where it mattered.

He should never have had children, ever. He should have left the MidWest and gone to live abroad. But he had stayed, and married, and fathered three children, because he had been born in Iowa, and he had lived for most of his life in Iowa, and he had no intention of dying anywhere else, or of being set to rest anywhere else, either.

He had been able to find only a few isolated instances of children who had escaped from Janek's greed – either because they had panicked, when they realized what their grandfather really was; or because Janek had miscalculated, and the children hadn't been home. Two of the children had been confined to mental institutions (Randy Touraine, of Vinita, Oklahoma, in 1936; and Caroline Drumright, of Pretty Prairie, Kansas, in 1951). Three others had been convicted of assault or homicide: James Bignor, who was now serving a life sentence in the federal penitentiary in Marion for killing a woman in her apartment in Creve Coeur, St Louis, Missouri, in 1964, and half-eating her heart; Kerry Blackman, of Kewanee, Illinois, who in 1966 had strangled and disembowelled three children she was supposed to be babysitting, and then cut her own wrists; David Colombotti, who had taken a 16-year-old girl to a cabin in Baker, Montana, in 1971, tied her and gagged her and then cut her abdomen open while she was still alive and partially eaten her uterus in front of her.

There was no doubt in Terence's mind that Janek's terrible appetite was hereditary; and that almost every case of cannibalism that had been recorded in the United States had been committed by descendants of the Green Traveller. At least one member of the ill-starred Donner Party of 1846 had been a grandchild of Janek-the-Green. When the snowbound emigrants were eventually found in the high sierra by a party of rescuers, a German farmer named Lewis Keseberg had been discovered boiling a young boy's liver and lungs while untouched ox haunches lay nearby. Terence had discovered that Lewis Keseberg's grandfather had been visited by Janek-the-Green and his entourage after a long wet summer in Westphalia had blighted his potato crop. The records of a local schoolmaster showed that Lewis Keseberg's grandfather and Janek-the-Green made '*eine gottlose und schreckliche Ubereinstimmung*' – an unholy and terrible agreement.

The schoolmaster hadn't said exactly what the agreement was, but Terence had been able to make an intelligent guess. There was only one kind of deal that an anxious farmer would make with the Green Traveller – a bumper harvest, in return for his wife's body and his children's lives.

Lewis Keseberg had escaped the Green Traveller by emigrating to America, but he hadn't been able to escape his own inherited appetite.

Terence had dreamed of human flesh, too. When he was adolescent, he had suffered hideous sleeping fantasies of gorging himself on the pungent fruits of opened-up stomachs. Wetness, warmth, connective tissue, slippery mucus. He had woken up gasping, sweating, with a huge erection, convinced that his lips were smothered in blood and that his throat was bulging with human tripe. But there had always been something in Terence's character which had kept that dream tightly contained, a dream and no more than a dream. Maybe he had inherited more of his mother's Calvinistic self-control than Janek-the-Green's grisly self-indulgence.

Maybe genetics had at last led the Green Traveller's birthline astray; and a new mythology was about to unfold. A stranger mythology, even more frightening than anything that gone before.

Terence was half-asleep when Luke, three guards and Terence's court-appointed attorney Wendy Candelaria appeared outside his cell.

'Terry,' said Luke, as one of the guards punched the combination to unlock the door, 'I want to have a few friendly words with you, if you don't mind.'

Terence sat up on his bunk, his hair frowzy, blinking at the unexpected light. 'I do mind. I don't have to talk to you. Nothing says I have to talk to you.'

Wendy Candelaria was a short, businesslike woman with a heart-shaped Italianate face, waves of bouffant brunette hair, and a line in tailored suits with wide shoulders and tight skirts.

'Terence,' she said, 'this could possibly help you quite a lot in your defence.'

'You're *my* lawyer, aren't you? Tell Bigfoot to leave me alone.'

Luke smiled. 'I want to talk to you about the Green Traveller: Janek-the-Green.'

Terence vehemently shook his head. 'No way, sir. Absolutely no way.'

But Wendy Candelaria sat down beside him, and laid her hand gently on his shoulder. 'Terence . . . the sheriff has already spoken to your wife. Your wife has told him that quite a long time ago – several years ago, in fact, and on several occasions since – you said things that could be construed by a jury as proof of your eventual intention to kill your children. Apparently she's prepared to repeat her testimony in court, as a hostile witness. You know what that means, don't you? That means you can be tried for premeditated homicide, murder one. And *that* means two consecutive mandatory life sentences, at the very least, plus whatever they give you for killing Mr and Mrs Loftus. You'll never leave Fort Madison alive.'

Terence raised his eyes. They looked drugged and unfocused. 'Iris? You've been talking to Iris?'

'That's right,' said Luke. 'We've been talking about all

kinds of things. The crops, the weather, the colour green. We've been talking about keeping the children quiet.'

Terence shivered quickly, and sniffed.

'I want to talk to you, Terry. I want to know all about the Green Traveller. I want to know what your father said to you when you went to Des Moines to visit him, just after you and Iris were married. I want to know why you killed your children, Terry; and who killed your sister-in-law.'

Terence looked at Wendy Candelaria, and whispered hoarsely, 'Do I have to tell him?'

'No, you don't,' said Wendy Candelaria. 'You don't have to say anything at all. But let's you and me have a lawyer–client discussion about it, right now, and decide if it might be better for you to plea-bargain with some of this information that the sheriff wants you to give him.'

Terence rolled his eyes. 'I'm not worried about Sheriff Friend. I'm not worried about Sheriff Friend at all.'

'So what are you worried about, Terence?'

Terence nodded his head towards the wall. 'Them. Out there. That's who I'm scared of.'

Luke said, 'Them out there can't touch you when you're in here, Terry. You know that. The only jail that has better security than Linn County is the federal pen at Marion; and I guess you've heard what that's like.'

Wendy Candelaria turned around. 'Sheriff – with all due respect, do you mind if I speak to my client in private? We might be able to achieve something of mutual benefit here, if you could just butt out.'

Luke grinned. 'All right, Ms Candelaria. These gentlemen will keep an eye on you, just in case. Call me if and when.'

He went back to his office, and sat down at his desk. In front of him, he had drawn a roughly-pencilled chart, interconnecting the murders of Lisa and George Pearson with those of Abner and Dorothy Loftus, as well as the death of Leos Ponican, the killing of Mary van Bogan, and the attack on deputy Norman Gorman.

They all interconnected like a well-made jigsaw. Only one snag. They only interconnected like a well-made jigsaw if you could bring yourself to believe that wandering mummers from medieval folklore had mysteriously reared their heads in the modern-day Midwest.

Luke opened his desk drawer and looked inside. A blue folder stamped Iowa State Commission on Substance Abuse. A dog-eared copy of *Police Magazine*, which included a profile of 'Linn County, IA's New Sheriff'. On top of both of these, however, a pack of twelve raspberry pastries, one gone already.

He looked at them for a long time. He could even *smell* them, fruity and sugary and almondy. Then he closed the drawer again, and turned the key. Come on, Luke: eating between meals was betrayal. Sally-Ann was trying so hard to keep him trim. She spent so many hours in the kitchen, making him fat-free chicken casseroles, tasty fish-and-pepper bakes, salmon ceviche and baked potatoes filled with *fromage frais*.

He traced his pencil around and around his chart. What other reason could there be, for somebody to have attacked Iris Pearson and Mary van Bogan? Maybe some unknown relative of Abner and Dorothy Loftus had decided to take revenge on the Pearson family. He jotted a note to himself to check out that possibility. Yet why would that same unknown relative have gone after Leos Ponican, too? Nobody except he and Norman Gorman had known that Leos Ponican was translating Terence Pearson's notes. And why would they have attacked Norman Gorman?

He covered his eyes with his hand for a moment, to rest them. Then, in one smooth uninterrupted movement, he unlocked his drawer, lifted out a raspberry pastry and crammed it into his mouth, before his conscience had time to realize what he was doing.

He sat back, chewing and swallowing in pleasure and guilt. It was no use: he had a big frame, he needed regular food.

He was still chewing, however, when the fluorescent light panels in the ceiling of his office suddenly flickered and dimmed. He couldn't be sure, but he felt that the ambient temperature had abruptly dropped, too, as if somebody had opened up a window.

He pressed his desk-buzzer, but his secretary had already gone. He stood up, and walked around the office, while the lights buzzed and flickered, and the temperature dropped lower and lower.

He listened. He could just about hear the whispering of traffic, and the occasional blarping of an automobile horn.

But he was sure he heard another sound, too. The softest of *scurrying* noises, almost as if they had rats running through the service ducts. Only lighter than that, crisper than that.

His chewing slowed almost to a stop. He looked down at the butt-end of pastry in his hand, and dropped it into his waste basket.

He crossed his office and opened the door. Outside in the corridor, the fluorescent lights were as bright as normal.

He didn't know why he felt so uneasy. He just had a feeling that something had arrived here; something deeply unpleasant; something cold and emotionless. He just had a feeling that something seriously bad was about to happen.

He was closing his office door when the corridor lights began to flicker too – while the lights in his office popped back to normal. He whipped open the door again, and was just in time to see a ragged, diagonal shadow crossing the green-painted wall at the end of the corridor.

Frowning, he left his office and walked down the corridor as quickly as he could. He was sweating by the time he got there: although there was still a hint of frostiness in the air. Again, right at the very end of the next bend in the corridor, he glimpsed a fleeting shadow, only the merest tip of it, a shadow like the triangular corner of a torn gauze scarf.

'Hey!' he called. 'Wait up a second! Who is that?'

There was no answer. Heavily, he jogged his way down to the next turn in the corridor. This time, he saw the hem of a white coat vanishing around the corner. He heard the swiftest, sharpest rustling sound. Couldn't be rats.

'Wait up!' he called again. He rounded the next corner just as the emergency exit to the stairwell slammed shut. He hoicked his gun out of its holster, and pressed his back close to the wall.

At that moment, deputy Bulowski appeared, from the opposite direction, still polishing her glasses on her handkerchief. She stopped and blinked at him.

'Sheriff? What are you doing?'

Luke lifted his finger to his lips. 'Hush up. I think we may have ourselves an intruder.'

'You *saw* somebody?'

'Glimpsed them, that's all.'

Edna Bulowski put her glasses back on her nose and took out her revolver. Above her head, the lights dimmed and almost died away altogether, and she looked at Luke in bewilderment. 'Are we having a brown-out, or is somebody tampering with the power?'

Luke edged his way towards the emergency exit, until his fingers were touching the handle. 'Cover me,' he said.

Edna Bulowski raised her revolver in both hands, and

pulled back the hammer. Her aim wavered from one side of the door to the other.

'I said cover me, not kill me,' Luke said, sharply.

'Don't worry . . . I never miss a single shooting practice.'

Luke took a deep breath, and then kicked open the emergency exit, jumping out onto the concrete landing with his gun held up in front of him.

The landing, and the stairs leading up to it, were deserted. Luke cautiously leaned over the green metal railing, and peered downward into the stairwell. Nobody there. Every flight, all the way down to ground level, was deserted.

'Anybody there?' asked Edna Bulowski, in a nervous voice.

'Can't see anybody,' Luke replied. But all the same, he had that creepy-crawly instinctive feeling that somebody was here. The lights were still flickering and buzzing, the air was distinctly chilled, and he was sure that he could still hear a scratching, rustling, whispering sound, right on the very edge of his hearing.

He looked upward. He couldn't see anybody there, either. All the same, he decided to walk up a couple of flights to take a look.

'Stay out here on the landing,' he told Edna. 'If you hear or see anything suspicious, give me a shout.'

'You got it, sheriff.'

Luke wiped his forehead with the back of his hand. Then, carefully, he began to mount the concrete stairs, his back sliding against the wall, his gun lifted. His thick composition-soled shoes made a squealing noise on every tread, and he winced and listened every time. If somebody was running up the stairs ahead of him, he wanted to hear them.

He reached the second flight. He looked back at Edna Bulowski and gave her the finger-and-thumb circle, meaning 'okay so far'. Edna Bulowski was nervously jerking her .38 from left to right in a passable imitation of Jodie Foster in *The Silence of the Lambs.* She glanced up at him and nodded, although she obviously didn't trust herself to say anything. Luke watched her for a moment, and was so amused that he almost relaxed. He just prayed silently that she wouldn't be tempted to pull the trigger: a ricochet in an eight-storey concrete stairwell could be seriously unfunny.

He was wondering whether it was worth going up any further when he heard footsteps. He was sure that he heard footsteps. The soft, chuffing footsteps of somebody climbing upstairs. He listened and listened. For a moment he couldn't hear anything at all but the *zizz* – pokk! – *zizzing* of the faulty lights, but then he heard them again. They were definitely footsteps, and they were climbing up the stairs, less than two flights above him, or even closer.

He tried to signal to Edna Bulowski that he had heard something, but she was too busy peering down the stairwell and waving her revolver around. He decided that she was probably more of a danger to him than she was to any intruder, so he didn't bother to alert her. Instead, he climbed further up the stairs, as swiftly as he could, his gun held two-handed now, muzzle lowered, his big hips moving snakelike sideways, his belly undulating under his crumpled shirt.

He had taken only three or four steps up the next flight of stairs when he heard the footsteps sharply and clearly. Rustling, busy footsteps, like the footsteps of somebody wearing a cloak, and dragging it behind them up the stairs. They were so close that he stopped in mid-step, and almost lost his balance. He didn't have to strain his ears any longer. The footsteps were right beside him, right *next* to him, even – that's what they sounded like. He leaned back against the wall and shouted out nervously, 'Who's there? This is county property!

If you don't have authorization, you're trespassing!'

His voice echoed from landing to landing. '*– you're trespassing! – espassing!*' But again, silence. The fluorescent tubes dimmed even further; until the stairwell was almost totally dark, except for an occasional stroboscopic flicker of greyish, metallic light. He edged across to the stair-rail and looked down. He could hear somebody's feet shifting, he was sure of it. *And they were close – very close – so close that they should almost have been breathing down his shirt collar.*

Yet where? He looked up and he couldn't see them. He looked down and he couldn't see them. Luke slowly stepped backwards until he felt the reassuring coldness of the painted breezeblock wall against his shoulder.

'Deputy Boo-lowski!' he shouted.

'Yes, sir, sheriff?'

'Deputy Bulowski, you go back and rustle us up some reinforcements! I want flashlights, too, and generators, if they're required! Tell officer Chadima to tighten up the front gate security, and to get some men on the roof!'

'Yes, sir, sheriff.'

She hesitated. Luke called, 'What are you waiting for? Move it!'

'Sheriff . . . I just wanted to save you the possibility of being embarrassed.'

'Embarrassed?' he called back. 'Why should I be embarrassed?'

His echo called back, '*– mbarrassed? – rassed?*'

'Well, sir, to tell you the truth, I don't really think that there's anybody here.'

Luke waited a moment or two before answering, and all the time he was waiting, he was congratulating himself on how restrained he was. At last, he called, 'Deputy Bulowski, there is somebody here. They may have authority to be here, in which case I take full responsibility for initiating a security alert. But in my opinion, anybody who had authority to be here would have announced themselves by now, in case they were shot by you.'

He made sure that his voice rose at the end of the last sentence, so that if anybody *were* here, they would easily be able to hear him.

Edna Bulowski returned her revolver to its holster, said, 'Whatever,' and retreated through the emergency exit.

Luke was now alone in the stairwell. The lights were faltering so much that he could hardly see anything, except the occasional zigzag image of concrete steps. He waited and listened. He could hear all the noises of the building around him: the whining of elevators, the rattling of air-conditioning, even the evening traffic crossing the Third Avenue Bridge.

Perspiration slowly trickled down the back of his neck and into his shirt. He was convinced that there was somebody here. He could almost feel them breathing. In fact, if he really strained his ears, he was sure that he could actually hear them breathing. Dry, regular and persistent. In and out. Somebody who was waiting for him to give up. Somebody who was waiting for him to give up and go away.

In the darkness, he heard a quick, sharp shuffle. He threw himself back against the wall, and lifted his gun, but there was still nobody there.

He took one step up. He heard another quick shuffle, almost at the same time. He took another step, and then another, and each time there was an imitative step from somewhere else. He stopped, the imitation stopped. They were trying to confuse him into thinking that all he was hearing was the echo of his own footsteps.

Or maybe they weren't trying to confuse him at all. Maybe they were the echoes of his own footsteps. Maybe Edna Bulowski was right, and he was alone.

'Anybody here?' he shouted out.

'– *body here?*' his echo replied. '– *body here?*'

He took another two or three steps up, as quickly as he could. This time, he was convinced that he could hear somebody else's footsteps – not quite synchronized with his own.

'There's no way out!' he shouted.

'– *way out!*' shouted his echo.

'The building is sealed off, top and bottom! You can't get away! You'd be better off coming downstairs with your hands where I can see them!'

'– *see them!*'

Still, there was no response. He heard a door thrown open right at the top of the stairwell, and a voice call out, 'Sheriff? This is Pete Fruehling! The roof is secure!'

'Thanks, Pete!' said Luke. 'Will you take a look down the stairwell for me – see if you can see anybody else but me?'

'Sure thing, sheriff.'

Luke cautiously stepped across to the handrail and looked upward, into the flickering gloom. He could just make out officer Fruehling's face, a pale expressionistic oval, like Munch's painting of *The Scream*. He raised his hand, and officer Fruehling raised his hand in reply.

'Anything?' he shouted.

'– *thing?*'

'Not so far as I can make out.'

'Anybody else up there with you?'

'Dan Ollinger.'

'Okay, then. Tell Dan to stay on the roof. You come slowly down the stairs to me. Be careful, though . . . I've got this strong feeling that there's somebody hiding here.'

'Don't you worry none, sheriff. I've got my shotgun. Besides it's my boy's birthday tomorrow, and I ain't planning on missing that.'

'*Hush up!*' Luke told him. He was sure that he had just heard the sharp, chipping sound of shoes on concrete.

Even if he had, however, any further sounds were blotted out by the racketing, echoey noise of the downstairs doors being flung open, and a strange, distorted voice shouting out, 'All secure down here, sheriff!'

'Okay!' called Luke. 'Now let's hold the noise down!'

Slowly, methodically, Pete Fruehling came down the stairs from the roof, his back sliding against the wall, his pump-action shotgun raised high. Luke stayed where he was, listening for the slightest sound of anybody trying to get away – the chuff of a shoe-sole on concrete, the pneumatic squeaking of a door. But there was nothing at all, only Pete Fruehling's steadily-descending footsteps, and the long sliding whisper of his shirt-back against the painted wall.

Eventually he reached the flight of stairs where Luke was waiting. He lowered his shotgun and shook his head. 'If there was anybody here, sheriff, they're long gone.'

'Okay,' said Luke, and holstered his revolver. 'But there was somebody here, all right. I saw them with my own two eyes.'

'Maybe it was the light,' Fruehling suggested. His face was just as pale and blodgy in close-up as it had been three floors above him: he looked like an unfinished portrait. 'When it's flickering on and off like this, it can play some pretty weird tricks. Give some folks fits, even.'

'I saw somebody, Pete. No mistake about that.'

They began to descend the stairs together. Officer Fruehling said, 'Could have been a cleaner?'

'Too early yet.'

Officer Fruehling glanced upward. 'You want a floor-by-floor search?'

'Let's just keep an eye open. And watch the exits.'

'Sure thing, sheriff. No problem at all.'

Fruehling went out through the third-storey emergency exit, leaving Luke alone on the landing. Luke was about to carry on down when he heard a sharp, rustling echoing noise. He stopped, listened, looked up. The lights dimmed, stuttered, dimmed again. He waited.

For a long, long time, nothing happened, except that the lights flickered. Then – through that fitful, stroboscopic dimness, he saw something falling, a small shower of leaves, in a leisurely seesaw motion, backward and forward, until they softly scattered at his feet. He didn't need to pick one up and look at it to know what they were. Bay leaves, of the species *Laurus nobilis.*

Luke heaved out his gun and took one wide step to the stair-rail. The lights were so dim now that he could scarcely see anything at all. But wasn't that something hanging suspended from the underside of the fifth-floor landing? Not from the topside: the *underside.* A ragged, shadowy shape, like a huge clump of Spanish moss, or a huge clump of mistletoe; or any one of those parasitic bushes that hung from tree branches.

Luke strained his eyes. Was it moving, this bushy shape? Was it creeping across the underneath of the landing, towards the corner? Maybe it was nothing more than shadows. How could a bush be hanging suspended from the underside of the stairs?

Unless – and this sudden idea froze him to the core – unless this bushy shape wasn't a bush at all, but something else. Something alive. Something that had escaped detection as it climbed the stairs because it had been climbing up the *underside* of the staircase, in direct defiance of the laws of gravity.

'Who's that?' Luke yelled. 'You come down from there, right now!'

There was silence for a moment, and then a sharp, ratlike rush of movement. Luke thought he saw a two eyes glittering in the darkness, but he couldn't be sure. His heart was pumping the blood around his body as if it were bailing out of a rapidly-sinking barge; his whole system was flooded with adrenaline.

He could have fired a warning shot – and he knew plenty of officers who would have done. But he had been taught by cautious, old-fashioned instructors, who believed in identifying your target before you opened fire, and he had seen the wisdom of that training in action, more than once. He wasn't Dirty Harry: he was Sheriff Luke Friend.

All the same, he kept his gun raised high.

'Did you hear me?' he shouted. 'If there's anybody up there, you come climbing down from there, right this instant, you got me? That means *now*!'

'– *means now*,' said his echo. '– *means now*.'

The bushy shape seemed to hang swaying from the ceiling for a while. Then, without warning, the stairwell was totally blacked out. Luke couldn't see the bush moving, but he heard a bustling chaos that sounded like branches and yard-brushes clashing together. A noise that rushed *upwards*, up the stairs, but on the *underneath*.

The lights flickered on again, but only gloomily. The bushy shape had disappeared from the fifth-storey landing, and for a moment Luke thought that it had gone altogether. But then he glimpsed a dark, raggedy shadow underneath the steps that led up to the seventh-storey landing, and he was sure that he could see a burst of leaves.

Luke yelled, 'Fruehling! Bulowski!' He started to run back upstairs, even though he knew that he didn't stand a chance of catching up with whatever this bushy shape was. At the fifth-storey landing he stopped, gasping for breath, and lifted his gun yet again.

He thought he heard leaves whispering. He thought he heard something that sounded like a soft, seething voice. A thin prickly branch of shadow reached down towards the seventh-storey exit, and the door swung inward, sighing on its hydraulic hinges. Only a fraction, two or three inches, then a little further.

Luke said, '*Freeze*,' but he said it under his breath, so that nobody could have heard him, and he slowly lowered his gun.

He watched in growing bewilderment and complete helplessness as the bushy thing appeared to crawl or slide down from the ceiling, and over the architrave of the emergency exit door. It made a terrible scratching sound, and shivered as if it had been shaken by a sudden gust of chilly wind. The light was so poor that it was impossible for him to distinguish whether or not it had any kind of coherent shape, if it had arms or legs or a body; or if it was nothing but a shadow after all, an optical illusion, an epileptic reaction to flickering light.

But he was sure that the thing heaved itself over the architrave, and disappeared onto the ceiling of the corridor outside, and crawled or walked away, upside-down, with its feet on the ceiling.

The emergency door hissed shut. Luke holstered his gun. For the first time in his life, he felt completely isolated, and very afraid. Even at school, when he had been teased day after day for being so big and so fat, he hadn't felt as frightened as this. This was serious shit. Ever since he had found Leos Ponican's body, he had known that this case had edged over the borders of reality. Maybe he should have been convinced after he had interviewed Emily, round at the Terpstras' house; but he had managed to persuade himself that he hadn't really seen a penis rearing out of her mouth. It had just been her tongue, a trick of the light, an optical illusion, a mirage. Seeing something so disgusting had made him feel guilty, as if he was some kind of pederast, and he had made a deliberate effort to forget it.

He leaned back against the wall. It was reassuringly solid and cold. He could feel his heart pounding and his circulation flowing through his veins.

'Jesus,' he said to himself. 'Jesus.'

He was still leaning back against the wall when deputy Bulowski appeared. Her glasses reflected the flickering light. 'Sheriff? Are you okay?'

He stood up straight. 'I'm fine, Edna – fine. But tell Pete Fruehling I want this building searched. Floor by floor, room by room. Nobody out, nobody in. And nobody goes home until it's done.'

Deputy Bulowski said, 'Okay, sheriff, if that's what you want.' Her shift had only twenty minutes left to go, and she was due to attend an Elks Lodge meeting where her husband Stan was going to be installed as Exalted Ruler and she herself was going to be honoured as Sweetheart of the Year. She said nothing, even though Stan would go crazy. She knew for sure that Stan would go crazy. But she didn't even flinch. The Elks served; but the sheriff's department both served and protected.

Luke went down to the second-floor landing and pushed open the door. A few minutes before, the corridors had been empty. Now they were jostling with police officers and secretarial staff. John Husband appeared, looking tired and bristly, and took hold of Luke's arm. 'What's up, Luke? Heard you've got yourself a suspected intruder.'

'I don't know. The lights are on the fritz. Maybe somebody's here; maybe they're not.'

'Well, it happens. Last week, we had a guy come in with a cushion stuffed down the front of his pants, tried to make out he was Perry Mason. What makes this one so special?'

'This one's special,' said Luke, in a voice that went every which way.

John tugged him to a halt. 'Does this have anything to do with the Pearson killings?'

'I don't know, John. Possibly. It may.'

'In that case, don't you think I ought to know about it?'

'It's nothing, John. Just a suspicion.'

'Still, you could have shared it with me, couldn't you? In fact, that's why I came to see you: to talk about liaison. I mean, liaison's critical, Luke, you're always saying that yourself.'

'For sure, John. Liaison's critical, I agree.'

'Then how come you talked to Iris Pearson and didn't tell me? How come I had to find out from one of the nurses?'

'Iris Pearson didn't tell me anything that would have helped you.'

'How do you know, Luke? This is a homicide investigation, Luke. The smallest detail could be critical.'

'John, if I had anything useful to tell you, I'd tell you.'

John hesitated for a moment, looking at him narrowly, and then released his sleeve. 'I'm trusting you, Luke. I'm trusting you to keep me informed.'

Luke caught sight of Rick Smith from the *Gazette* and lifted his hand in acknowledgement. 'What possible motive could I have for holding anything back?' he asked John.

John looked at him narrowly. Luke could read the answer to that question in his eyes, almost as clearly as if he had said it out loud. *You're holding something back because you want all of the credit for solving this case.*

If only John could have read in his eyes what *he* was thinking. *I daren't tell you what I've found out about this case, because you'd think that I was totally out of my mind – and so would the county attorney.*

Rick Smith came up and said, 'What's going down here, sheriff?'

'Nothing serious, Rick. We have a suspected intruder in the

building, that's all. Probably unarmed, probably harmless. Just another dipstick in the engine of life.'

'Too bad about Norman,' said Rick, jotting a couple of shorthand notes and then clipping his ballpen back in his pocket.

'Yeah, too bad.'

Rick suddenly reached his hand up, close to Luke's face, and Luke instinctively backed away, as anybody would do, particularly if they were trained in self-defence.

'Woah, don't panic,' said Rick. 'You have something in your hair is all.'

He carefully picked a leaf out of Luke's hair, and held it up. It was a bay leaf, *Laurus nobilis*. 'Been seeing a whole lot of these lately,' he remarked.

'Time of the year,' said Luke, dismissively.

'I don't know,' Rick told him. 'Didn't you ever hear that nursery rhyme, "*The town and country's filled with bay . . . the bushy man is on his way*".'

Luke cleared his throat, and wiped his forehead with the back of his hand. He was breathless and sweaty after all that climbing up and down stairs. 'Where'd you hear that?' he asked.

John Husband was standing on the other side of the corridor talking to two of Lukes deputies, but he must have picked up the hint of stress in Luke's voice, because he turned and looked at him expectantly, as if he wanted to hear the answer, too.

'It's Czech,' said Rick. 'You ask any Czech kids, they'll sing it for you. They have all kinds of nursery rhymes about hedges.'

Luke stared at him for a very long time, but Rick neither blinked nor wavered.

'What's your particular interest in Czech nursery rhymes?' Luke asked him, at last.

'What's yours?'

'I don't follow you.'

'Well, correct me if I'm wrong, but I did hear that a certain well-known local sheriff is suddenly taking an usual interest in Czech folklore.'

'So what else do you know?'

'Not much, except that I know how difficult it must be for an officer of the law to persuade the county attorney that folkloric characters were responsible for homicide in the first degree.'

'Who have you been talking to?' Luke demanded.

Rick tightened his lips and pulled an imaginary zipper across them. 'Privileged sources, sheriff. But it's true, isn't it? You've been talking to more than one expert in Czech superstition. As a matter of fact, a friend of mine told me. He helps with the library at the Czech Museum.'

Luke said, 'I've been filling in some ethnic background, that's all. I always do that, no matter what the crime is. Cedar Rapids is a mixed community.'

'You mean that only half of them work for Rockwell, while the other half work for Quaker Oats?'

'You know what I mean.'

'Do you really think that there's some kind of occult element involved in these murders? Satanists? Devil-worshippers? Something worse?'

'No, absolutely not. And you can quote me on that.'

Rick slapped his notebook shut. 'That's a pity. Even "maybe" would have made a better headline than "absolutely not".'

Luke laid his hand on Rick's shoulder and squeezed it just hard enough to hurt. 'I'll buy you a drink, Rick,' he told him. John Husband saw that the interview was over, and turned back to his conversation.

Wendy Candelaria rapped on the door of Luke's office and swept briskly inside without waiting for him to ask her.

Luke was hunched over his desk, tiredly finishing off his paperwork. A styrofoam cup of coffee was positioned under his lamp, so that the steam curled out of it in a sinuous, illuminated S. A lozenge-shaped patch of sweat darkened the back of his shirt.

Wendy perched herself on the chair directly opposite his desk. Black nylon tights zizzed against black nylon tights. 'I'd like to come back tomorrow morning. Terence is pretty tired right now, and he wants some time to think; but the chances are that he's going to volunteer some information that will help you to identify the perpetrator of the Mary van Bogan homicide, plus a whole lot more about his own alleged homicides.'

The lights momentarily flickered, and they both looked around the office.

Luke said, 'Ignore it. It's only a temporary glitch. What I want to know is, will Terry tell us *why* he killed his children, as well as *how*?'

'Is *why* so important?'

'Why is critical.'

Wendy stared at him, hard-eyed. 'There's something going down here, isn't there? I can feel it.'

'What you see is what there is.'

'No . . . I've spent the whole of my working life in police headquarters and county jails, and I know when there's something going down. You're worried about something, and it's more than Terence Pearson.'

Luke tried to smile. 'You have a vivid imagination, Ms Candelaria.'

'I don't think so. If you want Terence to tell you *why*, I think I need to know *what*.'

'Wendy –' Luke warned her. 'Don't get yourself over-involved. You could disappear up your own instructions.'

Wendy blew him a pouting, well-lipsticked kiss. 'Thanks for the caution, sheriff. But I think I'll play it my own way. I'll see you tomorrow, when Terence has had some time to mull things over.'

The lights flickered again, and this time the office dimmed so much that Luke could barely see her: only her eyes glistening, only the shine of her lips, only the gleam of her nylon tights.

'Maybe you've fallen behind with your local taxes,' Wendy suggested, with a slanted smile.

'Maybe it's worse than that,' said Luke. 'Maybe it's the end of the world.'

The rain trailed across eastern Iowa that evening like the bedraggled dress of an abandoned bride; cold and cheerless and never-ending. It soaked the corn and it flooded the culverts and it made the Cedar River rise by two clear feet, so that it burst its banks in nine separate places and washed out corn and soya and potatoes. On the Wesley Hog Farm west of Linn Junction, fifteen gilts were drowned in their pen. Traffic on highway 380 north of Cedar Rapids was almost invisible in veils of spray, and a Volkswagen bus carrying eleven Cub Scouts was crushed by a liquid oxygen tanker at the intersection of 76th Avenue and Tissel Valley Road, killing two of them and seriously injuring three more.

It was one of those dark, wet, tragic evenings when Luke felt that the world was turning against him, when reality became almost too much to bear; but unreality was even worse. He sat at his desk until way after eleven o'clock, and officer Fruehlinger came in to report that the building was clean; that there was no sign of any intruder.

'You're sure of that? One hundred per cent sure?'

'I'm telling you, sheriff, we checked every broom closet; every washroom; every stationery cupboard; every god-damned place you could think of, and a few besides.'

Luke was holding one of the bay leaves in the palm of his hand. He looked down at it for a while, and then he closed his hand and crushed it. He smelled the strange aromatic fragrance of bay; and he was surprised that he had never noticed it before, how distinctive it was, how green-smelling and how strong.

'Okay, Pete, let's stand everybody down now. If anybody's stayed on late, they can go now, and take some extra time off later.'

'Thank you, sheriff. Oh – and sheriff?'

'What is it, Pete?'

Pete Fruehling dug into his shirt pocket and produced a dull-looking coin, which he placed on the edge of Luke's desk. Luke picked it up and examined it, turning it from side to side. On one side, there was a crude double-headed eagle; on the other, there was a leafy bush. Underneath the bush were embossed the words *Zivot v Smrti*, Life Within Death.

Thirty pieces of silver, Mr Marek Senr. had told him. And this had to be one of them. One of the coins that Judas had been paid, for betraying Jesus. One of the actual coins.

The Green Traveller had been here, and some of his followers had been here, even if they had gone. This ancient silver coin was the evidence.

Luke said, 'Where'd you find this?'

'Do you want me to search the building again?' Pete Fruehling asked him.

'I said, where'd you find this?'

'Third floor, outside of the women's washroom.'

'But you didn't see anybody?'

'I said, "third floor, outside of the women's washroom". '

'What?'

'No, sheriff, I didn't. But I don't mind going through the building again, if you want me to.'

'Pete, what the hell are you talking about? Will you talk sense?'

'I said, I don't mind going through the building again. It's not a problem.'

Luke stared at him. 'Are you and I on the same wavelength, or what?'

'I'm just saying that I don't have any objection to another search.'

'Pete –' said Luke. Then he opened his fist and looked down at the coin. He lifted his eyes and looked around him. The room seemed unusually gloomy; and Pete seemed to be oddly out of focus, not so much blurred as *dim*, like a man standing behind a net curtain. Luke felt he was here, and yet he felt as if he weren't. He had a disturbing sensation that the floor was moving under his feet, like the swimming sensation of jetlag.

He dropped the coin onto the desk. The instant he let it go, he experienced a sharp rushing feeling; and then the lights were bright again, and Pete was clear again, and the sound of telephones ringing and air-conditioning humming were just as sharp as they had been before.

'I beg your pardon?' said Pete.

'You beg my pardon for what?'

'You just said that you and I weren't on the same wavelength.'

'Oh, yes. Did I? Maybe I was thinking of something else.'

'Whatever you say, sheriff.'

After Fruehlinger had gone, Luke sat back in his chair and swung himself thoughtfully from side to side. He looked at the silver coin with every swing, but he didn't pick it up. Mr Marek Senr. had told him what it could do, and Luke believed him. It was evidence. Hard, empirical evidence. The only trouble was, it wasn't evidence that Janek-the-Green was a real-life flesh-and-blood serial killer. It was evidence that all of the folk-stories were true: that there *was* a Green Traveller who could survive from century to century, that there *were* mummers who carried swords and knives and leather pouches of holy silver.

He had experienced the effect of one of those pieces of silver for himself, and he believed it. He believed it. For a few moments, while he had held that coin tightly in his hand, he had lived not *now* but *then*, a heartbeat behind Pete Fruehling, a heartbeat behind the whole of Cedar Rapids, and Iowa, and even his own wife and daughter.

He knew now that he hadn't imagined the shadowy, bushy creature that he had glimpsed in the stairwell, wherever that creature might have escaped to. But he also knew that there was very little that he could do. Unless he could actually corner the Green Traveller, and discover who or what he actually was, the Green Traveller would stay more of a myth than a man – more of a frightening fairy-tale character than a real-life perpetrator.

Luke didn't enjoy being evasive with John Husband and the Cedar Rapids Police Department, but he remembered what had happened four or five years back to Sheriff Dennis Molloy, over in Black Hawk County. There had been a horrifying series of sexual attacks on women drivers by a naked man who – according to every woman he assaulted – had his head 'fixed on backwards'.

Misled by an over-imaginative young deputy, Sheriff Molloy had become convinced that he was hunting a reincarnated gunslinger from the 1880s, Jack Allison, who had been hanged in Waterloo on the last day of October 1886. Allison's neck had been so severly twisted around by the hangman's rope that the mortician had laid him in his coffin sideways, so that he would be looking upward.

Sheriff Molloy had arranged an exorcism; and had even flown in a Haitian voodoo doctor from Miami, all at the county's expense. The hitchiker had eventually been caught, however, and had been found to be wearing a latex Richard Nixon mask back-to-front, with holes cut in it for his eyes.

The last thing that Luke wanted to discover was that the Green Traveller was a part of a strange and complicated hoax, with himself as patsy. He wasn't yet ready to join Sheriff Molloy in the sunset home for gullible law officers.

He took a plastic forensic envelope out of his drawer and carefully nudged the silver coin into it with his ballpen. He sealed it, and held it up. Encased in plastic, the coin didn't seem to affect him. He laid it on the open palm of his hand. Still no effect. He squeezed it. Nothing.

Well, that was something. It seemed as if the spiritual magic of the ancient world could be quarantined, if you used a modern material. He dropped the coin into the breast pocket of his shirt, patted it, and waited for just a moment to make sure that it didn't nudge him back into time.

Maybe a slight sense of vertigo? No. No dimness, no trembles. Everything was fine. But he still respected the power and the antiquity of what he was carrying in his pocket.

He was a churchgoer. He knew the words of Matthew almost by heart. '*Then when Judas, who had betrayed Him, saw that He had been condemned, he felt remorse and returned the thirty pieces of silver to the chief priests and elders. And he threw the pieces of silver into the sanctuary and departed; and he went away and hanged himself. And the chief priests took the pieces of silver and said, "It is not lawful to put them into the temple treasury, since it is the price of blood."*

'*And they counselled together and with the money bought the Potter's Field as burial place for strangers. For this reason that field has been called the Field of Blood to this day.*'

Luke felt humble, sober and deeply scared. After all, he was carrying around with him one thirtieth of the price of the actual Field of Blood.

Luke took a last walk around the building, listening, looking around. On the first floor he came across big, rawboned Joe Kroliekewicz, the building-engineer, who was checking a panel of circuit-breakers.

'Tracked down the problem yet?' Luke asked him.

Joe shook his head. 'It's weird. It's like an irregular series of surges, but I don't know why it's acting up this way. I've been talking to the power company, but they're not showing any fluctuations at all.'

'Okay, Joe . . . do your best.'

He made his way along the corridor, his shoe-soles squeaking, to the cells. There he passed the time of night with the duty officer (who was standing to attention, still wreathed in cigarette smoke, a copy of *Penthouse* half-concealed behind his back). He walked on through to Terence Pearson's cell, and stood outside for a while, watching Terence lying on his bunk, staring at the ceiling with his eyes wide open.

'How are you doing, Terry?' he asked.

'Bored,' said Terence, without even looking at him.

'Ms Candelaria tells me you might be interested in being helpful.'

'I'm thinking about it. What was all that commotion just now?'

'Nothing for you to worry about. An intruder, that's all.'

Terence flicked his eyes towards him. 'An intruder?'

'Somebody who left some bay leaves scattered around the place. Anybody you know?'

Now Terence sat up, looking seriously worried. 'Somebody came in and left bay leaves around? You're kidding me, aren't you? You're just trying to get me worried.'

'I saw somebody with my own eyes, Terry. Some guy who looked like he was dressed in a bush.'

Terence came right up to the bars, and gripped them tight, and searched Luke's face for the slightest hint that he might be ribbing him.

'You're serious, aren't you?' he said, at last. 'You've seen him! You've seen the Green Traveller inside of this building! Jesus! I thought you said this place was safer than Marion!'

Luke said, 'We've searched the building roof to basement. There's nobody here.'

'You think he'd let you find him? The Green Traveller can do anything he wants, go anyplace he takes a mind to! Listen, sheriff, you have to get me out of here. I'm not staying here if the Green Traveller's here. No way, sheriff. Absolutely no way.'

'I'm afraid you don't have the choice,' Luke told him.

'For Christ's sake!' Terence screamed at him. 'It's not a question of choice! It's a question of life and death! Do you know what the Green Traveller does to people? Do you really have any idea?'

'Terry,' said Luke, 'stop screaming, will you? You're as safe in here as anywhere. If you can't get out of that cell, then how the hell do you think that anybody is going to be able to get in? Even the Green Traveller can't get through solid steel bars!'

Terence circled his cell, colliding with the wall, colliding with the bars. He clutched his elbows and shivered like a child pulled out of a swimming-pool. 'He's here, for Christ's sake! He's here! I knew the weather would bring him! I knew the crop yields would bring him! I've been feeling him coming for years and years, and now he's here, and I'm locked up in this fucking cell with no way of getting out and he's going to kill me, sheriff. Do you hear me? He's in the building! He is right here in this fucking building, and he's going to find me *and then he's going to kill me*!'

These last few words were uttered in such a panicky falsetto that Luke could scarcely understand them. Terence came up close to the bars, his head held in his hands, and all of the blood had drained out of his face, so that his skin looked as grey as papier-mâché.

He took a pinched, nasal breath; tried to sound reasonable. 'Sheriff, the reason I killed them – the reason I killed them, was *because of him*! Because of the Green Traveller, that's why! I killed them because there was no other possible way. No choice at all. And now he's here!'

'You want to make a full confession?' asked Luke.

'*I want you to let me out of here!*'

'If you want to make a full confession, you'll be moved from out of this cell. We'll take you along to the interview room, and you can make your confession there.'

'Interview room?' asked Terence, suspiciously.

'Sure . . . it's much more comfortable for all concerned.'

'It's secure?'

'Sure it's secure.'

Terence looked around, thoughtfully sucking his cheeks in. 'I don't know, I don't know. This isn't a trick, is it?'

'Why should I trick you?'

Terence looked at him for one needle-sharp moment, and then began to smile. 'This *is* a trick, isn't it? My lawyer's gone home, you think you can say what you like. You went to my room, didn't you? You saw that picture of the Green Traveller. You put two and two together and now you're trying to frighten a confession out of me. That would save you a whole lot of work, wouldn't it, and a good few hours in court? Well, you can't fool Terence Pearson like that – not me, sir, you'd better believe it.'

'Terry,' said Luke, as patiently as he could manage, 'I saw

it with my own eyes. It was just like a bush. It was hanging from the ceiling.'

Terence came so close that Luke could smell his breath – the fetid breath of somebody in deep emotional distress: somebody who hasn't been cleaning his teeth properly or drinking enough water.

'You can't fool me, sheriff. Wendy Candelaria told you that I was prepared to think about a plea . . . that set you thinking, didn't it? If he's got some information to make a plea with, then he must be guilty, or at least an accessory. So I'll go down to the cells and scare the living shit out of him, so that he tells me what he knows without even having to give him anything at all in return!'

Luke hefted up his gunbelt. 'You've got it wrong, Terry. I saw it on the ceiling.'

'You read that. You read that in my notebooks, that walking-on-the-ceiling stuff.'

'We haven't finished translating your notebooks yet. We sure haven't found out anything about walking on the ceiling.'

'You're shitting me, sheriff!' Terence retorted. He was almost screaming. 'You're shitting me! I don't believe a word you say!'

Luke unbuttoned his shirt pocket and took out one of the bay leaves that he had picked up from the stairwell. He held it up in front of Terence's nose and said, 'What's this, then?'

Terence shielded his eyes with his hand as if he were a vampire being threatened by a crucifix. 'Where'd you find that?' he said, sucking in his breath. 'You could have found that anyplace at all. You could of bought that from a foodstore.'

'I could've, for sure, but I didn't. I found it in the stairwell, just after Janek-the-Green had climbed out.'

Terence kept his hand raised. 'I don't believe you. No way.

Just take that thing away and leave me be.'

Luke dropped the bay leaf back into his pocket. 'Ms Candelaria said you'd be having a think tonight. A good long think. Make sure that you do.'

Terence didn't answer. He was still standing with his hand fearfully raised when Luke turned around and left the cell-block, saluting the duty officer goodnight, and walking out of the lobby and into the rainy night.

He walked across the parking lot, holding his hat brim tight to stop the wind from catching it. He didn't know what to make of Terence Pearson. Maybe his first instincts had been right, and Terence Pearson was nothing but an out-and-out loony. On the other hand, Terence Pearson believed in the Green Traveller, and so did Luke; and in a bizarre way that made them co-conspirators. Not in homicide, but in bearing witness to the strangest and most frightening phenomenon that Luke had ever come across, in all his years.

He climbed into his car, and buckled up his seatbelt. Through the rain-starred windshield, he thought he could see a tall man in a white raincoat standing on the sidewalk of the Third Avenue Bridge. He switched on the ignition, and then the wipers, but when the windshield cleared, the man had disappeared. Faders, his grandfather used to call them: people who seemed to be there, and then when you looked they weren't there. His grandfather used to say that they were the ghosts of settlers who had died while trying to cross the plains of eastern Iowa in the 1840s, people with names like McCleod and Murphy and Smith and Brozik. Dead folks.

Luke reached into the glovebox and took out his driving glasses. He only needed them when his eyes were tired. He thought that he had probably seen too much tonight: more than any man should see in a lifetime. He wanted to do nothing more than get home and crack open a beer.

A little more than twenty minutes later, Terence was still sitting on his bunk, his head resting back against the grey-painted wall, his mouth open, half-sleeping, half-listening.

It had been a quiet evening in the cells. A black woman had been brought in just after midnight, laughing and weeping in turns, and then singing '*Sweet'n'Lo . . . sweet chariot . . . comin' for to carry me home . . .*' over and over, until a desperate man's voice had screamed out, 'For Christ's sake! It's *swing low*, not Sweet'n'Lo!'

Somebody else, somebody who sounded very young, had started sobbing. But on the whole the cell-block had been mostly quiet, with nothing but shuffling, and snoring, and the occasional racketing cough.

Terence dozed with the back of his head against the wall and dreamed that he was running across a hurricane-blown wheatfield in pursuit of Emily. He was swinging his sickle, his largest sickle, the sickle he used for cutting back the bramble-bushes. He was exhilarated, frightened. He knew what he had to do. The wheat-stalks whipped against his legs, stinging him. The sky revolved around him like a great black revolving carousel, with thunder-grey horses.

'*Emily!*' he was screaming at her. '*Emily, stop!*'

But Emily didn't stop. She reached the edge of the field and disappeared down the embankment, and then she was gone.

Terence reached the top of the bank, just above the ditch, and looked wildly around, his breath surging in his lungs. The highway curved away for miles and miles, and this time there was no pick-up truck, there was nothing at all. He turned back, confused. Where was she? One instant she had been running a few feet in front of him; now she was nowhere to be seen.

'*Emily!*' he shouted. '*Emily, where are you?*'

He waited, listened. The wind buffeted his ears. The wheat rustled and whispered like the sea. A long, long time went by, during which he remained sitting on his bunk-bed with his head against the wall and his mouth open, softly snoring, his palate collapsed into his throat.

Then he heard laughing. The gentlest of laughing, not raucous at all. Little girl's laughter, mocking but sweet.

In his dream, he turned around and there was Emily. But when she slowly turned around, she didn't have Emily's face at all. She had the white masklike face of a mummer, highly varnished, with pierced black holes for eyes.

Shocked, breathless, Terence woke up. And when he woke up, there they all were. They were standing silently outside the bars of his cell, watching him, as if they had been watching him for hours.

There were six; and five of them were masked in white. Terence said, 'God. God Almighty.' He sounded like a mountain-climber, running out of oxygen. He was so stone-frightened that he emptied his bladder down the left leg of his pants, hot and urgent and humiliating.

Their sudden appearance was frightening enough as it was. But what made them even more terrifying was the fact that they weren't completely opaque. They looked like ghosts of themselves, visions of themselves, rather than real people. If Terence peered hard enough, he could see right *through* them, a faint image of the wall behind. The bulkhead lights in the corridor illuminated them brightly, yet when they crossed in front of it, it shone dimly through their shoulders and their heads.

For Terence, this was proof enough. They were real, all right. But they existed a heartbeat behind him. What he was seeing was them as they *had* been, a second ago, not them as they actually were. That was what made them immortal; that was what made them untouchable. If he seized them, if he struck them, he would be striking nothing more substantial than a memory.

Closest to the bars stood the tall man in the white, white raincoat, his face glazed in white enamel. His right hand held the bars gently and casually, like a man holding the rail on a subway train. His fingers were long and dry and perfectly manicured, although the nails of his index finger and middle finger were stained dark amber from smoking. Beside him – only a little further back – stood a thinner, taller man, in a curious bag-like costume quartered in black and red, and a small black cushionlike cap, with a silk tassel at each corner. This man carried a long black velvet bag over his shoulder, and out of the neck of the bag protruded the crucifix-like handles of several swords.

Half-hidden behind this taller man was a small, crouched figure in a thick tarry habit like a 14th-century monk, his face completely hidden by the darkness of his cowl. But one hand was drawn up to keep his habit tightly to his neck; and this hand was soft and lumpy-fingered, as if his flesh had decayed like cheese. Although his face was hidden, Terence could hear his breath whining thickly through half-clogged nostrils; and he could see him sway slightly, as if he were in constant pain.

Off to one side, brightly illuminated by the fluorescent corridor light, so that they appeared to be unnaturally real – even more real than reality itself – stood two young people, a boy and a girl. The boy was wearing a silky skintight costume of scarlet and yellow motley. The girl's curly blonde hair was entwined with dead flowers, daisies and thistles and common St John's wort. She was dressed in a thick ragged jacket of animal pelts, and coarse grey woollen leggings, and boots.

Every one of them carried a small leather pouch around the neck; and for Terence that was the final dread authentication that these were the Green Traveller's special and chosen mummers; because the pouches contained the pieces of silver with which Judas Iscariot had been paid to betray

Jesus; and it was these that ensured their immortality.

Terence said, 'You came, then.'

He knew all of their names. His father had told him, in a quick, frightened whisper, who every one of them was. The white-faced Witness: the one who stood and watched the sins of greed and betrayal, and recorded them, every one. The Swordsman, who was executioner and eviscerator, the cutter-out of guts. The Leper, who carried every disease that man was heir to, the unclean one. The twins Knife and Naked.

Only two were missing. The Doctor, who could restore decapitated heads, and magically bring back the dead. And the Green Traveller, Janek, the bearer of fruitfulness and fertility, the inheritor of all the ancient and mysterious forces of greenness and growth.

Terence stood up. 'What do you want?' he asked. His throat felt tightly constricted, as if he were choking on fishbones, or burrs.

The Witness said nothing. The Swordsman said nothing. They were mummers, they never spoke. But the girl Naked said, from behind her smooth white varnished mask, 'You took what wasn't yours. You took two lives which were not your lives to take.'

'I saved them, that's what I did,' said Terence.

'You condemned them to nothingness, that's all. You don't think that heaven would have them, do you? Heaven is closed to Janek's children. And they could never find acceptance in the Dark Domain, either.'

'They weren't Janek's, they were mine.'

'They were Janek's line,' said Naked. She had a light, awkward, slightly Eastern European accent, and her voice faded and surged, as if he were listening to a radio broadcast from a very distant city, at night, when all the radio frequencies were warbling and singing with loneliness and desperation. There seemed to be a pause, too, between the moment he spoke and the moment she answered, a time-lapse.

Terence knew why; and it made him even more frightened. These were the actual followers of Janek-the-Green, the silent immortals, those who possessed the thirty pieces of silver that Judas had taken to betray Christ.

Naked insisted, 'Your children were Janek's descendants; and so they were Janek's. Your father had already promised that Janek could have them; and you, too, and yours.'

'He had no right,' said Terence. He could almost hear his father's voice now, scrapy with panic. '... *I thought I was doing the right thing, Terry, as God is my witness. I really believed it. I didn't think of the consequences once ... didn't think that they would ever come to get you, not for real ...*'

The girl Naked came closer to the bars. Terence could see her eyes glittering through the eye-holes in her mask. He was terrified that she might be able to walk right through the bars and touch him. It was a totally irrational terror, but all the same he backed away. A troupe of mummers who could enter the county lock-up without encountering any opposition whatsoever could well be capable of walking through steel bars.

She smelled of something, this girl. She smelled of half-decayed animal furs and old pot-pourri and sex. Behind her, the boy Knife said nothing, but he was standing with one hand resting on his hip in a way that gave Terence the impression that he was smiling.

'A promise is a promise,' said Naked.

'I didn't make any promises,' Terence protested. 'My father made them, before I was even born. It wasn't me.'

'Nevertheless, a promise is a promise, and a consequence is a consequence. Whatever you take from Janek-the-Green you have to pay back. It might be three hundred acres of winter wheat. It might be corn; it might be babies. It might be a single hog-peanut. You have to pay back, my friend; and you know it.'

Terence didn't know what to say. He was so frightened that he could barely speak. He kept on swallowing and swallowing and his mouth kept flooding with warm saliva, as if he were just about to vomit.

With a thin scratching sound, the Witness trailed his fingernails lightly down the bars of Terence's cell. Again, there was a hair-raising time-lapse. The scratching sound started before the Witness even touched the bars, and it finished while he was still running his nails down the metal.

Then the Witness stepped away, as if he had heard enough, and now, quite swiftly, the Swordsman stepped forward, reaching behind his back and drawing his swords out of their scabbard. Each of them made a high ringing noise when he drew them out; a noise that set Terence's teeth on edge. There were five swords in all, and the Swordsman deftly interlocked them, so that they made a criss-cross pentangle. He held them up in the air, so that Terence could see them shining. Terence knew why they were criss-crossed in this way. The victim's head would be inserted into the middle of the pentangle, and then the swordsman would draw them closed, like a camera shutter.

Terence raised both hands with his fingers interlocked in the same way as the swords. 'Stay away!' he insisted. 'You can't come in here! You're not invited – you have to be invited! And, besides, there's nothing green in here! Nothing!'

Naked said, 'We don't need an invitation, my friend. Janek is your father and your father orders you to let us in. Besides, there *is* something green in there.'

Terence kept his fingers lifted. 'There's nothing . . . I made sure.'

'We can all make a mistake,' said Naked.

Terence, horrified, glanced quickly around his cell. There

was nothing green in it: he was positive. He had checked and re-checked every day; and he always searched around obsessively before he went to sleep. He never ate green vegetables, he never read anything but paperbacks with the covers stripped off, in case there was a speck of green in the colour printing. For the same reason, he never accepted any wrapped candy. What could be green in here? What could be green?

A light draft blew through Terence's cell. As it did so, the bay leaf that Luke had intended to drop into his pocket came sliding out from beneath the bunk. It flipped over, hesitated, and flipped over again.

'Green,' said Naked. She pronounced it 'grin'.

The Witness touched the cell's combination lock with the fingertips of his right hand. In his left hand, he was cracking dice. He tossed them up, caught them, cracked them, tossed them again. He never took his eyes away from Terence's face. Terence was beginning to tremble. He kept his fingers raised to ward the Witness off, but he knew that it was no use any more. The Witness would toss the dice, and solve the combination.

The Swordsman waited patiently. The Leper stayed in the background, breathing as harshly as a man on his deathbed. Knife splayed out his fingers and scrutinized his nails; Naked laid a hand on his shoulder, and slowly massaged it.

'You can't do this,' said Terence. 'Jesus – you're not even *real*, you're a myth! You're a goddamned – fairy story!'

'Do you want to find out how real we are?' asked Naked. 'We are much more real than you.'

'I can shut my eyes and I can open them again and you'll be *gone*!' Terence screamed at her.

'I don't think so. Ask the Swordsman. Ask if you can test his swords, how sharp they are. Have you ever been cut by a myth? Has a fairy story ever drawn blood?'

The Witness threw seven. The dice seemed to jump and sparkle in the air. At the same time, Terence heard the first lever in the lock click free. The Witness caught the dice, and cupped them in his hand, and breathed on them; and then he tossed them again, and this time he threw nine.

'Four numbers, four throws,' said Naked; and came closer still.

The second lever in the lock released itself.

Terence gradually retreated, until his back was pressed against the wall of his cell. He kept his fingers raised in that same criss-cross pattern, and his eyes were wide with terror. '*Ab insidiis diaboli, libera nos Domine!*' he screamed.

'What's this?' asked Naked. 'Church talk? An exorcism? We were blessed by the Holy Father himself, my darling. Church talk is meat and drink to us.'

'*Ut Ecclesiam tuam secura tibi facias libertate seruire, te rogamos, audi nos; Ut inimicos sanctae Ecclesiae humiliare digneris, te rogamus, audi nos. Per unigenitum Filium suum Dominum nostrium Iesum Christum, qui cum eo uiuit et regnat in unitate Spiritus sancti Deus, per omnia saecula saeculorum.*'

'You have a way with languages, don't you?' said Naked; and the third lever clicked.

The Swordsman took a single step forward; with his shining pattern of swords lifted in the air like a religious talisman. The boy Knife let out a high-pitched laugh, as if he couldn't wait to see what would happen next. Terence stopped praying and appealing to God; but he still kept his fingers raised in that same criss-cross device, and he still kept his back to the wall.

'I don't believe in you,' he insisted.

'You believe in hell, don't you?' Naked asked him. 'You believe in demons? *Everye degree of devylls of lether and spirytis on cordis.*' She was taunting him now; taunting his research; taunting his obsessive studies of weather and crop-fertility. In the end, he was Janek's son, and Janek would claim him, no matter how long it took; no matter if the mummers had to bide their time for years.

The Witness threw four.

'*Four*,' breathed Naked; and the lever clicked open.

Terence dropped to his knees. The cell door swung ajar on thinly-oiled hinges, and the Witness stepped inside, followed by the Swordsman and the boy called Knife.

'Will you die here?' asked Naked. But Terence said nothing. All he could think of was Emily, rushing across the wheatfield, and the rain lashing coldly against his cheeks.

The Witness touched him, and his touch was truly hellish: cold and fierce, like a dead body that had been galvanized into life with thousands of volts of electricity. His touch made Terence's shoulder muscles contract and twitch and crawl with half-realized agony.

'Time for the reckoning now, I think,' said Naked.

The Swordsman held his array of swords over Terence's head as if he were going to crown him king.

Terence said, 'You're cowards, all of you. You hide your faces.'

But Naked retorted, '*Les visiteurs silencieuses se cachent quelquefois sous des formes bestiales, on se couvrent le visage d'un masque pour demeurer inconnus.*'

Terence felt a terrible sense of inevitability. He breathed in and out through his nose in short, shallow breaths. He had learned enough about Janek-the-Green to know where he had come from, he and his fellow mummers. They had first appeared in early Bohemia, in the 9th century, after the baptism of Prince Borijov. So they had come on Christianity's coat-tails. They were God-mockers. They came from the days of miracle plays and plague pits; from forbidden sabbats and fertility rites; from the dark Bohemian history of Podebrad and Ladislas; and terrible wanderings around Europe – wanderings which had at last brought them here, to the farmlands of the Middle West, where Christianity and Czech superstition still survived, almost uniquely, in the latter half of the 20th century – along with a desperate need for what Janek-the-Green had to offer.

Fertility; for nothing more than the price of a future life.

Prosperity; for the promise of an unnamed, unknown child that was still unborn.

The Swordsman stepped up to Terence, and slowly lowered his criss-cross pattern of swords around his neck.

Naked said, 'Janek wants you, my darling. You know there's no escape.'

Ten

Lily sat up. 'I'd better go. We have an action meeting tomorrow morning.'

'You're not planning another of your riots, are you?' asked Bryan. He was lying back on the pillows, luxuriously blowing cigar smoke at the ceiling.

It was 12.27 in the morning. Bryan had returned to the Collins Plaza just after eight o'clock in the evening, and had found Lily waiting for him in his suite. He hadn't been altogether pleased: he had spent two and a half hours that afternoon arguing with USDA officials over proposed cuts in agriculture stabilization and conservation services; and then another two hours arguing with hog and cattle farmers over Zapf-Cady.

He had been hoarse and tired, and not in the mood for bondage games.

There were less than two weeks to go to the final vote, and many hog farmers were beginning to panic. When Zapf-Cady was first mooted, it had generally been regarded as a midly eccentric piece of political correctness. But it had won such huge popular support that Bryan was no longer trying to work out whether he would win at all, but how large his majority would be.

Perhaps Zapf-Cady's greatest asset was that it was so hard for politicians to say that they didn't support it. If you came out in opposition to Zapf-Cady, it was tantamount to saying that you were in favour of vivisection and fur-farming and cruelty to animals; and that you didn't believe that animals had souls.

Lily walked naked across to the mirror, her large breasts swinging as she walked. Her thighs and her buttocks were still imprinted with Bryan's red fingermarks, and her wrists were encircled with crimson bruises. She stood in front of the mirror, primping her hair, licking her lips and pouting.

'Do you think I'm looking tired?' she asked Bryan. 'I think I look tired.'

'You look great. I don't know how you do it.'

'No . . . I think I'm looking tired. I'll be glad when this is all over.'

Bryan rolled over. His penis hung across his hairy thigh like a dark, exotic fruit. 'What's this action meeting all about, then?' he wanted to know. 'Nothing violent, I hope? We want to keep the media behind us.'

'Haven't you been reading your papers?' asked Lily. She went across to the gilt-decorated bureau and picked up a copy of the *Cedar Rapids Gazette.* The headline read SUPER HOG INJURES 2ND SCIENTIST.

Bryan picked a shred of tobacco leaf from his lip. 'I read that. So what? They'll have to close down the Spellman Institute in any case, when Zapf-Cady goes through.'

'But have you read what they've done to this poor animal? They've actually implanted human brain synapses, so it thinks that it's human.'

'That's what they're trying to suggest,' said Bryan. 'But I was talking to a couple of agricultural scientists yesterday and they don't seriously believe that it's possible. What you're getting is a hog with a brain that you can use for doing physical repairs to a damaged human brain – but a hog that thinks it's a human? I don't think so.'

Lily sat down on the bed next to him. Her nipple brushed his arm. 'You do love me, don't you?' she asked him.

He looked back at her, his eyes tightly focused. When he looked at her like that, she always thought that he gave himself away. It was supposed to be a look of unwavering sincerity; a look that said 'How dare you doubt me, even for a split second?' But to Lily it was a look that had no depth. It was like a mirrored vizor coming down over Bryan's face, so that all she could see was herself.

Bryan wasn't as hard as he pretended to be. He had the most unexpected softnesses, like his love of opera and his fondness for dogs and his endless grieving for his dead mother, which like Alph the sacred river ran through caverns measureless to man, down to a sunless sea. But he had overlayered his softnesses with vanity and more vanity, and then the greed for money, and the hunger for power. He could be inspirational. He was so handsome that he *should* have been evangelical, politically if not morally. But he protected himself with chitinous layers of cheapness and bullying and a highly-detailed selfishness that bordered on the psychotic.

He said, 'Of course I love you,' but then he was too selfish to admit that he didn't.

'You seem so distracted,' she said. She tried to stroke his hair, but he twisted his head away.

'I'm tired is all. It's been a difficult day. Nothing but hog farmers and agricultural environmentalists and accountants. Accountants, Jesus! Did you know that five thousand employees of the Department of Agriculture are accountants? The Department of Agriculture has so many fucking accountants, they do accounting for the General Accounting Office!'

'Bryan . . .' said Lily. 'I'm not an innocent. I can sense these things, much more than most.'

'What *things*?'

'I can sense when somebody's starting to question a relationship, like you are. I can sense when somebody doesn't really want to own me.'

'You want to be *owned*? A woman like you?'

'Of course. I always told you that, right from the very beginning.'

'For Christ's sake, Lily. I love you, but I'm going through a crisis. Give me a break. I want you, I need you. You're very special. You're *essential*. What else do I have to say?'

She lay down close to him. She touched his face. With the tip of her middle finger, she outlined his perfect forehead, his perfect nose. She tugged at his inky-coloured hair. 'I need you,' she breathed. 'I need you for everything.'

He blew smoke out of the side of his mouth, away from her. 'Lily . . . I know you need me. I need you, too. But right now, I'm really involved. I'm tired, too. My energy level's right down.'

She stayed close beside him, very close. Her fingertip caressed the grainy black stubble on his chin, his sharp triangular Adam's apple, the flat gym-trained muscles of his chest. It traced its way downward, to his navel, where she dipped it into his sweat, and then sucked it, as if she were sucking nectar.

He stretched across her and perched his cigar in the crystal ashtray. He wouldn't crush it out: it was too expensive and it was only half-smoked. He gave her a perfunctory kiss on the shoulder, and said, 'Listen, you're a beautiful girl. You have brains, guts, whatever it takes. You and I, we've worked good together, for the best of causes. But this is not going to last for ever. It can't. You have your whole life ahead of you, doing whatever you have to do; and I have other fish to fry.'

He kissed her again. 'For starters, I want to be President.'

Lily reached down between his legs and massaged him. Her massage was strong and relentless, and right on the very edge of being painful. She squeezed each testicle between her fingers until Bryan reacted with a quick, high intake of breath; and then she pulled and kneaded at his penis, until it began to rise.

'You couldn't live without me, could you?' she whispered. 'Come on, admit it.'

But all Bryan could say was, 'Lily – for Christ's sake, Lily, give me a – *second's* – break.'

Immediately, she let go of him, and swung her legs over the side of the bed. 'I'm sorry. I just thought that we were closer than that.'

'Sweetheart –' said Bryan. 'I don't know how close you imagined we were. Well, we're close, for sure. Of course we've gotten close. But once we've won that vote –'

Lily turned her head around and stared at him sharply. 'You do *believe* in this, don't you?'

He stared back at her, just as sharp. 'Of course I believe in it. Do you think I would've put in all of those months of hard work, if I didn't believe in it? Do you think I would've risked my career? Do you know how controversial this proposition is, especially for a senator who comes from hog-rearing country? It could've been suicide. But I believed in it; and I worked at it; and now it's going to happen.'

'And now you're going to leave me,' said Lily.

'Did I say anything about leaving?'

'No . . . but you're trying to prepare me for it, aren't you?'

'Lily –'

She leaned over him so closely that their noses were almost touching. 'You don't even know who I am, do you?' she breathed.

He didn't answer. He didn't actually know what she was

talking about. Of course he knew who she was. In the first week they had become involved with each other, Carl Drimmer had initiated a thorough check on her background. She was a fanatical animal rights activist, that much he knew. She was an orphan, the adopted daughter of Mr Karl Monarch, a prosperous insurance broker from Marion, that much he knew. She had attended elementary, middle and high schools in the Marion school district and achieved 23.6 for the American College Testing exam, against an Iowa average of 21.6, which itself was the highest in the nation. She had graduated from the U of I with an honours degree in social sciences.

He knew when she had lost her virginity; and to whom. (Seventeen years and three months old, to John Forshaw Jr., of her high school athletics team.) He knew her medical records, her dental records, everything. He had seen too many politicians brought low by bimbos. He had sworn that it would never happen to him.

'What are you talking about?' he demanded.

She turned away. 'What do you think I'm talking about? I'm talking about love. I'm talking about loyalty. From the moment you first made love to me, I belonged to you; and I always will.'

Bryan had never felt disturbed by a woman before, but he did now. He was beginning to suspect that there was more to Lily Monarch than met the eye; and that all the time he had been exploiting *her*, for the purposes of promoting Zapf-Cady, she had been exploiting *him* – although he didn't yet know why, or for what.

She was a stunningly beautiful girl; misty-focused and erotic and mysterious, like a *Playboy* centrefold, but intelligent, too, and highly perverse. She attracted all kinds of men: portly public officials, television directors, Hell's Angels, journalists, all kinds of riff-raff. She gave Bryan everything, including her trust. Yet she was able to say '*You don't even know who I am, do you?*; and he knew that she was telling the truth.

He didn't know who she was. Not for sure: not for certain. And with Zapf-Cady coming up for ratification by Congress, he wasn't sure that he wanted to know, either. He smelled trouble. He smelled something approaching him from blind-side. He didn't like it at all. It made him feel itchy.

'This action meeting,' he said. 'It's nothing to do with this hog, is it?'

'It might be,' she replied, with her back turned.

'You don't have to do anything about this hog . . . the second we ratify the act, this hog goes free.'

'But what better publicity could we get, than to set it free now?'

He lifted himself up on one elbow. 'You want to set it free *now*? Are you crazy? That means illegally entering the Spellman Institute and letting the hog out of there – also illegally. You'd be guilty of trespass, larceny, damage to property, God knows what else. For Christ's sake, Lily! There are probably laws in Iowa against hog-rustling.'

She swung around, flashed him a look. 'You're not going to stop us, Bryan. You always said that you were behind us. You said it on television, didn't you? You said it in *Time*. "I support Animals Have Rights Too", 101 per cent, that's what you said, and I can show you the clipping. We're going to let out that hog; we're going to set that poor animal free, and there's nothing you can do to stop us.'

There was a long, long silence between them. Far below, they could faintly hear traffic noise, and the tiny wailing of a far-away ambulance siren.

At last, Bryan said, 'Maybe we've made a mistake, you and me. Maybe we've kind of – I don't know – maybe we've kind of misunderstood each other.'

She was still standing in the same position, half-turned around, so that her face was brightly lit by the large crystal bedside lamp, so that her eyes sparkled, so that her right breast was fully moulded by shadows, so that her concave stomach was sculptured by light, curve sliding into curve, and her thighs too; and her sparse covering of pubic hair glowed like an unblown dandelion-clock.

At that instant, Bryan wished to God almighty that he understood her, because Lily was more than special: a prize, whether he loved her or not.

All the same, why did she have to be so wilful? Why did she have to be so possessive? Why did she have to insist that he owned her; because he didn't own her, and didn't want to own her, and never would. After Zapf-Cady, there were other prizes waiting.

'Lily,' he said, 'I never ordered you to do anything before. I never would have been so presumptuous. But I have to order you now. You and your whacko friends stay away from Spellman – please. Otherwise you could screw up everything.'

Lily said, 'That hog is almost a human, Bryan . . . he's locked up, tormented. We can't leave him there.'

'You have to. Got it? You have to. If you let him out, you could risk everything. You've read the papers. That hog is seriously dangerous. He's killed one doctor and he's injured two more. Supposing he kills some kid? Overnight, you could ruin everything, totally. Right now, we have the edge. But we could lose that edge –' he popped his fingers '– just like that, in seconds, because somebody did something ill-advised.'

Lily walked back to Bryan and kissed the top of his head. 'You don't understand animals, do you, God bless you. But you will.'

'Lily –'

'We're going to let him free.'

'*Lily –!*'

He didn't know what to say; he didn't know what to do. She stood by the window, still naked, looking down over the lights of Cedar Rapids, her hands pressed against her cheeks as if she were shocked, or thoughtful; or maybe both. He kicked back the sheet that was twisted around his left ankle, and climbed out of bed, and stood close behind her. She had a pattern of dark moles on her shoulder, like the constellation Cassiopeia. He nearly touched her, but then he decided not to.

He walked towards the bathroom.

'You own me,' she said, quite loudly. 'You're my lover.'

He stopped, turned, and spread his hands appealingly. 'I don't own you, Lily. Even if I wanted to own you, I couldn't. That's not the way it works. You push, you persuade, you bully, you bribe. You try all of the tricks in the book. But you never *own* people, never. It just isn't possible.'

He went into the bathroom and half-closed the door. He saw himself in the mirror over the washbasin and thought how masklike he looked. Haggard as hell. He went to the toilet and raised the seat, and he was just about to piss when Lily walked in.

'Come on, sweetheart,' he said. 'Give me a break here, unh? I'm tired. I need to catch some sleep.'

But she ignored him. She walked right up to him, and caught hold of his hair, and kissed him. Her tongue slithered in between his lips, and her saliva tasted of wine and cloves.

'Come on,' he pleaded. 'I need to pee.'

But she kissed him again, and then she straddled the toilet, facing him, and took hold of his cock, her fingernails digging into his skin, so that he couldn't escape. 'Pee, then,' she said; and her eyes challenged him like they always did.

He couldn't stop himself. His cock burst out with a hot fountain of urine, which Lily immediately directed onto her breasts. She tugged his cock from side to side, so that he pissed in turn on each nipple; and then she directed the stream downwards, so that he pissed on her stomach. With her left hand, she reached down and parted the lips of her vulva, so that the hot sparkling urine gushed directly into her open vagina, and ran down her thighs.

It was all over in seconds. He tugged himself away, genuinely shocked – so quickly that she scratched his cock with her fingernails, and drew blood.

'Jesus, Lily,' he told her. But she was completely unabashed. She stood up, wet and dripping, and embraced him, grasping his cock and his balls and squeezing them over and over. She kissed him, and smeared her hands all over him, and kissed him again, and bit his lips, and reared up her right leg so that she could massage the backs of his thighs and his buttocks with her foot.

They lay on the green-carpeted floor, sticky and wet, and Lily urgently rutted. But Bryan was exhausted, and all he could think was: please, I want this ended. This is more than I can take.

When, after all, it was ended, he lay on the floor staring at Lily's foot and the side of the bathtub, and thinking nothing at all, except that trouble was coming: bad, bad trouble.

He sat up. 'Lily,' he said, 'we'd better take a shower, don't you think?'

She smiled at him. 'If that's what you want. I'm content to smell like you.'

'But – *piss*? Jesus, who does that?'

She continued to smile, and now she looked almost dreamy. She massaged her own breasts, over and over, pulling and tugging at her nipples, as if she were remembering something erotic, thinking of something basic and crude, something which turned her on.

'Oh . . .' she said. 'Boars.'

'*Boars?*'

'The boar marks his female by urinating on her – the same way he marks his territory. It's proof of ownership.'

Bryan stared at her for a long time, and then slowly shook his head. He was seriously beginning to think that enlisting Lily Monarch and her animal activists might have been a very serious error of judgement.

She said, 'I have something to tell you. It's time that you knew.'

It was an hour later. They had both showered, and now Bryan was lying on the bed in the white fluffy hotel bathrobe, correcting a speech that he was due to make tomorrow to business students at the U of I. He sat in a small ellipse of light, his reading-glasses shining, his brown tortoiseshell fountain-pen poised over his script. His toenails were clipped: he smelled of Heritage aftershave.

Lily climbed onto the end of the bed – near enough to be intimate, far enough away for Bryan not to be able to touch her. She was wearing an ivory silk pyjama-top, no pants. If he had lifted his head from the pillow, he would have been able to see between her thighs, her heel buried in her sex, but he resolutely stayed where he was, glasses shining, pen in hand, waiting to hear what she had to say.

'You're finding this relationship difficult, aren't you?' she said.

Bryan took off his glasses and stared at her for a while. Not his cold, self-defensive mirror-stare, but a stare of genuine curiosity. It had been a long time since any girl had spoken to him like that.

'I'm finding it *unusual*,' he admitted, at last.

Lily traced a pattern on the bedspread with her long-nailed fingertip. 'I don't want you to give up on it, because of that. It's too important.'

'Important for what reason? Because you couldn't get another guy to put a vegetarian bill through Congress? Because you couldn't get another guy to piss all over you? What?'

'Maybe both of those things,' said Lily, softly. 'Maybe both of those things and something more.'

'All right, then. Tell me. Nobody ever accused me of being close-minded.'

'Do you remember the Hog Girl?' said Lily.

'The Hog Girl? For sure, everybody remembers the Hog Girl. What was that – twelve years ago, thirteen? Over in Prairieville or someplace like that.'

'Fifteen years ago, in Prairieburg,' said Lily.

'That's it. They found a young girl out on some real isolated hog farm, didn't they? Her parents had died and the hogs had brought her up. She was more hog than human.'

'That's right,' said Lily. 'The hogs fed her and foraged for her and kept her warm. They even educated her, after a fashion. She could communicate with them; she could understand what they wanted.'

There was a silence so long that Lily was afraid that Bryan was never going to speak to her again. He just stared at her with the arm of his glasses in his mouth, and his expression was unreadable.

'*You* were the Hog Girl?' he asked her.

Lily lowered her head. Tears began to slide down her cheeks.

'The Hog Girl was *you*?' he repeated, incredulously. 'All this time, I've been sleeping with the Hog Girl?'

Lily looked up, and swallowed. 'My real name isn't Lily Monarch at all. It's Virginia Lauterbach.'

'That was it, Virginia Lauterbach, the Hog Girl,' said Bryan. 'I had Carl check up on you. I had Carl check up on everything, down to the size you took in Dutch caps. How come he didn't find that out?'

'You had Carl check up on me? You couldn't trust me?'

'Oh, come on, Lily, you know how it is. I'm a senator. I want to be President. I have to take precautions. For your wellbeing, as well as my own.'

'You could have asked me. You could have asked me anything you wanted to.'

'Lily, I'm sorry, but I check up on absolutely everybody. My staff, my friends. Even the kid in the mailroom.'

Lily wiped her eyes with her sleeve. 'Well . . . I guess a senator has to do what a senator has to do. But you wouldn't have found out about me being the Hog Girl. Not easily, anyway. The Iowa state welfare department arranged for my adoption. They gave me a new past, and a new future, too. It was bad enough that I was brought up by hogs, without having to suffer everybody's morbid curiosity for the rest of my life. After they found me, it took me nine weeks to get back into the habit of walking upright. I still have this really comfortable feeling when I drop down on all fours. I was eighteen months in therapy before I started to speak.'

Bryan nodded and couldn't seem to stop nodding. 'I remember. I read about it in *Reader's Digest.* It was an incredible story. Truly incredible. And it's *you*? Jesus!'

Lily turned her face away. 'Maybe I shouldn't have told you.'

'Why not? It's incredible. It's exciting!'

'Stop saying "it's incredible". You're making me feel like a freak.'

Bryan tossed his speech to one side, and sat up in bed. 'Lily – you're not a freak, no way. What happened to you, that wasn't your fault. It was incredible that you managed to survive it. The Hog Girl, I can't believe it.'

'It isn't something you'd want to be reminded about.'

'Still, tell me.' He sat up, and reached across the bed, and held her wrist.

'You probably know it all, if you read the article in the *Reader's Digest.* My mother and father used to have a hog farm out at Amana, but things went badly and the Farmer's Bank foreclosed on them. Leastways, that's what I found out later. Late one night my father loaded up all of the hogs we had left, and we just packed our belongings and drove away.

'We were lucky, I guess. We found an abandoned farm near Prairieburg, and we squatted there. I grew up among the hogs because my father didn't dare to send me to school, in case anybody found out where we were. He always made me promise never to leave the farm, never, and of course I was scared to. I can remember standing by the hog-pens on a hot dusty day and looking toward the horizon and thinking *that's where the bad people come from.*'

Bryan shook his head in sympathy. 'Incredible,' he repeated.

Lily said, 'One winter it was bitter cold so my parents stoked up the stove to keep us warm all night and in the morning they wouldn't wake up. They died of carbon monoxide poisoning. I was four years old. I didn't dare leave the farm because my father had told me not to, and I didn't like to go into the house because my father and mother were lying there dead. So I went to the only friends I had; and they were the hogs.

'They accepted me and they took care of me and they treated me like one of them. I fed on sow's milk from the teat and scratched-up turnips and anything else the hogs could forage. One particular sow was always there to look after me. I loved her as close as I could have loved a mother. I was lost in the fields once, and twisted my ankle, and she came out and found me and lay beside me to keep me warm, until I could make it back to the farm.

'After my father and mother died, it didn't take the hogs more than a few weeks to revert from being domestic hogs to feral hogs; and by the time I was discovered, I was almost a feral hog myself. Well, a gilt, technically speaking. I hadn't had my first litter.'

It was obvious that Bryan was fascinated and aroused. He stroked her arm with the back of his hand, and then her shoulders, and then her cheek.

'So that was what all that business in the bathroom was all about? The sexual habits of a sow?'

'That was the way my mother behaved. My hog mother, I mean.'

'You never – not yourself – ?'

Lily looked him straight in the eye. 'Would it disgust you if I had?'

For the first time since she had known him, Bryan blushed. 'I'm sorry,' he said. 'I shouldn't even have thought it.'

'Why not? *I* would have thought it, if I were you. That's one thing that living with hogs taught me. Complete honesty. But the answer to your question is no, I never did. The boars simply weren't interested in me. They get sexually stimulated by smells. I smelled pretty bad, I guess, but I just didn't smell right.'

'How were you found?' asked Bryan, trying to change the subject.

'Purely by accident. A property agent came out to the farm, one summer afternoon, and there I was, lying asleep next to my hog mother, naked, filthy, skinny as a hairpin. He woke me up and the first thing I did was try to run away. I thought he was one of the bad people that my father had warned me about.

'Those hogs were intelligent; and unselfish; and kind, too. They can be scary when they're aroused. They can hurt you, too. But when you get to know them – when you really get to know them – well, they have such understanding, such natural sympathy, such *grace.*

'Now you can see why I feel it's my duty to let out Captain Black.'

Bryan stroked her hair. 'Yes, I can.'

He hesitated for a moment, and then climbed off the bed, and went across to the drinks cabinet. 'You want a whiskey?' he asked her.

She shook her head.

He poured himself a large one. 'I can see why you feel the way you do, I really can. I mean, that was such an incredible experience, living with hogs. But you're totally unique. Nobody can empathize with hogs the way that you do, nobody at all. That means that the public at large is not going to understand what you're doing, and if we're going to get Zapf-Cady through Congress, we need understanding from the public at large, and we need it bad.'

Lily said nothing, but sat on the bed, staring at him.

'The Hog Girl,' he said, swallowing whiskey. 'Who'd have thought it? I've been making out with the goddamned Hog Girl.'

Together, hurriedly, they walked along the corridor until they reached the emergency exit which led to the stairs. They left behind them a whirl of disturbed air; and the smell of half-rotted burlap, and damp-soured animal pelts, and plague. The entourage of Janek-the-Green, the Green Traveller, and their terrified prisoner Terence Pearson, rushing away.

They turned the corner and were suddenly confronted by deputy Bulowski, shrugging on her pink raincoat. They stopped, and stared at her, and she stared at them.

She looked first at the Witness, so tall and white. Then to the Swordsman. She hardly took in the Leper; or Naked, or Knife. But she did recognize Terence.

'Excuse me,' she said. 'But who are you? And where in hell do you think you're going?'

Terence said nothing; but Naked said, 'Leave us alone. You'll regret it, otherwise.'

'Excuse me?'

'Leave us alone, and forget. Go back to your home. That was where you were going, wasn't it?'

Edna Bulowski took a firm step forward, and reached into her holster for her gun. 'I think you're making a small mistake here, folks,' she told them. 'This man is under arrest, in custody; and you are not only trespassing but springing him out. Which is a felony.'

'Please . . . let us pass,' said Naked.

Edna Bulowski lifted her gun and slowly shook her head from side to side. 'No, sorry. That isn't possible. This man has to return to custody; and you guys have to come into custody, too. You're under arrest on suspicion of trespass into county property; and of aiding a suspected felon to escape from custody; and from the looks of you people, all kinds of other stuff, too. You want to know your rights? I'll read you your rights. But first, let's go quiet, now, shall we, and find some cells?'

The Swordsman stepped forward. The sound came first; his foot followed. Edna said, 'Freeze, sir, please. Stay where you are. Put your hands on the wall where I can see them.'

The Swordsman did nothing at all. Edna wasn't even sure that he had heard her. He seemed strangely indistinct, as if her glasses were fogged up. In fact, all of these people, except for Terence Pearson, looked almost *transparent.*

'You should let us pass,' Naked repeated, in the most helpful of voices.

'Is he deaf, or what?' Edna demanded, jerking her head in the Swordman's direction.

'Oh, no. Not deaf. He chooses not to speak, that's all.'

'Well, tell him that it would be a good idea if he also chose to put his hands up against the wall, and spread his legs.'

A heatbeat's pause, and then Naked said, 'He obeys only one master. All of us do.'

'He obeys only one master?'

Another pause. 'That is correct. He will not listen to direct orders.'

'Then maybe he takes *advice*, now and again?'

'Of course. None of us is too proud to ignore advice.'

'So tell him that my advice is that he puts his hands against the wall, and spreads his legs, because otherwise, on a count of three, I'm going to shoot him.'

Naked turned her face away – didn't even answer. The boy Knife pointed his toes, one after the other, in a stilted imitation of ballet steps. Edna licked her lips. There was something wrong here, something seriously wrong. She could actually see the wall through the boy's upraised arms. He was like a ghost, like a double-exposure. Terence Pearson stared at Edna sweaty and grey-faced, but he didn't speak, either. He was far more frightened of the mummers than he was of a short, bespectacled deputy sheriff with no back-up and no idea what terrifying plague-breathing creatures had come her way.

'One,' said Edna. Her throat sounded tight.

Still the Swordsman remained where he was. He didn't even seem to breathe.

'Two,' said Edna. She was praying very hard that she wouldn't have to shoot this man, but she was sure that he wouldn't leave her any other choice. Maybe he was carrying only swords while engaged in the commission of a crime.

She had every right to use fatal force, if she considered it necessary.

'Three,' she said. 'This is your last chance.'

She fired. In the confines of the corridor, the shot was thunderous. She must have hit the Swordsman, because she fired point-blank; yet the instant *after*, she had fired, and the bullet had chipped a lump of plaster from the wall behind him, he swung to one side. *After*, not before – yet he was still unharmed.

She aimed her revolver for a second shot. But the Swordsman's arm snaked behind him so quickly that she didn't even see it. She heard a high, teeth-ringing whisper of steel against scabbard. She consciously tightened her finger on the trigger of her service revolver, but by then the sword was already flying through the air towards her face, point-first, at a speed of nearly 60 m.p.h. With a brittle *chippp!* sound, it split the lens of her glasses and struck her directly in the right eye, pierced her skull from front to back, and stuck her to the grey plaster wall. Her gun tumbled, unfired, to the floor.

Edna was shocked, but not killed. She stood back against the wall, feeling utterly cold, although she couldn't think why. Even the inside of her brain felt cold. She wanted to move; she wanted to fall. She wanted to understand what had happened to her.

She saw blurry figures standing in front of her.

'What's happened to me?' she asked them; or thought she asked them. She wasn't at all sure that she knew how to speak.

One of them approached her very closely, so close that she couldn't focus on him. A voice said, 'You should have let us pass. We obey only one master, and it isn't you, I'm sorry to say.'

She felt a strong, bony hand on her shoulder, pressing her hard against the wall. What were they doing to her? Why were they pressing against her like this? But then she felt the chilly, grating sensation of the sword being tugged out of the plaster, and back through the side of her brain, and out of her eye-socket.

The pain detonated in her head like a white roaring fire. In fact she actually believed that she was burning. She slid sideways against the wall, leaving a semi-circle of blood, and the floor came up to her and hit her as hard as somebody rushing through a door.

She didn't see the feet that went shuffling past her: the feet of Witness and Swordsman and Leper; the dancing-shoes of Knife; the boots of Naked. The dragging laceless shoes of Terence Pearson, on his way to meet his nemesis, Janek-the-Green, walking with spastic reluctance, like a man on his way to be hanged.

They went out through the exit door. The light in the stairwell was still fitful; and it lent a particular air of darkness and evil to the five masked mummers. Terence looked down into the flickering shadows and said, 'Where are you taking me? You won't be able to get me out of here. The building's guarded too well.'

'Some can see us and some can't,' said Naked. 'Besides, we're not going downward. We're going *up*, to the roof.'

'We're going to the roof? And then what?'

'And then, my friend, you will see what you will see, and more besides.'

'We'll be trapped if we go up onto the roof.'

'Janek your father can never be trapped, never confined. He walks down the years as a sower of seed. He gives life, he gives growth. He is fertility itself. How can he ever be trapped? Is the root trapped under the paving stone?'

Terence said, 'I don't think I can make it.'

Naked was puzzled. 'You don't think you can make *what*?'

'I don't think I can make it to the roof. My legs are giving out.'

'My friend, you'll have to. You have no choice.'

As if to emphasize the point, the Swordsman unsheathed two of his swords, and held them upright, one in each hand. The light slid down their blades like quicksilver sliding down a crevice in the wall.

'All right,' said Terence. He felt a huge sense of hopelessness, as if everything that he had ever done was futile. All those years of studying bibles and history books and meteorological charts – all those years of watching and waiting – and yet here they were, the mummers he had always feared.

He hadn't believed his father at first, when his father had explained why he should never have children. '*You're not my son,*' his father had told him, in the twilight of his living-room, his face silhouetted agaisnt the net curtains, with their patterns of parrots and orchids. '*I let somebody else lie with your mother . . . it seemed like it was worth it at the time . . . I never thought that you would turn out to be you . . .*'

He had argued with his father all afternoon. He had even called his father's doctor. 'He says I'm not his son . . . I can't seem to convince him, no matter what.'

It was when his father's doctor had softly said, 'There was some question of paternity, yes. Don't quote me, because I'll always deny it, but your mother always said that you were somebody else's son. There was no affair. She'd only slept with him once, and that once was terrible. But once was enough.'

They reached the top storey. Knife opened the door, and stepped out onto the roof, and Naked followed.

'Come on,' she urged. 'You've always wanted to meet your maker, haven't you?'

Terence was so sick with fear that he leaned against the wall. 'I don't know . . . I can't do this.'

'He's your *father,*' Naked insisted.

Terence thought of breaking away, and making a run for it, but the Swordsman was standing in such a way that any attempt to escape looked distinctly risky, more than that – distinctly fatal.

Terence took the last few steps onto the roof; onto a glistening black tarmac lake. It was still raining, but clear, and there were views of Cedar Rapids on all sides. To the north, to the glittering oxbow bends in the Cedar River, and beyond, to Hiawatha. To the south, to the airport, and millions of acres of restless farmland, where things were always growing, and pushing up from underneath the earth, like dead folks who refused to stay buried.

Terence walked to the parapet, and looked over. The Swordsman followed him closely. Terence looked down at the traffic for a very long time, until the rain began to drip from the end of his nose, and then he turned and brushed the Swordsman aside and said to Naked, 'Where is he? What does he want?'

'He's here,' said Naked, and bowed, and stepped back, the rain sparkling on the fur of her rancid dog's-fur jacket.

And, sure enough, he was.

He came rustling out of the shadow of the elevator housing, and here he was, at last – the Green Traveller whom Terence had feared since boyhood. The creature who would conceive you, and then covet your intestines for year after year. The creature who believed that every one of his children belonged to him, in every imaginable sense.

The creature who came knocking on your door at night, knocking and knocking, because he wanted to feed on his own flesh and blood.

His face was concealed by a white-varnished mask, just as his entourage was masked, and his mask was painted with the same slyly-smiling face as the engraving that Terence had pinned to the wall above his desk. It was a peculiarly medieval face, smooth and Slavic-looking, and it frightened Terence so much that he could hardly bring himself to look at it. The face was surrounded by a bushy cloak of laurel, and the laurel was intertwined with brambles and nettles and old man's beard, the curly, fluffy clematis known as Traveller's Joy.

He approached Terence slowly, with a dragging, rustling sound, until they were standing face-to-face, only two or three feet apart. The wind rattled in his leaves, but all the same, Terence thought he could hear slow, painful breathing, like an asthmatic. The Green Traveller had the strangest smell, too, like herbs, and moss, and damp peat. And he was freezing cold. As cold as a hollow in the forest, on a January night.

The girl Naked came up close, and leaned close to the Green Traveller's mask. She nodded, and nodded again, and then she said to Terence, 'Janek is displeased with you. He wanted a son to be proud of. He says that you deprived him of something valuable and important that was rightfully his.'

Terence swallowed. He was almost about to cry. 'I wanted to save them, that's all. I didn't want them to suffer.'

'You didn't want them to suffer? They're suffering now. Their souls have no place to go. Their spirits have no place to rest. And it's all because of you.'

Terence insisted, 'I wanted to save them, that's all. They were my children, for Christ's sake!'

'Whose children?' asked Naked.

'Mine, my children. Mine. The children that Iris and I created between us.'

Naked leaned close to the Green Traveller again, and then she said, 'And who created you?'

Terence turned away. The boy Knife nodded to him, almost sympathetically.

'Who created *you*, Terence?' Naked repeated, in a much sharper tone.

'My mother created me. My mother and – something. Something that gave my family bad blood. It was all my father's fault.'

'Your father?'

'My mother's husband. James Pearson. Farmer, of Des Moines, Iowa.'

'But your *real* father?'

Terence clenched and unclenched his fists. He wanted to face up to the Green Traveller, he wanted to face up to that bland, mocking medieval smile, but he found it so hard. Whatever he said, however he raged, he knew that this was his real father, the creature who had impregnated his mother, and given him life.

Whatever this creature was, *he* was, too. There was no escaping it.

Naked leaned close to the Green Traveller again. She listened, but she hesitated before she replied.

'What is it?' Terence wanted to know. His voice was almost drowned out by the thunder of a plane, circling around towards the airport. '*What is it? Tell me, for Christ's sake!*'

'He says you make him angry; that you have disappointed him. He has never known one of his sons to behave like this before. All of his sons are obedient sons, they never plot so hard to deprive him of what is rightfully his. You are his flesh and blood. Why have you tried to cheat him?'

'He was going to kill us all,' said Terence. 'He was going to *kill* us! It says so in the Bible, it says so in every book, in every language! He was going to cut out our guts and eat them!'

'But he is your father. He gave you life: he has the right to take it away.'

Terence shook his head, again and again. 'No way, young lady. No way at all. He didn't have the right to do nothing like that. Once you're born, you're born, regardless of who your parents may be. Once you've got life, nobody can take it away from you – *nobody* – because life is sacred, each to his own.'

'But you killed your own children, didn't you? What right did you have to do that?'

'I had the right to protect them from pain. I loved them, God damn it to hell. I loved them! But they had bad blood! They had such bad, bad blood!'

Tears began to roll down his cheeks, and he jabbed his finger at Naked in fury and fear and frustration. 'He doesn't own any single part of me, not one goddamned fingernail! Because I'm me! Because I'm me! Because I'm *me*!'

There was a moment's silence. The Green Traveller

rustled, and stepped back; and then even the Swordsman stepped back, and the white-coated Witness, too. The Leper was already standing well away, close to the opposite parapet, silhouetted by the glow from the lights of downtown Cedar Rapids like a hooded, 14th-century nightmare. Knife took three cautious paces back, hesitated, then took another.

Terence said, 'What? What are you doing?'

But even Naked said nothing. A small whirlwind of leaves blew up, and rattled across the rooftop, and flew off into the sky. From out of the whirlwind, two grotesque hands appeared – hands that were flesh and bone and twigs, intertwined. Terence knew what the Green Traveller actually was; but to confront him for the very first time had nothing to do with books, or bibles, or historical research. To confront him for the first time was to understand the strange and terrifying power of Nature – a power that was governed by no laws but the laws of growing, and feeding, and growing again, and overwhelming everything that stood in its way.

Terence could see nothing of the Green Traveller but a turmoil of flying bay leaves, out of which his two hands were extended, like the hands of a man who was drowning in a leaf-carpeted lake. They were so pale, his hands, that they were almost luminous, the colour of vegetable tubers that have never seen the sun. Some of the veins were blue, where blood flowed through them. Others were wriggling white roots. Out of the sides of his fingers, and out of his nails, stiff woody branches sprouted, so that his hands became complicated claws of curved and broken sticks.

'Oh, God protect me,' said Terence. He was shaking so much that he could hardly stand up. This was terror. This was absolute cold-frozen terror. He watched these two hands rise in front of him, and his insides dissolved. The most frightening part about it was that he knew what was going to happen to him. He had studied it and researched it for so many years, expecting to avoid it. He had become such an expert on Janek-the-Green that he had somehow imagined that he would have some influence over him, if they ever met.

Instead, he felt total watery collapse; the melting-away of all of his resolve; the complete evaporation of his willpower.

Naked listened to Janek-the-Green for a moment, and then said to Terence, 'You like it here, up on the roof?'

Terence shrugged, unable to speak.

'Your father brought you here because he wanted to show you something.'

Terence wildly looked around. All he could see were the lights of Cedar Rapids; all he could feel was the wind.

Janek-the-Green rustled to the very edge of the roof, and climbed up onto the parapet. He stood silhouetted against the sparkling nightscape of the city, leaning into the wind to keep his balance. The wind caught the leaves of his cloak, and blew them into the air, so that a rushing, rustling tail of leaves trailed out behind him like a banner of war, and then scattered all over the streets below.

'He wants you to see the smallness of human life,' Naked breathed in Terence's ear, obscenely close. 'He wants you to see how frail you all are; little winking lights.'

They heard the echo of sirens in the street far below them. 'And, of course, who would think of looking for you up here?'

Terence stood and watched the leaves blowing in a dark windborne river from Janek's back. He knew that there was nothing he could do. Janek-the-Green was everything that the Bible had said about him; and worse. He was a ghastly miracle. And he was real.

And he was here.

And Terence could do nothing at all but wait for what his destiny had brought him.

Out on 76th Avenue, SW, about three miles west of the airport, a truck driver named Randy Gedge was driving westward with a full load of ninety-six double-fronted refrigerators, bound for Des Moines.

The rain had mostly eased off, but the spray on the highway was still bothersome, and he kept his speed down to a cautious 45. A few miles back, he had almost rear-ended a Toyota hatchback that had pulled out in front of him, and he was the kind of driver who preferred to feel frustrated than to end up killing a family of five. He had seen it happen all too often. A moment's anger; an ill-judged manoeuvre; and then one of those crashes where you couldn't tell where metal ended and people began.

Randy was 55 years old and this was his last year of driving for Hawk Eye Freight. He wasn't sorry. He wouldn't miss the highways, endlessly unravelling in front of him, and the days of appalling loneliness, although he would miss the wild, vulgar CB banter, and the truckstops, and the winter sun rising over the prairies. He would miss the freedom, too, because now he would have to return to his small green-painted house in Marion, and talk to Betty every day of the week, and go shopping every Thursday morning, and sleep in the same bed every single night, watching the headlights of other trucks swivel across the ceiling.

It didn't bode especially well, the future, but Randy was trying to be optimistic. What worried him more than anything else, though, was what he and Betty were going to talk about, day after day. He had never been a talkative man. He was handsome in the ugly way that Charles Bronson was handsome, and he was bow-legged and built like one of the refrigerators he hauled. He was opinionated, too. He had all kinds of opinions, especially if you wanted to argue ice hockey. But there was scarcely anything he wanted to say to

Betty. All that interested Betty was daytime television and shopping. The last time he had asked her out, he had told her that she could go anywhere she wanted, anywhere at all. The Sports Page maybe, on 1st Avenue, she loved the tuna salad; or Huckleberry's. But what had she asked him to do? She had asked him to drive out to Williamsburg, over an hour away, to the Tanger Factory Outlet Center, so that she could buy floral covers for the living-room couch.

The rain lashed against the windshield of his truck, and the wipers were hurtling from side to side at full speed. On the radio, a dead Roy Orbison was keening, *'Only the lonely . . . know the way you feel . . . tonight.'*

Randy thought, no they friggin' don't. The same Toyota that had pulled out in front of him on Edgewood Road had slowed down now, and was right in front of him, driving at 30 m.p.h. He flashed his main beams, but the driver took no notice: in fact, he slowed down even more. Randy didn't want to tailgate him, but he didn't want to lose his momentum, either. A rig this size, fully loaded, took well over a mile to get up to speed; and it was costly on gas, too.

'Come on, you sumbitch,' he breathed, changing down two notches.

But the Toyota drove slower and slower, until it was barely making 25. Randy came right up behind it, almost bumper-to-bumper, but the Toyota driver was either drunk or elderly or obstinate as all hell, because he kept up the same miserable speed, for mile after mile, until Randy felt that he was ready to ram him. What provoked him even more was the stupid 'Mr Smiley' face in the rear window, and the slogan JESUS NEEDS YOU NOW.

Randy was concentrating so hard on keeping his distance from the Toyota's rear bumper that he didn't notice the pale shapes crossing the highway up ahead of them – not until it was far too late. The Toyota couldn't have seen them, either, because it suddenly swerved sideways, and then jolted, and jolted again, and skidded onto the other side of the road.

Randy stepped on his airbrakes, and the tyres of his tractor-trailer gripped the macadam with a high shuddering howl. At the same time, however, he heard heavy, fleshy objects thumping into his front bumper and his radiator grille, dozens of them, and suddenly his windshield was sprayed with blood and bits of flesh, as violently as if somebody had emptied an abattoir bucket all over it.

The tractor jack-knifed, and the whole rig slewed through 180 degrees, its trailer colliding with the side of the Toyota. The Toyota was pushed right off the highway, and tilted nose-first into a concrete drainage ditch. At the same time, the rear doors of the trailer burst open, and six or seven refrigerators crashed across the road, two of them landing on top of the Toyota's roof.

For one long moment, Randy thought he could keep the rig under control. He spun the wheel into the skid, and almost managed to correct it. But the jack-knifing trailer had built up too much momentum, and it swung back across the highway, its tyres screaming, and toppled the entire rig over on its side. Randy felt it going. He knew it was too late to jump clear, but he flung himself sideways, across the floor of the cab, in a desperate effort to avoid being crushed.

There was a devastating crash, and the earsplitting sound of refrigerators dropping on top of each other. The tractor's windshield dropped out, like a shower of snow dropping from a winter porch, and Randy felt the cold stinging of the rain, and the blustering buffeting of the wind.

He felt something else, too. A pinching sensation in his left ankle. Not particularly painful, just pinching. He tried to lift it up to see what had happened to it, but he found that he couldn't. He looked down into the foot-well and saw that the tubular seat support had collapsed, pinning his ankle like a giant paperclip. He wriggled it, and it didn't feel as if it were broken, but all the same there was no way he could pull his foot out.

He sniffed hard. He couldn't smell fuel, thank God, but he still wanted to get himself out. The rig was lying right across the highway, with its lights out, and although it was five after eleven and there was hardly any traffic around, there was a hell of a risk that somebody would come barrelling along the highway and hit it.

At first, Randy was so shocked that it didn't occur to him to think what might have been obstructing the highway, and what he might have hit. There had been nine or ten distinct impacts, and a whole lot of blood. He hoped to God that he hadn't hit a whole lot of hikers, or a road construction gang. But it didn't seem very likely that anybody would be out walking or resurfacing the highway at this time of night, in this weather, and he certainly hadn't seen any warning signs.

But then, as he peered out of his glassless windshield into the rain and the darkness, he began to distinguish something moving. He began to see pale, mottled shapes milling around in the rain and the darkness, dozens of them, all around the wreck. He heard whining and crying, and then a high-pitched scream, and then another.

Two or three of the shapes turned around and approached him, and it was then that he realized what they were. Hogs, God damn it. A whole herd of stray hogs. One of them came up close, and Randy wasn't surprised that the Toyota driver hadn't seen them until it was too late. The hog was filthy and stringy-looking and its hair was all matted with rain and dirt. It looked undernourished, too, as if it hadn't been fed for weeks. Another one approached, its black eyes glittering in the darkness, and it was so skinny and spiny-backed that it looked more like a giant sewer-rat than a farmyard hog.

Another came up, and then another. They sniffed at the truck suspiciously, with drool hanging from their jaws.

Randy shouted out, 'Help! Can anybody hear me? I'm trapped in the cab!'

The hogs were startled, and they backed away a few paces; but they soon returned; and this time they were joined by more. Randy said to them, 'Come on, guys, give me a break, will you? I just want to get my ass out of here.' He wasn't afraid of them: his uncle had farmed hogs once, and he had often fed them and watered them and driven them from one pen to another, whipping their rumps with a stick.

With a lot of awkward struggling, he managed to reach his CB handset, but the set was dead. He shouted again. 'Anybody out there? I'm trapped!'

Still there was nothing but the rain and the wind and the grunting of an injured hog. One of the hogs came right up to the cab and poked its snout inside, only inches away. He could smell it, even over the stench of spilled diesel. It smelled ranker than any other hog he had smelled before.

'Go on, get out of here!' he snarled at it. But it didn't even flinch. It stood there, with its head inside the cab, staring at him as if it were actually *thinking* what it was going to do next.

Randy wrenched his ankle from side to side, but he still couldn't work it free. The hog was joined by another hog, and then another. It snuffled at him; cautiously at first, and then more avidly.

'Go on, shoo!' Randy shouted. 'Get your stinking carcass out of here!'

But the hog grew bolder. It lunged right into the overturned cab, and bit at Randy's sleeve. Randy shouted, 'Shoo, you bastard!' but the hog took no notice, and bit at his sleeve yet again. This time it tore through denim, and snagged his skin.

Up until now, Randy had felt irritated. Now he began to feel genuinely frightened. He struggled even more furiously to free his ankle, and at the same time he tried to reach up to the glovebox, where he kept a heavy-duty flashlight and a self-grip wrench.

But the hog went for him a second time, and this time it bit viciously into his wrist. He smacked at it with his open hand, again and again, and yelled, 'Get off, you bastard! Get out of here!'

Instead of retreating, however, the hog squealed and roared and went viciously wild. It forced its way further into the cab, and bit at his arm and his flailing right hand. At first, he felt nothing but a sharp stinging sensation, but suddenly there was blood everywhere, wet and warm. He hit at the hog twice more before he saw that all four fingers on his right hand were missing, and that only his thumb remained.

He screamed. A huge, lung-scorching scream. He hit at the hog again and again; but the beast went for him again, biting into his wrist, and tugging back its head, so that a long strip of flesh and muscle was torn away from his arm, all the way down to his elbow.

The other hogs had scented blood now. They crowded around the cab, pushing and wriggling and screeching, climbing on top of each other to reach him. All he could see was glittering eyes and slobbering snouts, and he was overwhelmed with pain and the fetid stench of pigs.

He screamed again, and waved the stumps of his hands around. But there were snatching teeth everywhere, and the living flesh was bitten in chunks from his arms.

One hog went for his face, and when that happened he knew he was dead; and wanted to die, too. He felt its breath on his face, and then it dug its teeth into his cheek and the side of his nose, and bit right through skin, flesh, cartilage and bone, and literally pulled his face away from his skull. Through half-blinded eyes, he saw the hog twisting its head away, with flesh hanging from its jaws; and then he felt the rain against his fleshless cheekbones.

His heart felt like a pendulum, caught by somebody's hand.

And released.

And swung.

And caught again, and held for a long, long moment.

And released. And swung. And caught again. And held for ever.

The hogs squirmed and crowded into the cab, and tore his body to pieces. They devoured every part that they could reach, pulling out his lungs in yellowish, tobacco-darkened shreds, burrowing into his pelvis to eat his intestines as if they were burrowing into a crowded trough. They even stripped and ate the bloodstained vinyl from the seats, and some of the foam rubber, too.

On the other side of the highway, down in the rain-filled drainage ditch, twenty or thirty more hogs were tearing at the bodies of the Toyota driver and his passenger. These two were luckier than Randy: the 55-year-old driver had died instantly when his automobile left the highway, his chest impacted by the steering-wheel. His passenger, a 35-year-old woman, had severed an artery in her thigh and died a few minutes later from loss of blood. All that they had known about hogs was when they had collided with the first half-dozen of them, as they had run across the highway in front of them.

In less than ten minutes, there was hardly anything left of Randy and the Toyota's occupants but three tangled arrays of blood and bones. Randy's eyeless, tuft-haired skull was lying against the door, staring blindly at his trapped ankle. The Toyota driver had been wearing pigskin gloves, which unaccountably the hogs hadn't eaten, considering that a ravenous hog will eat almost anything. One hand still clasped the steering-wheel: a hand that was attached to nothing at all.

There was a heavy rumble of thunder, and some of the hogs were already beginning to move on.

It was then that a 20-year-old college student called Rick McCready came speeding eastward along the highway in his father's saddle-bronze Camaro. Rick had promised to collect his father from the airport after a late flight back from Chicago, where his aunt had just given birth to twins. He was twenty minutes late already, and his father would be going ape, which was why Rick was speeding.

The rain was lashing diagonally south-south-west across the road, and even with his windshield wipers on full-speed, he was finding it difficult to see more than a quarter of a mile up ahead. But 76th Avenue was as straight as an arrow, and there was never anybody else on the road this time of night, not in rural east Iowa, where most people were tucked up in bed as soon as *Star Trek: The Next Generation* was over. Rick was travelling just over 80 m.p.h., nudging up to 85, and he was singing along with Nirvana's 'Heart-Shaped Box', and whacking his hands on the steering-wheel in time to the drumming.

He didn't see Randy Gedge's overturned rig lying across the road until it was far too late for him to stop. He slammed his foot on the brake, but the Camaro was still travelling at well over 70 when it crashed into the cab. The impact drove it underneath the tractor's engine, compressing the car so violently that the front part of the passenger compartment was reduced to less than a third of its original height. Rick McCready was compressed with it, instantly changed into a wide, flat thing of crushed-up flesh that even his father wouldn't have recognized, except that it was wearing Rick's college sweatshirt.

There was a strange hiatus, with only the sound of the rain and the wind, and the distressed squealing of injured hogs. Then Rick's gas tank exploded, hurtling two blazing hogs and a blazing back tyre up into the air. There was another hiatus, then another huge explosion. Fiery chunks of truck cartwheeled across the highway. Within a few seconds, the wreckage was ablaze from one side of the highway to the other. Burning hogs rushed hysterically around and around, screaming like children. One of them ran in a flaming zigzag into the cornfield beside the highway, twisting and untwisting itself in agony before finally collapsing and burning like an abandoned sofa.

Seventy-sixth Avenue was like a scene from hell. Thunder rumbled; rain came down in glittering sheets. And through the rain the blazing wreckage of truck and automobile luridly flickered; while the only voices were the terrible cries of injured animals.

Eleven

It had been pan-fried chicken that evening, with mustard greens, because Sally-Ann let him have one high-calorie meal every week, so that he wouldn't find his diet too dispiriting. If she had known about his illicit consumption of raspberry Danishes and sugared donut holes, she might have thought differently. But they all enjoyed a good old-fashioned family meal together, it brought them close, and Luke's obvious enjoyment was a reward in itself.

She was fondly watching the relish with which he mopped up his cream gravy with his freshbaked cornbread when the telephone rang.

He wiped his mouth with his napkin and started to get up, but she said, 'No, no. You carry on eating. Unless somebody's been murdered, you're going to finish your supper.' She picked up the receiver. 'Hallo?' she said, and listened. 'Yes, this is she. He *is* here, yes, but he's eating.'

'Who? Who?' asked Luke, pushing another piece of cornbread into his mouth. Nancy said, 'Daddy! Don't talk with your mouth full! You're always telling me not to do it!'

Sally-Ann listened some more, and then she brought the phone over to the table. 'John Husband. It's serious.'

Luke took the phone and said tersely, 'Go ahead.'

'I'm sorry, Luke. It's pretty crappy news. Somebody just sprung Terence Pearson.'

'What?' Luke burst out. 'How could anybody spring Terence Pearson?' But at the very same time that he was talking, he was thinking *the Green Traveller, I saw him, he was there, after all.*

'Even worse news,' said John. 'They took out five of your people, too.'

Luke stopped chewing. 'What do you mean, they took out five of my people?'

'They killed them, Luke. You have five officers down.'

Luke started to shake. 'When did this happen?' he wanted to know.

'Pretty hard to tell: we just discovered it. Mike Whipps went around there to give you his latest report on the Pearson case. Everything was normal on the front desk, but when he went up to the third floor, all he found was dead people, and blood. Then one of your deputies came up and told him that Pearson had flown the coop.'

'Tell me who's dead.'

'Verbick, Smittkamp, Engel, Sloan and Bulowski.'

'They killed Edna?'

'I'm sorry. I know that all of them were friends, as well as police officers.'

Luke said, 'Don't tell me any more. I'm coming right down.'

'I've alerted the State police, too; and the Highway Patrol.'

'I'm coming right down.'

He handed the phone back to Sally-Ann. She could tell that he was distressed. He stood up, kissed Nancy, kissed Sally-Ann, and went to the door. He was out of uniform: in a blue lumberjack shirt and easy-fit jeans, but he put on his uniform windbreaker and his hat and his gunbelt.

'Luke –' said Sally-Ann.

'Five dead,' he said, 'including Edna. Pearson's escaped, too, so keep the door locked. You never know with these nuts: sometimes they come after the people who collared them.'

'Oh, Luke, I'm sorry. I'm so sorry.'

He opened the front door. 'Thanks. Time for that later. Right now, I've got myself some work to do.'

The rain was coming down in drenching sheets by the time he reached the Third Avenue Bridge. The parking lot was crowded with ambulances and squad cars and press vehicles. Even the commissioner's limousine was here, for Christ's sake. Luke parked his Buick and jogged heavily over to the front entrance, where he was immediately surrounded by reporters and photographers.

'Just let me through,' he insisted.

'But, sheriff – does this mean that Terence Pearson was part of an organized gang of criminals? Or some kind of sect, maybe?'

'Do you know how your deputies died?'

'You always boasted that your cells here were real high-security. How could a mass murderer simply walk out of here?'

Luke answered none of their questions, but forced his way through to the foyer, where John Husband and Mike Whipps and a score of other officers were waiting for him, as well as the deputy commissioner, a florid-faced man with wavy silver hair and a nasty, repetitive cough.

On the floor by the front desk there were two humped sheets. From the body beneath each sheet, a thin river of blood had run, following the octagonal pattern of the marble floor tiles.

Luke ignored everybody else and took hold of John Husband's arm. 'Tell me what happened,' he said, under his breath. 'As much as you know. In words of one syllable. And don't say "sorry". That's two syllables.'

John said. 'It doesn't make any sense. It's like nobody saw anything. Smittkamp and Engel were on the front desk. Somebody must have just walked in and taken them out with a knife. Throats cut, both of them. Ear to ear, and a bit more besides.'

'Had they drawn their weapons?'

John shook his head.

'Any footprints?'

'No. Whoever did this knew how to handle a knife, I can tell you.'

'Both of them killed with the same knife?'

'Same type knife, by the look of it. But we won't know for sure until we take metal samples from the wounds.'

Luke walked around the desk, and looked down at the two humped sheets. For the first time in his career, he really didn't want to see what was underneath. He had been talking to Smittkamp and Engels less than two hours ago. He knew, however, that he would have to look, and look closely, because this was one of those incomprehensible incidents that, sometimes, no amount of detective work could ever explain. How could one man have cut the throats of two armed officers?

'More than one perpetrator, clearly,' said Luke.

'Nobody saw nobody.'

Luke paced around the foyer. His fellow officers and the press respectfully stood aside. He knew what he was looking for. He wasn't looking for fingerprints or footprints. He was looking for a sign that the Green Traveller had been here.

He stopped pacing and stood with his hand covering his

mouth, thinking. John Husband came up to him and said, 'You want to see the cell?'

'They didn't force the lock. They must have known or guessed the combination. Maybe one of them was a safe-cracker.'

'Yes,' said Luke. 'And maybe he wasn't, either. Maybe he was a dice-player. Dice-players have a way with numerical combinations, don't they?'

John Husband looked perplexed. 'I guess,' he admitted.

It was a grim night. He lifted the sheet that covered Edna Bulowski and stood and stared at her for a very long time. She had fallen in such a way that she appeared to be smiling at him, with her one blind and bloodied eye. He looked at the bodies of Sloan and Verbick, too, in the small room next to the cells where the night-duty officers brewed up coffee. The pinups on the wall were squiggled and sprayed with blood.

'Pretty weird business,' John Husband remarked.

'Terence Pearson was a pretty weird guy, with some pretty weird ideas.'

'Pretty weird friends, too, by the look of it.'

Luke said, 'No . . . these weren't his friends. He didn't have any friends. These were people who wanted him for something else.'

'They must have wanted him pretty damned badly.'

'Yes,' said Luke. 'I'd just like to know why.'

They went back to the front desk to talk to the medical examiner. It was the same snappy, short-tempered examiner who had dealt with Mary van Bogan, back at the Pearson house. He looked tired and out of sorts.

'Any ideas?' Luke asked him.

The ME shrugged. 'On superficial examination, it looks as if all four male officers had their throats cut by the same or exactly similar weapons. I would say that they were held from behind and that the fatal wound were inflicted very swiftly. The weapon or weapons were extremely sharp, almost preternaturally sharp. We're talking about a knife that could cut through a half-inch steel pipe here, not just a human neck.'

'What about deputy Bulowski?'

'Sword or very long knife. Some indications that it was thrown, rather than thrust. There were secondary cuts on the lower rim of the eye-socket that indicate that the blade dropped or reverberated after the initial intrusion. This normally wouldn't have happened if the perpetrator was holding onto the weapon's handle.'

'Anything else?'

'Not yet. We'll get you a full set of detailed reports as soon as we can.'

'Thanks,' said Luke. 'That's very co-operative of you.'

The ME looked at him over his half-glasses, and his eyes were cold and serious. 'These were *our* people, sheriff. You'll get all the co-operation you need.'

Luke was still looking around the stairwell and the corridors when Deputy Fairbrother came hurrying up to him. 'Sheriff? Sorry to interrupt you, but we've had a fatal traffic accident out on 76th Avenue South West. Tractor-trailer and two cars.'

'Anything that you can't deal with?'

'No sir, but I thought you ought to know the reported cause of the accident, sir.'

'Go on.'

'Well, it was hogs, sir. A whole herd of hogs, maybe a hundred or more.'

Luke shut his eyes for a moment, and squeezed the muscles at the back of his neck. 'Jesus,' he said. 'That's all I need. Hogs.'

Garth was bruised and groggy when Nathan and David came into his room at Mercy Medical Center, but he managed to raise a smile.

Nathan drew up a chair beside the bed. The covers were humped over a leg-frame, to protect Garth's broken ankle. His ribs were strapped right up to the armpits.

'You look like shit,' said Nathan, gripping his hand.

'Thanks. I feel like it.'

David said, 'We brought you these pecan candies . . . oh, and this, too.' He handed Garth a box of chocolate-coated nuts and a copy of *Playboy*. 'I said it might get you too excited, but Dad said you swore on the Bible you never ever looked at the pictures.'

'This son of yours is becoming too cute for his own good,' said Garth.

'Kayley been to see you?' asked Nathan.

'Sure. She brought me these flowers. She'll be back later, right after she's had something to eat.'

Nathan said, 'Tell me what happened.'

'You don't have to look so worried.'

'Of course I'm worried. I feel responsible.'

'Well . . . what happened was *painful*, I won't deny that, but it was really interesting. I went into Captain Black's pen and I started to talk to him. He was kind of edgy, but not particularly responsive. Not until I mentioned the name Emily to him.'

'Emily? That was the name of the Pearson girl, wasn't it? The one who survived.'

'Exactly. Why do you think I mentioned it? But that's when the captain went absolutely crazy. He went wild! He came after me like the Wabash Cannonball.'

'So what are you trying to say?'

'I'm trying to say that it must have worked . . . the xenografting. I know it's not conclusive proof, by any means. Maybe the captain just got pissed off. But his response to "Emily" was so immediate – so positive.'

'You really think that Captain Black has inherited little George Pearson's personality?'

'Maybe not his entire personality. After all, George's personality was only half-formed. But his memories, maybe. His psychological points of reference. Emily always protected him. Emily always looked after him. Maybe the reason he went berserk was because – this time, this one last time – Emily failed to look after him, and he died. Or at least, his physical existence as a three-year-old boy has come to an end. His brain, in part, has carried on.'

Nathan slowly shook his head. 'God Almighty, it's incredible. I mean, if you're right, it's incredible. I didn't think that this was going to go any further than a simple tissue transplant.'

'I'm not sure that I did, either,' said Garth. 'If you have any other kind of organ transplant, you don't acquire any of the characteristics of the donor, do you? It's not like those horror movies where people have the hand of some murderer sewn on to them, instead of their own, and go around strangling people.'

'But in this case – ?'

Garth cautiously patted his lips, to feel how swollen and cracked they were. 'In this case, yes. We really could have changed Captain Black's personality. If I can get him to make a positive response to – say – a dozen things that only George would have known about, then I think we'll be making some astonishing progress. I mean, if we can transfer personality characteristics and memories from one brain to another – think of the possibilities. We can revolutionize the treatment of mental disorders overnight.'

'Eat your heart out, Sigmund Freud,' smiled Nathan.

'Don't laugh,' said Garth. 'It could easily happen.'

'So . . .' Nathan asked him, leaning back in his chair and lacing his hands behind his head, 'what do you propose to do?'

'Get myself out of this place, as soon as possible. I hate hospitals.'

'You could do a whole lot worse than Mercy,' Nathan reassured him, and picked up his chart from the end of the bed. 'Hmm . . . says here you suffered a Pott's fracture. That's a bummer. They take weeks to heal, especially in old guys like you.'

'I love you, too,' said Garth. 'But I want to be out of here by tomorrow. I can't delay this experiment by even one day.'

'You're going back to it? After what Captain Black just did to you? After he killed Raoul?'

'Nathan, I have to. With Zapf-Cady going for the vote, we may not have very much more time. Besides, I know what to expect now. I'll play it safe.'

David said, 'Can I see Captain Black again?'

Nathan shook his head. 'I don't think so. He's turned pretty dangerous, ever since he's had this operation.'

But Garth said, 'Sure you can see him. Why not? We won't be playing Daniel in the Hog's Den any more. I'm going to rig up a way in which we can talk to Captain Black without putting ourselves at risk. Or him, too, for that matter. Sure you can see him. In fact, I think I'd really like you to. He liked you the first time you met him, didn't he? Maybe a younger presence could help to calm him down some.'

'I don't know,' said Nathan. 'If there's any risk at all –'

Garth lifted his hand. 'No risk, I promise. There's no way that I'm going through this again. No, thank you. Not even in the interests of science.'

'Well, I'll think about it,' said Nathan.

'Oh, come on, Dad,' David urged him. 'I told all my friends about him.'

'I said, I'll think about it, okay?'

They talked for a while about going back to school, and baseball, and then David went to buy himself a 7-Up. Nathan drew his chair a little nearer to Garth's bedside, and said, 'Let me ask you this seriously. Do you think that Captain Black has really acquired that little boy's personality?'

'I don't know for sure,' said Garth. 'But there are indications.'

'Do you know how bad this makes me feel?'

'Why should it make you feel bad? The boy was dead. Now some part of him is still alive. Surely something is better than nothing.'

'But he's alive inside of a *pig*, Garth! What kind of a nightmare is that?'

Garth lay back on his pillows. His face was drawn and pale and extremely grave. 'I don't know, Nathan. But I'm going to do my darndest to find out.'

'And if it turns out to be hell on earth, for a boy to discover that he's been reincarnated as a hog?'

Garth held Nathan's gaze with complete steadiness. 'If that's what it turns out to be, then we'll have to do to Captain Black what any good veterinarian would do: we'll have to put him out of his misery.'

'You mean little George Pearson will have to suffer the agony of being murdered twice over?'

'Nathan,' said Garth, 'You're being far too sentimental. Even if there is something of George in Captain Black's brain, it's probably not much more than a vague half-awareness.'

'Okay, okay,' Nathan nodded. 'I guess I'm just feeling guilty.'

'Story of your life, old buddy,' said Garth, and clasped his hand, and said, 'Thanks for coming. You and David both. Come on up to Spellman Saturday morning, and see for yourself how the captain's coming along. It'll be interesting. And safe, too, I promise you. This is the kind of experiment that happens just once in a lifetime, and you're part of it. You ought to be there.'

Nathan said, 'It isn't easy, you know, feeling responsible for other people getting killed.'
'You're not responsible. Raoul knew the risk he was taking.'
'All the same.'
Garth gripped Nathan's hand. 'Listen, there's something called fate, and however smart we are, we can't avoid it, because we make it ourselves. We have to, otherwise what would we be? Raoul made his own fate; and so, in her way, did Susan. She tried to drive to the hospital to save her child when she would have been better calling the paramedics. Who knows why she did it? We probably never will. But that was who she was, that was how she was always going to behave, and her fate was waiting for her down that slip road, the same way that Raoul's fate was waiting for him inside of that laboratory. So stop blaming yourself. For God's sake, Nathan, it isn't humanly possible to foresee the consequences of everything you do.'
'I guess,' said Nathan. But he still couldn't stop himself from thinking about George Pearson – tiny, bewildered George Pearson – opening his eyes to find that he was no longer a boy, not in shape, anyway; but a huge, lumbering hog. God, no wonder he went crazy. Anybody would go crazy. It was worse than Kafka's *Metamorphosis*, in which the young man turned into a giant centipede.
David came back with his 7-Up. 'You should watch the news,' he told his father, enthusiastically. 'There's some hogs got loose, and caused a pile-up out by the airport. The cops are saying there were three people killed, and the hogs ate them.'
Garth said, 'Jesus.'
'That must be wrong,' said Nathan. 'Hogs don't eat people.'
'I'm afraid I'll have to correct you there,' said Garth. 'They have been known to. In fact, when they're really hungry,

they'll eat almost anything. One of our research assistants left his folder in a pigpen two or three months ago, and that pig was squealing fit to burst itself the very next day, because it was shitting out undigested marker pens and chrome-plate springclips.'

Nathan stood up, and laid his hand on David's shoulder. 'Okay, Garth, I think that's enough for one night. We have to go.'

'Oh, chill out, Dad, I want to hear about the pigs.'

'I said that's enough for one night. I'll call you later, Garth. I'm glad you weren't bust up too bad.'

'I'm a survivor,' smiled Garth. 'Or hadn't you guessed that already?'

The black van turned into Vernon Drive and the driver switched off its engine and killed its lights. It was parked diagonally opposite the Pearson house, although the Pearson house was blacked out tonight. The trees thrashed in the gusty wind, and the tapes reading POLICE LINE – DO NOT CROSS were twisting and snapping like a ship's pennants.

In the back of the van, Terence sat with a gag bound tightly into his mouth, and his hands tied behind him. He was bruised and sore, and he was sure that he had lost some teeth, although his mouth was so swollen that it was impossible for him to tell. He was exhausted, too. He felt that this night was never going to end, that dawn would never break. The van's windows were darkly tinted, but all the same there wasn't the slightest glimmer of light from outside. Nothing but the sound of telephone lines whistling, and leaves rattling on the roof, and the intermittent slam-*pause*-slamming of a garden gate.

The floor of the van was heaped with dirty blankets and uncured goat hides, and Terence was crowded close to the Leper in his stinking tarry habit. The Leper said nothing, but breathed with a complex, clogged-up whistling, and occasionally scratched. Terence was sure that he could hear soft lumps of atrophied flesh dropping off him, but it he was probably imagining it.

On the other side of him, closer still, sat the girl Naked, with her ratty-smelling fur jacket and her hair that was crisp with dead flowers. She had scarcely spoken to him since they had left the sheriff's department, but occasionally she had stroked his cheek with the crooked fingers of her left hand, almost absent-mindedly, as if she were trying to remember what he felt like, what he looked like.

On the other side of the van, barely visible in the gloom, sat the Swordsman, his head in his hands, his bag of swords resting against his knee. Beside him sat Knife, posing, fidgeting, sighing from time to time. The Witness was driving; so that Terence could see only the silhouette of his back. He presumed that the Doctor was sitting next to him, in the front passenger seat. He had heard a thick, low dialogue in common Czech – not the Czech of book-writing or academic discussion, but the Czech of the less well-educated people of Bohemia and Brno, thick with trilled 'r's' and strong exhalations of breath, the sort of pronunciation that could make sense of words like *scrvkl* and *trpyt.*

He had guessed that this was the Doctor, because the same common Czech was also used by university students and intellectuals, although there were very few books or articles written in it.

He wasn't frightened by the Doctor, however. Not as much as he was frightened by the Swordsman; and not even a fraction as much as he was frightened by the bushy, scraping, rustling shape that sat right in the very back of the van. Janek-the-Green, pungent with bay; dark as a freshly-opened grave; a relentless and voracious presence that he couldn't even start to understand.

Where Janek-the-Green sat, the blankets were heaped with pungent soil. Naked had said, with laconic amusement, 'This is something for you to see . . . this is where the story of Dracula came from, carrying his boxes of earth with him.' She pronounced it 'Dra-*coo*-la', and it sounded all the more frightening for that, as if she had actually known him.

Terence was still shocked and bruised by their swift escape from the sheriff's department. They had rushed downstairs from the roof like the maddest of mazurka dancers, all six of them, flight after flight, until they had reached the fire exit to the street and collided out of it, into the storm. There had been nobody to stop them; no alarm; no shouts of '*Freeze! Police!*' They had run across the rain-lashed parking lot to their van, and clambered into it.

Terence had shouted out, 'Hey! I'm here! I'm here, for Christ's sake!' and it was then that the Witness had hit him a single devastating punch in the side of the face with the force of a billy-club and he had spun backwards on one foot, the other foot lifted in the air like a maniacal clown, and collapsed onto the rainswept concrete. Between them, Knife and Naked had heaved him into the back of the van; and here they were.

'What are we waiting for?' he asked Naked. His voice was snotty and thick.

'We're waiting for your little girl to start crying, and to wake up your neighbour,' whispered Naked. 'He will go to see your little girl, and ask her what the matter is. She will tell him that she has heard a frightening noise in the street outside. He will come downstairs, and unlock the door, and look out. It is then that we can enter his house without any bloodshed, and take your Emily away from him.'

'How do you know this?' said Terence.

'We know because a child of Janek can always sense that he is close by. You sensed it, didn't you, when you were locked in your cell? Emily senses it, too.'

'You should leave her alone,' said Terence, miserably. 'You shouldn't take her. You should leave her alone.'

'Well, now,' said Naked. 'And who are you to be saying such things? You, your father's son?'

Terence glanced at the dark, bushy shape in the corner of the van, and couldn't help shuddering, as if some prickly demon had whispered coldly into his ear and told him the date of his death. 'That's not my father. My father was a kind man, gentle. He never would of killed nobody, never.'

'Of course your father was a kind man. He still is a kind man. Look at him, my friend. He could have taken your life on the rooftop, yes? But he spared you, because he loves you. You are his flesh and blood, yes? His to kill; his to spare. And for the moment he has chosen to spare you, which is kind.'

Terence coughed, and shivered. Suddenly, the Witness raised his hand, and the Green Traveller gave a hideous, excited rustle. A light had been switched on in the Terpstras' house. After a moments, Mr Terpstra appeared briefly, crossing the upstairs landing in his red and brown striped bathrobe.

'There,' whispered Naked. 'Your daughter has started to cry.'

Terence accidentally bit his swollen lip, and winced. He closed his eyes and prayed to God that Janek wouldn't harm either of them, himself or Emily. *Oh God save me from the Green Traveller. Oh God save me from my own bad blood.*

Two or three minutes went by, and then they saw Mr Terpstra walking back across the landing.

'Now's the time,' breathed Naked. They waited for a few tense seconds more, and then, to Terence's surprise – and obviously to Naked's surprise, too – the landing light was switched off.

There was a sharp, disturbed rustling from Janek-the-Green. The Witness turned around in his seat, and even though he was wearing his expressionless, white-varnished mask, it was obvious that he was perplexed.

'What's happened?' asked Terence.

'Your neighbour has returned to bed. He hasn't gone to see your daughter at all.'

'So what does that mean?'

'That means we will have to enter the house another way.'

'You mean you're going to have to force your way in?'

'We can't do that.'

'Why not? There are five of you.'

'We simply can't. It's . . . not possible, that's all.' Naked sounded testy and anxious. From the scratching noises in the back of the van, Terence guessed that Janek-the-Green was growing anxious, too. Or maybe hungry. According to the old books that Terence had been studying, Janek needed to feed at least twice a week, and sometimes even more often.

'You will have to go to the door yourself and wait for your neighbour to invite you in.'

'Jesus, he won't do that,' said Terence. 'He hates the sight of me, always has.'

'You will have to try. There is no other way.'

'I don't think you get it,' Terence retorted. 'Quite apart from the fact that Terpstra hates my guts, he wouldn't ask a fugitive child-killer into his house, would he? He may be an idiot, but he's not stupid.'

'You will have to try,' Naked repeated.

By way of underlining Naked's request, the Swordsman drew out one of his swords and pointed it steadily and directly at Terence's forehead, so that the point dug into his skin. Terence felt blood trickling down between his eyes and sliding down the side of his nose.

'All right, then, I'll try,' he agreed. 'But you'll have to untie me first.'

Naked held her hand out, and the Swordsman passed her

a horn-handled knife. She cut the cords that bound Terence's wrists, and gave him a push with the flat of her hand. 'You won't try to escape, will you? I would hate to see you die.'

Terence said nothing. The boy Knife reached out and opened the van doors, and Terence climbed past the Leper and the ragged bushlike shape of Janek-the-Green. He hesitated for a moment as he passed Janek, but Janek didn't respond at all. Behind his mask he remained as chilly and as hostile as ever.

Terence stepped down onto the road. Naked said, 'Make sure you are invited inside. Janek will be very angry with you if you don't.' She pronounced it 'engary'.

'I think I get the message,' said Terence. He walked diagonally across the street to the Terpstras' driveway, massaging his wrists as he did so. His mouth felt as if it were ten times its usual size, and his right temple was throbbing. He stopped when he reached the Terpstras' front lawn, and turned around. The van remained blacked-out and sinister, and there was no indication at all that there was anybody in it. Terence glanced down the street, trying to calculate his chances of escaping. But the nearest side-turning was well over five hundred feet away, and he had seen for himself how fast and accurate the Swordsman could be, when he had killed that sheriff's deputy.

Besides, he would need not only the speed to escape, but the will, too; and he wasn't sure that he had that much determination any longer.

Terence limped to the Terpstras' door and pressed the bell. He had to press it six or seven times before the landing light was switched on again, and he heard Leland coming down the stairs grumbling, 'All right! All right! Don't you know what time it is, for Christ's sake?'

He didn't say anything until Leland Terpstra had opened the door, and peered out into the darkness.

'Who's there?' Leland demanded. 'What the hell do you want?'
'Hello, Leland,' said Terence, trying to sound quiet and conciliatory.
'Who's there?' Leland repeated. Then he said, '*Terence*, is that you?'
'Right first time, Leland.'
'I thought you were in jail,' said Leland, nervously. 'Did they let you out?'
'Something like that. They granted me bail.'
'After what you did? They granted you bail?'
'Leland, I'm tired and I'm hungry and I can't get into my house. The sheriff's department forgot to give me my keys back, and I forgot to ask for them.'
'I'm sorry, Terence. I can't help you. Dolly gave our spare set to the police. They said nobody should enter the house until after their investigation was all done.'
'I just don't know what to do,' said Terence. 'I don't have enough money for a hotel. I don't even have a dime for the telephone.'
From the upstairs landing, Mrs Terpstra called out, 'Leland? Who is it? What's going on?'
Leland Terpstra said, 'It's all right, Dolly. Nothing to worry about. Somebody asking for directions, that's all.'
But he looked fiercely at Terence and said, 'I'm sorry, Terence. I can't help you. Now leave us alone.'
Terence stepped nearer to the front door. Leland Terpstra kept it on the brass security-chain, and even closed it an inch or two narrower.
'Leland, you don't have to be afraid of me. I didn't do anything wrong.'
'You cut off your kids' heads and you don't think that's wrong? You're a maniac. You were always a maniac, the way you shouted at everybody; the way you used to treat poor Iris. But this time you've gone and done something totally beyond

the pale, Terence, and I don't want to have nothing to do with you. Nothing, you hear me?'

'How's Emily?' asked Terence, trying to sound reasonable, trying to calm Leland down.

'Emily's fine, no thanks to you. That poor girl's lucky she's not in a mental institution, the things that happened to her.'

'Is there any chance that I could see her?'

Terence looked around at the van. He knew that he was not supposed to invite himself in. The Green Traveller had to be freely asked: otherwise he was powerless to cross any threshold. He had influence only over those who readily agreed to what he had to offer; but it was remarkable how many people did. They were quite prepared to sacrifice the future of unconceived, unbaptized children, so long as they could have wealth and plenty now.

Still, Terence thought wryly, that wasn't so unusual. People were sacrificing the future of unconceived, unbaptized children every day of the week, and quite often they weren't even doing it for wealth and plenty, but just out of witlessness, or apathy, or malice.

There was no signal from the van, so he turned back to Leland Terpstra. 'Give me a break, Leland. I won't be guilty until a jury proves me guilty. Maybe I was all-fired crazy some of the time. But I wouldn't of hurt those kids, you know that.'

Leland peered down the street, first one way, then the other. 'How'd you get here?' he wanted to know.

'Some friends dropped me off. They left before I realized I didn't have my key.'

'Couldn't you just break in? It's your house, after all.'

'Well, maybe I will. But I'd sure like to know that Emily's okay.'

'Not possible, I'm afraid, Terence.'

'Leland – I'm her father. Whatever I've been accused of, I'm still responsible.'

'I said, "not possible". She's not here.'

'What do you mean, she's not here? The sheriff told me that he'd seen her here. He told me himself!'

'He did see her here. That was just after your sister-in-law was killed. But you didn't think they'd let her stay here, do you? The people from the county welfare services came and collected her. I don't know where they've taken her. Some children's home, I guess.'

'They didn't tell you which one?'

'If they did, I don't remember. We took her in for a couple of hours, that's all. We were just being neighbourly.'

Terence pressed his hand against his chest. He was beginning to hyperventilate. He didn't dare to guess what would happen if he had to go back to the van and tell Janek-the-Green that Emily had gone, and that he hadn't been able to gain admission to the Terpstras' house.

'You all right?' said Leland, staring at him more intently. 'That's a hell of a swelled-up lip you got there. And what happened to your head?'

'Leland,' he breathed. 'I really have to sit down.'

But Leland shook his head. 'I'm not taking you in, Terence. There's no way. I've seen you acting out of your skull and I don't want that happening in my house. Now you'd better leave this porch or else I'm going to call the cops on you and have you removed, and for a man on bail that wouldn't look good at all, now would it?'

'Leland, I'm begging you. I'm going to faint flat on my face, else.'

Leland hesitated for a long, long time. Terence closed his eyes and almost *willed* him to invite him in. At last Leland closed the door, slid back the security-chain, and said, 'Five minutes only, Terence. Not a minute longer. And no crazy stuff. You understand me?'

'Leland, that's all I'm asking.'

Leland opened the door. Almost instantaneously, Terence heard the van doors banging, across the street. Leland peered over Terence's shoulder and said, frowning, 'Who are those people? Looks like a fancy-dress party.'

Terence turned around. Crossing the street on swift, silent, determined feet came the Swordsman, the Leper, the Witness, and the twins Knife and Naked, followed closely by a small monkeylike figure in a dark velvet cloak whose face was hidden behind a mask varnished solid red, the colour of fresh blood. This must be the Doctor, he thought, and he knew what the Doctor could do.

When Leland saw that the entourage were walking into his driveway, he said, 'Shit, Terence!' and tried to slam the door. But Terence stuck out his elbow, and stopped him from closing it, and then he gave the door a hefty kick which sent it shuddering wide. 'Shit, Terence, what's going on?' Leland panicked.

The Swordsman was on him before he could say anything else. He seemed to have crossed the front yard instantaneously, in a single heartbeat. Tall and long-legged and unstoppable, he seized hold of Leland Terpstra's collar and wrenched him around and kicked him, so that Leland fell in a praying position onto the stairs. Leland let out a cry that was halfway between a cough and a scream, but the Swordsman kicked him again, his narrow black suede boot thumping between Leland's shoulder-blades so hard that Leland screamed for breath.

The rest of the Green Traveller's entourage crowded into the hallway, while the Swordsman dragged Leland into the living-room. The boy Knife drew the drapes tight together, and then switched on the overhead lights. From upstairs, Mrs Terpstra called, 'Leland? Leland! What's going on down there, Leland? What's all that banging?'

Naked glanced at Knife, and without any hesitation,

Knife left the living-room and went upstairs, silent and quick. Terence looked at Naked in alarm, but Naked lifted her fingers to her lips, to indicate that he should stay silent, say nothing. Terence watched helplessly as the Swordsman forced Leland to kneel in the centre of the room, and cuffed him from side to side. It sounded like a butcher beating out steaks.

Leland's cheeks burned fiery red. An ugly black bruise was swelling up on his forehead, and blood was sliding out of the side of his mouth. He turned to Terence in terror and sheer disbelief.

'It's real,' was all that Terence could tell him.

Naked demanded, 'Where is your daughter? You said that your daughter would be here.'

Terence defensively lifted his hands. 'The welfare services took her away.'

'The welfare services?'

'I swear it.'

Naked looked contemptuously around the neat, wax-polished living-room. She and the rest of Janek's entourage were so out-of-place in a room like this that even Terence had difficulty in believing that they were really here. They were so decayed, so decadent, so medieval. But their reality was confirmed by their strength, and their self-assurance, as well as the fact that they smelled like medieval people, of sweat and grease and filthy velvet.

Naked approached Leland Terpstra and stared at him with her vacant, white-masked face. Leland raised his eyes, and his Adam's apple worked up and down, as if he were trying to swallow a large lump of fat. 'What do you want?' he asked her. 'You're not going to kill me, are you?'

Naked laid a hand on his shoulder. 'What do you know about death?' she asked him.

'I don't understand what you mean.'

'I mean, are you aware of what happens to you, when you die?'

'I don't know. I really don't know. Some folks say there's a light, don't they? And they feel like walking into it, because it's so welcoming.'

'And do you believe in this magical light? If I were to kill you now, is that where you'd go? Straight into the light?'

Leland twisted his hands together, around and around. 'Please don't kill me. I've tried to be good, okay? I've tried to be fair and honest to everybody. If I'd've known that you wanted Emily, I'd've kept her here. What difference does it make to me? But I didn't know you wanted Emily, and the welfare people took her, and as far as I was concerned that was the best thing that could've happened.'

'Where is she?' asked Naked, in a foggy, appealing voice. She stroked his cheek with her knuckles, over and over. 'Why don't you tell me where she is?'

Leland was sweating and trembling. 'Ma'am, believe me, I'd tell you if I knew.'

She went on stroking him, more and more seductively, until his face was filled with despair. 'You must know,' she whispered. 'You must be able to remember.'

He shook his head again and again. He was so frightened now that he couldn't even speak.

Terence said, 'There aren't that many places in Cedar Rapids where they'd take an abandoned child. My guess is McKinley Children's Home, because it's close to Mercy Medical Center. That's where they're taking care of her mother. My wife. Iris.'

Leland said desperately, 'I just don't know. I just don't know.'

'Well . . .' said Naked. 'Not that it matters. We'll find her anyway.'

'I just don't know. I swear it. I just don't know.'

All the time that Leland was begging and babbling, the Swordsman was drawing his swords out of his scabbard, one by one, with that dreadful sliding, ringing sound. He drew out all five, and interlocked them, blade by blade, until they formed the pentangle that Leland himself had briefly glimpsed on the night that Mary van Bogen had been murdered, across the street.

The Swordsman held up the pentangle so that it framed his bland, masked face. Leland stared at him, and then at Terence, and said, 'What? What is it? What is he going to do?'

At that moment, Knife reappeared. He seemed to be short of breath. He looked across at Naked, and nodded, and Naked momentarily closed her eyes in silent acknowledgement.

The Doctor came across the room. His mask fitted badly, and his scalp was tufted and scabrous. He stood close to Leland and coughed – a high, phlegm-racked cough – and then he patted him on the shoulder.

'The Doctor says not to be afraid,' said Naked.

'Terence –' begged Leland.

Terence turned his back. He knew what was going to happen now. Leland had invited them in; and once Leland had invited them in, he had irrevocably placed his fate in the Green Traveller's hands. The Green Traveller was famished; his roots and tendrils were painfully wriggling where his stomach should have been; and there was only one food which his appetite demanded. Human viscera – Leland's viscera, because there was nobody else. Not as sweet as one of the Green Traveller's own children; not as mortally satisfying. But food all the same.

The Swordsman lowered the pentangle of swords over Leland's head, in the same way that he had lowered them over Terence's head, back in the cells. But back in the cells, the

Swordsman had done it only to warn Terence that his head was forfeit if he didn't comply. This time, Terence knew that the Swordsman was acting in his role as Janek's executioner. He closed his eyes for a moment, and under his breath he whispered, '*Heavenly Father, have mercy on him.*'

Leland was whinnying, a dreadful faltering sound that came out of one nostril. The pentangle of swords was lowered over his face until it formed a criss-cross collar of sharpened steel around his neck. He turned his head from one side to the other, frantically, trapped, and then he screamed. 'Terence help me! Terence, God help me! Don't let them kill me, Terence! No!'

Terence made the mistake of turning back. At that instant, the Swordsman closed the pentangle with the thinnest sound of sliding steel, and the swords cut through Leland Terpstra's neck as if it were no more substantial than a cabbage stalk.

There is always an instant when a decapitated head can see and understand what has happened to it; and Leland Terpstra's head was no exception. It stared at Terence, and its mouth began to open as if it wanted to say something. But then blood exploded out of the carotid artery, drenching the shoulders of his bathrobe; and the Doctor immediately snatched at the thinning hair and lifted up the head and swung it from side to side, so that blood sprayed all across the room, and up the wallpaper, and spattered the colour photograph of David Kirkwood Terpstra in the Terpstra family shrine.

'For God's sake!' Terence screamed at the Doctor.

The Doctor shrank back, pretending that he was afraid. He held out Leland's dripping head as if he wanted to give it to Terence as a peace offering. Terence had scarcely eaten anything all day: only the hamburger that they had given him in his cell at lunchtime, and his stomach tightened, and his mouth filled with grainy, acidic sick, which he had to swallow back.

'Tell him to stop it!' Terence coughed at Naked. 'Tell him to put that down!'

But Naked only giggled. Terence felt that he was living out a nightmare: that he had never slept, and that he never would again, because it wouldn't matter if he were asleep or awake. He tried to seize Leland's swinging head, but the Doctor whipped it out of his reach, and lifted up a skeletal, warning finger.

The Swordsman meanwhile had propped up Leland's headless body so that it was sitting on the floor with its back supported by the couch. The carpet all around it was so soaked with blood that it literally crackled, but the Swordsman took no notice. This was obviously part of a well-rehearsed ritual. Everything had to be prepared in the same time-honoured way.

Terence was shaking with disgust. 'God,' he kept repeating. 'God, you're sick. You're worse than I ever imagined.'

'We give people what they want, that's all,' said Naked. 'We don't ask for much in return.' She pointed to the blood-sprayed photograph of David Kirkwood Terpstra, on the wall. 'How many young people died in how many wars?' she asked, 'And what did their parents get out of that? Not an inch of land; not a single good crop. Janek-the-Green is a giver of life, not a taker-away. All he expects is what is rightfully his. What he has conceived, can he not consume?'

The Doctor meanwhile was holding up Leland's head in his right hand, and digging deep into the pockets of his cloak with the other. He came up with bunches of dried herbs and roots and flowers, some of which Terence recognized, others that he could only guess at. The Doctor crammed them into the gaping neck cavity of Leland's body, and at the same time traced symbols and patterns in the air.

From his years of research, Terence knew that the Doctor was using sage, rosemary and thyme, the herbs of marriage, and of binding things together. He was also using beans, which were traditionally placed in coffins, so that their sprouts would please the dead. There was snakeweed, for curing haemorrhages; rue, for reversing decisions; eringo, for healing lacerated flesh; and centaury, for creating delusions.

There was verbena, a herb so powerful that it was believed in the Middle Ages that it could turn the sun blue, if only it could be taken there.

Most potent of all, though, was male mandragora root, black outside and white inside. The medieval belief was that the mandragora grew out of the seed of the last involuntary ejaculation of a man being hanged. It was the root of extreme sexual potency and extreme violence.

By the time the Doctor had finished, Leland's neck aperture was sprouting out herbs and roots and dried flowers like some grotesque plant-holder.

Naked stepped up close to the body and chanted, '*Conjuro et confirmo, super vos angeli fortes, sancti atque potentes, sancti atque potentes, sancti atque potentes.*'

The Doctor raised Leland's head in both hands, held it for a moment, and then lowered it slowly onto the bloody pipe of his severed neck. It made a soft, wet kissing sound.

Terence had read all about the Doctor's restoration of decapitated heads. It was mentioned dozens of times in 14th-century Czech literature, and in some of the oldest books he had found, including the *Clavicules de Salomon* and *The Sacred Magic of Abramelin the Mage*, both prohibited by the Catholic Church.

He had read about it, but he had never really believed it to be true; and he had never imagined that he would see it for himself.

But the Doctor clasped his hands around Leland's neck, and held them there for a while, and then he took them away.

Terence shivered in shock; and couldn't help letting out a great retching bark. Leland's head was joined back onto his neck, but in a terrible lumpy awkward way. There were still sprigs of herbs and dried flowers protruding from his skin, so that he appeared to be wearing a choker of wispy leaves.

'You see?' said Naked, spreading her arms wide like a magician's assistant. 'The head is taken off; the head is put back on again.'

'But he can't be alive!'

'Why not? Of course he's alive! He's been healed!'

As if in response to Naked's claim, Leland groaned.

'That's nothing but air, coming out of his lungs,' Terence protested. 'You cut his head off! He *can't* be alive!'

But then Leland opened his mouth wider, and let out another groan, much longer this time. It wasn't just a groan of pain. It was a groan of utter despair. Even worse than the groaning of a man who knows that he has to die, this was the groaning of a man who knows that he is already dead. It made Terence's skin shrink.

'There!' said Naked, triumphantly. 'Now the Witness will call for your father, and your father will show this man what true suffering is!'

The Witness silently swept from the room.

Terence couldn't speak, couldn't even draw breath. He had felt that he was living in a nightmare ever since his father had first told him about the Green Traveller, but he had never thought that the nightmare would come to anything like this.

Leland groaned again, and gradually his groan rose higher and higher, until it was a harsh, unending scream. His eyes suddenly opened, and he stared at Terence with an expression of total mental torture.

'Kill me!' he screamed. 'Kill me, Terence, kill me! Kill me kill me kill me kill me!'

Terence took a stiff, semi-paralytic move toward him, but with one fluid movement the Swordsman lifted one of his long gleaming blades and pointed it at Terence's throat, warning him to keep away.

Leland kept on screaming, over and over, 'Kill me, Terence! Kill me! Kill me!' He twisted his head from side to side. His neck bulged, and fragments of the herbs which protruded from his skin dropped onto his blood-soaked bathrobe, sticking like midges caught in honey. 'Kill me kill me kill me kill me KILL ME, TERENCE!'

Terence tried another step forward, but this time the Swordsman dug the point of his sword right into his shoulder, almost half an inch deep. The cut stung like a hornet's sting, and Terence immediately stepped back again.

'Don't interfere, Janek's son,' Naked advised him, speaking much more loudly than usual so that he could hear her over Leland's screamed-out appeals. 'You don't want to displease your father too, do you?'

The Swordsman prodded Terence back and back and back, until he was forced to sit down in the armchair next to the fireplace.

'And *stay* there,' Naked admonished him.

Leland started to wave his arms around. He attempted to climb to his feet, but his beheading seemed to have deprived him of his balance and his physical coordination, and all he could do was turn himself around so that he was crouching over the couch. A thin string of blood and dribble slid from his mouth. He coughed, and he coughed out prickly dry hawthorn, and blood. 'Kill me,' he told the couch. 'Kill me,' he told the wall. 'Kill me,' he told the desecrated photograph of his dear dead son.

The door opened again and the Witness returned. He

looked down at Leland Terpstra, and then he beckoned to the thing that was following behind him.

A draught blew through the open door, and a clef-shaped curl of dried bay leaves rustled across the carpet. Then Janek-the-Green appeared, in his coat of bushes and branches. The branches scratched against the door-frame, and the leaves endlessly showered down around him. His mask remained as impenetrable and as sarcastic as ever, but under the bright ceiling light in the Terpstras' living-room, Terence could see the rest of him more clearly; and the clearer he appeared, the more terrifying he was. His hair was bone-white, almost greenish-white, but in patches his head was covered with clumps of damp green moss. It was difficult to see inside the darkness of his leafy cloak, but Terence could make out hanging roots, and soft pale shapes that looked like parasitic fungi. He stank, too. He stank of leaf-mould and rotten wood, and the sourish juices of crushed nettles.

The Swordsman took hold of Leland's shoulder and twisted him around, so that he could see Janek for himself. Leland's mouth opened and closed, and then he started screaming again, a scream that reminded Terence of a dog that he had once seen crushed beneath a truck.

Leland lifted one arm and reached out toward Terence in terror. 'Kill me, Terence! For God's sake, Terence! Kill me!'

Terence started to get to his feet, but the Swordsman turned around and gave him another warning wave of his sabre.

'Kill me, Terence!' Leland shrieked.

'Ask him!' Terence shouted back. Leland was obviously too hysterical to understand, because he kept throwing his head from side to side, and tearing at the couch cushions as if he wanted to rip them apart.

'Ask *him*!' Terence repeated, at the top of his voice, pointing to the Green Traveller. 'Listen to me, Leland, ask *him*!'

Leland kept on babbling for another few seconds; then he stopped, and stared at Terence with bulging eyes. Terence was still pointing to the Green Traveller, and this time he repeated, much more softly, 'Ask *him*.'

There was no time for Terence to debate the morality of what he was doing. He knew that Leland would die one of the most agonizing deaths ever devised; but if Janek didn't kill him then he wouldn't die at all.

Leland turned his head around on his lumpy, herb-necklaced neck, and looked up at the Green Traveller in awe. There was a long moment when Terence didn't think that Leland would be able to speak, but he would *have* to speak, because the Green Traveller could only kill by invitation.

Leland coughed – more blood, more herbs. Then he said, with extraordinary composure, 'Kill me.'

The Swordsman acted instantly. He pushed Leland back onto the couch, and ripped open his bloodstained bath-robe. He sliced open the pyjama-jacket with his horn-handled knife, and pulled it apart to reveal his thin white abdomen. Leland's chest was rising up and down in fright.

The Green Traveller approached the couch and reached down with one bramble-sharp hand. He scratched several thin parallel tracks down Leland's bare stomach – tracks that drew tiny beads of blood. Leland clenched his teeth, and breathed in and out in quick, sharp hisses. He was too frightened to speak any more. He had experienced death once tonight. All he wanted now was to experience a death that lasted and would give him peace.

The Green Traveller hunched his leaf-cloaked back, and half-turned away from Leland, as if he had changed his mind, and didn't want to kill him, after all. Leland kept on sucking his breath in and out, waiting to discover what the Green Traveller was going to do to him, his fingers digging deep into the cushions of the couch. Leaves fell everywhere, a never-ending autumn of the soul.

It happened so fast that Terence missed it. The Swordsman reached down with the thinnest of knives and sliced Leland open from his grey pubic hair to his sunken breastbone. The knife was so sharp that it stuck in his breastbone for an instant, and the Swordsman had to tug it backwards and forwards to get it out.

It was so swift, in fact, that even Leland didn't realize what had happened to him, until he lifted up his head and saw that his abdomen was hanging open, and that his lap was filled with glistening, ochre-coloured intestines, which seemed to rise and swell like some kind of steaming, repulsive pudding. The smell was so sweet and thick that Terence couldn't endure it any longer, and he retched twice, and then regurgitated everything that was in his stomach, painfully, on all fours, in the Terpstras' fireplace.

He heard Leland screaming and screaming. He didn't want to look again. He couldn't. But then Leland screamed, '*Terence!*' and he turned his head, his eyes blurred with tears, his sinuses clogged with blood and vomited meat.

He saw the Green Traveller bent over Leland's opened-up abdomen, one hand deep in Leland's intestines. With the other hand, sensuous cupped, like a man feeding off the richest of truffles, the Green Traveller had pulled up his dark, membrane-sheathed liver, and was cramming it into the slyly-smiling mouth aperture of his mummer's mask.

'*Terence!*' Leland screamed again. But Terence crouched behind the chair and covered his ears with his hands and tried to pretend that he wasn't here, that he hadn't been born, that even the worst of horrors have to come to an end.

Twelve

Emily lay in bed in the welfare home staring at the ceiling. It was well after three o'clock in the morning, but she hadn't slept all night. She had been listening to the rain gurgling in the downpipes like the voices of drowning men. The draught from the partially-open window made the net curtain ripple; and it played out a continous shadow-theatre on the ceiling of a hunchbacked creature with a huge head, accompanied by two elongated greyhounds, running and running beside him.

She was conscious that something momentous was happening to her but she couldn't understand what. She felt as if there were two of her; one inside the other. It was just as if two slightly-different photographic negatives had been laid one on top of the other, because both personalities were hers, yet one of them was darker, stranger, more obscure, as if she were covering her face with her hands.

This darker personality was growing, too. She could distinctly feel it growing. She almost felt that she could talk to it as if it were a separate person, yet it was her, too.

She had first felt this blurring of her personality on the night when Aunt Mary had been killed. She had woken up to feel a huge surge of alarm and delight, like riding a roller-coaster in total darkness. She had sat up in bed, her eyes wide, listening, and she had known that somebody who loved her was very close, somebody she had never met before, but somebody who would give her everything she wanted.

She had smelled something exciting, too, like aromatic

herbs, and woods in winter; and tasted an unusual taste on her tongue – starchy, pungent, slightly slimy.

She could remember talking to the tall white-faced man in the white coat in the yard, but she couldn't clearly remember how she had got there. She could remember how excited she had felt, how thrilled. Her father's father was coming! She couldn't wait to see him, couldn't wait to invite him in. He wasn't grandpa from Des Moines, he was a new grandfather altogether, powerful and wonderful and strange.

She could remember the leaves scuttling across the yard, more and more of them, and the way they caught in the chicken-wire. She could remember a long-legged girl in a shaggy jacket of rabbit and dog furs, and another man with a peculiar black cap.

After that, though, nothing seemed to fit. Had she seen her mother on the stairs? She had half an image of it, but she couldn't be sure. Had she heard Aunt Mary crying out? She didn't know. Her mind wouldn't focus at all.

She felt sorry for Aunt Mary. She had wept for her, quite bitterly, round at the Terpstras' house. But then she had stopped feeling sorry for her, and felt enormously pleased instead, because she had a feeling that her father's father was pleased.

She couldn't remember if she had actually seen her father's father or not. She had an indistinct recollection of something dark and thrashing and bushy, but how could that have been her father's father?

She thought about George, and Lisa, and that made her feel sad again. She could still picture them kneeling in the field, remember thinking they were praying, when all the time their father was going to cut off their heads.

She watched the hunchbacked creature bounding and leaping on the ceiling, and the thin, attenuated dogs running beside him. She wondered where he was running to, this creature – if he were running away from something even more terrible, or if he was hunting somebody down. A sudden patter of rain against the bedroom window made her jump, and she lifted her head to make sure that there wasn't a real hunch-backed creature peering over the window-ledge.

She knew that her new grandfather wasn't pleased with her father at all. She didn't know *how* she knew, she just did. It was in her head as if she had always known it. Her father hadn't done things the way he was supposed to. He hadn't behaved like a son. He had killed George and Lisa because he hadn't wanted their new grandfather even to see them; and if Emily hadn't run so fast, he would have killed her, too, and then things would have gone badly, terribly wrong.

Not just a little bit wrong; but wrong enough to change the weather, and the way the grass grew, and for people to get killed.

It was wrong for her to feel the way she did now, and she was keenly aware that the consequence of being *two* Emilys in one Emily were going to be catastrophic. Not just for her, but for her new grandfather, and all of the thousands of people who needed him. Emily thought of fields, and farms. But she didn't see soya crops flourishing, or corn rustling in the summer sunshine. She saw nothing but sour earth, and drought, and winds thick with eroded dirt. She smelled the smell of stagnant ditches, and rotting wheat, and freshly-excavated graves.

She asked herself who she was, and she wasn't sure that she could answer. She was sure that she was Emily. But she was also 'Emily'.

It was 'Emily' who had invited her new grandfather and all of his friends into the house, the night that Aunt Mary had been killed. It was 'Emily' who had talked to the sheriff, in the Terpstras' house. She couldn't even recall what 'Emily' had said to him; although she remembered an unpleasant gagging sensation, and the feeling that she was saying something wicked.

Tonight, now, she wasn't sure where Emily ended and 'Emily' began. She didn't even know if she ought to feel frightened.

The net curtain rolled in a sudden surge of wind, and the hunchback somersaulted and jumped and disappeared into a crack in the world, and the greyhounds jumped after him.

The door of Emily's bedroom opened an inch or two, and through slitted eyes she saw one of the beige-uniformed staff, checking up on her. There was a moment's pause, and then the door quietly closed.

Emily thought: *There are two of us here, can't you see us? The girl and the 'girl'. The weather's changing, the world's changing; and I'm changing, too.*

At a quarter past ten the next morning, the doorbell rang in Lily's house, and she went to answer it, still towelling her hair. Three bedraggled young men and one equally bedraggled young woman stood on the porch. Behind them, the rain was drifting across the puddly, roughly-paved end of Fir Avenue, and clinging in the trees like smoke.

'Hey, come on in,' said Lily. 'I just made some fresh coffee.'

The tallest of the young men took a long cowboy-booted stride into the hallway, and the others followed. He was thin-faced and dark, with long black hair that was tied back in a bushy pony-tail. He was dressed in worn-out black leathers, emblazoned with badges and pins and the letters AHR2 in metal studs. One of the other two young men, Henry, wore a woolly bobble-hat like Michael Nesmith from The Monkees, and the other, who called himself Kit, had a large nose and rain-beaded glasses. The girl was pretty in an anorexic, waiflike way. Her brown long-sleeved T-shirt was soaking, and she kept squeezing water out of the cuffs.

'Harriet, do you want to borrow something dry?' Lily asked her. She herself was dressed in tight blue jeans and a thick lumberjack's shirt, unbuttoned almost to the waist. 'You don't want to catch cold again, do you?'

'No thanks,' sniffed Harriet. She walked across the red and yellow Indian rug to the fireplace, where three ashy logs were giving their last faltering warmth. She slapped her wet sleeves around her to get her circulation going.

'I have so many T-shirts, you're welcome.'

'It's okay,' Harriet insisted, irritably. She was the serious martyr of the Animals Have Rights Too movement. She always said that if she ever killed any animal, even accidentally, she would slit her wrists. She had even begged Upjohn Pharmaceuticals to use her for vivisection, in place of a chimpanzee, because chimpanzees were equal to humans, and what difference would it make?

'How about you, Dean?' Lily asked the tall, dark young man. 'Is everything ready?'

'You bet. We have the ladders, we have the wirecutters, we have the boltcutters, we have the thunderflashes. John's ready to hit the main gate at 12.01 precisely; we'll hit the perimeter fence as soon as we hear his signal.'

'This is going to make front-page headlines all over,' said the young man in the woolly hat, triumphantly. 'I mean this is going to make us totally famous, worldwide.'

'What did the senator say?' asked Dean, in a voice that was dark as his mien.

Lily was brushing her hair in the seashell-framed mirror that hung next to the telephone. 'The senator wasn't very happy, as a matter of fact.'

'Did you expect him to be? Right now, he's exploiting animals almost as much as the research laboratories exploit animals. He's using them, same way he's using you.'

He came over and stood close behind her, watching her face in the mirror.

Lily said, 'It's not that he doesn't agree with what we're doing. It's just that he can't be openly associated with anything illegal.'

'Lily, he's a politician, and he can't be openly associated with anything illegal? You've got to be pulling my wire.'

'You have to give him some credit, Dean. If it weren't for him, we wouldn't have got any serious hearing at all – not from the media, not from Congress, not from anybody. We certainly couldn't have *dreamed* of a bill like Zapf-Cady, not in a million years. It goes to the vote in a week, and it's going to be passed. I'm sure of it.'

'And your precious Bryan Cady gets all the glory?'

'It doesn't matter who gets the glory. What matters is that millions of animals will be given the right to life.'

Dean put his arms around Lily's waist, and held her tightly against him. 'So what does that mean? That if I'd been able to put through a bill like Zapf-Cady, you would have kept on fucking me, too?'

She pushed down at his interlocked hands. 'Let me go, Dean. Whatever Bryan and I do together in private, that's our business, not yours.'

Dean reached up and squeezed both of her breasts through her lumberjack shirt. She twisted around and tried to slap at him, but he caught her wrists and laughed at her.

'You're a shit, Dean,' she told him, breaking free.

'At least I'm an honest shit. At least I'm trying to make the world better, instead of worse.'

'Oh yes? And where does grabbing my tits come on your list of global improvements?'

'Oh, come on, Lily, for Christ's sake. You know I can't stand to see you fawning over that bastard. I'm suffering, Lily. I can't help it.'

Lily buttoned up her shirt, and then went through to the hallway and took down a waterproof khaki windbreaker. 'Let's just get moving, shall we? There's an animal locked up at the Spellman Institute who's been suffering a hundred times more than you.'

Lily opened the scratched and battered door that led through to the kitchen, and was immediately and enthusiastically greeted by her two shaggy German Shepherds, who obviously thought that she was going to take them out for a walk. 'Stay, Rudi. Stay, Max. Mommy will be back later.'

'Maybe you should bring them along,' Dean remarked. 'They're the fiercest things on four legs I've ever seen.'

'I don't want to risk them getting hurt. You didn't come along to that rally in Denver, did you? Ron Short brought his Dobermann along. The first thing that happened was a security guard blew the poor dog's front legs off. It was just awful.'

Harriet was wiping her nose on a tiny scrap of damp Kleenex. At the same time she was looking up at the photograph that hung over the fireplace. It showed a large Berkshire sow in a half-collapsed pen, surrounded by six or seven piglets. 'I think you have a soft spot for pigs, Lily,' she said.

Lily smiled. 'They're my favourite animal. They're bright. They're kind. They have mortal souls.'

Dean checked his watch. 'Twenty-five after. It shouldn't take us longer than twenty minutes to get there.'

They left the small weatherboarded house and walked across the sloping front yard to the road, where Dean's mud-sprayed Cherokee was parked. They climbed aboard and headed westward.

'I can't take 76th Avenue because it's still blocked off by that accident. The fire was so bad they've got to relay the road. I'll go past the airport instead.'

'I saw that accident on the news,' said Lily. 'They said a whole herd of hogs had broken loose.'

'Your favourite animals,' Harriet gibed.

They drove the rest of the way to the Spellman Institute without exchanging more than two or three sentences between them. In spite of their bravado, they were all tense. The institute had some of the most aggressive security in eastern Iowa, and it had been tightened up even more since the last time Lily and her supporters had demonstrated outside. This demonstration, of course, was going to be far more risky. They had very little idea of what security precautions surrounded Captain Black. They had no idea whether he was under constant guard or not – nor how quickly the security staff could react to a break-in.

Usually, Lily and Dean planned their demonstrations down to the last inch and the last split second, but security was so tight at Spellman that it had been impossible for them to obtain any detailed information. They had found a sketchy architectural schematic that had been attached to the institute's annual report, so they knew roughly where the main pigpens were located, and they were going to try to break through the perimeter fence as close to them as they possibly could. But there was very little cover on that side of the institute, and they knew that their chances of slipping into the building without being spotted by a security camera were probably nil.

Quite apart from that, a Very Important Pig like Captain Black may not even be quartered in the same pens as the rest of Spellman's livestock, for fear of cross-infection.

Still, thought Lily, even if they failed to rescue Captain Black the very fact that they had tried would make headlines all over the country. She didn't underestimate her own newsworthiness, either. The principle of it repelled her, but she was a realist, too, and she was quite aware that if she unfastened her shirt buttons again the chances of a front-page photograph would be increased fifty-fold by each unfastened button.

Bryan Cady had once made the point to her by asking her to put on a lowcut dress and walk through a room in which he was giving a serious election briefing to twenty of his staff. Not one of them – not even the women – had remembered a word that Bryan had said to them. He said later, 'The most eloquent politician in the world could never make a point like a woman's bra.'

Under a slate-black sky, they left the road at the sign that said Aman Natu eserve, but instead of following the track that led directly to the front gates of the Spellman Institute they turned off southward, down a gently-sloping gully, through thistles and rain-beaten grasses, and then climbed at an awkward angle up the hill that overlooked the institute's perimeter to the south-west. The terrain was rough, and it didn't help that it had been raining so heavily over the past few days. The Cherokee whinnied and toiled, and Dean had to change down lower and lower until they were crawling up the last steep slope at less than 2 m.p.h.

'Are we going to make it?' asked Lily.

Dean checked his watch. 'Yeah, we'll make it. But only just.'

The Cherokee's tyres screamed as they tried to get a grip on the slippery vegetation and the slithering dirt. The windshield wipers flopped from side to side in an endless monotonous samba. Dean gunned the engine again and again, and muttered, 'Come on, you bastard. You can make it. Come on, you bastard. One more try.'

For nearly ten seconds, the Cherokee stayed where it was, tilted at the summit of the slope, its wheels spinning frantically. Lily was sure that they weren't going to make it: that the vehicle was going to slide backwards down the slope, and overturn. But Dean gritted his teeth, and slammed the gearshift down into 1, and stamped on the gas pedal again and again. At last the Cherokee scrabbled its way to the top of the slope, and onto the undulating field beyond it.

'That was close,' said Harriet. 'I thought we'd have to turn around and go back home.'

'You still can, if you want to,' said Lily.

Harriet shook her head. 'Just because I didn't approve of this particular demonstration, that doesn't mean I'm going to let you guys take all the credit.'

'What would you rather do? Let that hog go on suffering?'

Dean said, 'Harriet would rather blow her brains out and offer them to Spellman for research.'

'You're a shit, Dean,' said Harriet.

'So people keep telling me.'

The Cherokee bounced and jostled across the field, heading for a stand of oaks that offered them the nearest available cover to the institute's southern perimeter fence. They clung on to the grab-handles inside the vehicle, trying to prevent themselves from being thrown from one side to the other. Over to their left, occasionally visible through the rain, they could see the gleaming rooftops of Spellman's laboratories, and the prickly spires of shortwave radio antennae.

'Here we go!' Dean whooped, and they drove straight into the woods, with twigs and branches lashing furiously at their windows. They followed a jolting, spine-jarring course over roots and rocks and fallen branches, until at last they arrived at the very edge of the treeline, two hundred feet clear of the perimeter. The institute had cleared the woods back in order to discourage the very kind of assault that Lily and her friends were attempting now.

Dean killed the engine, and they sat in silence for a few moments, trying to assess the difficulty of the task that faced them. The perimeter fence was fifteen feet high, high-grade chain-link, topped with seven strands of razor-wire. Ten feet back, there was a second fence, also topped with razor-wire, and hung at intervals with signs depicting a skull and a lightning-flash.

Three hundred feet away, and fifty feet inside of the double fence, stood a tall steel pole, on top of which a remote video camera slowly turned from side to side, watching the perimeter like one of the Martians from *The War of the Worlds.*

Dean checked the slow swinging of the surveillance camera against the second-hand of his wristwatch. He checked it twice, and then he said, 'Thirty-seven seconds, from one side to the other. That means we have just over half a minute to be out of the woods, across to the fence, cut the wire, across to the second fence, cut the wire, and at least fifty feet into the compound.'

'It can't be done,' said Lily.

'I'm pretty damn quick with the wire-cutters,' said Dean.

'All the same . . . there are five of us, we'd never make it. Listen – they're bound to detect us breaking in sooner or later. But the longer we can give ourselves before they raise the alarm, the better chance we have of releasing Captain Black.'

'So what do you suggest?'

Lily looked around. 'Visibility's pretty poor, isn't it? And the storms have been tearing off quite a few branches. I'll take a large dead branch with me, tie it around my shoulders, run to the fence, then drop to the ground at the count of thirty-seven. With any luck, the camera operator won't see anything but leaves.'

Dean was about to protest, but then he shrugged. 'I guess it's not a bad idea, at that. Most of the time those security guards don't bother to watch their monitors, anyway. But I think I should go, not you.'

'I should go,' Harriet volunteered. 'I'm the smallest.'

'Can you cut through the wire, though?' asked Dean.

'I cut through the wire at Maybelle Cosmetics, didn't I? And that was way up on the roof.'

'I guess so,' Dean admitted. 'What do you think, Lily?'

Lily thought about it. There was a lot to be said for letting Harriet cut through the wire. It would go a long way to appeasing her, making her feel wanted. There was more than one Harriet in AHR2, and they had been growing more and more restless since Lily had started associating with Bryan Cady and gradually abandoning terrorism in favour of media hype and political lobbying. They wanted to throw red paint on mink coats, these Harriets. They wanted to firebomb meat-packing factories; and blow up medical research facilities; and assassinate people who made lipstick.

Lily knew that one bill like Zapf-Cady would achieve infinitely more than any number of acts of terrorism, but she didn't want to lose supporters, not even extreme supporters, not until Zapf-Cady was safely passed.

At the moment, the media adored her. But Bryan had warned her that the media turned quickest on those they adored the most, and that – given the slightest hint of weakness – they would happily tear her apart in a feeding-frenzy that would make a shoal of piranha fish look as tame as a can of tuna.

Dean checked his watch again. 'We'd better make up our minds. It's five to.'

'Harriet can go,' said Lily. 'In fact, I think she should.'

'Well, halleluja,' grinned Harriet, and gave Dean a contemptuous flat-of-the-hand slap on the back.

They climbed out of the Cherokee into the dripping woods, and after a brief search around the undergrowth they found exactly what they needed: a freshly-fallen oak branch, over five feet in length, with plenty of spreading foliage. They tied it to Harriet's back with nylon twine, and then they gave her a pair of heavy-duty wire-cutters and a pair of insulated industrial gloves.

'You look like a goddamned walking bush,' grinned Dean, as Harriet made her way to the edge of the woods.

'Remember *Macbeth*,' put in Henry. ' "Macbeth shall never vanquish'd be until/ Great Birnam Wood to high Dunsinane hill/ Shall come against him".'

'You know what your problem is, Henry?' Dean retorted. 'You're too fucking educated. Education is bad for the brain. Stops a guy thinking straight.'

They gathered together at the treeline waiting for noon. They shuffled their feet to keep warm, and watched the rain sweeping across the downsloping grounds that led toward the pigpens. Dean kept looking at his watch and saying, 'Come on, John, for Christ's sake.'

It was nearly a minute after twelve when they heard the high, shrieking whoop of a skyrocket, over on the far side of the institute. They briefly glimpsed it, glittering in the rain, and then it died away. Dean was timing the security camera, and he started to count out loud, '. . . thirty-three . . . thirty-four . . . thirty-five . . . thirty-six . . . okay, Harriet, *go*!'

Hunchbacked, trailing her branch behind her, Harriet hurried across the rough tummocky grass between the woods and the perimeter fence. Lily held her breath, willing Harriet not to stumble. Dean kept on counting as the camera slowly turned through its 180-degree arc of surveillance, reached the end of its swing, and immediately started to turn back again.

Harriet had reached the outer fence, and she was already crouched beside it, fumbling with her wire-cutters.

'. . . twenty-eight . . . twenty-nine . . .'

She cut through a link about four feet above the ground, and then began to snip the links downward, one at a time. They could hear the snipping sounds echoing in the woods behind them. The wire must have been very heavy gauge, because she had to struggle with each link.

'. . . thirty-five . . . thirty-six . . .'

Harriet dropped face-down on the grass and lay totally still. She looked like nothing more than a fallen branch. The camera's gaze passed over her and then turned back the other way again.

'Yesss!' said Kit, punching the air. 'We fooled 'em!'

'. . . eleven . . . twelve . . . thirteen . . .' Dean counted.

Harriet began to get the knack of cutting through the links, and this time she managed to cut right down to the grass before the return of the security camera had her dropping down onto her face for a second time.

She snipped a few links along the top, and then bent the wire back, to create a 'doorway' that would not only be large enough for the five of them to climb through; but which would be large enough for Captain Black to be driven out of – when and if they managed to set him free.

The camera came back. She dropped onto the grass in between the outer perimeter fence and the inner perimeter fence, and lay still.

'Let's hope they don't notice the hole in the wire,' said Lily. But over on the far side of the institute, they heard the crackling of more fireworks, and the wailing of sirens, and the chances were high that none of the Spellman security staff were paying too much attention to the movements of a fallen oak-tree branch on the southern side of the perimeter, unnatural as those movements were.

Harriet crossed to the internal fence, and knelt down in front of it.

'Gloves!' called Lily; and Harriet turned and gave her a quick wave of acknowledgement. She put on her insulating gloves and began to cut through the links in the same way that she had cut through the outside fence. With each snip, Lily saw showers of tiny white sparks, which indicated that the entire fence was electrified, not just the straining wires.

'. . . thirty-six . . . thirty-seven . . .' counted Dean, and Harriet dropped yet again.

She had finished her vertical cut when Henry suddenly tugged at Lily's sleeve. 'For Christ's sake,' he whispered. 'Look!'

It was something that none of them had expected. Walking towards them on the outside of the perimeter fence was a security guard in a dark-blue waterproof cape, leading a Dobermann on a heavy chain lead. He was already so close that they could hear the dog panting and the lead jingling and the guard's wet cape squeaking as he walked.

Harriet must have seen him at the same time, because she dropped flat on her face, even though they had reached a count of only seventeen. But the dog yelped and bounded, and the guard started to jog-trot towards the cut-open hole in the fence. He twisted the dog's chain twice around his left hand, and reached under his cape with his right hand to pull out a revolver.

'Hey!' he shouted. 'I want you out of there, hands over your head! I can see you, and I want you out of there!'

Harriet stayed where she was, cowering beneath her oak-branch. The guard cautiously approached the hole in the outer fence, and ducked through it. His dog was straining so fiercely on its leash that it was almost choking, and Lily could hear its throttled breathing as it tried to break free and rush at the intruder which it had been trained to attack.

The security man stood over Harriet and pointed his revolver at her head. Lily could see him clearly now. He looked impossibly young, with a pale podgy face and a little Burt Reynolds moustache. It was all he could do to stop his Dobermann from dancing and pirouetting and wrenching itself out of his grip.

'Come on, now, I see you there, you ain't hid very good! I want you to stand up with your hands where I can see them, nice and slow.'

Almost ten seconds went by while the rain kept on sweeping down; and the camera kept on swivelling blandly on its tall grey pole; and the Dobermann gasped and slobbered and clawed at the turf. Then – very slowly – with her hands in clear view, Harriet stood up, and faced the security guard with a pinched and muddied expression of defiance. She untied the nylon cord around her waist, and pushed away the branch that was tied to her back. She said something to the guard, but Lily couldn't hear it.

'That's it,' she said, touching Dean's shoulder. 'Let's just back out of here.'

'I don't think so,' Dean replied.

There was something in the tone of his voice that made Lily turn to him, and as she did so she saw him drawing out of his leather jacket an automatic pistol, a nickel-plated 9-mm Browning Hi-Power. She knew what it was because he had shown it to her before, twice – the first time, when she had told him that their affair was over, and he had threatened to shoot both of them. The second time, when they were going to break into the Schuyler Frankfurter Company, and they knew that they would face heavyweight security. On both occasions, she had told him to put it away. Guns had nothing to do with love or with the lack of love; or with saving the lives of innocent animals, either.

'Dean! No!' she snapped at him.

But he raised the automatic in both hands and pointed it with complete deliberation at the security guard and neither warned him nor wavered but pulled the trigger and fired.

There was a light *crack* noise like a branch breaking, and a puff of smoke. The security guard dropped heavily onto the turf.

Instantly, his Dobermann jumped forward with a loud yelp, and dragged the chain leash out of his hand. The dog launched itself at Harriet in a brindled blur, yapping and barking, and tearing at her arms. Harriet screamed, and tried to beat the Dobermann away, but it was wild with fright and fury, and it went for her like no dog that Lily had ever seen before.

'Dean!' she shouted. 'Dean! Shoot it!'

She started to run toward the perimeter fence. She didn't care about the security camera any more. Dean hesitated, but then he started to run after her.

'*Dean, shoot it!*' she screeched, almost hysterical. She could see blood flying; she could see Harriet's arm frantically waving.

Dean overtook her, holding the automatic high. But they were both too late. Harriet struggled to her feet, her face bloodied, her T-shirt in ribbons, and the Dobermann spun around and jumped at her with all the hideous hard-muscled athleticism of which a trained killer dog was capable.

Harriet didn't scream this time; but the dog's momentum knocked her clean off her feet, and backward into the electrified fence. There was an ear-splitting crackling sound, and Harriet flung up her arms and danced a sickening, jerky dance. Sparks cascaded over her shoulders like a fairy cloak. Her hair burst into flames, to give her a crown. She opened her mouth to scream, but her muscles were locked in electrocuted spasm, and all that came out was flickering light and a stream of smoke.

The Dobermann lunged at her again, and hit the fence full-on. There was another violent burst of sparks, and the dog was flung head-over-heels onto its back, more than twenty feet away, where it lay with its legs stiff, shivering, its fur charred, with smoke issuing from its mouth, its ears, and its anus.

They reached Harriet but she was clearly dead. Her face was blackened. She was too hot for them even to touch her. Lily stood up and there were tears running freely down her cheeks.

'Why did you have to bring that fucking gun?' she raged at Dean. 'God, you're such an aggressive, small-minded moron!'

'Don't you shout back at me, Lily! We needed protection!'

'Protection? Protection from what? You asshole, you had to bring that fucking gun! Don't you have any idea how *stupid* men look, when they carry guns? The only reason they carry guns is because it's against the law for them to walk around with their pants open, and in any case people would laugh if they did!'

'For Christ's sake, Lily, the guy pulled a gun on her!'

'Because he was an asshole, like you, and because we're all assholes, for allowing people to walk around with guns. But you were the biggest asshole of all, because you used it, and you killed him, and you killed Harriet too!'

Dean stalked around in circles, ashamed, angry. 'All right, all right. I blew it.'

Lily caught hold of his jacket and stiffly swung back her arm and slapped his face so hard that he shouted out loud. She paused, and then she slapped him again, and then again.

'You didn't blow it because I'm not going to let you blow it!' she screamed at him. 'Does that register, someplace in that apology for a walnut you call a brain? I'm going to make sure that Harriet didn't die for nothing! We're going down to those pigpens and we're going to let out Captain Black and you're going to help us do it!'

Dean lifted both hands in surrender. His left-hand cheek was fiery from all that slapping.

Lily said, 'We don't have any time at all. The security guards will have seen us now. Let's just do it, regardless.'

There was a moment when she thought that Dean was going to turn his back on her, now and drive away. But when he looked at her directly, she could tell by the wincing in his eyes that he couldn't. Even though he never saw her naked any more, even though he couldn't hold her in his arms, and kiss her, he still wasn't ready to leave. The day would come when he wouldn't think about her, even once, but that day wasn't today.

'Henry, Kit,' he said. 'Let's get to it.'

He picked up the insulated gloves that Harriet had dropped, and quickly snipped away the last links of the electrified fence. Sparks showered down onto the grass. He ducked through the opening and said, 'Come on. You said it yourself. We have to be quick.'

'The gun, Dean,' said Lily.

He shook his head. 'I'm keeping the gun. I killed a man, I need protection.'

For an instant, Lily almost didn't go. But in spite of Harriet's death – or maybe because of it – she was feeling dangerous and elated and full of adrenaline. Maybe she wanted to show Bryan something, too. She belonged to him, yes. She didn't mind that. She enjoyed being sexually owned. It could have been her extraordinary upbringing; it could have been the way she naturally was, but the thought of *having* to spread open her legs whenever he wanted her was fearfully arousing. But she had an independent mind, and strength of her own, and nothing in the world was ever going to stop her from expressing herself.

'All right,' she said, her voice quaking. 'Keep the goddamned gun. But keep the last goddamned bullet for yourself; because that's all you deserve.'

A security alarm was plaintively beeping in the near-distance. They could hear shouting and vehicles revving up. Together, the four of them ran as quickly as they could down the well-mowed slope that led toward the pigpen building, the soles of their trainers squeaking on the wet grass.

They had almost reached the building when Lily caught that sweet, unmistakable aroma; that aroma that had always excited her, no matter what. Dean was gasping for breath.

'Hyperventilating,' he said, wiping his forehead with the back of his hand.

'No time,' Lily panted.

They heard a Tannoy booming and echoing around the main buildings. It was impossible to tell exactly what it was saying, but it wasn't difficult to get the gist of it. The southern perimeter has been compromised. A security guard has been found shot. A known animal rights activist has been found electrocuted. Intruders on institute grounds.

They ran along the puddled concrete path that led to the main door of the pigpen building. Dean threw his back to the wall, Rambo-like, and then pushed the door with his hand.

'Well, would you believe it,' said Kit, in amazement. 'It isn't even locked.'

Captain Black had stayed in the darkest corner of his pen all morning, but Garth was still hopeful.

'He's sulking, is all. He's behaving like any three-year-old kid who can't have his M&Ms.'

Nathan glanced at Garth in something like surprise. He didn't know how he could be so forgiving, after what Captain Black had done to Raoul Lacouture, and to him, too. But maybe this was nothing to do with forgiveness. You don't expect God to say sorry when he takes your wife and your son away from you, without warning. Maybe you don't expect God's creatures to say sorry, when they kill your friends and bust up your ribs.

'Maybe we should try running through some names with him,' suggested Jenny. 'If he responded to Emily, he may respond to others, too.'

'That'll make a good starting point,' Garth agreed. 'Let's get this sound-system switched on.'

The institute's electrical engineers had installed a simple

two-way microphone and loudspeaker system so that Garth could talk to him without putting himself in any danger. The perspex viewing-window in Captain Black's pen had been cleaned of dried slobber and its scratches polished out, so that they now had a clear view into every corner of his pen.

Nathan said, 'Has he done anything *unpiglike*? I mean, anything that a boy would do, rather than a hog?'

'His sleep pattern appears to have altered,' said Jenny. 'He seems to need much more sleep much more regularly. It's too early to say if this has any significance. He's still on antibiotics, and it's been taking him quite a long time to recover from all of the anaesthetics we loaded him up with.'

'Anything else?'

'Yes . . . unusual copious activity of the tear ducts.'

David was watching Captain Black in total fascination. 'What does that mean?' he wanted to know.

'Well, I guess you could say that he's been crying a lot.'

David nodded. 'I think I would, if I was three years old, and I found myself stuck inside of a giant pig.'

Garth tapped the microphone, and it made a sharp popping sound. Captain Black grunted, and turned around, and Nathan could see his eyes sparkling in the grotesque shadows of his face. 'Testing, testing . . .' said Garth. 'A is for Adam, Alan, Arthur and Abigail. B is for Bob, Bill, Betty and Bert.'

Captain Black trotted heavily around in a circle, as if he found the sound of Garth's amplified voice to be extremely irritating. He shook his head like a wet dog, and let out a deep shrieking grunt.

'He doesn't seem to care for the loudspeaker too much, does he?' Jenny remarked.

'If he has a kid's brain, maybe he'd rather hear a kid's voice,' suggested David.

Garth made an appreciative face, and Nathan suspected

that this is what he'd been expecting to hear from David all along.

'All right,' said Garth, 'let's give it a try. Go through all of the names you can think of – but don't, just at the moment, say Emily.'

Garth swung himself away from the microphone, stiff-legged, and sat down on the wheelchair stencilled with the words Property of SIG. His ankle was encased in plaster, but it was still very sensitive, and he had to put only the slightest pressure on it for it to feel as if Captain Black were still standing on it, with his full weight, and refusing to budge.

Nathan put his arms around David's shoulders and said, 'Come on, then, let's give this a try.'

David leaned forward to the microphone, and nervously said, 'Captain Black? Can you hear me, Captain Black? It's me, David. We met before, remember? I stroked your ears. That was before you had the operation.'

Captain Black grunted, but showed no other signs that he recognized David's voice.

'Captain Black, I'm going to tell you some names, okay? What you have to do is nod your head up and down if you remember any of them, or shake your head if you don't. So here goes the first one, Adam, like in Adam and Eve. Adam. Do you remember that name, or don't you?'

A long silence followed. Captain Black remained motionless, huge and shaggy and black, but he didn't take his eyes away from David, not once.

'Okay, maybe you don't remember Adam. How about Billy, you remember Billy?'

Again, no response at all. Jenny said, 'I don't think this is getting us very far, do you? Maybe we should skip the language recognition stage and go straight through to the brain-scan.'

'No, no, this is fascinating,' said Garth. 'I want to see if I can elicit a pattern of responses that are positively identifiable as being George's. Or human, at the very least. Or not a normal hog's responses, at the very, *very* least.'

'What about Chris?' asked David. 'Christopher, Chris? Christine? Carole? Chip? Charles?'

Captain Black neither nodded nor shook his head, but he was showing *some* signs of response. He began to utter a deep, deep growling noise, a reverberating rumble that went on and on, and grew louder and louder, like an approaching earthquake.

'Daniel? Dick? Drew? David?'

Captain Black slowly began to trot towards the perspex window. His ears were aggressively lifted and his fur was bristling. David backed a step away, but Nathan gripped his shoulders to reassure him, and said, 'It's okay. He can't get out of there. No way.'

'He's *fantastic*,' said David. 'Look at him, he's *huge*.'

Garth said, 'It looks like he's waiting for something.'

'Food, maybe? Titbits?' Nathan suggested.

'He's just been fed,' said Jenny. 'He eats a whole lot, but he eats only what he needs, and then he stops. Pigs don't beg for scraps, the way that dogs do.'

'So, what?' asked Nathan. 'He's definitely expecting something. Look at him.'

Garth heaved himself out of his wheelchair and stood close to the perspex, but Captain Black ignored him. Captain Black had his eyes on David.

'He's waiting for David to do something,' said Nathan.

'Yes, but what?'

'George Pearson was there,' said Garth. 'Would he have known his alphabet?'

Nathan shook his head. 'He might have learned the first four or five letters from *Sesame Street*, but no more than that. Kids don't usually manage the whole alphabet until they're five.'

'He doesn't need to know the whole alphabet,' said Garth. 'So long as he knows that E comes after D.'

'I don't follow you.'

'I think he's waiting for David to say "Emily" '.

David glanced at him. 'Shall I say it?'

'Try a few other names that begin with E, and *then* say it.'

'Okay. Eddie. Edwina. Ellie. Erica.'

Captain Black's ears were still pricked up, his snout slightly raised, his teeth half-bared. He hadn't moved, not even another inch, but the tension inside him was almost tangible. Tons of muscle and tons of bone, locked tight as an overwound clock – all waiting for a child's brain-cells to respond to a single name.

'Jesus, it's awesome,' said Garth.

'Edgar,' said David. 'Esther, Egbert.'

'Now,' said Garth, and Nathan gripped David's shoulder a fraction tighter.

'*Emily.*'

Captain Black exploded into action. He hurtled at the perspex screen and collided with it, hitting it so hard that a six-foot section of aluminum frame dropped out of the side, and fell clanging to the concrete floor. He stepped back, and then charged again, and actually managed to crack the wall of his pen.

'He's gone crazy again!' Jenny cried out. 'I'll have to give him another shot!'

She picked up her metal veterinary case, laid it on a chair, and opened it up.

Nathan gently pulled David back from Captain Black's pen. The hog had charged a third time, and then stopped. There was blood on the window and Nathan suspected that he had burst some stitches in his head.

Garth said, triumphantly, 'He knows his sister's name. I'm sure of it. *He knows his sister's name!*'

'So what are you going to do now?'

'I'm definitely going to arrange for them to meet.'

Captain Black collided with the window again, spraying it with blood and thick, ropy saliva. 'You're out of your tree,' said Nathan.

'I don't think so,' Garth grinned. 'I think we're right at the beginning of doing something really fantastic. I mean, we've talked about the medical benefits and the psychotherapeutic benefits – but take this whole thing to its logical conclusion. If a loved one dies, you could have their personality transplanted into your family pet, your dog or your cat. You'd never have to lose them, not totally.'

'Are you *serious*?' Nathan asked him.

'I don't know. Maybe not totally. But stranger things have been known to happen.'

Captain Black thundered against the window again. Garth snapped, 'Jenny, are you ready with that metho yet?'

Jenny nodded, closed her veterinary case, and came forward with a loaded dart-gun. 'Let's just open the door quickly and give him a shot in the chest.'

Garth wheeled as close to the door as he could and punched out the combination. Jenny turned the handle, and was about to open the pen when a high, sharp voice called out, 'Freeze! Don't move!'

They turned around in bewilderment. Walking swiftly towards them along the length of the pigpens came a tall blonde girl in jeans and boots, two bedraggled young men, and another man, taller and darker, in a leather jacket. The dark man in the leather jacket was pointing a gun at them.

'What the hell is the meaning of this?' Garth demanded. 'Who are you? What the hell do you want? This is restricted property!'

Nathan recognized the girl at once – and as she stepped forward, and entered the closest pool of cool fluorescent light, Garth recognized her, too. Last time he had seen her was under the hot, eye-drying lamps of a television studio, where she had told him to his face that he was a butcher and a sadist.

'Well, well,' he said. 'We meet again. This is an honour. Is that what those sirens and fireworks have been all about?'

'Partly,' said Lily. She looked flushed and hot, and grim-faced with over-excitement. 'But the main reason we're here is *him*.'

She pointed at Captain Black. Garth turned and looked at Captain Black, too, and then turned back again. 'I'm not sure that I understand you.'

'It's very simple,' said Lily. 'We've come to liberate him. We've come to give him back his dignity, and his right to lead out his life without being used as a living experiment. We've come to set him free.'

Garth looked at Nathan, and then at Jenny, and then back to Lily. He was open-mouthed. 'You've come to set him *free*? I hope you're not serious.'

'I'm not in a joking mood, Dr Matthews. One of our supporters just died, trying to get in here.'

'A whole lot more are going to get hurt if you let this hog out of his pen. See for yourself, Ms Monarch. I have fractured ribs, a fractured ankle, a torn muscle, bruising, lacerations, and a headache from hell. Captain Black did all this to me, in a matter of minutes; and I was one of the lucky ones.'

'Open the pen,' Lily insisted. 'We've come to set him free.'

'Ms Monarch, Captain Black is one very dangerous beast. You can't set him free.'

'Open the pen,' said Lily. This time, Dean stepped forward, holding his automatic in both hands, with the hammer cocked. He pointed it at Garth's head and said nothing at all.

'Garth,' said Nathan, 'we'd better open the pen.'

'He'll kill us,' retorted Garth, looking directly into Lily's eyes. 'Look, you can see him, he's agitated enough already.'

Lily leaned forward so that Garth could smell her perfume (Red, by Giorgio, mingled with mud and rain and panicky perspiration). She had another smell, too, a male smell, as if she had very recently had sex.

'Open – the – fucking – pen,' she whispered.

Garth turned to Jenny and said, 'Open the pen, Jenny. Then stand well back, and don't even think about moving. Nathan – you and David do the same. Flat against the wall, don't move a muscle.'

Dean stalked over to Jenny and held his automatic only an inch away from her head. She closed her eyes, and swallowed. Then she pulled down the lever, and swung the door back. A fetid odour of hog-swill and sour urine flowed out with the draught, so strong that it made Nathan's eyes water.

Jenny retreated behind the door. Garth backed up his wheelchair, and then heaved himself out of it, and limped on his walking-stick across the floor, until he was standing close to Nathan and David. 'She's crazy,' he said, under his breath. 'If she lets that hog out, there's no telling what he could do.'

Captain Black roared and squealed, and crashed against the window again. Another length of aluminum dropped to the floor, ringing like a bell.

'What did I tell you?' Garth challenged Lily. 'He's out of his head. You can't let him free, he'll kill himself, as well as anybody else who gets in his way.'

But Lily turned and flashed him a blue-eyed look that immediately silenced him. 'What do you think I am, Dr Matthews? What the hell do you think I'm doing here?'

She approached the open door of the pigpen, and stood for a moment in a pose that was almost balletic, like one of the swans in *Swan Lake*. Captain Black was barging furiously around his pen, thumping against the walls, roaring and screaming. He was in such a frenzy that he hadn't realized yet that the pen door was wide open, and that he was free to leave.

Lily let out a high-pitched cry. It was so high that, at first, Nathan thought that he was imagining it. Gradually, however, it sank a little lower, and warbled – an eerie, animal cry that made Nathan's scalp contract, and sent cockroaches of tingling sensation crawling through his hair.

'What the hell is she doing?' he whispered to Garth. 'Is she calling him, or what?'

'That's not your usual hog-call,' said Garth, in awe.

'Then what is it? Listen, he's calming down!'

Garth leaned over to Nathan, and breathed, 'That's a mating call. A sow's mating call. I'm sure of it.'

'You mean – ?'

'She's got it off perfectly. Listen, he's calling her back! Yes, she's seducing him. That's what she's doing. She's turning him on.'

Lily slowly stepped away from the open door, still crying, still warbling, and as she did so, Captain Black appeared, bruised and crusted with blood, his bandages gone. His face looked like a huge, grotesque gargoyle cast in blackened bronze. His eyes were unfocused, and duller than they had been before, as if he were confused, or drugged, or tired of living. Saliva dripped from his jaws onto the floor, and his stomach rumbled like summer thunder.

Lily reached out and grasped Captain Black's ear, and stroked it. He snuffled at her arm, and dipped his head. Lily looked across at Garth, triumphant. 'You see? You don't have to be cruel, you don't have to be punitive. He's a mortal being, just like you and me.'

She laid her hand on Captain Black's flank, and said, 'We're leaving now; and I'm taking him with us. Don't try to stop us, please. We've had enough tragedy for one day.'

Garth said, 'You realize, don't you, that you're signing that animal's death warrant? The minute he leaves this institute, he's out of our protective jurisdiction. If he doesn't die of starvation first, he'll be hunted and shot. Let me put it this way: nobody who purports to be an animal-lover could possibly contemplate setting him free. He's a highly developed and highly-specialized domestic hog. Not a wild boar; not a razorback. A creature bred by humans and raised by humans and nurtured by humans.'

'All the more reason for him to rejoin the real world.'

'I don't think so,' said Garth.

Dean approached them with his automatic raised. 'Shall we be quiet here, please? We're taking this animal, and that's it.'

Lily gently took hold of Captain Black's ear and began to lead him along the central corridor between the pens. As they passed each one, the hogs inside started whining and grunting and screaming, until the entire building echoed with a cacophony of crying pigs. It could have been Purgatory: it probably was.

Henry and Kit walked on either side of Captain Black's slime-streaked flanks; while Dean brought up the rear, slowly sweeping his automatic from side to side, his eyes challenging any of them to call the alarm, or make a rush at him, or make any movement at all that would give him an excuse to shoot. He had shot and killed one man today. Another would make no difference. Another would give him more of a high. That crack, that kickback. That was something. And the guard dropping flat on his face, straight into the grass.

Garth looked at Jenny, who was slowly emerging from behind the pigpen door. Only a few inches in front of Jenny's right toe was the dart-gun – primed and cocked and loaded with enough metho to knock out one a half tons of enraged, thick-skinned hog. More than enough to knock out 195 lb of nervy, thin-skinned human.

Garth stared down at the gun in the most obvious way possible, his eyes wide. Then he jerked his head towards Dean.

Jenny immediately got the message, but it was clear that she didn't know what to think about the ethics of it. She shrugged and spread her arms and tried to look at him appealingly. But Garth repeated his head-jerk, and tried to mouth, '*Now!*'

Under his breath, Nathan cautioned, 'Garth, don't risk it. For God's sake. You don't want Jenny killed.'

And David said, 'Listen, Dad! Sirens! Police to the rescue!'

But at that instant, Jenny made her own decision and dipped to the floor and scooped up the dart-gun and fired it. The dart snapped so close to Dean's head that it flicked his hair. He clapped his hand to his head, quite sure for a second that Jenny had hit him. But then Henry, behind him, fell to the floor, and started kicking and shaking and convulsing.

Garth shouted, '*No!*' but Dean was totally wired and hopping stiff-jointed like a marionette. He shouted, '*Bitch!*' and fired his automatic twice into Jenny's face, blowing apart flesh and bone and cartilage. The shots echoed everywhere and the hogs shrieked and grunted in panic. Jenny fell sideways, her arms hanging limp, her face pulped, sliding down the door. Dean backed away, grey-faced, roaring; but at the same time, Garth screamed out, '*Emily! Emily!*'

Lily had managed to lead Captain Black halfway towards the pigpen doors, and so far he had followed her with pet-like docility. When Garth screamed '*Emily!*', however, he threw back his deep-set head and opened his mouth wide and let out a cry of anger and anguish that made even Dean lower his gun and look around in awe.

Captain Black bellowed again, a foundation-shaking rumble that rose to an ear-scraping shriek. He turned around, and stood up on his hind legs, tottering and balancing step by step. He towered over them all, black and bristly and furious-eyed, nearly eleven feet tall, nearly twice the height of a well-built man, but built like a thick tapering column of fat and muscle and black hairy skin. He was more like a nightmare than a living beast; the kind of ugly, glittery-eyed monster that pursued people when they slept.

But he was alive, and he was here, solid and reeking and furious.

With a clatter, he dropped back onto all fours.

Lily tried to start up her singing again, but Captain Black shook his head with obvious contempt, and her singing gradually petered out, and she backed away.

Garth called out, 'Ms Monarch! If I were you, I'd make a run for it! This is one angry hog!'

But Lily stayed where she was. 'We came to set him free! That's just what we're going to do!'

She waved her arms at Captain Black and cried out, 'Here sir, here sir, come on Captain, come on sir!'

But Captain Black roared and shook his blood-caked head, and then he suddenly went for Henry with all the rhythmic, quick, unstoppable speed of a small locomotive. Half-jokingly, Henry said, 'Hey, old buddy, take it easy!' and lifted up his hand to fend him off. But then Henry realized that he was trapped in a corner between two pigpens and that Captain Black was trotting towards him very, very fast, and that this wasn't a joke at all, but a threatening situation in which he could very easily get himself killed.

'Hey come on now, piggie!' he joked, as Captain Black trotted closer and closer. 'Only in fun, okay?'

But one-and-one-half tons of hog hit him at nearly 5 m.p.h., and his body wasn't built to withstand even a tenth of that impact. There was a serial crunching sound, from his chest to his pelvis. He tried to say something, but he found it impossible. There was no breath left in his lungs. He opened his mouth, and nothing came out but blood.

Kit put his head down and ran for it. He had disappeared out of the front door and into the rain before Captain Black had even managed to turn around. Dean hesitantly raised his gun, but it was obvious that he would have to hit Captain Black directly in the brain if he wanted to stop him dead, and Captain Black was a moving, threatening target. He started to back away, step by step; then he turned, and started to walk. Then he started to run.

Captain Black ran after him. His trotters galloped on the concrete floor like the hoofs of a heavy horse. He burst out into the rain; and Nathan heard shouts and pistol shots.

Lily was standing quite still, with her hands covering her face, shocked. Nathan pushed past her and ran after Captain Black. Outside, a small force of six or seven security guards were climbing the slope towards the pigpens, and two of them had already caught and arrested Dean. He was lying spreadeagled on the wet grass, his face contorted and darker than ever, like the face of a demon. One of the security men had his boot in the small of his back, and a Colt automatic pressed against the back of his head.

Captain Black ran at an angle towards the security guards; then hesitated; then turned southward. Two or three of the guards fired shots in the air. They echoed flatly in the wet morning air; but Captain Black didn't stop. In fact, he ran even faster.

David rushed up and caught hold of Nathan's hand and begged, 'They're not going to kill him, are they?'

Nathan lifted his hand to shield his eyes against the rain. He could see the perimeter fences; and suddenly he realized that both of them had been cut through. Not the narrow triangular type of cuts that a few stray intruders would have made: but wide, full-scale cuts, big enough to drive a Volkswagen through. The kind that Lily Monarch would have made, if she had really been serious about rescuing Captain Black.

'Shit,' he breathed, and started to run; but he knew that Captain Black was way too far ahead of him. One of the security guards had almost caught up with him, a mottle-faced panting man with a dark-blue beret and popping eyes and an awkwardly-carried Colt Commando. 'Call for an ambulance!' Nathan shouted at him. 'Call the police! There's a wild hog out there! Dangerous! You got me? Call the police!'

The man stopped, and stumbled, and stared at him. 'What?' he said, uncomprehending.

Captain Black must have been psychic. He galloped uphill towards the hole in the perimeter fence without any deviation at all. He made the ground shake. He dug up turf. He was more than an animal, more than a hog: he was the living embodiment of Garth Matthew's darkest dreams: all of those impossible possibilities that genetic science could conjure into life.

His head spun, like a speeded-up movie of clouds and sunshine and sky. He knew that he had to find em-el-ee, MLE, wherever she was, wherever she was hiding, because MLE was different, like he was different, and MLE knew why they had to die, and why they hadn't died, and who was coming and why they had to die.

He reached the first perimeter fence and barged through it with sparks crackling from his fur. Smoke burst out, and drifted into the rain. Then he barged through the second fence. He ran towards the woods, his shoulder muscles heaving like the great greasy-black pistons of a pumping engine. He disappeared into the trees; and by the time that Nathan and David and the rest of the security guards had reached the perimeter, he was gone.

'Damnedest thing I ever saw,' said the security man with the popping eyes. 'Damnedest thing I ever saw.'

Back in the pigpens, the telephone rang. Garth ignored it at first, but then he painfully hobbled over to answer it.

'Garth? It's Morton.'

Morton Hall was the director and chief administrator of the Spellman Institute: a haughty, correct man who respected Garth's abilities but generally found him eccentric and untidy and chronically lacking in what he liked to call 'corporate awareness' – in other words, doing what he was told.

'How can I help you, Morton?' asked Garth.

'I've had a report from Dr Goodman that your research with Captain Black may be subject to certain ethical irregularities. Until such time as we've had a chance to talk these over, I'd like you to suspend your research programme.'

'You don't want me to experiment on Captain Black any more?'

'Not for the time being.'

Garth looked at the empty, bloodied pen. Then he said, 'Okay, Morton, whatever you want.'

'You're not going to object?' asked Morton, in obvious surprise.

'No, Morton. I'm going to bow to your greater judgement.'

Morton was flustered, pleased. 'That's very co-operative of you.' He was about to hang up when he said, 'Do you have a security alert over there at the pens? I just saw one of the security vehicles driving your way.'

'Oh, nothing to worry about,' said Garth. 'We've just mislaid a couple of things, that's all.'

Thirteen

The rain had eased off for a while, and a sharp triangular blade of clear blue sky had appeared over Hiawatha as if it were a sign from God, but the mid-morning light was still gloomy and shadowy and strange, and the burned-out wreckage of Randy Gedge's tractor-trailer was still dripping like the raised *Titanic.*

Luke walked around it with his hat in his hand. Now and then he looked back at deputy Joe Freeman, as if he were expecting an opinion, but deputy Joe Freeman was far too raw to know that an opinion was expected; and far too raw to have one, anyway. This was only his second traffic fatality, and only the third time that he had worked with Luke.

'Witnesses say hogs,' Luke remarked.

'That's right,' said deputy Freeman, enthusiastically. 'A whole herd of them, crossing the highway unattended.'

'Plenty of hog carcasses to show that was so,' said Luke.

'Yes, sir. That's right, sir. Twenty-eight identifiable carcasses altogether, plus some burned-out bits that could have been hogs, or bits of hogs, but no way of proving it for sure, barring forensics.'

'Where do you think they came from?' Luke asked him. 'You're a local boy.'

Deputy Freeman pulled a face. 'Herds do get out, from time to time, but they don't usually go very far. They're pretty timid, as a rule, and they know what side their bread's buttered.'

'Meaning?'

'They won't go far from their food supply, and they're very picky about their food.'

'That's what I thought,' said Luke. 'So why did a hundred-odd hogs decide to cross 76th Avenue SW in the middle of a rainy night; and where the hell did they think they were going?'

'I don't know, sir. But there are two pretty big hog-farms nearby to here – Kravitz's and Johnson's.'

Luke picked a brown, crusted curve from the side of Randy Gedge's truck. He sniffed it, and then he suddenly realized what it was. He passed it over to deputy Freeman and said, 'Smell that. What do you think?'

Deputy Freeman cautiously smelled it, and then he blinked and coughed and noisily swallowed.

'Crackling?' he said.

Six or seven years ago, it had obviously been a prosperous hog-farm, with substantial outbuildings and pigpens and feed-stores, and a two-storey farmhouse with a red-tiled roof and a pillared portico in the style of Tara, in *Gone With the Wind.*

Now, however, it was shabby and weatherbeaten, with that exhausted greyness that affects both overworked men and overworked farms. The driveway that curved in front of the house was clotted with weeds, the barn windows were broken, and the windpump was lacking six or seven blades. The sign over the pigpens was so faded by sun and rain that it was almost impossible to distinguish the words 'Frank Johnson Fine Berkshires'.

Luke parked in front of the main house and climbed out of his Buick. The clouds were hanging low, like the sagging awnings of a bankrupt circus. It was still raining, very fine and wet, and Luke took out his handkerchief and wiped his face with it. He sniffed. There was a cloying, sweetish smell in the air, a stomach-unsettling mixture of pig-manure and well-rotted apples and bad meat.

On top of the pigpens, a weather-vane in the shape of a farmer chasing a piglet was plaintively squeaking from NW to NNW. More wet weather to come, no doubt about it.

He climbed the steps to the front verandah. The green-painted door was open, but he knocked all the same, and called out, 'Mr Johnson? Mr Frank Johnson? This is Sheriff Friend here!'

After a short pause, a bone-thin man appeared in the hallway, wearing grey dungarees and a faded red and white work shirt. He had a fleshless face and eyes that were almost colourless. A hand-rolled cigarette was stuck to the side of his lip.

'Frank Johnson?' said Luke. He took out his badge and showed it to him.

'We met before,' said Frank Johnson. 'My eldest son Roy was caught for drunk-driving 'bout three or four years back, you come over and give him hell.'

'I remember. Did it do him any good?'

'Not much. He's in Fairbanks, Alaska, now, doing who knows what, but making plenty of money at it. Still drinking. Still driving.'

Luke said, 'I came to talk to you about your hogs.'

'I don't have no hogs no more, sheriff. The farm's for sale and all me and Beth are doing is scratching what we can. I'm getting by repairing tractors and threshers and stuff like that, but it don't pay too much.'

'What happened to your hogs?'

'What do you think? Same as everybody else's hogs.'

'Sold?'

Frank Johnson shook his head. 'They wasn't in any condition for auction, sheriff. Even if they was, the price was down so damn low that I wouldn't barely have gotten my feed money back. Everybody knows that meat products is going to be banned, you can't sell a prime pork Berkshire this morning for more than twelve dollars and fifty cents, the whole damn animal, and next week, when they pass that damn Zapf-Cady bill, you won't be able to give a hog away, not to no one, because you'll be breaking the law.'

'So what did you do with your hogs, Frank?'

'Did what I had to do.'

'You slaughtered them?'

Again he shook his head. 'Too damned expensive to slaughter. Just stopped feeding them, that's all.'

Luke frowned at him. 'You did what?'

'Just stopped feeding them. Reckoned they'd die, soon enough, and those that died the first would be food for those that died later.'

'Jesus, Frank,' said Luke, in disgust. 'Do you know how cruel that is?'

Frank Johnson seemed unimpressed. 'There's no way around it. Pound for pound, feed is dearer than meat. It's called farm economics.'

'But what if Zapf-Cady isn't passed? There's a strong chance that it won't be.'

'Doesn't make no difference. The price of hogs has been too damn low for too damn long, and I couldn't make no go of it, nohow.'

Luke said, 'Let me take a look in those pigpens.'

'You want to? It aint a pretty sight.'

Frank Johnson led the way across the yard, pausing for a moment to relight his cigarette-stub with an oily-smoking Zippo.

'How many hogs did you have?' Luke asked him, as they approached the main doors to the pigpens.

'Over three thousand, give or take a sow or two. That was the minimum I could raise to keep this place in credit. So you think about the feed bill. Every growing hog eats five to six pounds of feed every day, that's eighteen thousand pounds of feed, day in, day out, Sundays too, and eighteen thousand pounds is the kerb weight of four and a half full-size Cadillacs which I don't even own one of, not any more.'

He yanked open the rusted, weathered door. Inside, it was dark, but Luke didn't have to be able to see anything to know what he was going to encounter. The smell of decaying flesh was so strong that he had to step back into the open yard, and take six or seven very deep breaths. Even there, the air was tainted with the smell of death.

'Working with hogs, you get used to it,' said Frank, laconically, puffing at his cigarette and waiting for Luke to collect himself. Luke's stomach kept going into spasm, and he would have given money not to have eaten those three cherry Danishes that he had awarded himself for having only toast and juice and black coffee for breakfast.

At last, swallowing saliva, he said, 'Come on, Frank, let's have some light on the subject, shall we?'

Frank shrugged, and reached inside for the lightswitch. The fluorescent tubes buzzed and flickered, and then popped on.

Luke opened his mouth, then closed it again. He couldn't think of anything to say that wouldn't be blasphemous. Frank Johnson's pigpen was like a nightmarish medieval battlefield; a charnel-house from hell.

It was almost three hundred feet in length, with a high corrugated-aluminum ceiling supported by triangular aluminum rafters. Its huge floor-space was divided by railings into hundreds of pens. In every one of these pens, at least one hog lay dead, and in some of them lay litters of six or seven. Their flesh glistened with millions of blowflies, literally millions of them, and most of them were heaving with maggots. Half-eaten hog skulls grinned at Luke from every side. One hog's mouth appeared to be moving, until Luke realized that its lips were simply rippling with maggots. Trotters, tails, haunches and heads, they were all jumbled together in grisly putrescence.

'Is that all of them?' asked Luke, beckoning Frank Johnson to slide the door shut.

'Most all. Some escaped a couple of days ago – maybe eighty, maybe a hundred. They're clever suckers, hogs. They worked out how to lift up the railings between their pens, and then they worked out how to nudge up the latch on the door.'

'Do you know where they went?'

'They went into the apple-orchard first off, foraging for

roots and apples. They did a whole lot of damage there, couldn't even count the cost of it. I wanted to shoo them out of there, but they was in a mean mood, and if there's nothing sweeter than a sweet-natured hog, there's nothing meaner than a mean one. They would've etten me given half a chance. 'Then as luck would have it the storm came and scared them off, and that's the last I saw of any of them. Reckon they're rooting someplace, they shouldn't be hard to find.'

'We've found them already,' said Luke. 'They crossed 76th Avenue last night and caused an accident in which three people were fatally injured.'

Frank Johnson looked at him, and sucked at his extinguished cigarette, and blinked. After a while, he looked away, like a man who's waiting for the decision on the price of a sow, and sniffed. It was then that Luke was sure that Frank Johnson had lost all sense of reality, a long time ago. It had slipped away, as it often did with MidWestern farmers, without anybody noticing it. Too many years of isolation, too many years of stress and toil and bank foreclosures; too many tornadoes, too much rain; too many years on the huge engulfing plains, feeling like a tiny twinkling speck in the vastness of the night, with nobody for company but your worn-out wife and *The Price Is Right.*

Luke laid his hand on Frank's shoulder. 'Frank, I'm going to have to consider arresting you for criminal negligence. But first of all I've got a whole lot of other things to do, and I want some officers from the ASPCA and the county agricultural office to come on down here and take a look for themselves.'

Frank Johnson nodded. 'I couldn't have shot them,' he said. 'The price of shells, I couldn't stretch to three thousand shells.'

'I know that, Frank. Just do me a favour, and stay put until you hear from me. Don't disturb anything, just leave it all as it is.'

'Whatever you say, sheriff.'

Luke climbed back into his car, switched on the engine, U-turned and drove away. He was less than a half-mile down the track when he started to sweat, and his stomach started to go into spasm again.

He sloughed to a halt at the side of the track, and stumbled into a cornfield, and vomited.

He was bent double for a long time while his spasms subsided. He could hear the fine rain crackling in the corn, and the thin, repetitive whistling of a cowbird. At last he stood up, and folded his handkerchief, and wiped his mouth.

He could still see Frank Johnson's pigpen from here. He could also see that smoke was rising from it, thick and dark and rolling with sparks.

'Oh, shit,' he breathed, and started bounding back through the cornfield towards his car.

He climbed in, and was just about to shut the door when he heard the sharp crack of a rifle-shot – then a moment's pause, then another. The shots echoed and re-echoed across the cornfield like applause.

Luke sat in his car with his head bowed and didn't even bother to start the engine.

Terence opened his eyes and saw daylight around the edges of the blind. He sat up stiffly. They had taken away his wrist-watch when they had arrested him, so he had no idea what time it was. He yawned and stretched and looked around the room. It was small and sparse, with a bare-boarded floor, a single rollaway bed, and a cheap varnished bureau. On the wall hung a foxed steel-engraving of a grim-looking man with a beard, with the caption *Bodeslas.*

He unfolded his pants and unsteadily climbed into them. He felt almost as if he had a hangover, but he knew that he hadn't been drinking. He lifted the blind, and found that he was looking into a narrow trash-cluttered alley between two single-storey concrete houses. There was a rusted gas barbecue and part of a sunbed and several cans of light green paint that were now half-filled with rainwater.

His bedroom door opened and Naked came in, still masked. She was wearing nothing except a rough linen shirt, crudely embroidered with red and black wool, and frayed at the edges. Her thin legs looked as if they had been stained with berry juice, and her toes were dirty. She looked even more transparent than she had before. On the wall, at an angle, hung a Firestone Tyre calendar, two years old, and he could clearly read part of the word 'eptember' through her shoulder.

'Today we must find Emily,' she said.

'Is it that critical?' asked Terence.

'Your father must find Emily.'

'You heard what poor old Leland Terpstra said. The welfare services took her; and if the welfare services took her, it's odds-on she's staying at McKinley Children's Home.'

'Then that's where we'll start searching,' said Naked, flatly.

She turned to go. Terence tried to catch her sleeve, but his hand went through thin air. As usual, she was a split second behind time; never quite catching up with him. Terence said, 'Janek's not going to hurt Emily, is he? If he's going to hurt her, I'm not going to help him to find her.'

'You don't have any choice. He's your father.'

'But why does he have to find Emily? Why can't he leave her alone? One child isn't going to make any difference, is it? He has scores of children.'

'Emily is different.'

'Oh, yes, and *why* is she so different?'

Naked was silent for a moment. Then she said, 'You should know why. You're different, too.'

'I still don't understand. Different from what?'

'Different from most of your father's other children. Rebellious. *Different.*'

Terence stared at her, wishing that she would come into full focus, so that he could see what she really looked like. So that was it. He was rebellious. It hadn't occurred to him before, during all his years of research, that he was the first and only child of Janek-the-Green who had devoted so much energy and so much fury into avoiding his destiny. The records showed that Janek had frequently met opposition from one of the farmers who had allowed him to impregnate their wives, especially after thirty-six years had elapsed and he had come to collect his visceral dues. But Janek had never before met any resistance from the children themselves. Quite the opposite: they had usually welcomed him. They had invited him in, and given themselves gladly.

Naked said, 'We'll be leaving soon. Are you hungry?'

'No, no I'm not,' said Terence, and sat down on the creaking rollaway bed. *He was rebellious.* Maybe Emily was rebellious, too; and that was why they wanted her so urgently. Maybe Janek had started something which he couldn't finish – created a line that didn't want to lie down, like all of the rest.

Terence had never known his mother too well. She had died when he was nine. But he always remembered a small, temperamental dark-haired woman with bright, deepset eyes and a sharp triangular nose, a real Grant Wood mother in an apron, a Daughter of the Revolution. And his father so slow and humble and defeated, a man for whom the rain refused to ease.

'Are you all right?' Naked asked him.

Terence nodded. 'Yes . . . yes, I'm all right. I just remembered something, is all.'

'Are you frightened?'

'What do you think?'

Naked paused in the doorway. 'It's nearly over, Terence.

You know that, don't you? It's nearly finished for good.'

'For sure,' said Terence, although he wasn't at all sure what she meant. What was over? His life? Emily's life? Or the Green Traveller's long and destructive journeys through Eastern Europe and Russia and the Midwestern plains?

She was almost sympathetic. But she was Janek-the-Green's voice and advocate, and she must have witnessed so much pain, so much suffering, so much feeding on the innocent.

Outside the window, the rain fell on the old gas barbecue, and dribbled from the guttering. In the room next door, Terence could hear the scratching of leaves and branches, and the low, conspiratoiral whispering of people who scarcely ever spoke. He had the feeling that he had learned something important; that he was capable of changing things.

He felt both excited and frightened; but what frightened and excited him even more was the fact that he didn't know *why*.

When Luke returned to his office, he found Professor Mrstik waiting for him, clutching a fat brown-leather briefcase under his arm like a baby pig. Professor Mrstik was tall, almost as tall as Luke, with thinning gingery hair and a face so white that he could have been surprised by a flour-bomb. He wore a gingery brown suit that was far too thick for the time of year, and smelled of damp.

He stood up and bowed when Luke came in, and gave him a damp, bony handshake. 'I gave myself ten more minutes,' he said. 'Otherwise, I would have had to call again next week. It is our special Czech weekend; we have folk-dancing, festivities, well, goodness knows what! It always brings a tear to the eye! Sometimes a headache to the head, too!'

'I'm sorry I'm late,' Luke apologized. 'We have a couple of serious ongoing incidents . . . I'm sure you can understand how it is.'

'Of course! All of life is a serious ongoing incident, yes?'

Luke took Professor Mrstik by the elbow, and steered him through to his office. There was a heap of messages, and his answer-phone was blinking, but he ignored them all, and dragged over a chair, so that Professor Mrstik could sit down.

'You want coffee?' he asked him.

'Tea, if possible.'

'Cookies?'

Professor Mrstik looked at him narrowly. 'You yourself want cookies, yes? But if I ask for cookies, then the responsibility is mine?'

Luke stared back at him, baffled. Professor Mrstik laughed. 'You have a diet book on your desk, yes? But you are plainly a man who cares for his food. So, very well, I will ask you for cookies with my tea, and you will be absolved.'

Luke pressed his intercom and without taking his eyes off Professor Mrstik, said, 'Janice? One coffee, please; and one tea; and a plate of those chocolate-chip cookies. That's right, the big ones.'

Professor Mrstik said, 'I have always wanted to play detective. And these notebooks you sent me from Terence Pearson, well, they whetted my appetite.'

'What did you think of them?' asked Luke.

'You want my candid opinion? I think that this is not a folk legend. I think that this is mostly true.'

Luke stood up. His chair squeaked and squeaked and then stayed silent. He walked across his office and then came halfway back again.

'You think that this is mostly true?'

'You are challenging me? In that case, I say yes, emphatically, this is mostly true. A few mistakes, because he cannot understand all of the subtleties of Czech language; but in substance, true, yes, all of this story of the Green Traveller, all of this story of mummers, and deals done to give good harvest, yes, this deals have been done, and proof! He has worked so hard, this Terence Pearson, to find proof! Newspaper, magazine, meterological report, harvest yield report, birth certificate, hospital record, death certificate, thousands of details, thousands.

He opened his briefcase and took out a thick, untidy sheaf of paper, and held it up. 'Proof! Janek-the-Green is true; and Janek-the-Green is alive; and it was Terence Pearson's fear of Janek-the-Green that was his direct motivation for killing his children.'

Luke took the papers, and laid them down carefully on his blotter, shuffling them top and bottom to collate them. 'Thank God,' he said. 'And thank you, too, Professor Mrstik. I was beginning to think that I was going out of my mind.'

'Some cakes short of a funeral, as they say,' laughed Professor Mrstik. Luke frowned at him, and he stopped in mid-laugh and said, 'Sorry . . . Czech humour is always a little different. We have some very funny jokes about poultices.'

'I'm sure you do. But meanwhile, this will be very helpful. Really.'

Janice came in with their coffee, tea and cookies. She placed the cookies close to Luke's elbow, but Luke said, 'No . . . they're for Professor Mrstik here.' Janice gave him a wan, disbelieving smile and left the office.

'Of course this was all very interesting to me,' said Professor Mrstik. 'I heard of Janek-the-Green when I was small. We used to sing "Cross your heart, cut out your guts, and hide from the bristly hedge". To find here evidence that this is true . . . well, you can imagine what it is like for me. It is like discovering that the Scissorman is true, from *Struwwelpeter*. It is like discovering that Dracula is true.'

Luke said, 'You understand, don't you, that this is all *sub judice*? You can't mention it to anybody, not yet.'

'Of course, of course, but I don't mind! The pleasure is in

the research, in the discovery! And I have done more research, with my friend Dr Schoenman, who is very interested in legend, but also in biology.'

Luke was beginning to grow a little tired of this. He wished his coffee weren't so hot; and that Professor Mrstik would hurry up and finish his tea, and leave him alone. He felt tired and ravaged; and agonizingly guilty, too. He should have seen the message on Frank Johnson's face. He had seen it so many times before, on so many farmers' faces, but this time he had turned away. He needed to think about that, alone, in private, and try to come to terms with it.

He needed to go fishing; or stand for a long time on the banks of the Cedar River, upstream by Blairs Ferry Road, out by the chain lakes, and watch the sun burning down toward the western horizon; in peace; in silence.

But Professor Mrstik said, 'The combination of animal and vegetable genes is not only a possibility but a reality, yes? Already food companies have discovered that they can insert genes from animals into plants, and vice versa, to make them grow this way or that way.'

He rifled through a bunch of news-cuttings and magazines until he found what he wanted. 'Here – look, the very latest conference by the Committee on the Ethics of Genetic Modification and Food Use . . . "it is now common practice for animal genes to be inserted into certain vegetable crops and vice versa . . . we are coming to the point where there will be viable food products that are neither distinctly animal nor distinctly vegetable." 'So you see Janek-the-Green is not just a story at all, but a scientific reality. What was created by the superstitious farmers of Bohemia was in fact a living, viable being. A terrible creature, both sad and frightening. But real, and capable of reproduction.'

'What did your friend have to say about Janek-the-Green's children, and his methods of reproduction?'

'Oh, well, not much. Dr Schoenman is only an amateur biologist, not a geneticist. But he suggested that you could ask some of the research scientists at the Spellman Institute, out in Amana. There you have one of the leading centres in genetic research in the whole country, yes, right on your doorstep?'

He licked his thumb and leafed through his file again. 'Here you are . . . he suggested two names, Dr R. Lacouture and Dr G. Matthews.'

'Dr Lacouture is dead. He was killed a few days ago, after one of the institute's experiments got a little out of hand.'

'Oh! I think I saw that on the news. Was he the scientist who was killed by the hog?'

'That's the one. But Dr Matthews is still with us, so far as I know.'

'Well, then, he could be your man.'

They talked a little more, and then Dr Mrstik handed Luke his completed translation of Terence's notebooks, and all the other material that he had gathered. 'You must keep me in touch with your progress, sheriff. This subject for me is one of great fascination. So many legends have been dismissed in the modern world; but it is only now that we are beginning to discover that many strange and terrible things have been hiding among us for hundreds of years. Why do they bother to invent impossible fantasies like *Jurassic Park*, when there are real miracles of genetics sharing our city streets with us?

'If you ever find this Janek-the-Green, you must let me see him. I insist. That is all I will ask in payment for this translation.'

'I'll think about it,' Luke told him. 'But there could be some personal risk, if Janek-the-Green gets to know who you are. The first person who tried to translate these notebooks was pursued by a person or persons unknown and he committed suicide.'

'Mr Ponican, yes. That was a great sadness. I knew him quite well.'

'We made the error with Mr Ponican of telling the media about him. We haven't made the same mistake with you. Nobody outside of this department knows that you've been doing this work. If I were you, I would make certain that it stayed that way. I believe in Janek-the-Green, *you* believe in Janek-the-Green, and I don't think that you'd want to answer a knock on your door at midnight tonight and find out that it's him.'

Dr Mrstik nodded soberly. 'I follow your meaning, sheriff; and thank you.'

Captain Black was heavier than any other hog in America: but he was superbly muscled and exceptionally strong. He had been bred to perfection. His heart and his lungs had been formed by the very best genetic combination of human and swine. Now, of course, he had something else, too – a mind that was capable not only of clever responses, as the minds of hogs always are, but a mind that was capable of *imagining* things.

He ran through the woods and the underbrush south-eastwards from the Spellman Institute, crashing through bramble and bracken like a huge black locomotive. His hide was streaked with rainwater, and his underbelly was caked with mud. His bandages had been completely ripped away, but his head was mostly healed now, and he suffered no more than the dullest of headaches. It made him irritable, but it didn't divert him from the single thought that had been throbbing in his brain ever since he had regained consciousness.

Emily, he thought. He had to find Emily. He had always known that Emily was different, and that one day Emily would have to die. Emily wasn't like Lisa at all. Emily wasn't like him. Emily was more like Daddy, she had Daddy's blood, and Daddy's blood was badder than Daddy knew.

Ever since his earliest days of awareness, ever since he had sat up in his crib in the sunfilled bedroom at Vernon Drive, he had known for sure that Emily was different, that Emily was *wrong*.

He loved her. He loved her dearly. But that was when she was 'sister', and not the other thing. When she was the other thing, when she was 'Emily', that was when she was strange and unlikeable and not like him and Lisa at all. He used to watch her sometimes and there was something in her eyes that made him feel anxious and hostile.

Thunder rumbled overhead, and the rain began to drift down even more heavily. He was lolloping along the northern shore of a small spectacle-shaped lake, his trotters cleaving heavily into thick black mud. On the far side of the lake, a cluster of ducks stood miserably under the trees, waiting for the storm to pass.

Captain Black knew that it wouldn't pass. Captain Black knew that the rain was set in till the end of the harvest, and that thousands of acres of eastern Iowa and Illinois and Missouri would be flooded. Captain Black had the brain of a Poland China hog, but he had the mind of George Pearson, and George Pearson was the grandson of the Green Traveller, the giver of fertility, and the taker-away, too, if he had the inclination.

Gradually, Captain Black began to work his way north-north-east. He had an instinctive sense of direction – partly animal, partly human, partly occult. He could feel the way the wind was blowing, he could feel the lightning crackling in the clouds. What was more, he knew exactly where he wanted to go. Back to Cedar Rapids, where Emily was. He couldn't let Emily get away. She had to be sacrificed, she had to be offered to Janek-the-Green. Daddy wouldn't do it. Daddy would rather chop her head off first, the same way that Daddy had chopped *his* head off.

He crossed the corner of a thousand-acre field, crashing and whipping through the sodden ears of rain-ruined corn. He clattered across a wet, deserted road. He heard a helicopter approaching from the west, and he ran into a small triangular stand of trees, and waited. The helicopter came slow and very low, flying under the clouds. The beat of its rotors made his head hurt, but he stood stock-still and waited patiently until it had passed, with rain dripping from his snout.

Once the fields were silent again, he trotted out of the trees and carried on running northwards.

He hadn't been running more than ten minutes, however, when he saw a group of dark, aimless shapes milling around in the field up ahead of him. It was raining even more heavily, and the field was misty, and at first he couldn't work out what they were.

As he ran closer, however, he caught a strong, familiar scent. He let out a grunt, and then another, and then a squealing roar. The shapes backed away, and then circled around him, thirty or forty of them. He stood in the middle of the field, and threw back his head, and let out a scream of challenge and assertion.

I'm here, I'm the strongest. Who wants to prove that I'm not?

The shapes came closer. They were emaciated and bedraggled, and they approached him with awe. They were hungry and disoriented and leaderless. Some of them were injured or burned. They were the last remnants of Frank Johnson's ill-fated Berkshire herd, digging for tiny swedes.

Captain Black screamed again, lifting his grotesque, werewolf-like face up to the clouds. The other hogs gathered closely around him, nudging against him, bowing their heads. Captain Black's huge red corkscrew of a penis slid glistening from its black shaggy sheath, and he urinated copiously onto the mud. The Berkshires milled around in the pungent steam, paying him homage.

When he moved off north, they followed him, running in a pack.

Bryan Cady was having lunch with William and Nina Olsen when he was called to the phone. Nina was feeding William with little forkfuls of pike quenelle, and she looked at her manservant irritably. 'Can't it wait, Newton? The senator's just started lunch.'

'I'm sorry, Mrs Olsen, but the caller said urgent.'

'Did he say who he was?'

'It wasn't a he caller, Mrs Olsen, it was a she caller. Ms Lily Monarch.'

'That deranged bitch. All breasts and no breeding.'

Bryan patted his mouth with his mint-green linen napkin, and raised a concilatory hand. 'Don't fret, Nina, it's probably just a last-minute technicality.'

'I shall be glad when Zapf-Cady is all over and done with,' snapped Nina. 'Oh, William, for God's sake, it's all dropping out of the side of your mouth! You're worse than a child!'

Bryan pushed back his Chippendale chair and walked the length of the oak-panelled dining-room and out into the hallway. The telephone was on a gilded 18th-century side table, underneath a huge George Luks oil-painting of dancing children, probably worth well over $1.5 million. 'Lily?' he said. Through the half-open study door, he could see a maid polishing William Olsen's desk, and a cat asleep on William Olsen's armchair.

'Bryan, this is my phone call.'

'What do you mean, "this is your phone call"?'

'I've been arrested. This is my phone call.'

Bryan's mouth went dry. 'You've been *arrested*? What the hell for? You didn't try that Captain Black stunt, did you?'

Lily began to weep. 'We tried, Bryan, but it all went wrong.

Harriet was caught trying to cut through the fence and Dean shot the security guard and Harriet's dead, too, she fell on the fence and it was electric.'

'For Christ's sake, Lily, slow down. Catch your breath.'

'It all went wrong, Bryan. Harriet's dead and Henry's in a coma. Dean's been charged with murder, and we've all been charged with armed robbery and assault and trespass.'

Bryan was squeezing his fist so tightly that his knuckles were spots of white. 'Where are you now?' he asked Lily, trying to control his temper.

'Linn County Sheriff's Department.'

'Have they read you your rights?'

'Yes.'

'Have they harassed you or bullied you or used undue force?'

'No.'

'I suppose you want me to find you a lawyer?'

'I just want you to get me out of here!'

'All right,' said Bryan. 'I'll do my best. But this is serious, Lily, believe me. I told you not to do it, for Christ's sake, but you thought you knew better, didn't you? This will probably cost us Zapf-Cady altogether.'

'We didn't mean for anybody to get hurt, Bryan. But it all went wrong.'

Bryan took a deep breath. *Don't lose your temper,* he told himself. *She's stupid.* She's over-impulsive. She's probably screwed up everything. But don't lose your temper.

'What about the hog?' he asked her.

'What are you talking about?'

'Captain Black. You didn't actually manage to let him out, did you?'

'Of course we let him out! That's what we went there for!'

'Oh, Christ, Lily. Tell me it isn't true.'

'Bryan, I'm proud of it! At least Harriet didn't die for

nothing! Do you know what they did to that hog? They cut open his head and gave him the brain of a three-year-old child! Can you imagine what that child must be thinking! Can you imagine what Captain Black must be thinking?'

'Jesus,' said Bryan. He pressed his fingertips hard against his forehead. He could see years of work and millions of dollars of campaign money sliding away from under his feet like sand down the side of a sand dune.

'Bryan,' said Lily, 'I know that I've acted impulsively. I know. But I couldn't let that poor animal suffer that kind of treatment any longer. You could tell how miserable he was, how frustrated he was. He was beating himself up against the walls of his pen. He was hurting himself on purpose. Hogs never do that, they're very self-protective. Not unless they're mad or they're miserable; and Captain Black is both of those.'

'So you've let out a mad, miserable one-and-a-half ton hog – a hog that's already killed one man and badly injured several others – and all in the name of animal freedom. For Christ's sake, Lily, what the hell did you think you were doing?'

'Captain Black is a mortal being, Bryan! A living, sentient creature, just like you and just like me!'

'He's a hog, Lily! That's all he is! A walking barbecue! Chops, shanks, butts, snouts and picnics!'

'You hypocrite!' Lily screamed at him. 'You don't really believe in any of this, do you? It's all politics to you! It's all wheeling and dealing!'

'What the hell does it matter?' Bryan retorted. 'You and your guerrilla tactics, you've screwed it all up anyway!'

He hadn't felt so angry for years. If there was one thing that enraged him more than disloyalty, more than deceit, more than any kind of political knavery you could think of, it was incompetence. And if there was one thing that enraged him even more than incompetence, it was finding himself obliged to support and to justify people who had acted incompetently.

For no sensible reason at all – apart from her unbalanced and over-sentimental attachment to hogs – Lily had put his whole political career at risk. When Bryan thought of all the time that he had spent on taking difficult opponents to lunch, on buttering-up the TV stations and *Newsweek* and the *Washington Post*, on lecture circuits and late-night radio shows, he was so furious that he could have smashed every single ornament within reach. He was almost hyperventilating, and there was a long, long pause in the conversation, although neither of them hung up.

After a while, Lily said, 'Bryan – I'm sorry if I've caused you any problems. I didn't mean to. But I had to make a statement of my own. I had to prove myself.'

'To whom? To Dean what's-his-name? To Harriet? To all of those other vegetarian fruitcakes?'

'I did a deal with the devil, Bryan. I did a deal with *you*.'

'You mean you formed an intimate association with a member of Congress in order to see your wacky minority ideals adopted as law?'

'Why are you being so horrible to me?' Lily screamed. 'You always told me that you believed in it, too!'

'Listen, Lily, I believe in political commitment! I believe in professionalism! I believe in getting things done! Most of all, I believe in not acting like a headstrong, wilful idiot and ruining months of planning and millions of dollars of capital investment! You're spoilt, Lily! You're self-indulgent! When you do a deal with the devil, it stays done, and you can never go back on it, never.'

Tearfully, Lily said, 'I still need a lawyer.'

'A lawyer, Jesus. You need the whole fucking Bar Association.'

'Maybe Captain Black will just come back.'

'In your dreams, Lily. This is real life. Think of the worst possible scenario, then double it. *Monster Hog Goes On Rampage In Children's Creche. Monster Hog Guzzles Novices In Nunnery Feeding-Frenzy.* Shit, Lily. Use your imagination.'

'But if we caught him again – if we said that we'd only let him out as a publicity stunt – ?'

'Lily, how are we going to catch him again? I'm wearing a three-and-a-half-thousand-dollar Cerruti sports coat, right? You want me to run out into the woods with a lasso and bring this giant hog of yours home in the back of my Ferrari?'

'Bryan, I know who he is. I know whose brain-section they implanted in him.'

'So how does that help?'

'*Listen,* Bryan. It was George Pearson, three years old. I heard the police officers talking to Garth Matthews when they arrested us. George Pearson was the boy who was killed by his father, out in a field.'

'Remind me.'

'He took all of his children out into a field and cut their heads off with a sickle, you must remember that. He killed some other people, but one of his daughters escaped.'

'Yes . . .' said Bryan, carefully. He was beginning to be interested. 'I remember that.'

'Well, when were right in the middle of liberating Captain Black, Garth Matthews shouted out "Emily" – really screamed it out. And Emily is the name of George Pearson's sister, the one who survived. Captain Black went crazy. Like, totally crazy.'

'He wasn't just frightened?'

'No, not at all. I'd been calming him, soothing him down.'

'But Garth Matthews shouted "Emily" and then he went wild?'

'That's right. And, later, I overheard Garth Matthews say to this other guy Nathan Somebody that Captain Black was probably going to go look for Emily.'

'Why would he do that?'

'Bryan, you don't get it. He may look like a hog, but inside of his head he has the intelligence of a three-year-old human kid.'

'You really believe that?'

'Yes, I've seen him. I really believe it.'

'And he's looking for his sister Emily?'

'Who else does he have, apart from his mother? And from what they told me at the sheriff's department, his mother's still in hospital.'

Bryan looked up at the painting of the dancing children. Such innocence, such glee. 'So what you're saying is, that Captain Black will be trying to locate his older sister?'

'Exactly. That's exactly it.'

Bryan was thoughtful for a moment. Newton appeared in the dining-room doorway and softly called out, 'Mr Cady, sir. You want me to keep your hors d'oeuvres warm?'

Bryan shook his hand, and said, 'No thanks, Newton.' He didn't like pike quenelle anyway; they tasted like half-congealed wallpaper paste.

'Listen, Lily,' he said, 'you know all about hogs, right? How they think, what they can do?'

'Of course, yes,' she said, cautiously.

'Do you think that Captain Black is going to be able to find his way back to Cedar Rapids?'

'I don't doubt it. Hogs have a really miraculous sense of direction.'

'He'd go back home, wouldn't he, to the Pearson house? He wouldn't know that his sister had been taken into care?'

'I guess he wouldn't, no. In any case he'd be sure to start by going someplace familiar.'

'Good,' said Bryan. He was thinking fast, calculating fast.

'All I have to do is arrange to have the Pearson house put under surveillance. If Captain Black shows up, I can have a team of hog-handlers and sharpshooters ready to deal with him; and the press on hand, too. Maybe we'll be able to salvage something out of this goddamned fiasco.'

Lily said, 'You never believed in any of this, did you?'

'What can I tell you?' Bryan retorted. 'I believed that you and I could work together for our mutual benefit. Now it seems that you had other ideas.'

'I had to set Captain Black free, Bryan. I had to show people how inhuman those experiments are.'

'Oh, really? You've probably put him through even more pain and even more fright than anything he ever suffered before. Listen – I have to make some phone calls, get this stake-out set up. I'll call you a lawyer, too. Meanwhile, just keep quiet, okay?'

'Bryan, I do love you, you know. I belong to you.'

Bryan let out a sharp, testy breath. 'It's a little late for that, don't you think? If Zapf-Cady fails to get through, I'll have lost millions of dollars and my political career will be effectively finished – and all because of you. Pretty funny way of showing your love for me, huh?'

'Bryan –'

'It's over, Lily. Forget it. I don't think it ever began. I'll have you bailed; I'll take care of your legal expenses. But that's it, that's as far as it goes. It's over.'

He didn't wait for her reply. Instead, he hung up and stood staring with unfocused eyes on the panelled wall. *Don't lose your temper,* he told himself. *Think clearly.* Then he picked up the telephone and threw it the length of the hallway, so that it smashed against the opposite wall.

Fourteen

The black van with the blacked-out windows drew up opposite the McKinley Children's Home in downtown Cedar Rapids. It turned, and then backed into a narrow alleyway between the Farmers' Bank Building and the Cedar Apartments. The Witness switched off the engine and stopped the wipers, so that the windshield gradually became blurred with rain.

'This is the place, yes?' asked Naked.

'Yes, well, yes. This is the place.'

'In that case, you and the Witness will go inside, and find out where your daughter is being kept.'

'Supposing she's under guard or something?'

'The Swordsman will accompany you, too.'

Terence turned to Naked. 'I can't do it. They won't let us in. They must have some kind of security. They'll call the police. They'll kill us.'

'You must,' said Naked; and her voice eerily reminded Terence of the tightrope dancer in *Elvira Madigan*, insisting to her lover Sixten that he shoot her. '*You must.*'

'They won't let us in,' Terence gabbled. 'They won't let us in! Look at us! With masks!'

'The Witness and the Swordsman will take off their masks, have no fear. And the Swordsman will carry a single blade, concealed.'

'I can't do it,' said Terence. He was very close to total panic. He felt as if his blood corpuscles were rushing around his body like freeway traffic.

'You must.'

'I can't, I really can't.'

'If you don't, my friend, many thousands of people will die. You can see for yourself what it is happening to the weather. Crops are already being flooded and flattened. You know why. Before he tends to anything, the Green Traveller must first tend to those people who threaten him – those people who threaten the purity of his ancestry. There are strong, straight plants and there are bent and corrupt plants, and you are the plant that has changed everything. You and your kin will one day destroy the parent, unless we destroy you first.'

In a vague, fragmentary way, Terence thought that he was beginning to understand why the Green Traveller wanted to find Emily so badly. He had read in some of his books about children of Janek-the-Green 'who had grown not straight, in the manner of the father'. In some children, these distortions were obvious when they were born, and they had been suffocated or drowned by their parents.

In 1632, in Bruges, in Flanders, a dead baby had been found floating in the canal under the Hoogstraat bridge. Its back had been layered with wet leaves; its veins and arteries had been penetrated by wriggling vegetable-roots. Its heart had been, literally, *green*, like a small pepper. Anthony Van Dyck had made a charcoal sketch of its body, which could still be seen today in the private room at the Groeninge Museum. For once, the plant genes that were inextricably tangled into the Green Traveller's physical being had visibly dominated the appearance of one of his offspring.

But there were other children whose perverted genetics were far less apparent. Only when they reached adolescence did they exhibit any signs that the Green Traveller's inhuman side had affected them so strongly. Terence had discovered a 19th-century German pamphlet called *Unheiligen Kinder* in which a case was reported in Drensteinfurt, a village close to Munster, Westfalen, where a young farm girl had been discovered by her parents 'writhing in her bed, with the skin of her face peeled off, to reveal a cleft green skull . . . while sharp thorns and branches pierced through her nightgown *from the inside*'. Her suffering had been such that her father had been obliged to kill her with an axe.

It was children like this of whom the Green Traveller was deeply afraid, and it was those children that he was always determined to hunt down, and destroy in a ritual of 'fire and sword'.

The Green Traveller craved humanity. He was like a hideously-driven narcotics addict, who needed more and more human viscera to slow down the inexorable growth of the roots and tubers that tangled through his system.

Terence wasn't sure what kind of threat Emily could possibly be to him, but he certainly appeared to regard her as one – and if that were true, he must regard Terence himself as something of a threat, too. If Terence had fathered one child like Emily, he could father another. That must be why the Green Traveller had spared Emily on the night that he had killed Mary. He had needed her invitation in order to feed on Terence, but Terence hadn't been there.

Terence had felt driven to kill Emily because she was Janek's granddaughter, and he had been terrified that she would have invited Janek to come into the house and slaughter the whole family. But now he realized that Emily could be his one salvation.

Janek rustled and shifted in the back of the van. Terence couldn't imagine anything more unnatural and misshapen than *he* was; but he knew that it was critical to Janek's survival that he keep his progeny pure. The children must never rebel. They must always submit to Janek's will. The first child who refused to open the door to Janek's knocking would be the first child to starve him of life, and to deprive him of the possibility of ever being human again. The first child who refused him would allow those roots to wind into his arteries, even deeper; and those branches to claw into his brain.

'Are you ready to go?' Naked whispered. 'You will know great pain unless you do.'

'All right,' Terence whispered. His face was clustered with sweat. 'But you won't hurt us, will you?'

'Perhaps, perhaps not,' said Naked. 'But Janek will let both of you survive, provided that you participate in the ritual of cleansing of the line, and that you swear not to have children, either of you, and also provided that you go far away from this place, to a city where there are no farms or pastures. You are the corrupt, distorted plant; and your Emily is your corrupt and distorted offshoot.'

'When has Janek ever let anybody survive?' asked Terence.

'This time, he may. But he must be sure that you have taken part in the cleansing and that you will leave this place for ever.'

Terence turned around and stared at the dark, bushy outline of Janek-the-Green. The rain drummed on the van roof and the Leper coughed and spat. Terence knew that Janek was wily and untrustworthy, and it was hard to believe that he would actually let him and Emily go free. But he had very little choice. He knew from his reading that when people had refused to give the Green Traveller what he wanted, the consequences were usually catastrophic. All across Central Europe, in the late Middle Ages, a potato blight had led to hundreds of thousands of deaths from starvation – and all because a farmer had burned his daughter alive in a hayrick, rather than let the Green Traveller have her.

The rain kept on drumming on the van roof and Terence knew that it wasn't going to let up until the Green Traveller had found his granddaughter. Already, the Missouri had burst its banks in twenty-eight different places, and thousands of acres of farmland were deep under water.

Terence checked the clock on the dash. It was 2.17 and he

was growing hungry and thirsty. 'Okay,' he said. 'Let's do it while we can.'

The Witness removed his mask. Underneath, his face was almost as white as the mask, with smooth skin the texture of bisque porcelain, and black, Slavic-looking eyes. His mouth was the thinnest of slits, and quite expressionless. He saw everything, the foulest of human vices, the most appalling deceit and treachery, and yet his face registered nothing at all. He witnessed: and remained unmoved.

The Swordsman took off his mask, too. His face was altogether different. Angular, densely scarred, with a sharp pointed nose and glittering grey eyes. He had a scraggly grey goatee and a thinning grey moustache. Although he looked at Terence in a quick, defensive and lively way, his face had the appearance of dead flesh, as if it would feel cheesy and decayed if he had the nerve to touch it.

'Go,' said Naked. 'Take every care.'

The Green Traveller let out a thin, piping noise, followed by a trickling sound. Terence didn't dare even to look in his direction.

The boy Knife opened the rear doors and they climbed out of the van into the rain. The Witness and the Swordsman walked on either side of Terence as they crossed the noisy, wet-slicked street, even though Terence could actually hear their footsteps just ahead of him. In the light and glitter of the night, they were barely visible, more like two moving shadows than two dangerous medieval rascals.

They entered the swing doors of the McKinley Children's Home, and the brown-carpeted vestibule was brightly lit, with pegboards on either side decorated with children's art. The founder of Cedar Rapids was honoured with a lurid painting entitled *Osgood Shephard Builds A Cabin By The Cedar River*, in which the first settler's house was depicted in stunning purple. A lopsided drawing of a factory was described as *The North Star*

Oatmeal Mill, 1872, Now The Quaker Oats Company (Where Daddy Works).

Terence crossed to the high formica desk where a formidable black woman with upswept spectacles was typing on a word-processor.

'Help you?' she asked, without looking up. Then she did look up, and took off her spectacles and stared at this unholy trio with undisguised disapproval – particularly at the Witness, at whom she narrowed her eyes and frowned as if she thought she could frown him into non-existence. And she almost could: because his outline was still shadowy and fluid, and his eyes were suspended in the air like the blood clots in a fertilized chicken egg.

'I'm looking for a girl called Emily Pearson,' said Terence. 'I was told she might be staying here.'

'I can't give information to anybody except relatives,' the receptionist told him.

'But you could tell me if she's here.'

'No, sir, I couldn't. I can't give information to anybody except relatives.'

'I know that. But I'm Emily's – uncle.'

'You're her uncle? You can prove that?'

'Not exactly, no.'

'I can't give you any information about Emily Pearson until you can prove that.'

'Then she *is* here?'

The receptionist shook her head, and went back to her word-processing, her crimson clawlike nails clicking on the keys. 'I told you. Information to relatives only.'

The Swordsman leaned over the counter. Terence didn't even see him draw it out, but he was holding a long, thin, brilliantly-shiny dagger, and its point was just dimpling the side of the receptionist's neck. She froze, her nails poised over her keyboard, her eyes wide.

Terence said, 'I think it would be a good idea if you told me if Emily Pearson was here or not.'

The receptionist swallowed, and then nodded. 'She's here, yes. Brought in yesterday.'

'Very good,' said Terence. 'So where is she now?'

'They just had supper. She's probably in the dayroom, watching TV.'

'So where's the dayroom?'

'All the way through to the back, up that left-hand staircase, then it's the door right in front of you.'

Terence glanced towards the street. Then he said, 'You won't call the cops, will you?'

'Unh-hunh,' said the receptionist, rolling her eyes downward so that she could see the blade that the Swordsman was pricking into her neck.

'What did you say?' Terence pressed her.

'I said I'm not going to call no cops; that's what I said.'

'That's what I thought you said.'

He turned to the Witness and the Witness indicated with a nod of his head that they should go to the rear of the building and find Emily. Terence turned back to the Swordsman just in time to see the point of his dagger emerging from the back of the receptionist's neck – only two or three inches of it – and then slipping out of sight again. The Swordsman wiped the blade on his upraised sleeve, and then dropped it back into its scabbard. He didn't even look interested in what he had done. The receptionist continued to sit upright for a few moments, but as they walked away she suddenly keeled over and dropped to the floor. Her shoulders were caped in glistening blood.

'Did you have to *kill* her?' Terence protested, in a fierce whisper. 'She didn't do anything to you!'

The Swordsman pushed Terence in the back, to indicate that he would do what he liked, whenever he liked. Terence stumbled, and then continued along the corridor, in between more childish paintings, and a large noticeboard announcing We Are McKinley Children: We Are Happy & Loved.

They heard children's voices singing. '*. . . what is your one-oh? Green grow the rushes-o!*' Then they climbed a short flight of stairs, and pushed open a pair of swing doors. The room inside was gloomy and crowded with children sitting on tattered armchairs and couches and bean-bags. They were watching *Indiana Jones and the Temple of Doom* on a huge old television. They were so engrossed in the human-sacrifice scene that hardly any of them turned around when Terence and the Witness and the Swordsman walked in and stood urgently looking from child to child, trying to identify Emily.

Terence thought: *please God, don't tell me she's not here.* But then a girl sitting on a bean-bag close to the television screen turned to see what was happening, and it was her.

It was almost like slow-motion. Her eyes widened and her mouth opened and she rose from the bean-bag and started to run towards the door at the opposite end of the dayroom. Terence cupped both hands around his mouth and shouted, '*Emmmiiiillllyyyyy!!!!*' The Witness bounded across the room, his white coat furling and unfurling like the foresail of a ship at sea, and the Swordsman drew his knife.

The knife tumbled slowly thought the air, flashing and flashing as it turned. For a split second, Terence thought that the Swordsman had killed her, that he would pierce her heart. But the knife went right through the sleeve of her pink gingham blouse and nailed her to the door, with a thud that sounded like a coffin lid closing. Terence shouldn't have worried. He knew that the Swordsman couldn't kill her: not until she had offered herself freely. And he also knew that he wouldn't kill her: not until she had offered up Terence's life, as a gift to her voracious grandfather.

'Daddy,' said Emily, her face white, terrified. Some of the

children began to scream, some of them started to cry, but most of them remained silent.

Terence came slowly across the room. She shrank away from him in fear, her eyes darting feverishly from side to side, looking for a way to escape. He could understand why. He wished there were some way of explaining it, but there simply wasn't. I have to take you away you because your grandfather is half-man, half-bush, and he needs our guts to keep himself alive? I have to take you away because thousands of people will lose their livelihoods if you don't, and hundreds more could lose their lives?

I have to take you away because your life was pledged from the moment you were born, and you don't have any choice at all, but to suffer the consequences of your grandparents' greed and your father's fecklessness?

'Emily,' said Terence, holding out his hand, 'they're going to let us go free. I'm not going to hurt you, sweetheart. I don't have to any more.'

The Swordsman gripped Terence's shoulder and jabbed a finger at the door, indicating that they should take Emily and leave the building immediately. Then the Swordsman stepped up to Emily, tugged his knife from out of her sleeve, and pushed her towards Terence as if she were a sack of flour.

Terence tried to take hold of her, but Emily twisted herself away. '*No!*' she whispered.

'Sweetheart, you don't understand. It's different now.'

She looked up at him and there was something in her eyes which he didn't understand; something which frightened him. For an instant she didn't look like Emily. She looked like a mummer's mask, with somebody else peering out from behind her eyes. He stood aside, and frowned at the Witness, but with chilly impatience the Witness beckoned him out of the dayroom, and together they pushed their way through the doors, and down the stairs, and passed the reception desk.

Terence tried not to see blood, but he couldn't help it. The Swordsman knew more than swords: he knew arteries, too, and where to find them, and how to nick them so they geysered out pints of blood in no time at all.

They left the building and crossed the road. A taxi driver honked his horn at them and shouted out, 'Hey! You got some kind of death wish, or what?'

The Swordsman stopped, and turned around, and stared at him. The taxi driver's jaw slowly opened, and then closed again, and then he accelerated up 10th Street with a squeal of wet tyres.

Terence kept his head down and said nothing. The Witness was close beside him. He ushered Emily into the alley, and opened up the van doors.

Emily said, in a voice that was papery with fright, 'Daddy – you're not going to cut my head off, are you?'

Terence said, 'No, sweetheart, I'm not. But I don't know what's going to happen next. Your grandfather's here. Your real grandfather, the Green Traveller. And what happens next – well, it's up to him.'

The Swordsman and the Witness climbed into the van. The Witness replaced his mask, and sat in the driving seat, and started the engine. The Doctor turned around, his face as pale as a lamp.

'Daddy I'm scared.'

'Me too, sweetheart. But let's take the chance. The Green Traveller's offered to spare us. He's going to let us go, so long as we leave Iowa and go to live in the city, maybe Cleveland or someplace, or Indianapolis.'

'That's all we have to do?'

'I think so.'

Emily climbed into the van, and Terence climbed in after her, and Knife closed the doors. Terence should have known then that there was something different about Emily. No other girl of eleven years old could have climbed so readily into a blacked-out van, one corner of which was occupied by a dark and rustling bush, and another corner of which was occupied by a greasy cowled figure, diseased and coughing and fetid with leprosy.

They drove off into the rain. Naked reached out and touched Emily's hands and said, 'You're cold, my darling.'

'I'm not your darling and I'm always cold.'

'You know why you're here, don't you?'

'Yes.'

'Something's gone wrong, Emily. It wasn't your fault. When he was born, your father didn't turn out quite right, and so you and Lisa and George, you didn't turn out quite right, either.'

They turned south-east on Mt Vernon Road. Emily looked across at Terence as if she were seeking confirmation of the truth of what Naked was saying; but Terence deliberately looked away, out of the front windshield. He didn't know what the Green Traveller had in mind for them; but all he knew was that ritual atonements were far from easy; and that there was a good chance that he and Emily would both be killed. Crops were always more important than the people who grew them; and all across eastern Iowa, the ground was thick with the bones of those farmers who had given their lives for a generous harvest; and some who had given their souls, too.

Emily said, 'Where are we going?'

'Back to your house,' said Naked. 'Then we can knock, the same way we knocked before, and you can let us in.'

'Supposing I don't let you in?'

'You will,' said Naked, behind her mask. 'Good girls always do.'

Luke knocked loosely on the door and then stepped into the office where Garth and Nathan had been reading for the past hour and ten minutes.

'How's it going?' he asked them, resting one huge buttock cheek on the edge of the desk.

'Fascinating,' said Garth, rubbing his eyes and dropping the last few pages of Professor Mrstik's translation onto the blotter in front of him. 'Absolutely and totally fascinating. This is the first conclusive connection between mythical characters and provable genetic science that I've ever seen. I mean, who knows what's next? Maybe we can prove that fairies exist.'

'So you believe it's true, all this stuff about the Green Traveller?'

'Not entirely,' said Garth. 'Some of the legend is pretty far-fetched. But there's obviously a central core of truth in it. Pearson seems to have checked out most of the more recent historical connections. And I believe that there was some kind of original ceremony of turning a man into a tree – that appears in seven or eight separate accounts, all of them written at different times. Mostly it happened in Dominica and Haiti and British Guyana, but there were isolated cases reported throughout the Northern Hemisphere, especially in Bohemia and Romania.

'What interests me most of all is the genetic evidence, which is very substantial and very consistent. I mean, these books that Terence Pearson was studying were fifty, sixty, a hundred years old, some of them. But they're all very specific that "man and bush were truly mix't, so that the two were not escryable, one from the other". We've done some animal–vegetable gene combinations at Stillman. We produced a frog that literally had lichen on its back instead of skin. But it can go further than that, much further. We're talking about animals that can partially photosynthesize; and plants with rudimentary thinking. It's all possible, it's all being done today.'

Luke said, 'I thought you would laugh. I thought you wouldn't believe me.'

Garth shrugged. He looked pale and tired, and bruised, too. 'Ten years ago, even five years ago, no, maybe I wouldn't. But we've made huge strides in genetics since then, and we're trying something new practically every day. Look at Captain Black.'

'I would, Dr Matthews, if I knew where to find him.'

'I think he's headed for home,' said David.

'Oh, yes, and what makes you think that?'

'I think he's headed for home because he has noplace else to go.'

'Dr Matthews?' asked Luke.

Garth shrugged. 'That makes sense. Maybe you should keep an eye on the Pearson house, whatever.'

'I'll send a couple of deputies out there, just to keep an eye on things.'

Garth said, 'You will let me know as soon as anybody sights him, won't you? Raoul and I spent the best part of our careers developing Captain Black. We always thought that his behaviour might be less than amenable, once we'd inserted human brain-material. But now we have this wild card in his genetic make-up, too: the fact that he could be directly related to this Green Traveller that Terence Pearson keeps rambling on about. Quite frankly, there's no way of telling if he's hog or boy or mythical mummer, or what particular combination of all three.'

Luke said, 'What I want to know is, how come you could use little George Pearson's brain-section without Terence or Iris Pearson's permission?'

'You don't normally need or seek permission to use fractional amounts of tissue from dead bodies,' said Garth. 'For instance, it's common practice to take the pituitary glands out of corpses, grind them to a powder and make hormones out of them. They use them in fertility drugs or growth-promoting substances. The last figures I saw, we regularly remove the pituitary glands from anything up to a million corpses every year. We also regularly take brain tissue out of dead bodies and use it in several types of neurosurgery, such as dural grafting.'

'Without anybody being asked?' said Luke, in surprise.

'You can't take it with you,' put in Nathan.

At that moment, officer Jean Lehman knocked at the open door. She was a podgy redhead who always reminded Luke of Loretta Swit. She was escorting Lily Monarch, who was looking bruised and pale and distressed.

'Ms Monarch asked to see you, sheriff. Said it was urgent.'

'All right, then,' said Luke, easing himself off the edge of the desk. 'What can I do for you, Ms Monarch?'

Lily said, in a very quiet voice, 'I need to talk to you. It's about Captain Black.'

'Let's find ourselves an office, then,' said Luke.

'No, no. I don't mind talking here. Dr Matthews and I have been enemies when it comes to vivisection and animal experiments, but – well, maybe he ought to hear what I have to say. Maybe he can help.'

'Okay by me,' said Garth. 'Do you know these other two gentlemen? This is Nathan Green, he's a pathologist from Mercy Medical Center. This is his son, David.'

Lily gave them a quick, dismissive smile. 'I've just made my phone call,' she said.

'You can tell my deputy the name of your lawyers,' said Luke.

'I haven't talked to my lawyers yet. I phoned Senator Bryan Cady. You probably know that he's kind of a friend of mine. Or was, anyway.'

'Go on.'

'Bryan's upset with me because I let Captain Black go free. He thinks it's going to jeopardize his chances of passing the Zapf-Cady bill through Congress next week. So he's decided to recapture Captain Black himself.'

'Oh, yes? And how's he going to do that?'

'He's going to stake out the Pearson home with hog-handlers and sharpshooters. And of course he's going to call the media. He thinks that if he catches Captain Black, that will make him something of a hero.'

'So Senator Cady thinks that Captain Black is headed for home, too.'

'That was my suggestion.'

'Young David here suggested it, too. He was trying to imagine what a three-year-old kid would do.'

'And I was trying to imagine what an adult Poland China boar would do.'

There was an odd intonation in her voice when she said that, which Luke didn't miss. She was trying to tell him something; something that was deeply important to her, but something that wasn't particularly easy for her to say.

'How could you possibly imagine what an adult boar would do?' he asked her.

She was silent for a few moments, and then she said, 'Maybe you should look me up in your files.'

'Oh, yes? And what in particular should I be looking for?'

'The Hog Girl,' said Lily. 'You remember the Hog Girl?'

Nathan said, 'I remember that. It was fifteen years ago, wasn't it? Up in Prairieburg or someplace like that. They found a seven-year-old girl out on some real isolated hog farm, didn't they? Her parents had died about three years before but the hogs had brought her up. She was more hog than human.'

'That's right,' said Lily. 'She learned to communicate with them; she could understand what they wanted; and she could imagine where they would go when they were alone and afraid and needed company.'

Luke stared at her. 'You're trying to tell me that Hog Girl was *you*?'

Tears sparkled in Lily's eyes. 'Yes, that Hog Girl was me.'

'But the way I heard it, that little girl was almost a hog herself. She needed years of psychotherapy just to believe that she was human.'

'I'm still having it. If you doubt my word, you can call Dr Cohen at the Cedar Institute.'

'I will,' said Luke. 'It's not that I don't believe you, but I think I ought to check. I don't want you getting yourself mixed up in something that puts back your therapy programme. The county could find itself liable for damages.'

Briefly, she told Garth and Luke what she had told Bryan Cady – about the way that her parents had died, and the way in which the hogs had reared her. They listened in silence, and when she had finished they both looked at each other, moved and impressed.

Luke tapped his forehead with his finger. 'So . . . what you're saying is, Ms Monarch, knowing what you know about hogs, you should be able to predict what Captain Black is going to do?'

'I believe so.' She wiped her eyes with her sleeve.

'You let him out; why should you want to help us to catch him again? He'll only be sent back to Spellman.'

'I want to help you catch him again because I made a stupid error of judgement about Bryan – about Senator Cady. I don't want Senator Cady to have any of the glory.'

Garth said, 'Presumably Senator Cady is worried that being associated with people who raid animal research institutes is going to affect the passage of his bill?'

Lily nodded. 'He called me all the names you can think of, and then some.'

'Well, I could call you a few names, too,' said Garth.

Lily said, 'I don't care if they don't ratify Zapf-Cady, not any more. I thought Bryan was an idealist. I thought he had social convictions. But the fact that Zapf-Cady has been drafted to protect animals is only incidental. It's just another bandwagon. Zapf-Cady is about the furtherance of Bryan's political career, and that's all.'

'Seems like the scales done fell from your eyes,' Garth remarked, drily.

Luke checked his watch. 'All right,' he said. 'I think we need to see what's happening over at the Pearson home. You can come along, too, Ms Monarch, but I'm going to have to insist that you wear handcuffs.'

'You're going to do your best to take Captain Black alive?' said Garth.

Luke looked at him with his dour, unimpressed sheriff's expression.

'Come on,' said Garth. 'This animal has cost us millions. He's a miracle of xenogenetic surgery. Dr Lacouture sacrificed his life, rather than see this hog die.'

'All I can say is, we'll have to play it by ear,' said Luke.

'But I can tranquillize him, given the chance. Then you won't have to kill him.'

'All right, then, if you want to bring along the necessary equipment to tranquillize him, then please do. But I'm not making any promises.'

'Can I come?' asked David, excitedly.

Garth said, 'It could be a good idea, sheriff. David has a way with Captain Black . . . or maybe with young George Pearson.'

'So long as you stay in the car and keep out of the way,' Luke insisted.

Lily went across to Garth and held out her hand. 'I want to say that I'm sorry for the way that things have turned out.'

Garth looked up at her. 'You don't get it, do you? You've just put my entire life's work at risk for the sake of some sentimental airy-fairy ideal. Of course I know that hogs are mortal. Of course I care when they suffer. But the human suffering that they can relieve is millions of times greater.'

Lily withdrew her hand. 'I'm still sorry, all the same.'

The telephone warbled. Luke picked it up and said, 'Yes? What is it? I'm busy.'

'Deputy Walsh here, sheriff. I've had two reports – one from the airport, one from downtown.'

'Good news or crappy news?'

'I guess crappy. A private helicopter pilot spotted something like a hundred stray hogs east of the airport headed roughly north-north-east, towards the city. They sound like the same hogs who caused that wreck on 76th Avenue last night. The only difference is, they appear to have a leader – a very much larger hog, a big black bastard, three times the size of a normal boar.'

'Captain Black,' said Luke, wryly. 'Sounds like he's found himself an entourage. Have we sent out our own surveillance?'

'We tried to send out a helicopter but the weather's closed right in. Even the airport's shut down. We've sent out a couple of 4×4s, but they're crossing some pretty damned difficult terrain.'

'Shit. Well, do your best. What's the other report?'

'You're not going to like this, sheriff. Three men broke into the McKinley Children's Home just twenty minutes ago. They fatally wounded the receptionist and then they went into the dayroom and kidnapped guess who.'

Luke covered his eyes with his podgy hand. 'I don't believe this,' he said. 'Not Emily Pearson?'

'Got it in one, sheriff.'

'Anybody see these guys?'

'Several passers-by, most of the children, and a taxi driver. Two of them were white-faced and tall and kind of scary-looking. The other was slightly built, pale, with short-cut hair.'

'Terence Pearson,' Luke breathed.

'Yes, sir. Taxi driver made a positive ID from a mug-shot. Said he remembered him anyhow, from the newspaper.'

'How about the other two?'

'The taxi driver wasn't so sure. Said he couldn't see them very good, for some reason.'

'Anybody see the getaway vehicle?'

'Black late-model Chevrolet van with dark-tinted windows. No registration plate.'

'Headed which way?'

'Turned north-east on 4th Avenue, then disappeared into traffic.'

Luke put down the phone. He said nothing at all.

'Anything wrong?' asked Garth, helpfully.

'Yes, I think the fertilizer is just about to make contact with the fan.'

The Cedar Mall backed onto a wide, scrubby strip of waste acreage that grew boggier and boggier until it eventually gave up trying to be land and sank into a muddy, flooded tributary of the Cedar River.

Although it was still only four in the afternoon, the rainclouds were so low that all of the lights around the mall had been switched on, and they gave a high multi-coloured gloss to the rainswept surface of the parking lot, and reflected red and green in the brackish pools and puddles of the field behind.

Captain Black stood knee-deep in one of these pools, his heavy black shoulders hunched, his ears and his snout dripping. The other hogs circled cautiously and respectfully around him, occasionally grunting and barking.

Captain Black knew what George Pearson had known – that shopping malls meant food. Captain Black hadn't eaten since mid-morning, and his stomach was hurting. Although he usually ate up to 15 lb of feed a day, he didn't usually expend so much energy, both running and keeping warm.

He lifted his snout and sniffed the air. The north-west wind carried the aroma of freshly-baked bread from an instore bakery; and of grilling hamburger patties and French fries. He let out a deep, rumbling cry, and began slowly to walk through the muddy, overgrown field towards the mall. The other hogs followed him, although many of them were too hungry and exhausted to keep up.

They trotted across the parking lot and their trotters made a rattling sound like devils approaching, on cloven hoofs. A family dressed up in waterproofs was just leaving the main entrance, their heads bowed against the wind and the rain, their shopping-carts stacked high. One of the children shrieked out, 'Lookit! Pigs!' and the father and mother backed away in fright and astonishment, their carts colliding together.

The hogs came out of the rainy gloom and their eyes glittered black in the light from the mall's interior. Their hides were plastered with thick greasy mud, and saliva dripped from their snouts. The automatic glass doors slid smoothly apart for them, and they came running into the mall, nearly a hundred of them, before anybody could think how to stop them.

The mall was warm and dry and bright and crowded. It was built in the configuration of a cross of Lorraine, with one long central promenade and two smaller ones branching across it. The floors were tiled in white marble and all down the centre of the main promenade there were marble planters with palms and fountains and semi-abstract statues representing the cultural heritage of Cedar Rapids – Native American canoes and Scottish bagpipes and Czech glassware.

Black as Satan and filthy as hell, Captain Black stood in the centre of the mall and let out a harsh, high scream that drowned out the chatter and laughter and even the syrupy orchestrated version of 'I Can't Help Falling in Love with You' that was pouring from the loudspeakers.

He screamed again and again, and so did the wild, bedraggled herd that had gathered around him. A woman screamed, too, and children started to cry. A man shouted out, 'Holy shit! It's a goddamned monster!'

To people brought up on *Them* and *The Thing* and *Jaws*, there was only one conditioned response, and that was to panic. A hideous shout of collective fear went up, like the shouting of airplane passengers who are convinced that they are going to die. People began to run down the central promenade, their feet scuffling and drumming on the tiled floor. Children were picked up; shopping-carts abandoned; bags and baskets dropped everywhere.

Captain Black saw the people running and he started to run, too. Running was exhilarating. He wasn't yet running *after* them. Unlike the lean and vicious herd of Berkshires who started running beside him, he hadn't yet been reduced to eating anything and everything that he could conceivably digest.

He ran down the central promenade, scattering shopping-carts and seats and abandoned baby-buggies. He crashed through the palms and the fountains, and one of the sculptures scored his left side, drawing blood. He roared and screamed, and the Berkshires screamed, too.

Shoppers scattered in all directions. Two or three of the Berkshires ran into The Bakery Shoppe and started ravaging the cakes and the bagels. Crumbs and broken cookies exploded everywhere. The Italian manager tried to beat the hogs off with a broom-handle, but then four more of them came rushing into the store. They collided with his knees and knocked him off-balance, and the next thing he knew he was lying on his back, with hogs tearing at his pants and his apron.

'You get off me! You get off me!' he yelled at them, in anger and fright. But then one of the Berkshires tore at his ear with its teeth, and ripped it clean away from the side of his head, along with part of his scalp, and first blood was spilled. The rest of the hogs abandoned the smashed and ruined pastries, and came after the manager with screams of greed.

Hogs burst into McDonald's and clambered onto the counters, tearing at hamburger buns and cheeseburgers, ripping open polystyrene boxes and pokes of French fries. One Berkshire tried to snatch the hamburger patties right off the grill-plate. His snout sizzled, and he screeched and rolled over, all the way across the grill, his bristles shrivelling and smoking, his legs kicking in agony.

Twenty or thirty hogs chased half a dozen children into Baby World. The hogs were so ravenous that they struggled and fought with each other to get through the door. There were no survivors in Baby World, and no witnesses, either. But the front window with its baby toys and rocking-horses and New England-style crib display was suddenly drenched in blood and pieces of torn flesh.

Captain Black had eaten now. Three or four of the Berkshires had brought loaves and sausages and hams, and dropped them at his feet, and he had stood his ground and eaten with dignity. The mall was almost completely deserted, and he walked slowly down the central promenade, growling in the depths of his throat. *I used to come here before, I remember it – but that was before –*

Before what? He still couldn't grasp what had happened to him; or who he was; or *what* he was. He felt strong and powerful, and yet he felt frightened and small, too and he couldn't understand why.

Emily. Emily would tell him what he was.

He was still stalking along the mall when he heard strange wailing noises. Not like hogs, not like animals at all. They reminded him of something exciting, but he couldn't decide what. He kept on walking. In one of the storefronts next to him, five Berkshires were bloodily feeding on a fallen girl.

They looked up and their eyes were terrible, and blood was dripping thickly from their smothered jaws. He turned away. They disgusted him. He thought they were weak and vicious, but he knew that they had to feed, too.

He heard men shouting, doors opening. He saw red and blue lights flashing. He had almost reached the end of the mall when he saw seven or eight men come rushing in – *men*, he knew they were called *men*. They stood in a line at the end of the central promenade and they shouted at him.

The one in the middle shouted the most. 'Jim! You got that elephant-gun ready? This baby takes one more step, he's headed for the packers! Rob, you start sweeping through those stores. Any hogs you see, you shoot to kill!'

Captain Black stared at the man in the middle and tried to speak to him. Back in his pen, the man and the boy had tried to speak to him. The boy had told him lots of names, and then said 'Emily'. Sometimes their voices had soothed him; but not very often. Most of the time they had driven him crazy. He couldn't think what 'men' were. He couldn't think what 'he' was.

But he knew that he didn't like this man in the middle, this man who kept on shouting. He took three threatening steps towards him, and bared his tusks, and screamed until he almost deafened himself, because he felt like screaming.

The man in the middle was Chief of Police John Husband. He had been driving home from a long meeting with the city's traffic planning department when he had intercepted an emergency call from Cedar Mall. He had immediately U-turned and driven back here; and he had been one of the first officers on the scene.

He could hardly believe what he was looking at. He had seen photographs of Captain Black in the papers, but he had never realized that a hog could be so huge – or so hellishly ugly, either. Captain Black was almost the size of a VW minibus; he took two or three steps forward and his wet slimy hide was literally steaming.

'Back off!' John yelled at him. But Captain Black showed no signs of backing off at all.

One of the officers was carrying a shotgun. John shouted, 'Kusak – blow his head off! The rest of you, start targeting those other hogs!'

At that instant, Captain Black started running at them. His trotters squeaked and galloped on the marble floor. His eyes were fixed directly on John, as if he wanted to glare him into submission. John raised his .44 Magnum in both hands, aimed at Captain Black's head and fired. The bullet left the barrel at 266 feet per second and Captain Black's left ear exploded in a chaos of blood and gristle. The bang was earsplitting.

Sergeant Kusak fired too, hitting Captain Black in the left shoulder with a full charge of shotgun pellets. A huge hunk of muscle flapped up, and Captain Black screamed in pain.

Captain Black was almost on top of him now, running at full tilt, and John fired again, but the bullet ricocheted off the floor and smashed the huge reinforced-glass window of Petrie's Pharmacy. John tried to duck out of the way, but his old bullet-wound let him down at the very last second and his leg buckled beneath him. Captain Black collided with him at nearly 20 m.p.h. and drove him through the window of the Country Cosmetics Store.

John didn't even have time to scream. Captain Black forced him the length of the store and drove him into a huge wall-mirror. John felt everything inside him crush, as if his chest were filled with nothing but eggshells. The last thing he felt was Captain Black's tusk driving into his ear.

Captain Black roared, and backed away. John slid down the mirror, leaving a triple trail of blood.

For a long moment, Captain Black stood amongst the litter

of broken perfume bottles and spilled face-powder and scattered lipsticks, and stared at his own reflection. He saw a terrible frightening beast, a beast that frightened even himself. Cautiously, growling in his throat, he stepped away. His shoulder hurt, and he knew that he needed to find Emily even more urgently than ever.

The mall crackled with gunfire. The Berkshires were being cornered and shot, and they were squealing in panic. Captain Black stepped out of the cosmetics store to find himself confronted by half a dozen men holding shotguns and revolvers.

They lifted their weapons and Captain Black knew that they were going to hurt him. He let out a huge, furious roar, and charged directly at them.

He heard their guns banging. He felt the heavy, painful thumping of bullets. But he wasn't hurt so badly that they could stop him. He ran towards the side entrance of the mall, still roaring, heading for the lights and the rain and the sparkle of traffic.

Sergeant Kusak shouted, 'Keep those doors closed!' and another officer pulled down the circuit-breaker that locked the automatic doors.

'Ready – when he turns around – fire!' ordered Sergeant Kusak.

They raised their guns again, and aimed. But Captain Black didn't turn around. Captain Black didn't even falter. All he saw ahead of him was open air and freedom, and he hit the plate-glass doors without even breaking stride.

With a massive crash, three tons of glass detonated into millions of sparkling fragments. For a second, they seemed to hang in the air, like a curtain of diamonds. Then they dropped to the floor in a spectacular shower, and Captain Black had disappeared like a thunderous shadow into the gloom.

Sergeant Kusak was almost screaming into his personal radio, 'Officer down! Officer down! Hog headed out of here! Get me some heavy artillery, for Christ's sake! Elephant-guns, whatever! And get some more paramedic units down here! And somebody who can really can shoot!'

The black van drew up outside the Pearson house and waited for a few minutes with its engine running. The street was wet and deserted. Over at the Terpstras' house, the windows were dark and the morning newspaper was still lying in its plastic wrapper on the front lawn. Obviously nobody had noticed yet that the Terpstras hadn't appeared since yesterday.

At last Naked touched the Witness on the shoulder and he switched off the engine. 'I think it's safe now,' she told Terence. 'We can rest for a while. The ritual must always take place in the eleventh minute of the eleventh hour. Eleven was a sacred number to the Bohemians. We can wait for the most mystical moment.'

They waited. In the front seats, the Witness and the Doctor eventually slept. Then the Leper's cowl drooped forward, and his breathing developed into a thick, unhealthy rasp. Knife stayed awake, and from the scraping, rustling sounds in the very back of the van, so did Janek-the-Green. But Naked's head dropped sideways by slow degrees, until her hair was resting on Terence's shoulder.

As she did so, the soft leather pouch that she carried around her neck fell against Terence's arm. He heard the coins inside it clinking. He waited in the darkness for a long, long time, listening to the mummers as they slept, listening to the hideous scratching of Janek-the-Green.

Then, with extreme care, holding his breath, he reached across with his left hand until he felt Naked's purse. The leather thong around the top was drawn very tight, but he managed to push the tips of his index finger and his middle finger into the neck of it, and gradually ease it open. Knife was staring at him all the time, but it was far too shadowy inside the van for any one of them to be able to see what he was doing.

He cupped the pouch in the palm of his hand and gently shook it. The coins rolled out, three or four of them, and dropped soundlessly onto the blankets that covered the van's floor. He tried to catch one of them, but it slipped between his fingers.

He sat back, and tried to relax, even though he was trembling. He wouldn't be able to deprive any more of the mummers of their coins, but at least one of them was now killable. Any chance was better than no chance at all.

At a quarter to eleven, Knife reached over and shook Naked's arm. At first she tried to push him away, but then she opened her eyes.

'How long have I been sleeping?' she asked. 'I feel so tired.'

Terence didn't answer; and neither did Emily. But knife lifted ten fingers and then one more, to indicate that it was almost eleven o'clock.

'It's time for you to go,' Naked told Terence. She sounded irritated, distracted. Terence knew why, but of course he didn't tell her. She was no longer carrying her share of Judas Iscariot's money, the coins that had been struck from the bands of the pillars of the tabernacle of the covenant. She was no longer living a heartbeat behind time. She was mortal again, although she didn't yet realize it.

'Hurry, you have to go!' Naked insisted. Terence reached out and tried to hold Emily's hand, but she pulled it away. 'I'm sorry,' he said, and he didn't just mean that he was sorry for trying to hold her hand.

The boy Knife opened up the van. Between them, Knife and

Naked and the Swordsman escorted Terence and Emily across the lawn, and up to the front door.

'You know what you have to do?' asked Naked. She took off her mask, and looked up at him. Her face was very pale, almost silvery-grey, but she was very beautiful in a Slavic-looking way. The rain sparkled on her tangled hair, and on her eyelashes, and touched her lips.

'We have to wait for you to knock,' said Terence, in a tight voice. 'Then Emily has to invite you in.'

'You know that your father will spare you, don't you? He can be forgiving, when he so desires. But he will need blood, to complete the ritual.'

'How much blood?'

'He will take it from your vein. You won't even know that you have lost it.'

Terence took a deep, frightened breath, and then coughed. 'If it's the only way.'

'It is, believe me,' Naked assured him.

Terence went to the front door, and then suddenly turned around, and let out a nervous laugh. 'I don't have a key. How can we invite you in if we can't get in ourselves?'

Without a word, the Swordsman stepped forward, and slid out his shining dagger. He wedged the point of it into the side of the door, and then hit the pommel with the flat of his hand. The wood splintered, and the Swordsman kicked the door with his booted foot, and it juddered open.

'Now, go inside and turn on the lights,' said Naked. 'Make it welcoming.'

'How long before you knock?'

'That depends on your father. But not long, I assure you.'

Terence and Emily went inside, and Terence walked from one room to another, switching on lights. The house felt cold and damp and deserted, and Terence was sure that he could still smell death. Death was a very difficult stench to get rid of. It clung to your soul as well as your house.

Emily stood in the centre of the living-room, her hands demurely clasped in front of her, looking around. 'It doesn't seem like our house any longer,' she said.

'It isn't, not really. The Green Traveller came calling, and that was the end of it.'

'Now I know why you killed Lisa and George, and why you wanted to kill me.'

Terence went to the small tray of drinks beside the television and poured himself a bourbon. The neck of the bottle rattled nervously against the glass. He swallowed, coughed, and then poured himself another one.

'You can understand,' he said. 'But can you forgive?'

Emily was watching him strangely through her BandAid-bound spectacles. 'Why do you want me to forgive you?'

'I guess everybody who hurts people wants forgiveness.'

'We have bad blood, don't we?' asked Emily.

'We have Janek's blood, yes. Janek's my father; and your grandfather; and he conceived us all for the specific purpose of feeding on us.'

'Do you think he's going to try to feed on us now?'

'I don't know. He promised not to. The legend says that he doesn't *have* to feed on his children if he doesn't want to. Once, not too long ago, he fell in love with one of his children, and he didn't feed on her. Another time, in the 10th century, he let a whole family of seven children survive because their parents paid him with the thirty silver coins that Judas was paid for betraying Jesus, and those helped him and his followers to live for hundreds of years.

'But even if it's not money, he always wants something . . . a piece of skin, a finger, a toe, a plait of hair, or blood. He can never leave you with nothing at all. He's given part of his life, you see, to make your parents' crop grow . . . he has to take some kind of life in return.'

Emily looked thoughtful, almost sly. 'Who was the girl whose life he spared?'

'What difference does it make? It was supposed to have happened in 1947 or 1948, just after World War Two, in Illinois, I think.'

'Who was the girl whose life he spared?' Emily repeated. Terence frowned at her and put down his glass.

'Why do you want to know?'

'It's important.'

'I don't know. It's in one of my books upstairs . . . that's if the cops didn't take it.'

'Find it. Tell me what her name was.'

'Emily –'

'*Find it!*' Emily demanded. Her voice was suddenly throaty and blurred.

'Okay, if that's what you want, but I can't guarantee that –'

'*Find it!*'

Terence was just about to leave the living-room when there was a loud, insistent knocking at the back door.

'It's them, already!' he said.

'Find the girl's name first,' insisted Emily.

'But aren't you going to invite them in?'

'Not until you find the name.'

The knocking went on and on and didn't let up. The Swordsman was at the door. The Doctor was at the door. The Leper was knocking; so were Knife and Naked. But most frightening of all, the Green Traveller was here at last, knocking and knocking, and waiting for Emily to invite him in.

Terence went upstairs and his legs felt as if they were filled with water instead of muscle and bone. The knocking seemed just as loud upstairs as it did in the living-room. He went to his study and took down the key and unlocked it. He turned around, but Emily hadn't followed him. He hesitated, and then he switched on the light, and went across to his bookshelf.

The sheriff's department had cleared his desk of files and diaries and pictures. But they had left most of his books behind, including his bibles. The book he wanted was still there: *Rural Mythology in Modern-Day America*, by Holzberger and Wendt. He took it down, and looked up Jack-the-Green in the index.

The knocking continued, and it upset Terence so much that he could scarcely read. But gradually, following the words with his fingertip, swallowing and swallowing with fright, he managed to decipher what they said.

'Jack-the-Green was supposed to have arrived in America sometime during the early part of the 18th century, although there are many contradictory accounts of the way in which he and his fellow mummers crossed the Atlantic . . .

'One of his last reported appearances was in Millersburg in western Illinois, in the spring of 1947. The story goes that he arrived at a small farm to offer his usual bargain, only to recognize that the farmer's wife was one of his own descendants . . .

'She was a Czech immigrant who could trace her lineage back to one of Jack-the-Green's daughters, whom he had sired in the mid-17th century when he was travelling through Bohemia. He had passionately loved this daughter, and given her an incestuous child in the hope of perpetuating her looks, century after century, daughter after daughter, so that he would never lose her . . .

'They had been separated by wars and thousands of miles of travel, but Jack-the-Green recognized this girl at once . . .

'The modern myth claims that – in return for a healthy harvest – Jack-the-Green gave an incestuous child to the farmer's wife in Millersburg, and that Jack-the-Green's incestuous line of daughters and granddaughters persists in

Midwestern America even today. Their looks are supposed to be very distinctive.

'It is interesting to note that medieval versions of the legend of Jack-the-Green invariably warn that his downfall would come, like Narcissus, from loving his own image, and that his own flesh and blood would one day rise up against him.'

The knocking at the door was so penetrating that Terence felt as if the Green Traveller were hammering inside his head. He pressed his left hand against his ear, to block out the noise, but he had to use his right hand to leaf quickly through the pages of *Rural Mythology* in search of any name. *Find the name*, Emily had urged him; and he knew that he had to.

There were no names mentioned in the main body of the text, but he turned to Sources and Appendices, and looked up page 243, where Jack-the-Green's incestuous relationships had been described. '*Peoria Journal-Star*, March 17, 1947: Farmer's Wife Blames "Bush-Man" For Violent Attack. – The wife of a farmer in the small community of Millersburg, Ill., complained to sheriff's deputies Wednesday that she had been assaulted by a man wearing a disguise made of leaves and branches. Mrs Karolina O'Neill, who came to Illinois only last year as a refugee from Prague, Czechoslovakia, said that the man had knocked at her door in the early hours of the morning and that she had invited him in, believing that he was a traveller who needed directions or assistance.'

Terence skipped down to the bottom of the footnote. It said, baldly, 'Mrs O'Neill was well-known to members of the Czech community in Peoria as Miss Karolina Ponican.'

He closed the book. He stood quite still, listening to the knocking. The Green Traveller wasn't going to go away. He would knock and knock until Emily invited him in. But why didn't Emily invite him in? Emily was the Green Traveller's granddaughter, after all, and didn't the Green Traveller's grandchildren always beg their parents to let him in? *He's holy, let him in.*

But maybe they wouldn't let him in if they were different. Maybe they wouldn't let him in if their character was far too much like his. If they were inbred; if they were strange; if their blood was bad. Hereditary lines are weakened and genetically altered by repeated incest, and maybe the time had come when Janek-the-Green was going to pay the price for having perpetuated the one face he really loved, apart from his own.

Karolina Ponican was Leos Ponican's sister; and that was how Leos had known what agonies were in store for him, if the Green Traveller came after him. But Karolina Ponican was also Karolina O'Neill, and Karolina O'Neill was very well known to Terence: as Carol O'Neill, his mother-in-law.

Iris was Janek-the-Green's daughter, just as he, Terence, was Janek-the-Green's son. They were half-brother and half-sister, and between the two of them they had given birth to three children whose paternal grandfather was also their maternal grandfather, and who was genetically bizarre beyond all imagination.

The knocking went on. Still Emily ignored it. Terence went back downstairs, back to the living-room, and she was standing there staring at him with her fists clenched and her mouth as tight as a clipped-up purse.

'How did you know?' he asked her.

'How did I know what?'

'How did you know that your momma and I were brother and sister?'

She nearly managed a smile. 'I didn't know. I felt it. It's like being two people, one on top of the other. I'm wrong. I'm something else; not Emily at all. I'm "Emily".'

'I could of killed you. I could of cut off your head.'

'You didn't; that's all that counts.'

'What are you going to do? Are you going to invite them in?'

Emily nodded but her eyes were very negative. 'He loves me but he knows that I'm wrong. He doesn't understand why. He loves me, but he's going to try to kill me, I'm sure of it. I frighten him.'

'*You* frighten him?'

Knokkk-knokkk-knokkk-knokkk-knokkk –

'He's going to wake up the whole damned neighbourhood.'

'I hope he does. Then he won't have very much time.'

'Why didn't he try to kill you before? When he killed Aunt Mary?'

Emily shook her head. 'He couldn't, because he needed to kill you first, you were his son, and you know that he couldn't kill you without being invited.'

'Are you going to invite him to kill me now?'

Emily gave a weird, airy shrug. 'I don't know. Do you think that I ought to? You said you wanted forgiveness.'

'Forgiveness from you, not him.'

'I don't forgive you. Why should I? Children should never forgive their parents. They don't have the right to. Besides, it's not necessary.'

The knocking was so loud now that it was making Terence feel deaf.

'Are you going to let him in now? Or what?'

Emily reached out and took hold of Terence's hand, and squeezed it. Her own hand felt very cold, and slightly slippery, as if she had been handling fish.

'I think I'm going to let him in.'

She walked, she *glided* to the back door. She opened it, and a rainy draft blew in, and scores of bay leaves scurried across the floor.

'Come in,' she said.

Naked came first. She had replaced her mask, but from the way she was standing, Terence could tell what her facial expression was like. Arrogant, amused, and beautiful. Then came Knife, and the Doctor, and then the Leper, breathing like a punctured leather bellows. Janek-the-Green came next. His entrance was slow and dramatic, in flurries of falling leaves. Terence had never seen him under such bright light before, and he was shocked by the way in which the vegetable side of his body had ravaged the human side. His face was still concealed behind a mask, but the roots that wriggled out of it on all sides told of a man who was gradually losing his battle against the forces of Nature.

Behind him came the Witness, and the Witness closed the door.

Naked said, 'You kept us waiting.'

'Yes,' Terence admitted. 'I'm sorry about that, but –'

Emily interrupted him by raising her hand. 'Welcome, grandfather,' she said.

Janek-the-Green rustled uncomfortably.

'What do you want of us?' asked Emily.

'A ritual,' said Naked. 'The ritual of blood-sharing, so that Janek may drink of his offsprings' goodness; and continue to wax healthy; and to survive for ever.'

'And that's *all* you want? You swear it?'

'We swear,' said Naked, pressing her hand against her breast. The Swordsman dragged five swords out of his scabbard, one by one, and noisily interlocked them.

Terence said, 'Let's just get it over with, shall we?'

'Very well,' Naked agreed, and stepped forward, and rolled back Terence's shirtsleeve, baring his wrist. Terence couldn't help noticing that strong smell of wet animal furs and flowers and male sperm, as if she had just climbed out of somebody's hot bed. It was arousing and frightening at the same time.

Janek-the-Green crept forward, and held out his hand too:

a tortured combination of greenish fingers and splintered hawthorn twigs. Their fingertips touched, father and son, the supernatural incest between plant and human. Terence could see that his own hand was trembling, but there was nothing he could do about it. It was beyond his control, he was frightened.

The Swordsman approached them. He was maskless now, and he stared at Terence with that grey, scarred face, and Terence saw nothing in his eyes at all. No pity; no hope; not even anger. Just a dreadful deadened cruelty – cruelty for its own sake, not even for sexual pleasure, or revenge.

The Swordsman gripped Terence's wrist, and cut it so quickly that Terence wasn't even conscious of seeing a knife. Blood ran diagonally across his skin and dripped on the floor. The Swordsman lifted his arm a little, and held it steady, so that the Green Traveller could extend one of his branchy fingers and dig it into Terence's vein. It hurt: and Terence shouted out loud.

The Swordsman relentlessly held them together, gripping each wrist, and strongly massaged Terence's wrist so that the blood pumped out more quickly. The Green Traveller shuddered and sniffed behind his mask – dry, nose-thumping sniffs.

Emily waited and watched. Naked stood close, and watched her, too.

'You should be doing a ritual,' said Emily. 'There's chants and stuff, for doing this.'

Naked smiled. 'The simple fact is, Emily, we don't really care. Bleeding your father is just another way of weakening him. We will have his guts, my darling; just as surely as we will have yours, too.'

'You can't!' said Emily. She took off her glasses and threw them aside, a gesture of suddenly-realized strength.

'Oh, yes, we can,' said Naked. 'You've invited us.'

'Don't you know who I am?' said Emily, glancing quickly and anxiously at Terence's wrist.

'Of course: you are the one whose face has always been adored. But sometimes we have to sacrifice that which we adore in order to survive; and your grandfather has had to make that decision. He admits his own folly. You should respect him for that.'

Emily took one step away from Naked, and then another. The lighting in the living-room was very flat and bright, and they all looked like characters from a 1950s TV play, stilted and monochromatic. They looked even clearer because they were no longer living in the past. They were no longer protected from death by a heartbeat's pause; by the fact that they would never get there.

But Terence was suddenly beginning to feel floods of weakness. His legs had been watery before: now they seemed to be melting away altogether. He had been willing to offer the Green Traveller a little blood, just to escape him, but he felt as if every vein and artery were being emptied, as if his life were flowing out of him, blood and dreams and memories, all mingled.

Emily croaked, '*Stop.*'

They didn't hear her at first, or didn't understand her. '*Stop,*' she repeated, in the same deep croak.

Maybe the Swordsman understood, because he lifted his pentangle of sword blades, and held it over Terence's head, like a halo.

'*Stop,*' Emily said, for a third time.

She stretched open her mouth, wider and wider. Her eyeballs suddenly filled with green – like liqueur glasses filled up with green Chartreuse. Her lips peeled back over her gums, and her gums were greenish-white, too. Out of her throat swelled a huge distended penis, slick with mucus, two or three feet of it, rising and rearing and unravelling, and dragging behind it a sticky string of folded leaves, like green bunting, more and more of it, until it dropped and heaped on the floor, piles and piles and piles of it.

The living-room was thick with the stench of amniotic fluid and chlorophyll. Emily literally poured herself inside-out, her mouth stretching wider and wider until her scalp unrolled over her skull like a green rubber bathing-cap, and her jaw dislocated so that a narrow arch-like ribcage could force itself out of her mouth, followed by swaying, glistening intestines and a pelvis the shape of a gravedigger's shovel.

There was a final sucking noise, and then the real Emily stood in front of them, a hideous concatenation of human and plant, the incestuous child of greed and want and mystical genetics. She looked like a quivering mantis at first, but then her leaves dried and began to unfold, and roots began to wriggle down her arms and legs, and they knew that here, truly, was her father's daughter.

She let out a noise that was unlike any cry that Terence had ever heard, human or animal. She swayed, and moved, and then she lashed at Naked with an arm that was half-claw and half-root-structure. Naked dodged away, but then 'Emily' lashed at her again, and this time her claw caught her cheek, like razor-wire, and lifted flesh away from bone. Naked screamed. She had never known pain like this before, because she had always been one single heartbeat away from pain; and from any retribution.

'Emily' moved nearer, with a complicated clicking of bones and roots, and lashed at Naked again and again and again, until Naked's animal-fur pelt began to fly off her back, in lumps of fox and rabbit and coyote, and her hair began to be soaked with red, and ribbons of skin danced from her thighs. Naked screamed and screamed and then suddenly stopped screaming and that was even worse.

The Green Traveller dragged his branch-like finger out of

Terence's vein. Skin snagged against twig. Terence swayed, and tried to fall sideways, but the Swordsman's pentangle was now around his neck. He felt the chilly, razor-sharp blades against his Adam's apple, and tried to stand up straight again.

There was nobody to speak to him, nobody to grant him forgiveness, nobody to tell him what sin he might have committed, just by being born. The mummers wouldn't speak, and Naked was lashed to death, and his own daughter had become what he was, a helpless, vicious victim of his own ancestry.

He opened his eyes just once, and said, 'Forgive me,' but nobody did, and the Swordsman's pentangle slid shut, and cut through his neck, and his head dropped onto the floor. He clearly thought, as his head toppled: *They've killed me, I'm dead,* and then he was.

'Emily' and the Green Traveller stood facing each other. The Leper shuffled towards the back door. Knife retreated too, one hand raised in self-defence. In the distance, sirens were scribbling, and they could helicopters beating, too.

The mantis-like thing called 'Emily' lashed out at Janek, and then at Knife. But then it hesitated, and looked down at the headless body that had once been Terence. A wide pool of shining blood was swelling across the floor, and crept surreptitiously along the skirting-board. At that moment, 'Emily' didn't know if she were 'Emily' or Emily, if she were human or plant, if she wanted peace and sleep or furious activity.

While she was hesitating, the Green Traveller started to churn with life. His leaves began to quicken and blow, his hands started to grow even more branch-like, the claws of a vicious tree. The lights in the living-room dimmed and flickered, and a wind started to rise. The floor trembled. Ornaments and vases rattled in their cabinets.

'Emily' uttered a scream that was partly the scream of a human girl and partly the scream of a female plant – the same agonized scream that female mandragoras emit when farmers pull them, still living, from the soil.

The Green Traveller let out a scream, too – only his scream was more like a thunderous roar. The roar was followed by a rushing sound, and the Green Traveller was enveloped in a blizzard of dry bay leaves, until he was almost completely hidden from sight. He grew in size, branching and spreading and creaking. The room was plunged into darkness, fitfully punctuated by a dazzling flash of greenish light. The whole house shook on its foundations, until windows fell crashing from their frames, and shingles slid from the roof, and the brick chimney-stack toppled and collapsed all over the yard.

In the kitchen, the refrigerator fell thunderously flat on its front, and cupboards dropped from the walls. All of Iris's copper saucepans fell, too, like a peal of discordant bells.

Through the hail of bay leaves, 'Emily' lifted her pale, glutinous green head towards them. She let out a hideous groan. She wanted to die now; she didn't want to live like this. She didn't feel like Emily at all. She felt only like 'Emily' – a grotesque parody of a girl, wracked with pain, every nerve screaming with the agony of metamorphosis. It was like being born all over again, except that it was even worse than that. It was like being born *inside-out*, with every muscle twisted, with every nerve-ending nakedly exposed.

She had done what she needed to do: she had shown the Green Traveller that his descendancy was genetically perverted beyond recovery, and all that lay ahead for him was to be gradually overgrown by the roots that grew inside him, until the last glimmer of humanity had been strangled for ever.

She didn't have to wait more than a few seconds for her absolution. The Swordsman slid out a single long blade, and lifted it high. He chopped, and chopped, and chopped again. Sometimes his blade chopped flying leaves, as well as flesh. Fingers and bones and fragments of leaf flew everywhere.

'Emily' accepted her execution silently. She did nothing to defend herself. She collapsed and folded and shrivelled, green flesh contracting like hot-blanched cabbage leaves, twigs broken, roots stripped; the daughter of fertility hacked into blood and bone and branches.

The Swordsman didn't stop, though. Not until the floor was littered with branches and chopped-up human organs and lumps and strings and things that were half-human and half-vegetable and glistening with mucus.

The Green Traveller whirled from the room, whirled away from the house, and burst off into the darkness. Lightning crackled; thunder slammed. Over towards Hiawatha, the sky was the colour of blood and papal robes.

The Swordsman hesitated, and then seized hold of the Doctor's shoulder, and the Witness's too. For a moment, they held each other close, very close, in silent camaraderie, which only mummers could have understood. Nobody else had travelled together for as long as they had travelled together; over thousands of miles of snow-swept steppes, over mountains and prairies and landscapes bleaker than the moon. Nobody else could have seen Wenceslas, lying in state, and heard Mozart, too. Nobody else could have walked through London, in the grip of the Black Death, masked and hooded, and crossed the Atlantic in the hold of 19th-century immigrant ship.

They said nothing, but they knew that they had reached a critical moment in their lives – a moment when comradeship might not be enough. They hesitated for just a moment longer, and then they ran out into the night.

Fifteen

They ran across the rainy front yard and suddenly searchlights popped on, and froze them. A helicopter thumped noisily overheard, circling and watching.

They ran to the right, and a siren whooped, and lights flashed, and they ran to the left.

Luke heaved himself out of his car and took out his shotgun with him. He turned to Nathan and David and said, 'Stay where you are – okay? I've had enough casualties already.'

'Yes, sir,' said Nathan. 'No problem.'

Lily, sitting in the back with deputy Lehman, said nothing at all.

Luke hadn't expected anything; not even Captain Black. But here were the bastards he had been looking for – the people who had scavenged across Europe and England and middle America for hundreds of years, offering dice-games, gewgaws, and flourishing crops for human lives. Janek's people, the mummers, cornered at last. They were running across the brightly-illuminated lawn in front of the Pearson house, a man in white, a man in a monk's habit, a man with swords on his back. The rain sparkled on the grass. He could see their breath. He could hear them panting.

'Freeze, police!' he bellowed at them, but they didn't stop. Two more patrol cars slithered to a halt, lights flashing, sirens droning. The helicopter turned at the end of the street, and then came thumping back towards them.

'Freeze!' Luke shouted. It was almost impossible to make himself heard over the noise of the helicopter. But they must be aware that he was telling them to stop.

The boy Knife pulled open the back of the van. The Doctor and the Leper climbed inside. The Witness ran around to the front, and yanked open the door. Luke lumbered forwards with his belly jumbling and his revolver raised and shouted, 'Stop! Freeze! Hands over your head!'

They ignored him. The Witness slammed the door and gunned the engine, and the black van snaked away from the kerb with smoke and steam billowing out of its tyres. Luke didn't want to do this. He could have fired and deliberately missed, but if he didn't act decisively now, then the life of some other law enforcement officer could be jeopardized tomorrow, or the day after, or in another year's time. So he fired and he hit it, right in the gas tank, with a straightforward .357 125-grain jacketed hollowpoint.

The van was travelling at nearly 40 m.p.h. when it blew up. The bang pressed on Luke's eardrums like somebody closing an automobile window at high speed. Pieces of burning debris whirled across Vernon Drive. The main body of the van hurtled along the road for another fifty feet, a blazing tumbril, its tyres spraying out fire like Catherine-wheels, until it finally rolled to rest against the kerb, and rocked backward and forward, still roaring with flame.

The van's darkened windows cracked and exploded, and flames jumped hungrily out of the window-frames and licked at the roof. Luke could see the mummers inside the van, immersed in flames, and he could see them moving. But they weren't moving hysterically, or frantically, in the way that most fire victims do when they catch alight. They seemed to be moving around quite calmly, trying to open the van doors.

They were immortal. They were each carrying the pieces of silver that kept them a heartbeat away from their destiny. They were unharmed by anything that could happen to them – totally unscathed, totally unmarked, like the woman who jumps from a sixty-storey building, a split second before she hits the sidewalk, except that *their* split second lasted for ever.

The van's passenger door opened up, and fire licked out of it in hot orange tongues. For a moment, Luke thought that the mummers were actually going to climb out of the van and get away.

But it was then that he heard somebody screaming. A terrible inhuman howl that went on and on, and grew even more terrible by the second. He had heard people howling like this before. People trapped in burning buildings, people locked in blazing cars. This was the howl of absolute agony, as layers of skin and nerve ganglia were burned away, and fire turned a human being into a raw and cauterized lump of meat.

There was another scream, and then another. The mummers were burning. The mummers were actually burning. Luke shielded his eyes from the heat and watched them helplessly as they danced a last agonized dance inside the framework of their van.

The heat, he thought. *That's what it was. The heat.*

Silver can withstand any degree of frost. Silver oxidizes but it never rusts. To all intents and purposes, silver lasts for ever. The only thing is, silver melts at 961.5°C, and is the most heat-conductive of all the metals.

Fanned by the storm, fed by the wind, the heat inside the van had melted the mummer's coins, and turned the silver coins of Judas Iscariot into drips of smelted ore. No longer symbolic, no longer potent, no longer blessed.

Two deputies came running forward with fire-extinguishers, but Luke snapped, 'Leave it! Let it burn out! That's an order!'

The deputies hesitated, and then retreated.

Nathan came out of the car and slammed the door. He stood looking at the burning wreck with its fire reflected in his eyes.

'God,' he said.

Luke sniffed, and holstered his revolver. 'We haven't yet found what we came for,' he said.

'Still . . .' said Nathan, 'I never saw anything like that before.'

'You never will again, if God's on your side,' Luke replied. The wind was rising even more furiously, and he had to hold onto his hat. Lightning crackled from cloud to cloud, like a Van der Graaf generator.

Luke walked towards the house. One of his deputies came running up, a blond young man with a bright red face. 'Search the back yard,' Luke ordered him. 'I want roadblocks on Mount Vernon Road, east and west; 5th Avenue at Wellington, Grande at Fairview, Washington at 35th.'

'What are we looking for?' the deputy wanted to know.

'A guy dressed up in leaves.'

'Pardon me?'

'Is that so difficult to understand? A guy wearing leaves!'

'Leaves,' the deputy repeated, deeply confused.

The van blazed hideously. The air was thick with gasoline smoke, and the smell of old, charred meat. The wind blew the smoke into dark, blinding spirals, and Luke found himself breathing the people he had just killed.

He entered the Pearson house and walked into the living-room. The paramedics were already there, and so was the medical examiner.

He saw a man with no head and a girl in a ratty fur jacket and a bloody heap of sticks and meat that looked like a blown-up barbecue. There was so much blood and human tissue on the floor that he had to stay in the doorway, for fear of stepping in it.

What he could distinguish, though, was poor little Emily Pearson, or part of her. Her face was spattered with blood but was almost untouched. It looked like the deathmask of a child saint, framed with coppery-coloured curls.

The ME took off his glasses and shrugged at him. 'Don't ask me, sheriff,' he said. 'This time I don't have any idea.'

'Makes a change,' Luke retorted.

'We got heaps of leaves, though,' the ME told him, lifting up a bloodstained bay leaf. '*Laurus nobilis* strikes again. We got other vegetable material, too. Like tofu, or something, but I'm not going to hazard any guesses, not just yet.'

Luke squatted down so that he could get a better view of Naked. Her face and her shoulders and the back of her head had been lacerated with something that could have been a whip, or could have been razor-wire, or could have been rose branches, thick with thorns. From the ears back she was flayed to shreds. Her face lay in a pool of blood but like Emily she still looked peaceful, as if she were asleep. She was quite beautiful, too, and she reminded him of someone he had known a very long time ago, maybe not in this life, maybe not in any life. Maybe the kind of girl that he had only ever met in dreams. Her own blood reflected her beautiful face.

Luke stood up. He felt infinitely weary. So many people had been killed since Terence Pearson had first attacked his children; and Luke had very quickly suspected why. He was intuitive, he was experienced. Ever since he was seven, he had believed in the unbelievable, and all the time he had been right. Yet he hadn't been able to save Norman Gorman's sight; nor Mary van Bogan's life; nor Leos Ponican; nor any of his dead deputies; nor Terence Pearson; nor Emily Pearson; nor poor Frank Johnson, the hog-farmer.

Then there was poor John Husband, and all the innocent people who had died at the Cedar Mall. The State police were handling it right now, but Luke knew that he would have to drive down there as soon as he had caught Captain Black.

He felt like the official recorder of death itself, the writer of names in the book of epitaphs.

He walked out of the Pearson house into the gale. The press had arrived, and so had a charcoal-grey Cadillac limousine, with its opera-lights glimmering, and so had a red Toyota pick-up crowded with tough-looking men with rifles and red plaid sporting coats and lariats.

Luke walked across to the limousine and tapped on the rear window with his knuckle. The window hummed down and revealed the handsome but tight-mouthed face of Senator Bryan Cady.

'I'm sorry, senator, you can't park here. We're having ourselves kind of a homicide investigation.'

'Who's died?' Bryan wanted to know.

'Can't tell you that until later, senator. We haven't made positive identification yet.'

'You don't have any idea?'

'No. I'm sorry. You're going to have to leave.'

Bryan looked agitated. 'Listen . . . I have all these men here.'

'I can see that, and in just a minute we'll be checking their firearms permits.'

'You don't understand. You know that hog that escaped from the Spellman Institute? The one that killed all those people down at the Cedar Mall?'

'You mean that hog that was sprung out of the Spellman Institute by animal activists?'

'Whatever.'

'Of course I know it, senator,' Luke said, grimly. 'That's why I'm here, to catch it. It killed one of my very best friends, Chief John Husband, so I can assure that it isn't going to get away.'

Bryan said, 'I want to help you to recapture it. It was let out of the institute in the name of animal rights, okay? But I also believe that there's a limit to animal rights, when they infringe human rights. That hog has to be caught for everybody's safety, and its own protection.'

'Don't fret about it, senator, we'll do it.'

Bryan looked up at him. He had come across Luke many times before, and he was quite aware how shrewd he was. There wasn't any point in bullshit.

'Let me put my cards on the table, sheriff,' he said, 'I've spent a whole lot of time and a whole lot of money in furthering the interests of animal rights. Zapf-Cady is going to be the most momentous piece of legislation since the Fourteenth Amendment.'

' "No state shall deny to any person within its jurisdiction the equal protection of the law?" ' asked Luke.

'That's right, sheriff. But now you can change that to "any person or animal".'

'All right, senator,' said Luke, patiently. 'But I'm still going to have to move you on. We've had a multiple homicide here, things don't look too pretty, and I'm in a very upset mood.'

Luke was still talking to Bryan when one of his deputies came up and said, 'A word with you, sheriff.' He took Luke aside and said, 'The State police have confirmed it. All the stray hogs are accounted for now, except for Captain Black. He was sighted about twenty minutes ago. It looked like he was losing a lot of blood, but he was still running, and he was running this way.'

'Thanks,' Luke nodded. Then, 'That limousine . . . that belongs to Senator Bryan Cady. That pick-up truck, that belongs to his hired hog-catchers. Somehow, Senator Cady has come to believe what *we* believe, that Captain Black is going to make his way his way here. I want him and his hog-catchers out of here, but quick. *Comprendo?*'

'You got it, sheriff.'

He walked back to his Buick. *John's gone,* his mind kept hammering at him. *John's gone.*

Nathan said, 'What's happening? This is pandemonium.'

Garth arrived, too, limping along with the aid of an ebony walking-cane. 'Any news of Captain Black?'

'We've had a pretty bad multiple homicide here, which may or may not be related to Captain Black. But I've had some information that he's headed this way, or could be. He went berserk with a herd of other hogs, down at Cedar Mall. A whole lot of people killed, I'm afraid.'

'Yes, I heard the bulletins on the car radio,' Garth nodded.

Nathan said, 'I feel so bad about this. I feel like every one of those deaths is my personal fault.'

Luke said, 'Dr Greene, from what you've told me, I don't think that any of this is your fault. Okay, you took a brain-section out of a dead body without permission from your employers. But it seems to me that taking all kinds of bits and pieces from dead bodies is generally regarded in the pharmaceutical business as standard practice.'

'I'm afraid that's true,' Garth agreed. 'What Nathan did was ill-advised, to say the least. But come on, Nathan, let's put it in perspective. Maybe that brain-section made Captain Black go berserk, maybe it didn't. But what you did isn't half as bad as those big drug companies who put even one diseased gland into their hormone drugs. They can end up by contaminating thousands of doses, and those doses get injected into women and children who don't know what the hell they're being injected with. So feel guilty if you want to, okay? But don't feel *that* guilty. You're not alone.'

Nathan shook his head.

'Just because other people are mass murderers, that doesn't make me any less of a mass murderer, now does it?'

Garth said something, but a helicopter drowned him out. Its

searchlight lit them up for a moment, and then flicked away again.

Flashlights flickered inside the Pearson house like summer lightning. The police photographers were taking pictures of the bodies. Terence Pearson's head, under the drinks table. Terence Pearson's severed neck. Scatterings of bay leaves, sticky with blood. Naked, as young as sin, staring at her own reflection. The face of Emily Pearson.

Luke shouted, 'Haven't you chased that limo out of here yet?' But then he heard somebody yelp, a yelp like a stepped-on dog, and he turned his head and saw something down at the very end of Vernon Drive, where it intersected with Ridgeway, a huge black shape moving slowly towards them in the rain, a shape so enormous that he couldn't believe that it was alive, and real.

There was huge drama in the way that Captain Black approached them. He should have had drums, he should have had fifes, he should have had dead-black banners. They stood still and watched in awe as he came slowly up Vernon Drive, a one-and-a-half ton hog, with the face of the devil and the glittering eyes of a thousand-year-old mummer. The rain dredged across the street and dripped from his snout, and nobody moved, nobody spoke; everybody watched him in deep respect.

He walked up to them, and then he stopped. He was looking for Emily, but nobody knew that. He was exhausted, and wet, and every bullet and shotgun wound burned in his hide like fire. But he was home; and if he was home, then his mother would take care of him, his mother would make sure that everything was warm, and cosy, and stop the burning for him.

Lily came out of the crowd and walked right up to him. She was still handcuffed, she was completely defenceless, but she approached him and she was unafraid.

Luke snapped, 'Ms Monarch! You back away from there! He's dangerous!'

But Lily didn't even turn to look at him. She said, 'Captain Black? Can you hear me, Captain Black?'

She didn't say it in English, though. She said it in another language – a language which he really understood. It was a language of warmth and emotion and deep security: a language which reminded him of straw and food and comforting bulk, the flanks of his mother, the heavy dark shape of his father.

'You're safe,' said Lily. 'Can you understand me, you're safe.'

To everybody who was watching, it sounded as if she were singing to him, cooing to him.

Captain Black arched his head back, so that the rain prickled his eyes, and tried to cry out '*Emily! Emily!*' but his throat was incapable of forming her name; and he hurt too much.

Lily took one step forward, and then another. Press cameras flashed; television floodlights swung around. Captain Black was illuminated in the rain in all his grisly glory, and Lily, too.

For Bryan Cady, it was too much. He could see tomorrow's newspapers already, with Lily and Captain Black on every front page. He let out a whoop, and came running from his limo to seize the moment. He snatched a rifle from one of his hog-handlers and ran towards Captain Black with the hand-held cameras suddenly running after him, cameras and sound-engineers and lighting-cameramen. Panting, Bryan stood in his black Armani suit only seven or eight feet away from Captain Black. He worked the rifle's bolt, and lifted it, and aimed it.

Lily screamed at him, 'No! He's had enough, Bryan, no!'

Bryan hesitated, and turned to her. And realized that he

had blown it. Because Captain Black stood totally still, and simply stared at him, and what was he supposed to do? America's most fervent animal rights supporter, shoot down a wounded, stationary animal in cold blood? Even as he stood in the rain with his .397 rifle raised, he was writing the headlines in his mind: ANIMAL RIGHTS SENATOR BUTCHERS DEFENCELESS HOG. And for what? To rescue Lily, who was obviously unafraid?

He lowered the rifle, and turned his back on Captain Black, and grinned at the television cameras. 'Guess he's decided to come quietly,' he said.

But it was then that Captain Black took four quick steps towards him, and hit him a bristly, muddy blow with his front leg, and knocked him into the roadway.

Lily shouted, 'No, Captain Black! No!' and whooped a command in hog-language. But Captain Black was wounded and his mind was a jumble of rage and pain and childish fright. He snatched at Bryan's jacket with his teeth, and tore off his sleeve.

Bryan twisted around, dropped his rifle, picked it up again.

'*No!*' screamed Lily, but Captain Black was far too quick.

He stepped onto Bryan Cady's face. In pounds-per-square-inch, his muddy trotter had enough force to punch a hole clean through an automobile door. It drove through nose and jaw and palate and brain-pan. There was a high-pitched crunch. Creamy yellow brains squirted out of Bryan's ears like liquid cod roes. He jumped and jerked and flailed his arms in the air, but nobody could look at him because everybody knew that he was dead.

'*Fire!*' Luke screamed.

Garth shouted out, 'No! Don't hurt him any more!' But he was instantly drowned out by a crackling, burping barrage of shotguns and revolvers and semi-automatic rifles. Pieces of bristly flesh flew off Captain Black's back, and his huge pendulous belly shuddered as bullets thumped into it. The barrage seemed to go on and on; but at the end of it, Captain Black took three steps forward, dripping with blood, but unstoppable, and threw back his head, and screamed.

Lily approached him again. Luke shouted out, 'Ms Monarch, for your own safety, you back off there!'

But Lily turned and shook her head, and Luke could see by the expression on her face that she was calm and completely confident, and she knew what she was doing.

Captain Black stood with his head bowed, dripping blood, while Lily shushed him and sang to him in a strange, high voice.

Luke came up and stood beside her. The smell of blood and hog was so strong that he almost retched.

'What are you saying to him?' asked Luke.

Lily said, 'I'm telling him that I love him; that everything's going to be fine.'

'Do you think he's going to stay docile?'

'I think he's dying.'

Captain Black tossed his head, and uttered a low, complicated growl.

'Is he talking to you?' asked Luke.

'In a way. That's the cry that hogs make when they're looking for their own families. I guess in this case he's looking for his sister.'

Luke turned towards the house. A deputy with a shotgun was standing guard by the door. Luke called out, 'Deputy! Have them bring out the girl! The young one, not the one in the fur jacket! Put her on a trolley and wheel her out here!'

'Sir?' replied the deputy. 'That girl's all over the place.'

'Tell the ME to shovel up whatever he can find and put in

a body bag, just so long as there's a face on it. Then wheel it out; and quick.'

The deputy looked pale. 'Yes, sir, sheriff, sir.'

Captain Black stayed where he was, his breath wheezing in punctured lungs. A few minutes later, two paramedics came out of the house, pushing a trolley. On it lay a body bag, joggling lifelessly with every bump in the sidewalk.

'Over here,' said Luke, beckoning.

Cautiously, they wheeled their burden in front of Captain Black. Lily touched his snout and caressed his cheek, and almost sang to him. He stood staring at Emily and snuffling, and even Luke could understand that this was where the strange and contradictory elements in his personality all came together – hog and boy and mythical mummer.

Without any warning, the rain started to drive down even harder. Lightning creaked and crackled only a mile away, and thunder fell down on them like a whole regiment of drummers dropping drums. Luke shouted, 'Where's the guy from the Spellman Institute? Dr Matthews? He's supposed to be anaesthetizing this mother!'

The thunder rumbled again, and the rain dredged down, but now Luke heard another sound as well – the sharp, scurrying rattle of dried leaves. He lifted his head, and saw that the air was whirling with bay leaves, millions of them, as thick as locusts.

There were shouts of warning from the police officers and State troopers and sheriff's deputies. The leaves swept through them in a ferocious blizzard, lashing their faces and stinging their hands. There were so many leaves that some of them staggered and dropped to their knees. A patrol car tried to back away from them, and collided noisily with a parked station wagon. Two more patrol cars collided. The air was so dense with leaves now that it was black, and even the house lights all around them were blotted out.

Luke cupped his hands over his eyes and strained his eyes to see what was happening. Nathan and David stayed close beside him, and Lily, too, although Lily kept her face completely hidden in her hands. The leaves were scratching and whipping at them so fiercely that Luke could feel blood dripping from the backs of his hands.

Captain Black uttered a massive cry of pain and desperation; but there was something else in his cry, too, so distinctive that Luke turned to Lily and shouted at her, 'What's he saying? Do you know what he's saying?'

Lily opened her hands for a moment and shouted back, '*Grandfather!*'

'What?'

'Hogs have sounds for *father*, meaning their own father, and then *big father*, meaning grandfather. That's what he's saying! *Grandfather!*'

Captain Black cried out again. Nearly half a minute went by; and then something huge and dark appeared in front of them, close to the burned-out van. It was an intense concentration of storm and leaves and Nature's unshackled fury. It was the power of the planet Earth itself, its energy, its growth, its mysticism, its explosive all-consuming energy. Saturn might eat his children; but Earth ate its children and its children's children, and this was how it did it.

The night was a blinding torrent of leaves and rain. Thunder rumbled and rumbled and never seemed to stop. The air was intoxicating with the smell of ozone and laurel and freshly-dug graves.

The huge dark shape came closer; like a slow-boiling tornado. The asphalt pavement under Luke's feet seemed to crawl away from it, as if in fear.

'For Christ's sake,' Luke breathed; more to himself than to anybody else. 'Janek-the-Green, in person.'

The man who had once been Janek had at last lost his battle with the roots that had been planted inside him. Now that his entourage had been burned to death, and his native soil sterilized by fire, he had nowhere left to go. Centuries of suppressed growth had burst out, all in one night, and what was left was a storm of branches and leaves and lashing thorns. In the stroboscopic flicker of the lightning, Luke saw fragments of a man amongst the vegetation: a white face, like a saint's face, with black, half-closed eyes, surrounded by a cage of brambles; shreds of red bloody thigh-flesh, and two emaciated martyr's feet.

There was an echoing rattle of pump-action shotguns being cocked, but Luke bellowed, 'Hold your fire!' He was scared, but he was fascinated, too. He wanted to see this Green Traveller alive; he wanted to see what such a creature could possibly be. Besides, what would they be shooting at? Branches? Brambles? A hailstorm of leaves?

The dark whirling tornado of bay leaves came closer and closer. The noise was deafening. It was now that Captain Black cried out yet again, a high-pitched call that ended in a grunt.

Lily caught hold of Luke's hand, and held it tight. 'He's saying, *kill me.* I've heard it before, when a hog was injured, or when it was sick. It's the same cry. *Kill me.*'

David was standing close by. 'No!' he shouted. 'He mustn't! He's going to be all right! He's a *boy*!'

Luke turned around to the deputy with the red face and yelled, 'Get this kid out of here!'

But before the deputy could snatch his arm, David started running towards Captain Black, running through the leaves, screaming, 'Don't kill him! Don't kill him! He's a boy!'

Luke said, 'Shit!' and started to run after him. The leaves were flying through the air so densely that he could scarcely breathe, scarcely even see. His stomach jumbled from side to side, his heart thumped like a one-man pillow-fight. Suddenly he collided with David and Captain Black's stickily-bloodied flank.

'David, we have to get out of here! There's nothing we can do! Come on, kid, for Christ's sake!'

Searchlights criss-crossed through the leaves and the rain. The ground trembled and tilted under their feet. Luke could hear officers shouting; Captain Black shuddering and grunting.

Lightning flashed and dazzled, and David screamed. Right in front of them, only two or three feet away, so close that they could *smell* it, reared a huge dripping distorted head. It was a gigantic parody of a human head, six or seven feet from cranium to chin, with milky-green eyes and pale green cheek-bones and a gaping mouth, with long curved thorns for teeth, and cuckoo-spit dribbling from its lips. It had a beard, almost, of glistening tendrils and trailing creepers and slug-infested leaves.

It was Janek's face, the same face that Luke had seen in Terence Pearson's engraving, medieval and sly, but grossly grown. Vegetable genes had overwhelmed his humanity, and turned him into this – a living, agonized creature made of fibre and flesh.

Janek's head swayed from side to side, supported on a thick rope of vegetable tissue. Its eyelids rolled down, and then rolled open again, and its jaws stretched wide. Then the lights flicked away and the lightning died and it was plunged into darkness.

'Run!' Luke roared, his face blizzarded with leaves.

David screamed, 'I can't!'

'Just run! Forget about Captain Black! Just run!'

'I *can't*! Something's caught hold of me!'

Luke turned, tried to pull out his gun, but then something as hard and as powerful as an automobile-bumper knocked him on the shoulder. He staggered, lost his balance, staggered, and then managed to stand up straight. At that instant, something that felt like fifty strands of barbed wire hit him directly in the face and ripped open his shirt.

'David!' he shouted, into the roaring darkness. 'David, get out of there for Chrissakes, just get out of there!'

David was screaming, but Luke couldn't see him. The leaves were too thick; the night was too dark. He dabbed his hand against his chest and felt warmth and stickiness, and knew that he was wounded. His shirt and his undervest had been ripped right through, his chest was lacerated. Even his shirt pocket had been torn half-open.

Inside his pocket, he felt the plastic envelope, with the silver Judas coin inside it. At the very same instant, David screamed again, and the lightning blitzed, and he saw David snared up in impenetrable brambles, and the grotesque head of Janek-the-Green stretching its jaws wider and wider, so wide that its sinews cracked.

Janek's thorn-teeth were even more savage than those of a Great White shark, row upon row of upcurving hooks. Liquid sap dripped from the green-ribbed roof of its mouth.

Luke thought: *Jesus forgive me, for doing this,* and snapped open the plastic envelope between finger and thumb.

He held the coin in the palm of his hand and squeezed it tight. He felt an odd, delayed jolt. He had the oddest sensation that he was here, right in the middle of this storm of wind and rain and bay leaves, and yet not here, either. He took three long strides towards David, and caught hold of him, and pulled him free from the brambles. Janek screeched, and its eyes peeled open, and brambles lashed wildly at Luke's left shoulder. But this time, the brambles passed clean through his muscles without even touching him. At that instant, Luke wasn't yet there.

Darkness. Leaves, and grit.

Luke rolled onto the wet asphalt, clutching David close to him. He rolled, and rolled, and rolled again. Suddenly there were flashlights lancing through the leaves, and voices saying, 'Sheriff! Sheriff, you okay?'

He let go of David, heaving for breath. David climbed to his feet. Nathan held out his hand and helped Luke up, too.

'What the hell happened?' he shouted, over the storm.

'Shotgun!' Luke demanded.

'What?' yelled his red-faced deputy.

'Give me a shotgun!' Luke repeated.

'Sheriff, you're hurt!' said Lily. 'Look at you! Your shirt's all covered in blood!'

'Shotgun!' Luke roared. 'I'm the only one who can do it!'

His deputy threw him a 12-gauge. He caught it, and turned back into the darkness and the storm of leaves.

The wind was shrieking like a chorus of a thousand tortured nuns. The bay leaves were flying so furiously that they lacerated his cheek. The storm had moved away: the lightning was flickering to the south-west now, and so the eye of this particular tornado was darker, and much more frightening. Luke edged forward with his 12-gauge held in his right hand and his silver coin held in his left.

And Jesus said, 'Forgive them, Lord, for they know not what they do.'

He saw Captain Black standing motionless amidst the whirl of leaves. He saw Janek stretching over him, even larger, even more grotesque, as centuries of pent-up genetic energy flooded through his system. In the dim light of distant lightning, he saw two hideous creations that only man could have made, by meddling with his own creation.

He struggled right up to Captain Black, and stood beside him, and screamed out, '*Janek! Janek-the-Green!*'

Janek's head swayed and angled, and looked down at Luke with emotionless eyes.

Luke lifted the shotgun and aimed it directly at Janek's misshapen skull. He wished he could think of something to say, like 'Make my day', but he was so exhausted and bruised and angry that he couldn't think of anything to do but roar, at the top of his voice.

Janek-the-Green whipped out at him in fury, brambles, creepers and thorns as thick as bullwhips. Luke instinctively lifted his arm to protect himself, but he didn't need to. They lashed right through him, as if he simply wasn't there.

He fired. The first shot blew a huge chunk of greenish skull-matter from the side of Janek's head. Then it went totally dark. He fired, and pumped, and fired again. In the intermittent muzzle-flash he glimpsed Janek's eyes, Janek's teeth, Janek's gaping jaws.

All the time he was roaring and he kept on roaring.

There was a moment when he felt as if he were going to be totally drowned in leaves. They caught in his hair, caught in his shirt, caught in his mouth. He reloaded, and fired one more time, and this time the muzzle-flash illuminated nothing, only darkness.

He heard the most extraordinary *sucking* noise. He felt as if the whole world were imploding. He couldn't see anything at all, except a few jumbled lights, but he could feel leaves rushing past him, and a sense that everything was being drawn towards Janek-the-Green, as if Janek-the-Green were a total vacuum, rather than a living being.

The rushing noise went on and on, and the leaf-blizzard grew fiercer and fiercer. Suddenly, there was a deafening bang like a cathedral door slamming. The night seemed to compress itself into one intense bible-black square. In that instant, Luke thought that he almost understood God, that he almost grasped the fundamental meaning of time, and history, and why the human race had struggled and warred for so many centuries against itself, and against nature.

The bang reverberated, but its reverberations grew fainter and fainter, and the night grew lighter, and even the air seemed to relax. The wind blew the leaves away in clattering, snaking curls, and then most of them were gone, and the street was bright, and the storm had passed south-west towards Iowa City.

Nathan came forward, looking around him in amazement.

'What happened? One minute it was dark; now it's all light again.'

Luke coughed, and wiped his forehead with the back of his hand. 'That's what we call law enforcement.'

At that moment, however, Captain Black shifted around, and let out a harsh, pitiful cry. He looked exhausted, spent, like a locomotive ready for the breaker's yard.

'That cry – what does that mean?' Luke asked Lily.

Lily was close to tears. 'He wants to die, sheriff. He's hurting, and he's had enough. Whatever happened there – whatever that thing was – that was his very last chance. Please, it's all over. Please.'

Garth said, 'No, sheriff. Not here. We can take him back to the institute.'

Lily turned to Garth and blazed at him, 'Just for once in your life, Dr Matthews, can you please do the decent thing instead of the progressive thing!'

Garth was about to blaze back at her, but then David said, 'Please don't keep him alive any longer. He's a boy too.'

Captain Black took three unsteady steps backwards. He growled, and tossed his head, with blood dripping out of his jowls. There was a moment's hesitation, when everybody stood in the strangest of tableaux, wondering what to do next. The officers looked to Luke for the order to open fire. Luke looked at David, and then at Nathan, and then at Garth, and finally at Lily.

'He's a mortal being, isn't he?' he asked her. 'He's just like you and he's just like me. That's what you've been arguing all along. What right do I have, to kill another mortal being?'

But Lily said, 'He knows it's all finished. He's alone now, he knows he's going to die.'

'He told you that?'

'Sheriff, if there's one thing I learned from living with pigs, it was this: that most animals would happily live with human beings, if they could trust them.'

Captain Black started to walk away from them, huge and tragic. The road was glossy with rain and blood. Luke knew that there was only one way to end this carnage, and that was quickly.

'I want every officer here, now!' he yelled. 'All available firepower!'

Their shoes and boots rattled on the tarmac. They caught up with Captain Black, and surrounded him, and Captain Black stopped again. The helicopter roared and retreated, roared and circled back again.

Luke walked up to Captain Black with Lily beside him. Lily wanted to go closer, but Luke held her arm. 'I know you can understand him. I guess he can understand you, too. But he's done some damage today, killed some people. I don't want you to be a casualty, too.'

Lily called to Captain Black – a high, ululating cry that made the hairs on the back of Luke's neck rise up. It went on and on, higher and higher, and then it died away.

Captain Black didn't respond. He stood and waited and snuffled blood, and that was all.

'What did you say to him?' asked Luke.

Lily turned away and her eyes were filled with tears. 'I told him he was safe now; and that I love him.'

Luke stepped back, and lifted one arm. 'On my mark, fire,' he called out. He turned to look at Lily, and Lily nodded, and mouthed the words, 'Thank you.'

Garth turned his back, and crossed himself, in memory of Raoul Lacouture.

Thirty officers opened up with everything they had. The noise was thunderous. Blood and flesh sprayed everywhere. Captain Black sank slowly to his knees, and still they kept on firing at him, until smoke poured out of his gaping mouth. At last Luke shouted, 'That's it! That's it!' and the officers backed away, leaving the bloodied carcass lying on its side.

Nathan came up and stood close to Luke. 'You know how this all started?' he said.

Luke took out his handkerchief and wiped his face. Then he blew his nose.

'It started with a favour,' said Nathan.

Luke looked at him, and then he clapped him on the back. 'That's how most trouble starts.'

Gradually, the rain began to ease. The black van lay smoking by the kerbside; Captain Black lay ripped apart and silent in the middle of the road, his legs stiff, his eyes misted over. Of Janek-the-Green, there was nothing left but wind-blown leaves. Out of his pocket, Luke took the coin imprinted *Life Within Death* and dropped it amongst the leaves.

'Payment in full,' he said, softly.

Then he walked back to his car, followed by deputies and news cameras and jostling reporters.

Rick Smith shouldered his way next to him. 'It paid off, then?' he asked. 'The Czech mythology bit.'

Luke said, 'Don't know what you're talking about, Rick. We had a road traffic situation; we had a berserk hog situation; that was all.'

'I saw different. So did a lot of people.'

Luke stopped, and looked him up and down. 'No, we didn't,' he said, reassuringly. 'We didn't see nothing at all.'

He climbed into his car, and slammed the door. Rick Smith looked at him through the rain-beaded windshield. Then he lifted both hands in mock-surrender, and Luke started up his engine, and he knew that it was over.

Carl Drimmer, aide to the late Senator Cady, called up William Olsen the same evening and said, 'Have you heard the news?'

Nina Olsen, who always picked up every call, said, 'Yes, and I can't say that I'm sorry.'

Carl said, 'I don't like to speak ill of the very recently dead, but he could have picked a very much less controversial issue, couldn't he, and still had a good chance of reaching the White House.'

'Do *you* have any bright ideas?' asked Nina.

'Me? Thousands. Most of Bryan's ideas were mine.'

There was a pause. William was feeding Pallas with pig's-caul, and the bird's beak was stretching it out into thin, unappetizing ribbons.

'Come see me, then,' said Nina. 'Maybe we could do some business, you and William and I. Especially you and I.'

Iris lay in her hospital bed and watched the airplane lights circling over Cedar Rapids. The rain had stopped: it was a clear night now.

She felt strangely refreshed, as if all her problems were over. All she had to do now was to look forward to having her baby.

Afterword

All of the medical and xenogenetic procedures described in this book have either been carried out already or can already be achieved. My special thanks to the directors and staff of the Spellman Institute for Genetic Research, Amana, Iowa, for their kindness and generosity. Thanks also to the Linn County Sheriff's Department, the Cedar Rapids police, the Cedar Rapids *Gazette*, Mercy Medical Center and the Czech and Slovak Museum and Library.

It is a matter of Congressional record that Zapf-Cady was put before the House of Representatives fifteen days later and heavily defeated on its first reading.